Ormesson 93347
At God's pleasure.

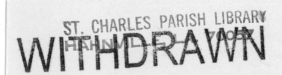

Also by Jean d'Ormesson

THE GLORY OF THE EMPIRE

This is a Borzoi Book
published in New York by Alfred A. Knopf.

At God's Pleasure

Jean d'Ormesson

AT GOD'S PLEASURE

TRANSLATED FROM THE FRENCH
BY BARBARA BRAY

Alfred A. Knopf   New York   1977

Library of Congress Cataloging in Publication Data

Ormesson, Jean d', (Date).
At God's pleasure.

Translation of Au plaisir de Dieu.
I. Title.
PZ4.0717At   1977   [PQ2629.R58]   843'.9'14   77-75016
ISBN 0-394-49899-2

To the memory of my father, liberal, jansenist, republican

and to the memory of my uncle Vladimir.
God's pleasure did not allow him to read this book.

Thus saith the Lord:
Behold, them whom I have built, I do destroy:
and them whom I have planted, I do pluck up.
And dost thou seek great things for thyself?

JEREMIAH 45:4

Toutes ces choses sont passées
Comme l'ombre et comme le vent!

VICTOR HUGO

O saisons, ô châteaux,
Quelle âme est sans défauts?
O saisons, ô châteaux,
J'ai fait la magique étude
Du bonheur, que nul n'élude.

ARTHUR RIMBAUD

Regarde-moi qui change!

PAUL VALERY

Quels livres valent la peine d'être
écrits, hormis les Mémoires?

ANDRE MALRAUX

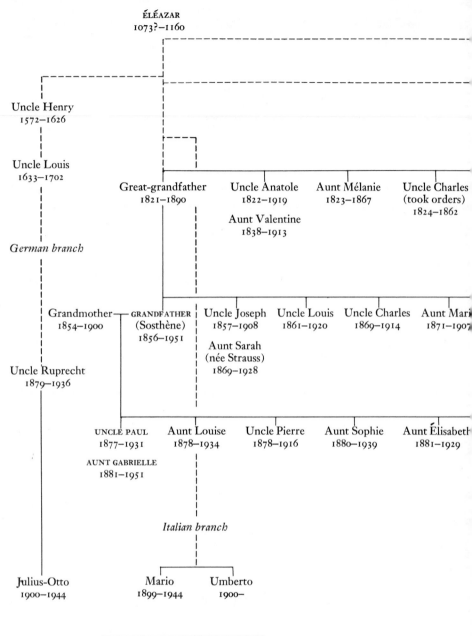

ÉLÉAZAR
1073?–1160

Uncle Henry
1572–1626

Uncle Louis
1633–1702

German branch

Great-grandfather
1821–1890

Uncle Anatole
1822–1919

Aunt Mélanie
1823–1867

Uncle Charles
(took orders)
1824–1862

Aunt Valentine
1838–1913

Grandmother
1854–1900

GRANDFATHER
(Sosthène)
1856–1951

Uncle Joseph
1857–1908

Uncle Louis
1861–1920

Uncle Charles
1869–1914

Aunt Mari
1871–1907

Aunt Sarah
(née Strauss)
1869–1928

Uncle Ruprecht
1879–1936

UNCLE PAUL
1877–1931

Aunt Louise
1878–1934

Uncle Pierre
1878–1916

Aunt Sophie
1880–1939

Aunt Élisabeth
1881–1929

AUNT GABRIELLE
1881–1951

Italian branch

Julius-Otto
1900–1944

Mario
1899–1944

Umberto
1900–

The Ancient Line

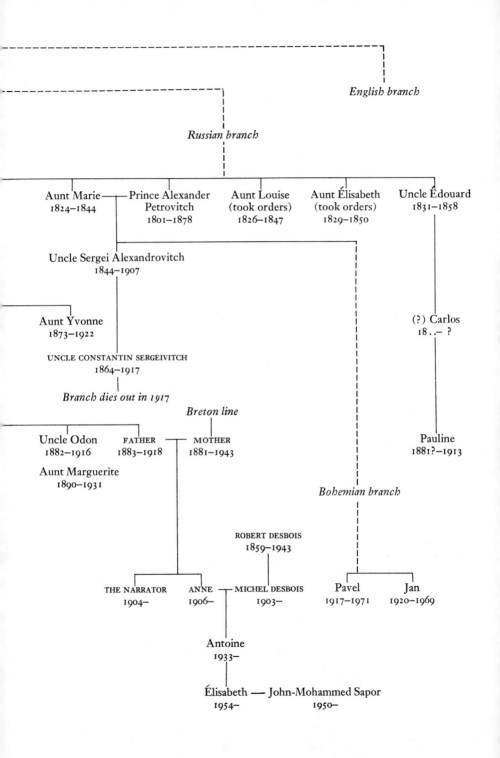

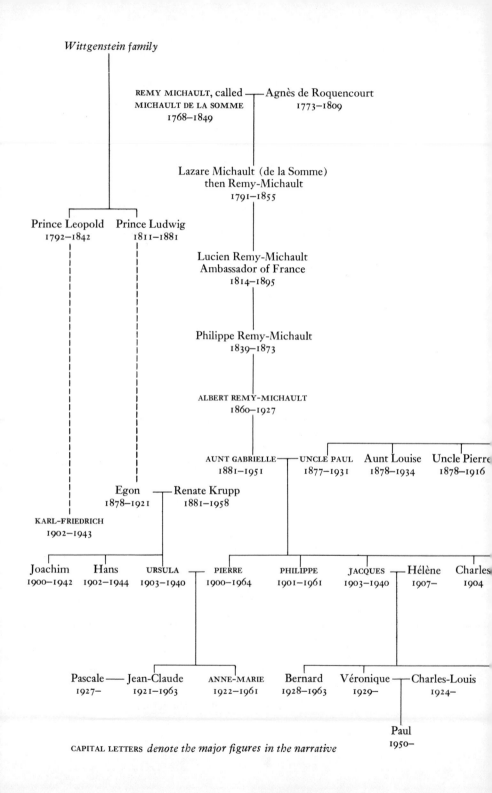

Wittgenstein family

REMY MICHAULT, called —— Agnès de Roquencourt
MICHAULT DE LA SOMME   1773–1809
1768–1849

Lazare Michault (de la Somme)
then Remy-Michault
1791–1855

Prince Leopold   Prince Ludwig
1792–1842   1811–1881

Lucien Remy-Michault
Ambassador of France
1814–1895

Philippe Remy-Michault
1839–1873

ALBERT REMY-MICHAULT
1860–1927

AUNT GABRIELLE —— UNCLE PAUL   Aunt Louise   Uncle Pierre
1881–1951   1877–1931   1878–1934   1878–1916

Egon —— Renate Krupp
1878–1921   1881–1958

KARL-FRIEDRICH
1902–1943

Joachim   Hans   URSULA   PIERRE   PHILIPPE   JACQUES —— Hélène   Charles
1900–1942   1902–1944   1903–1940   1900–1964   1901–1961   1903–1940   1907–   1904

Pascale —— Jean-Claude   ANNE-MARIE   Bernard   Véronique —— Charles-Louis
1927–   1921–1963   1922–1961   1928–1963   1929–   1924–

Paul
1950–

CAPITAL LETTERS *denote the major figures in the narrative*

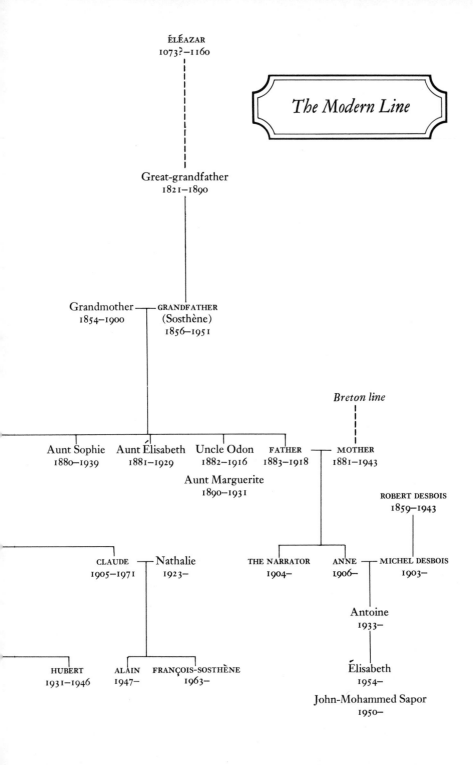

ÉLÉAZAR
1073?–1160

The Modern Line

Great-grandfather
1821–1890

Grandmother ——— GRANDFATHER
1854–1900   (Sosthène)
                    1856–1951

Breton line

Aunt Sophie   Aunt Élisabeth   Uncle Odon   FATHER ——— MOTHER
1880–1939   1881–1929   1882–1916   1883–1918   1881–1943

Aunt Marguerite
1890–1931

ROBERT DESBOIS
1859–1943

CLAUDE ——— Nathalie   THE NARRATOR   ANNE ——— MICHEL DESBOIS
1905–1971   1923–   1904–   1906–   1903–

Antoine
1933–

HUBERT   ALAIN   FRANÇOIS-SOSTHÈNE
1931–1946   1947–   1963–

Élisabeth
1954–

John-Mohammed Sapor
1950–

ONE

Eleazar, or the Mists of Time

Heredity, the only god whose name we know.
                                                    —Oscar Wilde

I WAS BORN INTO A WORLD THAT LOOKED backward. The past was more important than the future. My grandfather was a fine upstanding old gentleman who lived in his memories. His mother had danced in the Tuileries with the duc de Nemours, the prince de Joinville, and the duc d'Aumale, and my grandmother had danced at Compiègne with the Prince Imperial, son of Napoleon III. But it was to the legitimate monarchy that all my ancient tribe had remained passionately devoted, through disaster, barricades, sieges, and rebellions. They cared nothing for alluring prophecies. The age of gold was behind us, together with the art of gracious living which still echoed faintly in our legends but which the youngest of us had never known.

The silent presence of the king was always there among us, or rather hovering over us. The older members of the family would still talk about him in the evening, as of a pure and kindly master whose servants had sometimes taken unworthy advantage of him. Five or six times every century he used to speak some trivial word to a great-grandfather who was a brigadier general, or a great-great-uncle who was governor of Languedoc, or a great-great-aunt who was a freethinker. We never tired of repeating such phrases. Indeed, they gave us so much pleasure we sometimes invented new ones.

Ours was an old family. I wondered about that rather mysterious description as a child, and asked my grandfather whether some families were older than others. Was there some dim distant past, perhaps guarded by angels with flaming swords, which had contained nobody but my ancestors, and where others were not allowed, so that they had just had to spring suddenly out of the void? No—all families were really equally old. Everyone had a father and mother, two grandfathers and two grandmothers, and eight great-grandparents. But some people still bore traces of their ancestors' passage through time. And so I learned about our debt to memory.

The past was a marvelous great forest, full as far as the eye could see of the overarching branches of trees which led down to ourselves. Often, during dinner, my father would talk of people I didn't know—uncles, aunts, cousins—and their names all mingled in my head. They made up a fascinating but rather frightening world of melancholy gaiety. Before I ever read Balzac or Proust, the shades of my own past made me dream of human adventure.

My family's appearance in history was a sudden one, an abrupt emergence out of the darkness. By a stroke of genius the king—or perhaps it was only his brother—took the first of our name with him to the East. A charming début! Frightful tortures, heads blown off, plague and leprosy. This first figure was Eleazar, head of our house and marshal of the faith and of the army of God. Devotees of truth, uncertain and variable as it always has been throughout history, lost no time in informing me that the great Eleazar, pride of our clan, was a mere, or perhaps one should say a distinguished, rascal. His reputation was far from high, it seems, around Damascus and between Tyre and Sidon. But my aunts mentioned him in their prayers, beside their patron saints and guardian angels. It didn't take me long to find out, through these legends, that history is deceptive.

The world began with Eleazar. All was vague before that, because we hadn't yet been born. I told myself that Eleazar too must have had a father and mother, two grandfathers and two grandmothers, and eight great-grandparents. But they didn't exist because they didn't have a name. People and things had a meaning, as far as we were concerned, only through the names they bore. Names in themselves contained the notions of order and hierarchy that we were so attached to. One of the many reasons why we mistrusted the Jews was that, for motives I didn't understand, they sometimes changed their names. For us, to change one's name was to undermine the order of things. The first thing the Almighty did when he created the universe was to give a name to plants and animals and the first man and woman. Our only criticism of God was that he hadn't given our name to Adam and Eve. For that reason the couple's claim to antiquity rather annoyed us. The history of the world before we came on the scene was not very important. Nor was it all that long. Authoritative works put it at five or six thousand years. Quite enough for those uninteresting ages before we made our appearance.

By some mystery which we didn't try to explain, the Greeks and the Romans were our ancestors. We could recognize ourselves in their well-bred violence, their genteel insolence, their lofty superiority. We thought with distant familiarity of Uncle Alcibiades and Uncle Regulus. We didn't go in for the woolly theories which trace the purity of the race back to the Teutons. We didn't take much stock in philosophizing. We were lucid, and put good sense before genius, and the light and sun of the Mediterranean above the mists of the North. We didn't have a very high opinion of thinkers. We liked painters, architects, men of war and of God. My grandfather had never been to Rome or Athens, but he spoke about them as if he'd lived there all his life. Marius was rather common, and we were ashamed of Verres, but Plutarch and Sulla, Pericles and all the Horaces including the poet, had always been old friends of the family. They were the sort of people we'd have frequented if only we'd been there. But with a charming simplicity and respect for the truth we acknowledged that we hadn't come into being until the Crusades.

We were descended, distantly and confusedly, from the builders of the Acropolis, Caesar's legions, and a Jewish revolutionary whose name we revered almost as much as our own. This was another mystery. He was the only revolutionary we did accept; we even modeled ourselves on him. The rest of them didn't count. What did

we care about the Aztecs and the Incas who'd entered this turbulent
world after us? We knew that Negroes, Eskimos, and people with
yellow skins existed, of course, but we'd never seen any of them. It
wasn't until the Colonial Exhibition that my grandmother first met
a real Negro. She found him delightful. But one couldn't really
suppose that these people were the same as us. The Almighty,
usually so indulgent, must have had some good reason for creating
them with this disadvantage. The Americans themselves were only
badly brought-up children who made one smile. My grandfather's
great-grandmother, who'd written her memoirs, often quoted
Chamfort and Rivarol, Madame de Staël and Chateaubriand. But
she never said a word about Benjamin Franklin, though we know
for certain that she met him at Versailles. My grandfather followed
her example, and sometimes pretended to forget that America was
no longer British. He wasn't very fond of the English, but he'd
learned to distrust even more the suspicious eagerness with which
the colonies tried to throw off their masters. "Such a young nation,"
a neighbor in the country used to observe about the United States
—she wanted to be thought up to date. "The worst of it is," my
grandfather would reply, "that it gets younger every day." And he
used to add that if he'd been Christopher Columbus he would have
kept quiet about his discovery. Apart from our own, there was only
one race that deserved attention and perhaps some respect, and that
was the Chinese. They'd invented gunpowder, the compass, fire-
works, and kites, and it was possible to regard the mandarins, safely
established amid their rigid traditions, as a set of silent, distant
counterparts of ourselves, half cousins and half accomplices, kept
safe by ancestor worship and intense individualism from the threat
of revolution which had been hanging over the West ever since
Luther and Cromwell.

We led an extremely simple life, in which the important things
were the parish priest, riding to hounds, reverence for the white flag
of royalism, and the family name. We didn't see anything remarkable about our existence: it had been familiar so long that we
couldn't imagine any other. And yet I only have to summon up one
season, one day, one hour of it, and I come up against all the

mysteries concealed beneath that apparent limpidity. It had taken a long time for everything to become so easy. It had taken a lot of suffering, a lot of blood and sweat, for me to be able to ride my bicycle on the white roads around the great stone pile with its towers and ramparts which the local people called the castle. And they were right. That's what it was.

It seemed perfectly natural to us to live in a castle. My father had been born there, and so had his father, and so had his father's father. Each generation was born there, and we went back there to die. One of my great-grandfather's brothers had been for several years a charming and fabulous crook; only a couple of photographs of him had been allowed to survive. He'd sold dozens of houses, boats, racehorses, and even women that hadn't belonged to him. He'd gone off to South America with the dowries of three young women in a row, all of them, of course, from the best circles of society. His sainted mother was said to have died of grief. She died, like all her family, at Plessis-lez-Vaudreuil. And he too came back from Argentina a few years later, despite the police, and creditors, and the fathers and brothers of his fiancées, to die there in the peace of God, who spent all his time forgiving us our crimes and follies and mistakes. And so there grew up around us our own time and space— a time which flowed ever backward towards its sources, a space centered on the family cradle to which we were all returned by death.

The castle of my father and grandfather, and of his father and grandfather and their great-grandfathers through the ages and the generations, was, as may be imagined, crammed with the successive legacies of the past. Chests like coffins, rolltop desks, French-polished or marquetry consoles, kidney-shaped or semicircular or cylindrical tables, escritoires, chronometers, Aubusson and Flemish tapestries, portraits of ancestors in full-dress uniform leaning casually on a desk holding a letter on which could be clearly read the sacred words "To the King"—these, and all the other things heaped up in the rows of attics full of dust and enormous trunks where we weren't allowed to hide and where family ghosts floated among the cobwebs, had been deposited there by wave after wave of generations. Buying and selling were rather dubious transactions, both imprudent and vulgar. Montaigne boasts somewhere of never having acquired anything and never having gotten rid of anything. Nor did we: we never bought and we never sold. Things just accumulated through marriages and deaths, dowries and legacies. Our style of elegance consisted in remaining uninvolved in all this. Our fortune, like our name, sprang out of the mists of time.

Every country or family or individual lives by a certain mythology which colors its existence. Our myth was the castle, which played an enormous part in our daily lives. It might have been said to be the incarnation of our name. Both were steeped in the same sacred awe. The castle was the name rendered in stone. It didn't consist merely of the walls, the towers, the great inner courtyard, the spiral staircases which François I had ridden up on horseback on his return from captivity, and the moats full of the same carp which had been alive in the good old days of the legitimate monarchy. It extended to the lands and forests which enclosed it as a case encloses a jewel. Every so often my grandfather would take me up the highest tower, from which one looked down on all the surrounding country. The sun shone, and my grandfather would show me what the centuries had bestowed on us. In the distance we could see Saint-Paulin, and Roissy, and Villeneuve, and the graveyard at Roussette where we were all buried. My grandmother said it was all very French, and my grandfather said it was the sort of country celebrated by Ronsard and La Fontaine and Péguy. I looked at it. I saw fields and trees and gentle hills. It was the corner of France which belonged to us.

After God and the king and the family name, there was one other character which tended to haunt the castle: this was France itself, often looking rather disheveled. Our relations with France were somewhat ambiguous. Naturally, France was not so old as the name we bore. And it was not so old as the king who'd created it out of nothing. Nor was it so old as God. But even before the great slaughter at the beginning of this century, one of my uncles and two cousins had died for France in the rice fields of Asia or the sands of Africa. Ours was no niggardly union with France. We had married the monarchy and the Church. Modern France was like an old mistress to whom one has become attached through many arguments and sacrifices. It was all the more necessary to get along with her because the king was no longer there. We used to run France down as much as we could, but it was considered good form to go and get killed for her. To die for what took the place of the king was for us a custom and a calling rather than a duty or a token of love.

But France, unfortunately, was occupied by the Republic. In the name of France, the real France, my grandfather maintained a tiny, more or less clandestine army which bore but a distant resemblance to the splendors of the monarchy and the heroism of the Chouans. It consisted of a dozen gymnasts who walked in procession behind their buglers on the feast of Joan of Arc. One evening, by some unhappy concatenation of circumstances, when my grandfather was entertaining a minister of the Republic, the visitor, on entering the drawing room, picked up, out of quite understandable professional habit, a newspaper which happened to be lying on a table. He found it to be a copy of *L'Action française*, which day after day, with scrupulous regularity and much insult, called in question his morals, his financial integrity, and his political ability.

"Good heavens!" said the minister. "Do you read this rag?"

"Every day," said my grandfather.

"As an emetic?" said the minister.

"No, Monsieur. As a stimulant!"

It was an understood thing that we got killed for France, but although we ranged ourselves with the nationalists, France was not really our country. We felt just as much at home, perhaps more so, in Bohemia, Poland, Baden-Württemberg, Schleswig-Holstein, Belgium, Italy, Vienna, Moscow, and Odessa. My father used to say that the Church, pianists, Jews, socialists, and we had no homeland. Wars, religious persecutions, marriage, and chance had scattered the family all over Europe. There was an English branch which pronounced our name with an absolutely killing accent, an Italian branch which had boldly added a Neapolitan "o" onto the sacred syllables, and a Russian branch which had followed the maréchal de

Richelieu to Odessa and married, alternately, German grand duchesses and a whole series of French actresses from the famous Michel
theater. Above all, we had a German branch.

One of my great-great-great-uncles, going back twelve or fifteen
generations, had married a sister of Admiral Coligny, and a whole
section of the family had gone over to Protestantism. There were
quite a lot of them, and they were all killed on St. Bartholomew's
Eve with the exception of a child aged three months, called Henry,
whose nurse had saved him by hanging him up, at the risk of
suffocation, in a huge chimney which the drunken soldiers fortunately didn't light because of the heat of that terrible August day.
Louis, Henry's grandson, went to Germany at the revocation of the
Edict of Nantes. The wars of Napoleon, Bismarck, the Kaiser, and
Hitler slaughtered his great-grandsons and the grandsons of his
great-grandsons. But around the beginning of the present century
there were still a good dozen or so of them left to fight duels with
ferocious elegance, to study philology at Heidelberg and Tübingen,
and to marry young ladies from the Krupp family.

All the members of the Germanic branch of our family were
shrouded in mystery. We never knew where they lived or what
passports they held. They drifted about between the plains of
Silesia and the mountains of Bohemia, and were to be found at
Marienbad and in the Black Forest, in the castles and palaces of East
Prussia and on the banks of the Rhine, and also in Venice and
Palermo, where through their womenfolk they clung to fantastic
memories of Emperor Frederick II and the Hohenstaufens. In November 1918 one of my grandfather's brothers, then a lieutenant
colonel on the staff of Marshal Foch, was surprised to see, alighting
from a big black Mercedes to discuss the conditions of the armistice,
a German vice-admiral of the Baltic fleet whose name was the same
as our own. It was Uncle Ruprecht. His son, Julius Otto, was to earn
a certain obscure distinction in the German nationalist movements
after the war. He fought against the communists with Kapp and
General von Lüttwitz, then with Ernst von Salomon, author of *The
Outcasts, The Cadets,* and *The Questionnaire,* and with General
Ludendorff. Julius Otto went along with Hitler throughout the

thirties, but managed to end up a hero: he was decapitated with an ax and hung from a butcher's hook after having helped his cousin, Colonel Count von Stauffenberg, to plant a leather briefcase containing a bomb under the Führer's desk on July 20, 1944.

Such were our contacts, beyond the castle and the forest, with the world around us. One of the secrets of our ancient family was that it conjured up for us, living there in that remote corner of the French countryside among our gymnasts and our parish priest, our chambermaids and our kennelmen, a Europe that was dying and a world that was dead. Everything that had been our strength and glory at the courts of Vienna and Versailles, in the drawing rooms of London and Rome, in camps and monasteries and cathedrals, on battlefields and most of the seven seas, was disappearing swiftly into deepening darkness. A few scraps survived, thanks to memory and kinship, the first still vivid and the second brilliant. But they only misled us about our fate. By dint of dining every evening, in our imagination, with the regent and the Kronprinz, with Cardinal de Rohan and Prince Metternich and the surviving remnants of the Marlboroughs and the Yusupovs, we were able to go on thinking that our family name was the center of the universe. We led a truly poetic, a dream existence. We lived far away from ourselves in space and time. And we weren't alone, in the evening, in the big murky drawing room among our priceless furniture, gazed down upon by the marshal who'd saved two kings and the great-grandmother who'd initiated three. The old house was filled with the shades of those no longer there.

But though they belonged to another age, my father, grandfather, and uncles didn't have an inordinate idea of their own importance. I never saw them anything but disarmingly courteous to everybody, never heard them raise their voices. Monseigneur the archbishop, doing us the honor of staying in the blue room once a year when he came to perform the sacrament of confirmation, was treated by them with exactly the same deference as they showed toward the daughters of the keepers and farmers of La Paluche. My people had no pride as individuals—they kept it all for the family as a whole. Perhaps a large part of the story I have to tell can be explained in terms of the unimportance of the individual in our collective life. What mattered was the stock which had started one day at practically the same time as history, and which spread across the world in so many different countries, so many different forms and uniforms, and always, by some fascinating mystery, at different periods and yet simultaneously. My cousin Pierre had played rugby a lot with the Catholics in Ireland toward the end of the twenties, and he used to say it reminded him of the family: the achievements of the individual belonged to the side as a whole, and what mattered was not distinguishing oneself but helping the team to win. Forward passing wasn't allowed. And the efforts of the family were back passes too.

Since everyone nowadays thinks about almost nothing else, I must say a word about money. With us you might have thought it didn't exist. It didn't exist, of course, because we had it. But no one would ever have had the effrontery to talk about it. Or, naturally, to make it. Money, like cancer or tuberculosis or venereal disease, was dealt with by never being mentioned. This silence provided us with an image of the world which was somewhat vague, but utterly charming. Later on, at about the time these reminiscences begin, money was to make a triumphant entrance among us with the marvelous Gabrielle—Gaby—Uncle Paul's wife. Millions would then flow past the windows of the castle, in the shade of the ancient limes. But they would be harbingers of the final catastrophes, like those unexpected and deceptive remissions which may precede the fatal crisis. In our heyday, though, we knew nothing of money. It was simply there. None of us could have said by what mysterious means it managed to change itself into new tiles for the roof, fancy-dress balls for the cousins from England, and hunting twice a week for six months of the year.

There was a very important person whose job it was to look after these strange transmogrifications. He had started quite young, and would die at an advanced age, at the dawn of the new era. His name was Monsieur Desbois—the rough equivalent in English would be Forester—and he was the steward. Unlike the huntsmen, La Verdure and Rosée, and the head gamekeeper, La Loi—their names might be rendered, respectively, Leaf and Dew and Law, and strangers exclaimed at their aptness—our steward had been called Desbois from time immemorial. In this case the name really was providential. For our money came not from the numbers racket, drugs, or white-slave traffic—except in the case of our uncle in Argentina—nor from industry or trade or speculation on the stock exchange. It came exclusively from houses and land, but above all from trees. It sprang out of fields and forests and stone, placed itself meekly in Monsieur Desbois' hands, and left them again in the form of coachmen, footmen, cooks, and gardeners. It was so easy to be rich! We owned a fair amount of the department of Haute-Sarthe, admittedly one of the smallest departments in France, and a few buildings scattered about in the area between the rue de Monceau and the avenue de Messine in Paris. I found out later that Proust, when he was young, had been our tenant at 102 boulevard Haussmann, and that two members of the French Academy, a world boxing champion, and three ministers of the Republic—one of them a socialist—had contributed to our support. I won't go into the number of crooks and prostitutes: Monsieur Desbois himself never succeeded in counting them.

Every now and again, of course, we would go to Paris. But we felt considerable mistrust and contempt for the capital, something that was quite the opposite of the great ambitions of people like Julien Sorel or Eugène de Rastignac. They went to Paris in search of fame. We left our fame behind at Plessis-lez-Vaudreuil, and it would still be there when we came back. No—we didn't go to Paris for glory. What we went for was dancers and new boots. It was very little, really—shopping and the needs of nature. We also took the opportunity to show ourselves at Longchamp, at drag-hunts, at the house of the eternal duchesse d'Uzès, at Aunt Valentine's tea parties, and at the charity bazaars run by the ladies of the Sacré-Coeur. Perhaps these pages may in their modest way help to show how things have changed between the Middle Ages in which we lived then and the modern times whose advent we obstinately refused to admit. The change was a very obvious one, a detail both small and crucial: it consisted in the organization of time. We used

to spend autumn and winter at Plessis-lez-Vaudreuil, because that
was the hunting season. But we came to Paris just before the hottest
season of the year, between spring and summer, because that was
the racing season, and the season for the receptions of which our
tenant in the boulevard Haussmann was so fond.

We never traveled. We went to Paris by carriage, or later by
train. That was all. It would never have entered my grandfather's
head to go to Syria or India or Mexico. There was something
unsettled and somehow vulgar in moving about. Ever since the
Crusades and the corsairs we had scarcely stirred from Plessis-lez-
Vaudreuil. You went to the Côte d'Azur only if you had something
wrong with your chest—and then, of course, only in winter, when
you might meet the Empress Eugénie or the Empress Elizabeth at
Cap Martin, or Queen Victoria at Cimiez, or the Empress of Russia
at Nice, sea-bathing behind a screen of sixty Cossacks. To be seen
at Cannes or Nice between May and October was a disgrace it
would be difficult to survive. There could be but three reasons for
a trip to North Africa: if you'd committed murder or theft; to
escape the invader, if you were from Alsace; or if you were a
homosexual. Travels in Italy and Greece were the only exceptions.
President de Brosses, Chateaubriand, and Edmond About served as
examples and excuse there. Those who weren't afraid of being
called bohemians might embark at Marseilles or cross the Alps to
go and wander among the ruins.

On the other hand, people often came to see us. We had lots of
guestrooms. There was the blue room, where we put the archbishop; the pink room; the yellow room, where Henri IV once slept
—Henri IV has slept at every genuine chateau; the carnation room;
the marquise's room—because Madame de Pompadour spent one or
two nights there; the two rooms in the tower; and the room without
a name. There was no running water in any of them. Running water
was so "common": no wonder it scared away ghosts. I was used to
seeing my grandfather break the ice on the top of his water jug
before performing his morning ablutions, when I visited for the
Christmas holidays.

But still friends came. There was something quaint and traditional about us. People came, often from a long way away, to savor
the somewhat strong aroma of a forgotten past. The first bathroom
was installed in 1936, when Léon Blum was prime minister. Social
progress ought to be good for something, my grandfather said. He
had a sense of occasion, a feeling for the right moment and for
propitious encounters. The first pigeon shoot took place in the
grounds on February 6, 1934. And no sooner had Stavisky put a
bullet through his head than the chauffeurs and cooks, who had
hitherto just been given lump sums to cover their expenditures,
were asked to keep a few accounts. This was a staggering innova-
tion, a sarcastic tribute to the decadence of the age. Everyone was
amazed, and perhaps rather shocked.

Friends, cousins, members of the Austrian or Polish branches of
the family, didn't come just for lunch or the weekend. They stayed
for a couple of months. Of course, they had a long way to come.
One fine day twenty-two of the Poles turned up, with so much
baggage that the stationmaster at Roussette had to press the under-
taker and two woodcutters into service. There was one Russian
cousin who settled himself in for good. He still lives at Plessis-lez-
Vaudreuil, though the upheavals of our modern age have forced
him into an occupation he never dreamed of during the parties and
suppers at Tsarskoye Selo and the Winter Palace: for twenty years
he's been chief of the fire brigade.

If I wanted to put our life in a nutshell, I'd say it was both strong
and precarious. Strong, because it was based on things which had
never trembled in the past and which could never be doubted in the
future. Between the world and us, our own ideas and us, us and
ourselves, you couldn't have slipped one of those rice papers my
grandfather used to roll his own cigarettes. We stuck together.
Doubt, intellectual uncertainty, bad conscience—we didn't know
what they were. We'd had a lot of misfortune. The Reformation
was one misfortune. The Revolution was another. Dreyfus's innocence was a calamity, Caillaux's introduction of income tax a minor
disaster. The Pope's condemnation of "L'Action Française" was a

major one. But these ordeals had no effect on our belief in immemorial values and the honor of the family name.

But as the years went by, we were less and less convinced that everything would work out in the end. For a long time we'd thought it would; now we weren't so sure. However, we knew for certain that things were going wrong whenever they upset us, and that we were always right. God and the king were on our side. This great coalition vouched for the past. It might be that it had less control over the future. Well, what did it matter? We lived in the past anyway.

But there were certain episodes in our history which we didn't know whether to regard as good things or bad. The most striking example was Napoleon Bonaparte. We couldn't agree about the Corsican elevated to emperor. Some of us hated him because he hadn't brought back the king and because he'd murdered the charming duc d'Enghien, who was in a way our cousin. Others liked him for having driven out the speechifiers: they preferred a soldier who shot people to lawyers who guillotined them. Another ambiguous case was the uncle who married Aunt Sarah. Aunt Sarah was a Jewess. And this represented a cruel misfortune, an inexplicable blow on the part of Providence, a divine affliction. My grandfather and grandmother didn't go to the wedding. No one did—only the archbishop of Paris, who sanctified the union, and the four thousand five hundred guests who were invited to the reception at La Bagatelle. It turned out, however, that Aunt Sarah was not only very beautiful and full of family feeling, but also extremely pious and right-thinking. She had close connections with lots of German grand dukes and princes, and with the archbishop of Paris. And she was very rich. What was one to do? A wealthy Jewess, even more of a monarchist than we were, a convert, naturally, and the bearer of our own name!

I shouldn't like people to think I'm making fun of the family. Perhaps, now that things have changed, as the reader suspects and will shortly see, I might be allowed to say quite seriously that nothing could have been more noble, serene, and worthy of love than that blind race into which I was born. It had its weaknesses.

What has not? Was Monsieur Daladier so wonderful? It had its absurdities. I won't say anything about Monsieur Blum: he was a prince, like us. But the republicans too were often laughable. It had its cruelties. Were the hands of the Revolution as clean as all that? We had behind us such a wall of memories, tradition, and prejudice that we had to stand up straight. We stood up very straight. We were strong. We knew how to die. The ordinary people liked us.

It will be objected that they didn't understand, that they were stupefied with religion, that they hadn't attained self-awareness. I'm not here to argue. I'm here to tell a story. And I say the people liked us. I don't know whether they liked the Condés, the Richelieus, the La Rochefoucaulds, or the Talleyrand-Périgords. But I do say they liked us. And they showed as much during the Resistance and at the Liberation. We had the whole district behind us. Half was for my grandfather, who was on the side of Marshal Pétain. And the other half was for my cousin Claude, who led the Maquis.

People loved us for a very simple reason. We loved them. Yes, we did. And I won't let you laugh when I'm only telling the truth. We weren't socialists and we weren't democrats. We hated both socialism and democracy. But we were Christians. Roman Catholics, of course, but Christians too. And we loved our neighbor. But the idea of our neighbor didn't extend very far, then, beyond the limits of the castle and estate. We couldn't have cared less about little Algerians and the children in the Congo, the floods on the Yellow River and people starving in Peru. But we did love our own people, the ones in Plessis-lez-Vaudreuil and Roissy, Villeneuve, and Saint-Paulin.

Perhaps I'm not being quite fair. My great-grandmother used to make us save up the silver paper from our bars of chocolate to send to the children in China, and I remember quite clearly that everyone said she had an especially soft spot for the natives of North Africa. It will be said that this was just another kind of racism. To tell the truth, I must admit she preferred the Berbers and the Kabyles—especially the children—to Arabs. Much later, at the time of the great quarrel between the sultan of Morocco and the pasha of Marrakesh, I couldn't help thinking she would certainly have been on the side of the Alaoui, because he wasn't an Arab. The thing was that she had elective affinities with the lords of the Atlas and the mandarins of China, the sort of sympathy somewhat crudely explained by Marxists nowadays as class conspiracy. But as we know only too well now, no one is ever completely free. We too were influenced by history, probably even more than other people. But we did what we could to love the little brothers the Lord had sent us.

No, we couldn't be called unfeeling. We knew less about the distant places of the world than devotees of television do. But then we were less inclined to snivel and do nothing about it. Our attitudes were the opposite of those of today. My grandmother didn't bother too much about what was happening in Africa or Asia or Latin America—we called it South America then—but she never spoke of misfortune without immediately trying to find a way of relieving it. We had cooks who insisted on being called chefs, and they wore big white caps which were starched by chambermaids in lacy aprons. We had butlers and footmen, tutors and gardeners, chauffeurs and scullions, gamekeepers and kennelmen. But none of our people—that's what we called them and that's what they called themselves—not one of our people ever died without my grandmother or my mother or some other member of the family standing by the wooden bed, under the crucifix and the palm, to hold the dying person's hand at the very end. Our people belonged to us. But we belonged to them, too. In those days you didn't change maids as casually as you changed shops or cars or shirts. Those who came to work for us didn't need social security, or pensions, or clinics, none of which existed yet. Anyone who came to work for us knew he'd never be unemployed or without means of support; he knew that he'd be looked after if he was ill, and protected against risks and dangers, and that if he died his children wouldn't be abandoned. How could it have been otherwise? As soon as he came to us, to warm the beds or rake the garden paths, he became one of the family.

We didn't maintain the icy protocol that reigned in the great houses of Austria and England, where the hierarchy in the dining

room was strictly reproduced in the order of precedence in the
kitchen and the servants' hall, and where, so we heard, visitors'
domestics were known by the name of their master or mistress. We
—my grandfather and his keepers, my grandmother and her chambermaids, my uncles and their kennelmen—were one big solid family whose members were interdependent. It extended to all the
neighboring villages. The woman who kept the draper's shop in
Villeneuve, the woodcutters in Roussette, the foresters, the men
who tiled the roof, the men who mended the roads, all belonged to
the same structure as our cousin in Pomerania who was a general
of Uhlans, and the elderly assistant at the Papal Court, our great-
great-uncle of Romagna and Lucania. We didn't look down on
anyone, not because we were virtuous but because we formed an
ancient edifice in which every stone was joined to all the rest by a
mortar immemorial, and in which only God and the king—in the,
alas, distant days when he was legitimate—were different from
anyone else.

We lived in a definite structure, a system—a tacit, rather mysterious, almost secret system completely incomprehensible to modern
minds. It was the system of honor. It was just as rigorous as Marxism
or Hegelian philosophy. But no one ever referred to it. Explanation
was frowned on. We were too close to the land and the horses and
the ancient trees to be very fond of ideas. But that taciturn life of
ours was animated throughout by a faith of which we never spoke:
a faith in continuity, survival, the permanence of objects and men
in the context of God's great design, of which the family name was
clearly one of the highest embodiments. We were only just beginning to realize, with some bewilderment, that God's great design
had always been called in question. Defeat, disaster, and treason
hadn't been too much of a threat. We weren't afraid of disasters—
we'd seen too many. We weren't afraid of betrayal—we'd sometimes betrayed with the best of them, and carried it off with an air.
Such imperfections were never of very great importance. No—
what, slowly at first and then ever faster, had undermined the order
willed by God was an army of termites, nasty, insidious, unhealthy
little insects and rodents: ideas. Caesar in Gaul, the Barbarians in

Rome, the Turks in Constantinople, the French in Moscow, and the
Russians in Paris, plague, flood, famine—these hadn't done much
harm. What had done damage was Luther, Galileo, Darwin, Karl
Marx, Dr. Freud, and Albert Einstein. This terrible blacklist contained six names. Three were Jews, two were Protestants (though
one of these was an atheist), and one was as good as a heretic.
Another name was added later, for having destroyed the human
face. This was a certain Pablo Picasso, who gave himself out to be
a communist. We reproached the Jews not so much for their
money, their long curls, Christ's blood, or the hooked nose—which,
incidentally, was completely absent from the captivating countenance of Aunt Sarah—as for thinking. We did very little thinking.
My grandfather loved to tell the story of how one of his brothers
came on a cab driver, probably a socialist, reading *La Pensée* by the
pale light of a street lamp. "Take me to Maxim's, thinker!" he cried.
A voice from far away in time and space told us not to think.

We owed our marvelous health, which had brought the family
name safely through so many centuries, to the absence of ideas. By
stopping the sun from going around it, and by saying that we
ourselves were descended from monkeys, Galileo and Darwin had
dealt a fatal blow to the stately edifice crowned by God and the
emperor, the king and the Pope, the cardinals, the marshals of
France, the dukes and the peers, and us. Was it sensible to represent
an ape and an orangutan as the progenitors of old Aunt Melanie,
who'd married one of the Spanish Bourbons and whose stunning
and proverbial beauty had killed two cousins, one after the other?
The Japanese were much wiser and more seemly in having their
emperors descend from the sun and moon. But we felt so sure of
our strength that we didn't really believe in the scientists' nonsense.
They were often republicans, anyway. Deep down in the bottom
of our hearts we'd always really agreed with the Inquisition. For
century after century the sun had risen and set on the glory of the
family. We weren't going to start revolving around *it* at the behest
of some rather low Italian. The case of Darwin was even simpler:
he was just a scoundrel. We used to wonder very coolly and calmly

what sinister ulterior motives were behind this mania for humiliating us. Probably something to do with the Jews or the Freemasons.

Any chinks in the edifice, any faded trappings in the great procession of glory, any patched breeches or limping old men or rebellious slaves or broken-down horses, we didn't see and didn't want to see. You do believe me? We weren't fighting for money, but for a certain image of the world that was beyond dispute. Comrade Karl Marx may have been right when he said that my grandfather and his like were merely defending an economic position. But he needed to call in Dr. Freud too, for we had no idea that that was what we were doing. God, the king, the past, and the family honor constituted an impenetrable wall between us and money.

Although our universe was still strong, the termites that were gnawing away at its foundations had made it precarious. It was full of holes. We'd already stopped living in the intoxicating world of reality, and our dead branches had withered on the tree. We didn't work. Life went on without us. We'd lost our grip. We'd left active service to indulge in melancholy reminiscence. Everything conspired to encourage this withdrawal. My grandfather, the head of the family, hadn't even been able to follow the one profession which he'd been taught by eight centuries of tradition: he hadn't even been able to be a soldier. He was born in 1856—he was two or three years younger than my grandmother—and so was fourteen in 1870: too young. In 1914 he was fifty-eight: too old. But he was eighty-nine in 1945, and there was still enough life left in him for him to see, through the joys of victory, the end of the world he had passed through as an onlooker. The story I tell is the story of the end of a world. Nothing can be sadder.

We were frivolous—Lord, how frivolous we were! We were charming, often handsome, always impeccably well bred, very tall, very strong, and very weak; marvelous huntsmen, sometimes pale and weary but always indefatigable, with inordinate appetites and limitless zest for anything that amused us. We were Aztecs, Incas, kulaks, Cathars, Bogomils, Georgian princes, merchants from Balkh or Merv in the age of Genghis Khan, heroes of Atlantis—we were all the races who were doomed and didn't know it. The irony of it! We thought we were princes and nobles and the Right instituted by God the Father, and we were really only what we most despised: the Jews in Poland in 1939. With our ancient chateaus and our elegant manners; our friendship for craftsmen, chairmenders, and potters; our mad ideas about honor and our scorn for money and work; our Almanach de Gotha under our arm, our God in the form of an idol, and our love of the land and the past in a world bent on a future from which trees, horses, patience, infinity, and respect were banished in advance—with all these, we were condemned to death. Like the Jews, the communists, the gypsies, and the Freemasons, all we were fit for was the ax, a bullet in the back of the neck, and the concentration camps. But the others would have their revenge; whatever happened they had some hope in the future. But we'd never have any hope again. Did we know this? I think it must have been like the idea of death for most ordinary people: we knew we would have to die, we had a vague suspicion that we were already dead, but we couldn't and wouldn't believe it. So we hid our dreadful fate from ourselves, hid it behind our clothes, our hunting, the cult of tradition, and a particular form of absurdity to which the shadow of death lent a certain grandeur.

A ridiculous grandeur—perhaps that's the quality I see in my great-uncles Joseph and Louis, and my great-great-uncle Anatole, with their whiskers and their high wing collars, their morning and frock coats, their inimitable accent, their devotion to the legitimate monarchy, the rigidity of their judgments and beliefs, their impeccable honesty, and their incurable blindness. They weren't ignorant. They spoke Greek and Latin much better than I did, though I'd spent a good ten years in the schools of the Republic trying not very successfully to learn them, and they'd read everything that had been written right up to the beginning of the eighteenth century. But after that their choice grew more and more restricted. To start with, a few were ruled out—like Rousseau and Diderot—for insolence and bloody-mindedness, and after '89 only a handful were admitted. Joseph de Maistre, Vigny, Barbey d'Aurevilly, rare swimmers, remained afloat; at a pinch, Bonald, Octave Feuillet, Victor

Cherbuliez, Maurice Barrès, and Léon Daudet; and of course, greatest of all, the vicomte de Chateaubriand, whose works all my family knew by heart from beginning to end, as they did those of the duc de Saint-Simon (who was connected with us through his wife, Marie-Gabrielle de Durfort, daughter of the maréchal de Lorges and sister of the duchesse de Lauzun). Our family liked everything about Chateaubriand: his birth, his ideas, his loyalty, his style. And also his follies, his moral rigor, his countless mistresses, his penchant for suicide and ruins, his irresistible melancholy interwoven with drollery, his devotion to lost causes—all these made him their man. Loyalty makes him my man still. No, we weren't ignorant. But we were dead. We had been overtaken by time.

I think I've given you a fair idea of the world we lived in. It had scarcely changed in almost a thousand years. And the last thing we wanted was that it should change. But despite the fact that we lived in our dreams and shut our eyes to anything unpleasant, our world was no longer what it used to be. We talked about it as if it were some elderly uncle suddenly struck down by an incurable disease. We looked at each other and shook our heads and said: "How he's changed!" We didn't profess any opinions, but deep down in the unfathomable depths within us we cherished a philosophy of silence and immobility. The saying that ideas make their way among men is very true. But in this dubious progress which philosophers—socialists, naturally—greeted as an advance in awareness, we saw as a slow sapping and undermining of our cathedrals. Yet, above such disasters, we still went on parading our empty lives. We didn't expect anything any more. We were just trying, always in vain, to slow down time and the passage of the sun over our heads. But God, our God, refused to perform this miracle for his latterday Joshuas. We weren't afraid, because centuries of courage on every battlefield forbade such a thing. But there was a divorce between the world and ourselves. Without respite, with ostentatious avidity, even, the world was committing an unforgivable crime. We had stopped, and it was going on.

2

The Breach

⬩ BUT IN THE END, ONE FINE SPRING DAY toward the end of the last century, modernity swooped down upon the family. To win us over, it had assumed the form of a fair-haired girl whom the Duke of Westminster and Monsieur Basil Zaharoff's nephew had noticed at hunts, at court balls in England, and at the charity bazaars organized, of course, by a lot of ladies out of the top drawer, always the same ones. Whether imported or exported, the women of our family are often beautiful. My Uncle Paul, who'd never lifted a finger except to serve mass in the castle chapel and be in at the death of a stag after three or four hours' hunting through ponds and thickets, met Gabrielle in a scene straight out of a novel by Georgette Heyer. He threw himself at a runaway horse in a forest in Sologne, and the daughter of an arms and orange merchant fell swooning into his embrace. He married her. She was delightful, of more than average intelligence, talented, and immensely rich. To no purpose. This attractive combination of qualities didn't please anyone. The family at once let it be known that it wasn't satisfied. And the arms dealer wasn't satisfied either.

Marriage was one of the clues to our ancient universe. For century after century we had married our peers. But as time passed, it became more and more difficult to find other families as old as ours.

Practically all of them had died out. The Revolution had gobbled up those few lingering survivors who might have aspired to ally themselves with us. So we'd been reduced to intermarriage. No one else still lived as we did. No one else found favor in our eyes. In less than two generations the family tree became horribly complicated: almost all husbands and wives were cousins, or uncle and niece, or aunt and nephew, and, to the great delight of archivists and country cousins, there were sometimes three- or fourfold relationships between the twigs of the branches. The unwritten laws of marriage were reducing the globe and its inhabitants to one clan.

Money didn't count for much in these alliances. What did count was blood. Antiquity was something that flowed in the veins. Family papers took the place of bank accounts. When other people talked about stocks and shares, we thought about the Crusades, and the only bonds we were interested in were those of feudalism. We had kept up the ancient traditions, and if one branch of the tribe got too impoverished, there were always convents and monasteries to restore the balance. The Church, like war and germs, helped to control population and balance budgets. But the Revolution dealt the financial equilibrium that no one ever talked about a blow from which we never recovered. One of the major catastrophes in our overlong history was the abolition of the law of primogeniture.

For a long time the function of women and younger brothers had been merely to make up the numbers and die. They were just instruments, tools, cogs in the wheel, and if necessary, replacements. It didn't really matter very much if a daughter or a little brother died. And a woman having a baby was quite free to succumb as long as she left a son behind to carry on the name. Daughters weren't important because they lost the name. And they lost the name because they weren't important. Eve's serpent swallowed its own tail. The sole *raison d'être* of women and younger brothers was to minister to the glory of the family of which the eldest brother was head. He was the only one who really mattered, since he both embodied and carried on the race. Everything was organized so as to concentrate all the group's resources on him. When brothers and sisters suddenly began giving up dying and going into monasteries,

when they stopped being silent and started claiming their shares of
the inheritance, the family, or at least our conception of it, was dead.
All that was left for us to do was to try to patch things up and get
out of it as best we could.

For many people, fashionable marriages were an essential part of
this process. But we still clung to our dreams of the past. We looked
on in scorn as American, bourgeois, or Jewish young ladies set on
their feet the descendants of high constables and princes of the
blood who were in trouble with their banks or their tailors or their
bootmakers. We were able to hold out, thanks to the boulevard
Haussmann and the farms in the Haute-Sarthe. True, the arrival of
Aunt Sarah had brought a certain amount of disturbance, as well
as money, into our immutable order. But her husband, Uncle Joseph, my grandfather's brother, wasn't an eldest son. Anything he
might do, however foolish, was of no consequence. Moreover,
though we lived on our memories, we also knew how to forget.
Very old families are like very old people: they fall into second
childhood and are threatened, or perhaps protected, by senility. In
the end we forgot about Aunt Sarah's origins. Her brother had
married a Châtillon-Saint-Pol, and her sister had married a Bourbon-
Vendôme. We mixed up the generations and fancied, more or less
genuinely, that her father was a Châtillon-Saint-Pol and her mother
a Bourbon-Vendôme. Thus, by a subtle combination of constancy
and inconstancy, the family presented as united a front as ever,
despite modern times, when Uncle Paul, my grandfather's eldest son
and the future head of the family, fell for the pretty arms manufac-
turer's daughter in Sologne.

For the past hundred years the rise of the Remy-Michaults had
been dazzling. But a hundred years was nothing, and people in our
family didn't rise. Everything we had was there from the beginning.
The basis of our fame was with us in the cradle—we never added
anything. A rise that covered a century, or perhaps a little more,
was nothing. And anyhow it had begun under the Empire, or worse
still, under the Revolution. Albert Remy-Michault was the equal of
the Schneiders, the Wendels, and the Sommiers. He was one of the
most elegant men of his day. Like Charles Haas, he was one of the

models for Proust's Swann. He was the head of a vast enterprise, he employed twenty thousand workers, and his fortune was no laughing matter. He was a commander of the Legion of Honor, and frequented the most exclusive clubs in Paris. But the only thing my grandfather cared about was that he was a republican. For eight centuries or more the family had got along very well without republicans. And what had been should continue to be. Such a long and laudable habit was not to be given up just because of a chance encounter with a girl who let her horse run away with her.

There was an even more serious objection. Everyone knew that the first of the Remy-Michaults, who was then called simply Remy Michault, was a prefect under the Empire before becoming minister for trade and public works under the Citizen King, Louis-Philippe. But many people had forgotten that earlier still, when he was twenty-five, he'd been a member of the National Convention. My grandfather's memory was as long for evil as it was for good. Somewhere between the table of dukes and peers and that of the marshals of France he kept a copy of the blacklist of regicides. It didn't take him long to find out that on January 20, 1793, Michault de la Somme (Remy) voted for the king to be put to death. There was a thunderclap in the sky over Plessis-lez-Vaudreuil. The marshals' batons, the wigs, and the damsels on swings shook in their frames and glass cases. My mother still used to tell me about it forty years later. My grandfather nearly had a fit at the thought that he might have a grandson who was the descendant of a regicide. One of the oldest families in France, one of the most loyal to the king —we didn't deserve it.

But the Michaults, then the Michaults de la Somme, then again the Michaults, and then the Remy-Michaults—"Don't even know their own name," said my grandfather—had left their mark in the history of France. True, the mark was on modern, almost contemporary history, and it was sticky with blood and money. Michault de la Somme, the son of an innkeeper and a milkmaid, not content with voting for the death of the king, had soon afterward sent several of his own colleagues to the guillotine. He was the associate of men like Sieyès, Barras, and Tallien. The First Consul noticed his efficiency as assistant to Daru in the commissariat, and he was made prefect of the department of the Marne, and then of his native department, the Somme, where he asked for and obtained the hand of a former nobleman's daughter. This was the first great triumph of Baron Michault's career. Under Fouché and Talleyrand he, together with Alexander and Metternich, worked clandestinely for the overthrow of Napoleon, to whom he owed everything, and for the restoration of the Bourbons, whom he'd once wanted to exterminate.

The former regicide's second apotheosis occurred under Louis-Philippe, the son of his erstwhile accomplice, the duc d'Orléans, a member of the National Convention and a regicide under the name of Philippe Egalité. Louis-Philippe, "king of the French," soon detected a good servant in this monarchist republican who had been connected for so long with the Empire. He gave him a ministry— a good one: first trade, then public works. Baron Michault made a fortune speculating on the railways. He was tempted to resume the name Michault de la Somme—the title was flattering, and might be useful too. But it stirred up too many old memories. So he decided to call himself Remy-Michault: a hyphen was almost as good as a particle. Baron Remy-Michault's always calculated splendors did Orleanism proud. His son, Lazare Remy-Michault, went to North Africa, and added a colonial fortune to the one his father had amassed in industry. A few more whirligigs of time, a few more massacres, and the Remy-Michaults were ready to invade the Third Republic as conquerors. They of course became as comfortable there as they were everywhere. All regimes suited them except those that had fallen. And they liked revolutions as long as it was they who ran them. We, on the other hand, for a long time had been on the side of power, but now that we were losers we naturally preferred those who were loyal and vanquished to those who were clever and victorious.

The Remy-Michaults were clever—they had a sense of occasion, they knew when to stretch forth their hands and grasp hold of history. They too had their family traditions: these consisted first and foremost in not having any traditions, so as to be sure of never missing anything. All was grist to their mill. They seemed to get fat on the very air. First they halted the Revolution for their own purposes, then they turned to their advantage a shaky monarchy, a revived empire, and a republic in its infancy. We'd been dead for a long time. But they were all alive and kicking! Always vivacious, active, alert, energetic, and even bold in a cowardly sort of way, they were marvelously intelligent, versatile, and adaptable. First prefects and ministers, then ambassadors and councilors of state, they also represented a certain image of France. A different image, but an image, and even quite a brilliant one. But we would rather have died than recognize ourselves in it.

My grandfather had only one word for the Remy-Michaults: riffraff. They had betrayed the king. They had betrayed the Church. And they had betrayed the enemies of the king and the enemies of the Church. And the trivial crime of having betrayed the king's enemies didn't atone for the monstrous crime of having betrayed the king. A friend of the Remy-Michaults came to plead their cause. He explained that the first of the Michaults had been one of the handful of men who destroyed Robespierre. He was told: "I'll sum up the story of Thermidor for you in a couple of words. It was the murder of one lot of scoundrels by another lot of scoundrels." Nothing could have been more foreign to us than the qualities which had made the Michaults' fortune in the course of thirty or forty years: flexibility, power to adapt, understanding of the ways of the world, versatility, talent, and perhaps intelligence. We weren't very intelligent. We had no talent. The Michaults, despite or perhaps because of their baseness, were cut out for success. We, after so much glory, admired only failure. And we called it loyalty.

The Remy-Michaults were mad for success. Office, fortune, glamour—they had to have all of them. The grandson of the member of the Convention, the son of Lazare and grandfather of Albert Remy-Michault, was French ambassador in Bavaria, and entertained Bismarck at the chateau of Ferriès in 1870. As always, his outstanding talents charmed everyone, including the Iron Chancellor himself, who sings his praises in a letter to Thiers. But his closest ties were with the Rothschilds of the day. After the war he left govern-

ment service and was given a job in the bank by barons Alphonse
and Gustave de Rothschild. All the major transactions of his time
passed through his hands: the payment to Prussia of five billion in
war reparations; the setting up of Suez; the preparation of Panama.
Between 1882 and 1886 he became managing director of the mines
at Anzin and Maubeuge, of the iron works at Riquewiller, and of
the steel works at Longwy. He was in on the founding of the
International Company of Wagon-lits and the big European express
services. He was one of the first people to take an interest in tourism.
He developed the colonial operations of Lazare Remy-Michault:
from Fez to Kairouan, he owned whole stretches of palm, olive, and
orange groves, and the finest plantations of lemon and mandarin
trees. A large part of the trade in citrus fruits between France and
North Africa was handled by companies over which he had either
direct or indirect control. Forain observed characteristically that,
for the Remy-Michaults, a couple of million oranges a day kept the
doctor away. He might have added that a war here and there didn't
do them any harm either.

Have I been fair to the Remy-Michaults? There's nothing so
difficult as trying to make words represent events, ideas, passions,
and feelings. All expression is betrayal. After having seen St. Louis
transformed into a brigand, Joan of Arc into a hysteric, Stalin into
the father of his people, tolerance into violence, and violence into
liberty, we can't help mistrusting language and writing. I too would
be perfectly capable of showing the criminal as victim, and then the
victim as criminal. We have seen plenty of these wearisome conjuring tricks in our time. To represent men and their actions justly calls
for an art that is almost divine, or at any rate, one which is much
more difficult than that of shining briefly at satire or apology. The
Remy-Michaults had one god, and that was success. There's no
getting away from that. But they were expert at all the rites necessary for gaining access to their divinity. Effort, hard work, a zest
for competition and struggle—in these chilly waters the great-
grandsons of the revolutionary splashed about with delight, having
been introduced to them by the Swiss nurses and inscrutable Jesuits
who brought them up. In addition to flexibility and skill, succeeding

generations had gradually acquired a strict sense of discipline, the most bourgeois kind of honesty, integrity, almost honor. "Honor!" stormed my grandfather. "Honor! Where would they have got it from? The moat at Vincennes, perhaps, when they shot the duc d'Enghien?" But as the years went by—we counted in centuries, the Michaults counted in years—the memory of regicide and the thirst for money gradually gave way to the conservative virtues of work and tradition. What they lost in brilliance they gained in solidity and persuasiveness. The word of a Remy-Michault was as dependable as a bar of gold. Values, in the bank sense as well as the ethical sense, took the place of audacity. Like us, they too started to obey the dim law of their own kind, and tried to organize as well as possible the ground which had been annexed by the conquering generations who had gone before. But whereas we were at the end of that long process, they were right at the beginning. I suppose my grandfather held them guilty of two almost opposite crimes: first, of being parvenus who'd built their fortune out of the death of Louis XVI, and second, of having ceased to be parvenus—having little by little managed to make everyone, themselves included, forget their original sin, so that imperceptibly, in their way of living, their interests, and their ideas, they were absorbed into a social class—which was also an ethical, metaphysical, and mythical class—that was eminently sacred in our eyes and ought to have been so in theirs: our own class.

Family legend has it that two parallel speeches were delivered practically simultaneously by my grandfather and Albert Remy-Michault, to their son and daughter respectively, in the style of the palinodes of tradition. "My boy," said my grandfather, who wasn't averse to a touch of pomposity now and again, "you are toying with the idea of a very profitable marriage. But money has never mattered or played any part in the history of our family. If we had enough to maintain our position in the world, well and good. If we hadn't, too bad. Eleazar's son couldn't raise the money to ransom his father from the Infidels. So Eleazar did without it, and escaped. He crossed deserts and oceans and came back to fight again by his king's side. We were never so poor as we were at the end of the fourteenth

century, and never more glorious. Once and for all, at the beginning
of our line, we replaced money, which may belong to anyone, by
honor, a kind of honor peculiarly ours: fidelity. Should there ever
be the smallest chink in the still incomplete edifice of our continuity, the day of its utter collapse will be at hand. We've already taken
a Jewess into the family. Do you now want us to take in treason and
regicide? If the death of God and the death of the king are to be
accepted as peccadilloes which may be forgotten, what will become
of the purity of blood and remembrance, what will become of the
values our family is built on? There is nothing in the world so fragile
as honor. It's at the mercy of the slightest shortcoming. The idea
that good and evil are evenly balanced is a dreadful illusion. Good
can be destroyed by evil, but evil is not destroyed by good: it
remains forever like a stain that can never be removed. That is why
it is so important to defend honor against all attack. I couldn't bear
the family name to be handed down through the centuries by the
descendants of a regicide. It would mean wiping out a thousand
years of honor and loyalty at a blow. Don't you see—our family's
whole idea of history and the world is now in your hands. Each of
us is only a link in one long chain. Woe to him who is a tarnished
link, and who weakens the whole chain! We ourselves don't count.
What counts is the family. One day we shall have to hand over
intact to our successors the honor we have inherited through the
ages from our predecessors. Don't let passion or self-interest jeopardize, at one blow, all that accumulation of integrity."

Meanwhile Albert Remy-Michault, with a tinge of vulgarity, was
addressing his daughter in more or less the following terms: "You
don't really want to marry this boy, do you, Gaby dear? Don't you
realize they're all frauds and good-for-nothings? I have no son, and
I need a son-in-law to succeed me. Your great dope of a Paul
wouldn't be any good. He can hunt—agreed. Dance, in a pinch. But
work! That's a different kettle of fish. I don't need a genealogist, a
huntsman, someone who knows how to blow a horn. I need a lad
who knows how to control machines and men. They must have
known how to rule men once. But they lost the knack through
doing nothing and thinking themselves better than everyone else.

As for machines ... Listen, if I couldn't have a graduate of the Polytechnique or an expert from the ministry of finance, at least I'd rather have a foreman, a workman, someone going up the ladder instead of coming down. For eight hundred years, as they themselves would say, they've been doing nothing but descend—descending from one generation to another, true, but that's descending all the same. And then they have the nerve to look down on us! Come now, don't cry. Were you as set as all that on being a duchess? Of course, you'd certainly have been prettier than all the old oil paintings in their salons. You'd have given those crazy degenerates some new blood. Come on, don't cry! Forget about it. Listen, shall we go on a trip to Venice or Salzburg or New York?"

Six months later, Uncle Paul married Aunt Gabrielle, just back from New York. The reason for this was that a new force had appeared in this fragment of social history to which I am endeavoring to make a modest contribution. Love. Love has always played a part in the history of man. It was found, of course, in Christian marriages. But as an effect rather than a cause. It didn't create families, regimes, and societies; it tended, rather, to destroy them. Racine's son Louis, in his memoir on his father's life and works, says admiringly of his marriage: "Neither love nor self-interest played any part in his choice." But now, for the past half-century, inextricably mingled with various camouflaged interests, love had entered into the social and economic arrangements of the industrial bourgeoisie. It was the element of dream in a world of machines. The great plains had been covered with factories, the trees cut down, mountains and seas already invaded and sullied, but love, injected into society at the beginning of the nineteenth century by romanticism, was having a triumphant career as a counterbalance to the world of technology. Man was hemmed in by machines, and soon would be hemmed in also by cars, communications media, and publicity, but he was capable of passion. What a relief! Love was nature's revenge and alibi in a world which was already aware, and somewhat ashamed, of its mechanized future. The myth of love, which was to nourish the cinema, literature, and popular song, and to be first another and genuine opium of the people and then be transformed into a religious and political weapon, was beginning to enter into the calculations of mothers of families and captains of industry. It usually did so with a great deal of good sense and willingness. Marriages of reason had created nations, shifted provinces, and built up fortunes. One of the triumphs of the conquering bourgeoisie was the channeling, domestication, and annexation of love. By some miracle the Tristans and Isoldes of bourgeois tales and legends never quite lost all sense of proportion and social propriety. Novels dwelt on the ravages of extreme cases of passion, such as those of Mathilde de la Mole in *Le Rouge et le Noir* and Anna Karenina. But I never heard of a Remy-Michault falling in love with a Negro, a farm laborer, a layabout, a noted prostitute, or an ex-convict. They might descend as far as a country doctor, a model, an actress, or a divorcee, but never any lower. No prince ever married a shepherdess who couldn't be made presentable. The heart had its reasons and reason was aware of them. It brought together only those who were likely to be suitable, and broke through only those barriers and prejudices so shaky already that they needed the merest touch to overthrow them. It would unite a notary to a squire's daughter, the son of a radical professor to the sister of a Catholic colonel, a Jewess to a Protestant, the daughter of a Freemason to the nephew of an archbishop, and my family to the Remy-Michaults. You'd have sworn it knew what it was doing every time; and it did know. The time for great upheavals hadn't yet come. I suspect that my grandfather and Albert Remy-Michault realized straightaway, perhaps with a tinge of regret but also with resignation, that despite the contrast between their ideas about people and the world, they were fated for each other. They indulged in a few more rearguard actions, but each kept ready, in the false bottoms of the unconscious, a peace treaty and a marriage contract. The family of the high constables and marshals of France was in need of money, and the children of the regicide hankered after some of the dusty glory of old furniture stowed away in noble attics. New classes were coming over the horizon of history. It was time to present a united front. My family's entry into the republican bourgeoisie heralded the advent of modern times, in which one could no longer afford to be too particular. It was necessary to form a sort of holy alliance or national front for the maintaining of privilege. Our contribution to the coalition was the castle and the name, one or two ghosts, some glorious memories of battles long ago, poetic imagination, tone. The Remy-Michaults supplied intelligence, hard work, desirable situations, and money. On one side was all the prestige of the past, and on the other all the promise of the future. Small-minded observers might say the arrangement catered to snobbishness and self-interest on both sides. But I hope I have shown that the pattern of this family chronicle was somewhat more complex than that. Of course, seen from the outside, passion and social status seemed to have arrived at a satisfactory compromise. Yet my grandmother, who was said to have espoused my grandfather once but his opinions a hundred times, died of grief less than three months after the wedding. No one was very surprised at her premature death: she herself had predicted it. The comment of Sauvagein, the worthy family doctor, was perspicacious. Turning, puzzled and perhaps slightly reproachful, from the hollow cheeks, the obstinate silence, the tear-filled eyes, and haggard features of my grandmother, he whispered to my grandfather: "If she were twenty, I'd say she was dying of love." He was not so wide of the mark. My grandparents were both quite innocent and had maintained their patriarchal ways in all their purity, and it was a love which seemed to us ignoble that made her die of grief. Six months later was born, at Plessis-lez-Vaudreuil of course, the future head of the family, in whose genealogy there were two saints and three bankers, Eleazar and a regicide, and a whole string of dukes and peers on the father's side, and, on the mother's, a lot of people no one had ever heard of. The child was called Pierre. Our family had had two marshals of France called Pierre, one under Charles IX and the other under Henri III. Also one of Louis XVI's chaplains.

From Tarass Bulba's Son
to Dean Mouchoux's Fritters

♦ THE EDIFICE OF OUR TRADITIONS AND
myths, more fragile than we knew, was threatened not only from
within, by people's private lives and the vagaries of youth. The
government too—you should have heard the loathing with which
we pronounced the word—did its best to bring it down, with elections and decrees and all sorts of institutions referred to far from
tenderly in the family circle. The Republic, in its scorn for our
privileges, had invented two or three terrible destructive and leveling machines in particular, and made them compulsory: these were
universal suffrage, military service, and mass education. In an increasingly hostile world where our natural superiority was being
attacked from all sides, our only hope of salvation lay in isolation.
Eventually we had become the only ones who still believed in us.
That was why we lived, hunted, and married just among ourselves.
People thought we were proud, but really we were shy. We were
afraid of other people, and of a future which was going to be the
opposite of the past. We shut ourselves up behind doors opening
onto a world which had become too big for us and for hopes bound
up with memory. But school and the army forced us to open the
doors again.

The army didn't bother us too much. We preferred officers to professors, NCOs to teachers, soldiers to students, and generals to academics, scientists, and winners of the Nobel Prize for physics, literature, or peace. We had a long, traditional affinity with soldiers. We'd been Chouans, émigrés, aristos. We felt closer to adversaries in uniform than to supporters in civvies. The fraternity of combat linked us to the armies of the Republic. We liked their order and hierarchy, their smartness and power. It wasn't our own order or hierarchy; it wasn't our sort of power. And of course it wasn't our sort of elegance either, for that was incomparable. But we put a brave front on it and my grandfather invited to Plessis-lez-Vaudreuil, for luncheon or to go hunting, such generals and colonels and captains as, though they might have no names to speak of, held views, either open or concealed, which were close to his own.

Beneath the lofty ceilings of the salons, under the eye of dukes and peers and marshals, the conversation would circle around a couple of terrible topics which everyone avoided like the plague. By some obscure instinct even the boldest—newcomers, young lieutenants, hotheads—were careful not to broach them. The delicate subjects were the flag and the "Marseillaise." My grandfather had of course continued to revere the white flag of the monarchists. But the officers with whom he surrounded himself were serving under the tricolor. You can imagine the effect on this elderly monarchist of the words of the national anthem. He used to pretend to confuse it with "La Carmagnole" and "Ça ira," two revolutionary songs, or, ironically, with the "March of the Toreadors" from *Carmen.* Later, much later, when some young members of the family started to spit on the flag and hiss the "Marseillaise," I found myself remembering, with a tinge of melancholy but also much amusement, how my dear grandfather had paved the way for these demonstrations.

The army was to play an increasingly important role with us. We found to our delight that it still preserved some relics of the *ancien régime.* Only the army and the Church still spoke to us of our ancient virtues, whispering the old refrains of the past in our ear, often in extremely odd guises. When the Dreyfus affair started to

rend the nation, we flung ourselves in on the side which you may
easily guess. Not, despite what superficial observers have thought,
because of fanatical anti-Semitism, but because of our desire to
defend the army. It so happened that it was a Jew who was threatening it. Was that our fault? We didn't even claim that he was really
guilty. We didn't know anything about it. In our view, it wasn't a
question of guilt or innocence: we simply thought it was the duty
of the individual to put society before himself. It really was too bad.
There were only two hierarchies left in France, the Church and the
army, and along comes some obstinate unknown captain and tries
to demolish the soundest of our traditional institutions on the ludicrous grounds that he was innocent. "And what about the dead?"
said my grandfather. "Those who were proud to die on the battlefield—weren't they innocent? Captain Dreyfus would do well to
regard himself as on active service before the tribunal." We were
beginning to lay down the law again to our fellow countrymen.
The Dreyfus affair drew us imperceptibly into the arena of public
debate from which hitherto we had been so careful to hold aloof.

Unfortunately, this return of ours from inner exile was not a
dazzling success. We might lay down the law, but no one obeyed.
Once again we'd backed the wrong horse. There seemed to be a
curse on us: nothing had gone right for us since the death of the
king. It should be added, by way of either excuse or condemnation,
that we were distantly related to Major Marie Charles Ferdinand
Walsin Esterhazy, who himself was related to the Galanthas, the
Fraknos or Forchensteins—so smart, names that were translated!—
the Cseszneks and the Zolyoms, and was a descendant of a family
of princes of the Holy Roman Empire going back to the Crusades
or perhaps even Attila, with an age-old right to the titles of
"Durchlaucht" and "Hochgeboren." The fact that he was in debt
didn't bother us too much. He'd been to stay at Plessis-lez-Vaudreuil
for a fortnight, and had spoken somewhat harshly of his colleague
Alfred Dreyfus: he hadn't a very high opinion of his abilities, and
he couldn't stand his voice or the look of his eyes. Ten years or so
later, we discovered that Major Esterhazy was only related in the
female line to our Esterhazy cousins. The last of the French Ester-

hazys had given birth during the Revolution to a natural son whose father was Jean-César, marquis of Ginestous: this child was the major's grandfather. The mother had taken advantage of the reigning confusion to give her son the illustrious name of Esterhazy. No one ever really succeeded in persuading my grandfather that Major Esterhazy was guilty. Right up to the end of his life he went on maintaining that the business of the memorandum was never quite clear. But it was with some relief that he discovered the illegitimate origins of the name which had been so sullied and which, combined with Dreyfus's innocence, had done the army so much harm. It was a small consolation, but for him vital.

With the Dreyfus case we had made a mess of our return to public affairs. But we did much better the next time. The second opportunity was also provided by the army. The army and war went together, and war was our province. And it was the Great War which at last brought us back into the arms of France after our long estrangement. Of course we'd have preferred to fight on the side of Germany, where we had so many relatives, and against England. Especially against the United States, where we knew practically no one. But we were beginning to realize that we were no longer being consulted. And it was some consolation that we were fighting with the support of the czar and Holy Russia. It was time at last to learn to bow to circumstances. We set off for the front with an enthusiasm which may have owed something to the murder of Jaurès.

It isn't too hard to guess what made us march against a country which was dear to us in various ways. What drew us to the frontiers was one of the oldest reflexes in our age-long history: the drawing together of the lands that were France. We much preferred the court of the king of Prussia and emperor of Germany, with its large staff of barons and counts and its sumptuous uniforms, to our own regime of lawyers and veterinarians. We felt more at home in the towers along the Rhine than in the taverns on the banks of the Marne; we felt nearer to the Teutonic Knights than to anglers or bowlers. But the spiked helmets, the long leather coats, the fur caps and death's heads of the Uhlans were eclipsed by an even brighter vision: the blue line of the Vosges, with the forests and plains below. For centuries the object of our existence had been the acquisition of land. That passion had taken us to the East, Italy, beyond the Rhine, and into the heart of Europe. Alsace and Lorraine were as sacred to us as the farms at Villeneuve, Roussette, Saint-Paulin, and Roissy. France was a hoard, a property, and it was our job to increase it. The fall of Napoleon III hadn't grieved us overmuch, but it was unbearable that the territory amassed by our kings should be dismembered. The Republic was able to gather us to its bosom because, under our wigs and coats of armor, in our chateaus and at Versailles, with our forests and our hounds, despite our dreams and because of them, we had never ceased to be peasants.

My grandfather had lost a brother in the battle of the Marne, one nephew in the battle of the Somme and another in the Dardanelles, two sons at Verdun and another wounded at Eparges and then killed at the Chemin des Dames—this was my father. He was thirty-five when he died, and I was just fourteen. I had an idea he was on Dreyfus's side, and that he wanted to live. But his life and ideas were of no great importance, because he was not an eldest son and what mattered more than anything else was the name he bore. The bonds created by honors and privilege are not so strong as those forged by sacrifice and loss. Through the death of its children our family, which had been excluded for about a hundred years, was brought back again into the history of France. True, there were whispered but half-proud rumors among us that one or another family hero had been found scratching out the word "Republic" and the image of Marianne from his medals. We were quite ready to die for them, but we drew the line at wearing them on our bosom. It didn't matter. My grandfather, who'd been bereaved six times in less than four years, was present with all the rest of the family at the victory parade. Monsieur Poincaré and Monsieur Clemenceau shook hands with him. Never before had we been at such close quarters with a radical socialist, a militant though converted member of the republican extreme Left. My grandfather remained a monarchist, but he began to love France. Some say he was even seen saluting the tricolor and standing up for the "Marseillaise." But it was not that patriotism had made him accept the sacrifice of his children. On the contrary, it was the death of his children which had reconciled him with his country. "I only hope," he said to Monsieur Desbois, "I only hope I don't become a socialist."

No, he didn't become a socialist. He discovered, to his astonishment, a new aspect of socialism: bolshevism. In 1912 or 1913 Uncle Constantin Sergeivitch, marshal of the royal household, president of the Zemstvo of the Crimea, owner of twenty or thirty thousand souls—whom as a matter of fact he had freed—and of so many flocks of sheep he himself didn't know how many, had come to visit us at Plessis-lez-Vaudreuil. He hired two railway coaches, of a staggering luxury even for those days, which were coupled as required to every train in Europe. He'd traveled via Vienna, Marienbad, and Baden-Baden to Nice, still full of Russians and Englishmen, and there he'd taken a suite for himself and his entourage—from October to May, it goes without saying—three whole floors in the largest hotel. The first floor was for the servants, the second for himself and his family, and the third was left empty, so that they shouldn't be bothered by noise.

There was something terrifying about Constantin Sergeivitch's fortune, and about his generosity, his recklessness, his wild prodigality. He had no idea of the extent of his wealth, and would hand out to dancers, hairdressers, and chambermaids diamonds and emeralds which nowadays would be star items in any collection or national museum. By a vagary of history this same Uncle Constantin was regarded by us as a rather advanced liberal. The Russian branch of the family had had a somewhat ambiguous relationship with the Romanovs. In 1825 they'd been involved in the Decembrist plot against the emperor Nicholas. Several had been sent to Siberia, and they had saved various socialist or anarchist revolutionaries. The great salons at Plessis-lez-Vaudreuil echoed with endless arguments between my legitimist grandfather and Uncle Constantin, who admired England, liberal philosophers, constitutional monarchy, and the regime of Louis-Philippe. We were for the czar, and he stood up for the Poles. He wasn't against Mirabeau, Thiers, or the memory of Talleyrand, whereas we loathed them all out of loyalty to the traditional monarchy which still prevailed in his own country but which he would have liked to change into a form of liberalism, almost of democracy. He and my grandfather were fond of each other, but the only thing they agreed about was the Franco-Russian alliance, and then it was for contradictory reasons: our Russian uncle admired the Republic, and we admired the autocracy.

In 1917, when the wretched Kerensky overthrew the Romanov regime, my grandfather exclaimed furiously: "There goes Constantin again!" A few months later we learned, with a horror we could never forget, that all the Russian branch of the family had been murdered in the Crimea. Prince Constantin, his wife, his six children, his seven grandchildren, his brothers and sisters and cousins, and some thirty of his servants had been shot by the Bolsheviks next to graves they had been forced to dig themselves. They had started with the youngest—little Anastasia and Alexander, aged two months and eighteen months respectively. After seeing all his family collapse in pools of blood, Uncle Constantin was the last to die, together with an old coachman whom we used to call Tarass Bulba. Four or five years earlier, his wide-belted greatcoat and fur hat had been the object of great wonder at Plessis-lez-Vaudreuil. The only surviving member of the Russian branch of the family was a young cousin who happened to be staying with us. Later, perhaps out of a hereditary liking for uniforms and helmets, he became an officer in the fire brigade.

The prince's last words had been for my grandfather, whom he loved dearly despite their differences, and for the Russian people, and for freedom: "Tell Sosthène," he said, "that nothing is lost, that Russia will be born again strong and great, and that the name of the future is liberty." My grandfather's comment: "That's where liberalism gets you."

Tarass Bulba's son was one of the few to escape the slaughter, about which for more than a year we had only the vaguest reports. He managed to hide, escape, and get to Constantinople, and he arrived at Plessis-lez-Vaudreuil toward the end of the spring of 1919. That evening there was a big dinner party at the castle, followed by a ball: the first festivity of that kind since all the losses of the war. My grandfather had just asked one of his Harcourt or Noailles cousins to dance a waltz when the door of the grand salon opened to admit Monsieur Desbois, followed by a shaggy young man dressed in rags and covered with mud. It was history entering, though we didn't recognize it—the links that had once made it so familiar having become so tenuous. The orchestra stopped playing. Silence fell. My grandfather turned to his steward with an air of bewilderment and displeasure. Monsieur Desbois stammered something, and ushered the stranger forward. Boris advanced, bowed, and then, before an astonished circle of onlookers, in the very room which Uncle Constantin had once filled with his noisy joviality, said rapidly, all in one breath, with a strong Russian accent: "Your grace, the prince is dead. He told me to tell you that nothing is lost, and that the name of the future is liberty." It was astounding to hear such words at Plessis-lez-Vaudreuil. Only a great catastrophe could make anyone dare to pronounce them in my grandfather's presence. Tarass Bulba's son was a lad of outstanding courage and intelligence. My grandfather had him taught French and provided him with the means to continue his studies. He soon turned out to be very brilliant, and in less than twenty years he became one of the most eminent physicists of his time. He eventually worked with Louis de Broglie and Joliot-Curie, and in 1961 Tarass Bulba's son, now a professor at the Collège de France and a commander of the Legion of Honor, was unanimously elected a member of the Academy of Sciences. If my grandfather had still been alive he would have been at the same time moved, delighted, and amazed at the way times had changed. Already, though, even these times were showing signs of wear and tear. Examples of boldness and novelty which still astounded us were already things of the past. Two or three years later, just before his fall from power, Nikita Khrushchev invited a delegation from the Institut de France to Moscow. Boris was one of them, and was received with great enthusiasm by his former compatriots. He toasted Ivan the Terrible, Peter the Great, and Comrade Lenin in vodka and joined his hosts in bitter

but delicious tears over the fate of ancient Russia. To spare my
grandfather the contemplation of such a spectacle, the Almighty in
his mercy had gathered him in.

The Great War had other consequences besides the fall of the
Russian Empire and my family's reconciliation with France. It also
brought the end of the Hapsburgs and Austria-Hungary, another
monarchy and another dynasty which had always played an important part in our private history. Out of hatred for Orleanism and
so as not to have to serve Louis-Philippe, my great-grandfather had
for four years, under the July monarchy, worn the white uniform
of the Austrian army. He'd been in Venice with the army of occupation, and fallen in love with an Italian countess who lived in a
Gothic palace on the Grand Canal, between the Rialto and St.
Mark's Square, almost opposite the Accademia. His adventures,
fictionalized, of course, were to inspire one of Lucchino Visconti's
most famous films, for the Austrian hero in *Senso,* Alida Valli's
lover, was my grandfather's father.

Austria-Hungary, like Russia and Germany, was one of the countries where we felt at home. Agreeing for once with Talleyrand, we
regarded Austria as Europe's House of Lords. We were horrified by
its collapse. Czechoslovakia, the new Hungary, the larger Yugoslavia which arose out of its ruins, were all profoundly foreign to
us. Blissful ignorance is sometimes able to see farther than intelligence and skill, and my grandfather, who didn't know anything,
predicted the disasters that would soon ensue as the result of the
destruction of the Middle Kingdom and the Empire with Two
Heads, of all that vanished world which had fought so many battles
against the Slav and the Turk and held so many celebrations in
honor of the two K's we still loved so well: *Kaiserlich und Königlich,*
imperial and royal. Something of our own past and our own heart
perished with the Hapsburgs. The war had given us one country,
France, but it had caused us to lose three others, with Germany an
enemy and vanquished, Holy Russia drenched with blood, and
Austria-Hungary in pieces. Victory shrank and altered the world
we had loved even more than defeat. History, which had so long
been on our side, was so no longer.

And that wasn't the worst of it. We loved the past so dearly we would willingly have renounced both present and future if only our memories at least had been left to us. But the Republic was snatching them away from us through compulsory education. We naturally disliked universal primary education because it might undermine the caste barriers which meant so much to us. But we disliked it not only because other people's children now had to go to school, but also because ours would have to go there too. Unlike the bourgeoisie, we didn't set any store by education, either for others or for ourselves. For centuries we'd seen the world the way we chose to see it, and what we said went. And now academic scribblers, radical professors, and socialist intellectuals had gotten hold of things, and were trying to make us measure up to their standards before they would let us start out in life. "I don't know what future's in store for my children," my grandfather used to say, "but at least I mean to leave them a past I chose for myself." But already over our old simple horizon of loyalty and honor were arising new values for which we were ill prepared: the values of truth and freedom.

We hated freedom. It had no meaning for us, except insofar as it was connected with rebellion, the right of choice, individualism, anarchy. As long as we were the power in the land, we only scorned and mistrusted liberty. "Tolerance!" my grandfather would say. "I suppose they mean licensed brothels." It wasn't until we were driven to it by the socialists and the liberals that we too came to demand the formerly detested freedom. But we still found it hard to accept it as a principle, and employed it merely as a tactic. I've always been told my grandfather was the inventor of the famous phrase, "I demand my own freedom in the name of your principles, but refuse you your freedom in the name of my principles." We were slightly ashamed at using the devious path of demagogy and freedom to get back to the true sources of temporarily obscured but immutable order. But what were we to do? In a mad world where everything was going to the dogs, we were only making use of freedom to reestablish authority. Since other misguided people used force and guile and numerical superiority to impose an intolerable tolerance upon us, we had to use what means we could to restore truth in the midst of all the lies.

Freedom was just a question of method. Truth posed very different problems. I think the best way of putting it, though perhaps rather provocative, is that truth and ourselves were one and the same. I don't want to exaggerate. Put it that truth was divided between God and us. Ever since I began these reminiscences of days gone by, two spheres, two constellations, two mixtures of reality and myth, have solicited me, at once because of the strength of their presence and their ambiguity. It wasn't a matter of morals, integrity, intelligence, or love of humanity. All that had changed, but we were comfortably installed in more or less consistent systems which we could manage without too much difficulty. No, what's hardest to explain now, because we didn't find it easy even at the time, is the relations we had then with money and with God. I've already talked about money, and we shall find the subject presenting itself again. Now let's say a word about God.

We weren't overburdened with piety. We'd known too many popes, cardinals, bishops, and even saints, had in fact provided too many of these ourselves, not to regard them with a certain familiarity. This didn't rule out respect and deference, or even reverence. But it did imply that we and they were collaborating in the same order, the same system. We respected the king because he respected us. We respected the Pope and the Sacred College because they respected us. We dealt with them as one power with another. Between the Church and us, between God and us, there was a whole series of reciprocal treaties. We were the eldest sons of the Church, the Lord's anointed. They protected us, and we in return protected them. I wouldn't say it was tit for tat, because we were after all committed unconditionally to obey all the decrees of Divine Providence. But it was plain that, when the worst disasters struck, Providence didn't lump us together with those the Church somewhat slightingly called the mass of the faithful. We didn't think of ourselves as part of that mass. I wouldn't like to say God was our equal or our partner, still less our client in the Roman sense of the word. No, of course not. But he had obligations toward us.

One fine day, visiting Rome, my grandfather's mother was to receive communion from the hands of His Holiness. Just before mass was due to begin, a monsignor came and told her that the Pope was either not well or detained, I don't remember which, but that the dean of the Sacred College proposed to take his place. My great-grandmother declined succinctly: "For us, it's the Pope or nothing."

The relations between the monarchy and the Jesuits, and with Gallicanism and Jansenism, the rivalry between Bossuet and Fénelon, Philip the Fair's struggle against the Templars, and the insult at Anagni had left their marks. But so too had St. Clothilde, the oak of St. Louis, the papal Zouaves, and the conversion of the Abbé Ratisbonne at the funeral of Uncle Albert de la Ferronays at San Andrea delle Fratte. As they say of velvet and other fragile, ancient fabrics, we marked easily. All aspects of the past, whether French, Catholic, or Roman, had left permanent traces in us. Of course, sometimes one kind of trace would predominate, sometimes another. Certain branches of the family had gone in for extreme piety, mysticism, bigotry. Others inclined more toward Voltaire. Unlike Diderot and Rousseau, Voltaire wasn't on our Index of French Literature. Some members of the family—my great-great-uncle Anatole was one—were great Voltaireans, and a tinge of anticlericalism wasn't altogether incompatible with the cult of the family name. But in general we didn't run to excess. It was still a matter of seemliness and loyalty. We loved God because it was clear that he loved us better than other people. How rude it would have been not to show our gratitude to someone who'd done so much for us for so long! And perhaps behind our allegiance to the Pope, the archbishop's ring covered with our kisses, the Sunday dinners with Dean Mouchoux, there lurked the dim but ancient fear that God might love us less if we loved his legates less. It was because Eleazar had escaped the Infidels, because the single male member of the family had not died at Agincourt, because two of us—quite enough to carry on the line—had escaped the guillotine, in short because we had found favor in the Lord's eyes long before the Bourbons, that Dean Mouchoux came every Sunday and indulged himself in the delicious, light yet creamy fritters with raspberry sauce which he loved so much. Right at the end of his life he told me that when there was any misfortune in the family—the advent of Aunt Sarah, Uncle Paul's marriage, Uncle Pierre's death at Verdun and my father's at the Chemin des Dames—the fritters with raspberry sauce would be replaced every Sunday for a few weeks by a rather boring fruit salad. The dean was sure, and indeed it wasn't impossible, that the change of menu was a sort of reprisal. Perhaps, through the dean's weak spot, we were punishing God for having abandoned us. When things improved again or we'd had time to forget, our piety regained the upper hand. We forgave God. We kissed the hand which had struck us. And Canon Mouchoux enjoyed his fritters once more.

Of course there was never any question of not paying God himself the respect due to his rank. Mass, vespers, the stations of the cross, the Corpus Christi and Assumption processions, and the cult of the Virgin Mary were as much a part of our world as hunting and family portraits. But it was not, or not wholly, a matter of piety. It was also part of the show. We were setting a good example. This played a crucial and at the same time paradoxical role in our lives. It was paradoxical because we didn't work, and crucial because we always came out on top. The eyes of everyone else were always on us. They imitated us. What we did was good, what we didn't do was bad. "Behave—people are watching you"; that was the refrain dinned into children from generation to generation. Perhaps we were proud? I'm not sure we weren't, rather, crushed into modesty and humility by the weight of our greatness. God was part of the greatness. And of the humility. We were never so great as when we were throwing ourselves at his feet. In humility we had no rival. We groveled in the dust, and God, who knew us, took us by the hand and raised us up to him.

It would be an absurd error, which of course many fools have rushed into, to accuse us of hypocrisy. Hypocrisy consists in pretense, disguise, assuming sentiments which you don't really feel, hiding those which you do. But we hid nothing, disguised nothing. Those members of the family who didn't believe in God made no bones about saying so. The others made no bones about getting killed for him. Most of us did believe in God with all our might. There were a few skeptics who didn't fast on Friday (but who usually made good deaths), yet most were believers. We had the believer's obstinacy and constraints and sometimes follies, often his blindness, always his intransigence. How could we not have believed in a God who had made us what we were? When our prayers rose toward him, our acts of grace and bursts of fervor, we knew he was there to receive them and to watch over our destinies. To doubt God would have been to deny ourselves. The thought never entered our heads.

By a marvelous coincidence, we rediscovered for ourselves the classical order of the great age of reason, of Descartes, about whom we knew almost nothing. For us, too, God was first and foremost the guarantee of all other certainties, the keystone of the whole edifice in which, through the Lord's help, we occupied the loftiest quarters. God had created everything and went on doing so, maintaining every moment the immutable order of beings and things. Not to believe in God was to cut oneself off from the world, to abandon oneself to madness and to violence both futile and doomed. An atheist couldn't understand anything about the organization of the universe, the history of mankind, ethics—of course—or even geometry. The ground gave way under his feet. But we—we walked in the sight of God, with his blessing and doing his will. Not that we deserved much credit for it, since what he willed was our greatness.

But the price of this greatness was sometimes high. If the truth must be told, perhaps we were Pharisees, not through hypocrisy but at the worst through pride. But sometimes there's heroism in being a Pharisee. Despite our moments of ill humor, despite Dean Mouchoux and his fritters with raspberry sauce, the will of God was sacred to us. We might be surprised when it didn't happen to suit us. We were even known to protest against such of his decrees as did us injury. But, just the same, it was a foregone conclusion that we would submit to them. The family motto was: "At God's pleasure." It is still to be seen on silver plate, on goblets, particularly on

books, on many buildings. It appears, in French, on a lintel of the
little oratory of San Giovanni in Oleo in Rome, built by a cardinal
bearing our name on the spot where, according to a tradition
derived from Tertullian, St. John the Evangelist emerged unscathed
from torture in boiling oil. Anyone can still go and look at this
evidence of the family and its presence in Rome, right next to the
pretty church of San Giovanni a Porta Latina. In a way, the motto
suited us very well: for centuries, with the aid of the big battalions,
God's pleasure had worked to our advantage. Of course, it was
important to prevent the Almighty from turning his coat or losing
his knack. It was clearly understood that the pleasure of God should
for the most part consist in being useful to us. But after all, we too
were the prisoners of the system. There was an order in the universe, and it involved the death of children, suffering, grief, and also
the possibility of the downfall of the radical socialists in France and
the Bolsheviks in Russia. We accepted it, like soldiers, without
hesitation or murmur. We liked the sound of the words "soldiers of
God." It wasn't just a question of linking together the saber and the
censer, the army and the Church. It was a deeper matter, of fighting
and accepting, of victory through obedience, of trusting God because, in all the thousand years he'd been looking after us, he'd
shown he was to be trusted.

Family feeling, love of God, a habit of accepting the force of
circumstance—these things hadn't done much to develop in us a
belief in free will and responsibility. God was responsible, and decision was up to him. As for liberty, that was moonshine. Everyone
was governed by his past, his memories, the present absence of the
dead, by all the weight of tradition. It was a kind of Marxism, in
which economic necessity and the call of the future were replaced
by moral obligation, the whisper of vanished generations and the
fascination of the past.

And so God shared with us the burden of truth. Unfortunately
it was very difficult to communicate with him. Religious outpour-
ings, direct contact with the Bible, the Protestant tête-à-tête with
the Godhead—we knew what these proud manifestations of human
impetuosity led to: they led to personal opinion, individualism,

interpretation gone mad, critical analysis, doubt, anarchy. Doubt and anarchy were two monsters that we greatly dreaded. In morals, the Church, politics, and art, we were in favor of certainty and organization. The pyramid, the obelisk, the Holy Spirit and the Holy Father, the idea of a head, the family, nature—all these things suited us very well. The spiral, democracy, homosexuality, dialectic, symbolism, Impressionism, modern and abstract art, Renan in his own day and André Gide later—all these we spat upon. Luckily, God's truth expressed itself in tangible forms, without ambiguity and ever stronger, reinforced instead of undermined by time. These forms were memory and tradition. As God decided everything and had allowed history to unfold as it had, history must be good. Truth had a face, and that face was to be found in the past.

But the past itself became complicated suddenly, as the result of a disaster. Up to 1789, we could regard history as Hegelians. The history of the world was the judgment of God. But a horrible thing happened in 1789, heralded by Luther and perhaps by Galileo— man's revolt against history as willed by God. Our task became more difficult. Until the Revolution we were for history and God: as St. Augustine, St. Thomas, and Bossuet had said, they were one and the same. But after the Revolution we were for God against history. It was a day-and-night struggle, full of anguish.

History was sacred for us, but we spent our time correcting it: reintroducing God, the family name, continuity, eternity—all the things which senseless others had expelled. We patched it up, and still managed to lean on it. It was gradually moving farther and farther away from reality, intellectual evolution, and the forward movement of science. But that didn't matter. What we lived by was true history, true values, true traditions, which were no longer those of men in general. We lived in a real country which was not the country of republican elections, of Monsieur Gambetta or Monsieur Blum or Monsieur Daladier. The rhythm of history had become as out of joint as that of the seasons and of well-bred weather—it was quite capable now of raining in July. The present was no longer something which would turn, tomorrow, into a past yet to come. It was something else—a monstrosity, an aberration.

The future was quite changed. The best we could do now was try to link a sadly distant future with a sadly distant past. The present was nothing but a long and dreary parenthesis. We lived by a history of God and by a family tradition which made us strangers in the world about us, alienated knights of a bygone mythology.

The truth had nothing to do with what was suggested by observation, experience, scientific instruments, dialogue. Descartes was far away. We were Cartesians in that we believed in the fundamental idea of divine guarantee, but far from Cartesian in our rejection of experience, and even intelligence, as a means for discovering truth. For us, truth was history as God would have made it—with our help, of course—if mankind in its folly had not done all it could to hamper him. Naturally, God was almighty, and let himself be taken advantage of out of kindness, and perhaps also out of a sort of weakness which we somewhat resented. But the awakening would be a terrible one: he was putting men to the test, and one day he would strike them down. And he would seat us at his right hand because we had never doubted, never doubted either God or ourselves. It was to avoid doubt that we'd given up thinking.

This notion of truth was clearly very far removed from the liberal and scientific methods of republican education. I remember my grandfather's constant fury against teachers and their crimes, against the primary and secondary school syllabuses, which not only jeopardized the future but—far worse—laid waste the past. The republicans and socialists and atheists ought to stick to their wild predictions, their vile politics, their elections, and their disgusting literature. They were welcome to them. But they should keep their hands off two things—the army and history. For, in our eyes, this pair prepared the way for the future as well as reflecting the past. My grandfather derived bitter satisfaction from observing the excesses of academics and scientists and what was beginning to be referred to as the "teaching profession" (he pronounced the term with a sneer). They'd begun by criticizing the *ancien régime,* had gone on to praise the Reign of Terror, and were now calling in question Divine Providence and the historical existence of Jesus Christ. He could only wonder how far they would carry their ravings. Not very much farther, perhaps. Things had gone so far, the situation had become so mad and horrible, that reaction was inevitable. In his optimistic moments, which alternated with attacks of depression at the moral and intellectual decline all around him, my grandfather dreamed of the day when men's eyes would be opened, when order would be reestablished around the Church and the throne, when everyone would be restored to his proper place (including us, of course, in the top rank), when officers and men, craftsmen and peasants, painters and writers, would all feel themselves part of one organized diversity, and when the family name would once again be held in reverence.

Compulsory education in a falsified history which mentioned merely in passing the names of our saints and marshals, and often grudgingly at that, drove him literally wild with rage. Even our own worthy schools—the monks, the Marists, the lycées Stanislas and Franklin, and the Jesuits in the rue des Postes—were gradually yielding to fashion and starting to talk about Danton, Robespierre, and Marat as if the best homage to such creatures were not to pass over their memory in silence. I remember how angry my grandfather was to find that the family name was not mentioned once in the sixth-form textbook of the famous Malet and Isaac series, though it referred three times—"the number of times Peter denied Christ"—to the loathed Michaults de la Somme. The French Revolution was no longer a parenthesis speedily closed by the return of the king twenty-one years or so after the death of Louis XVI. On the contrary, it was now put forward as one of the highest points in French history, or, worse, as a new point of departure. My grandfather noted with consternation that children were offered a course in history which culminated when they reached sixteen—just when they were beginning to be really aware—in the study of the Revolution, and that success in examinations depended on that period to the exclusion of the Renaissance, the Counter Reformation, the seventeenth century, the Capetians in the direct line, and the wars in Italy. What was there left to hold on to if the craze for destruction no longer spared what was by definition over and done with and was forever to be treated with respect—namely, the past

and the dead? Yes, everything was certainly changing. The present
didn't matter—we were used to trials and the need for courage and
individual sacrifice. The future was more serious. But when it came
to history, that was a scandal so outrageous that it might jeopardize
all possibility of survival.

To block all the doors opening onto a disintegrating universe, my
grandfather decided to confront the contemporary age as Noah
had confronted the Flood—in an ark against which the waves could
dash themselves in vain. Plessis-lez-Vaudreuil was transformed into
a redoubt, a fortress, a blockhouse. While the Remy-Michaults
spread out everywhere and quartered the world by car, train,
steamer, and after a little while by air, we huddled in on ourselves.
Eventually we came to be regarded as eccentrics even by our peers.
Our chief companions were faithful old retainers who, like us,
shook their heads wistfully over the spun-sugar and nougat palaces
of the good old days. One day when Uncle Paul's father-in-law was
telling about one of his hunting parties in some distant, overelegant
dream setting, and how an army of beaters had driven the game into
the guests' very arms, I overheard my grandfather muttering to
himself: "I wouldn't boast about it if I were in his shoes." And I
remember a postcard, also from Albert Remy-Michault, on a cruise
in the Greek islands, which arrived one fine summer's day at Plessis-
lez-Vaudreuil. It smugly enumerated the useful relationships its
author had managed to build up in the shade of his main jib and
fore-royal. "I've seen the Etienne de Beaumonts, the Montesquious,
the Greffulhes, and a very charming young Ford ..." It was too
much. My grandfather sent a postcard with a stag on it to General
Delivery, Santorin, which said: "I've seen Jules. He sends you his
best." Back came a letter from Mykonos: "What Jules? If you mean
Jules de Noailles, give him my love. But perhaps you mean Jules de
Polignac—I traveled from London to Monte Carlo with him three
weeks ago." My grandfather then splurged with a telegram: "Keep
all your Juleses, and the rest. I'll stick with mine. He's been gamekeeper at Plessis-lez-Vaudreuil for forty-seven years."

Jules was a character who'd played an important role in the
family saga, from father to son, ever since the Restoration. Albert

Remy-Michault got his own back with a story—entirely invented
—about my great-grandfather, which I've already recounted elsewhere and which in its time kept Paris laughing two whole days.
According to the story my great-grandfather and Jules—he was
young then, or perhaps it was his father, who was also called Jules
—climbed to the top of the highest tower at Plessis-lez-Vaudreuil.
It was summer, and the sun was shining down over all the landscape
my grandmother had loved so much. Roussette, Roissy, and Villeneuve nestled drowsily among the fields and woods. Ponds and
rivers gleamed like mirrors.

"Jules," my great-grandfather is alleged to have said. "Look."

"Yes, your grace."

"What do you see?"

"Trees, lakes, meadows, farms."

"What else?"

"Hills in the distance, more woods, more ponds, and then trees
and meadows as far as the eye can see."

"Well, Jules, all that belongs to me. Now shut your eyes."

"Yes, your grace."

"Now what do you see?"

"Nothing, your grace."

"Well, Jules, that belongs to you."

The anecdote eventually came to my grandfather's ears, but he
just shrugged his shoulders. "Vulgar bourgeois invention," he said.
"What nonsense. What belongs to us belongs to Jules."

That was a slight exaggeration. But there may have been some
truth in it. Because we hadn't yet discovered mankind as a whole,
we did the best we could with the family. And, when all was said
and done, it worked. And Jules was one of its most important
members.

So we disputed every inch of the ground against the world and
the times. We organized ourselves, and did all we could to find some
last remaining scraps of tradition to cling to. We did our military
service in the cavalry, because horses were more faithful than men
to memories of the past. Old priests who didn't know anything, and
whose eyes God had mercifully kept shut against the horrors of the

age, came and taught the younger members of the family about the noble deeds of the Romans, of our kings, of Charlotte Corday and Monsieur de Charette; about the justice of St. Louis, the simplicity of Henri IV, the courage of Bayard, and the victories of Turenne. We stopped bothering about a despised present and a doomed future. We kept our eyes fixed on the past, lest it too should suddenly fade away, disappear, slip between our fingers.

4

The Clockmaker from Roussette and Aunt Gabrielle's Double Life

IT SEEMS TO ME I CAN LOOK BACK FOR centuries at the big stone table that stood under the walls of the castle in the shade of the ancient limes. Time left no mark on it; it drifted on through eternity. After lunch and dinner too, in the summer when the weather was fine, we used to gather around it, through bereavement and disaster, to re-form the family circle. We had gathered there in wigs and three-cornered hats, in toppers, bowlers, and boaters. We'd gathered in military caps, and now we gathered bareheaded. It was like a film in which the generations imperceptibly melt into one another, disappearing into the void only to come to life again as children who themselves turn ceaselessly, over the years, into parents and grandparents and great-grandparents. Champaigne once painted us sitting around the stone table, and so did Le Brun, Rigaud, Lancret, and Nattier. Watteau painted us, between two Pierrots, and so did Boucher and Fragonard. Remy Michault de la Somme preferred to be depicted by Louis David—another member of the Convention, another regicide. But we kept Madame Vigée-Lebrun for ourselves. We were just falling into the arms of Bonnat when Nadar appeared with his bulb and tripod, to disappear immediately beneath his little black veil and fix us. Then we stepped down from our stiff frames of wood and gilt, into leather, soon plastic, albums where we looked just like anyone else. How right we were to loathe technology! We hated it just as we hated progress. Unfortunately we weren't much attracted to talent or genius either. We looked like people by Berthe Morisot or Degas or Vuillard or Bonnard, but we never suspected it. For us, painting like everything else had come to an end with the monarchy. Delacroix and Courbet filled us with mistrust. They painted with ideas. We preferred Ingres and Gainsborough. It was whispered that one of the cousins frequented houses of ill fame and painted terrible things there. We weren't all that surprised. We didn't know much, but we could still guess that there must be some secret link between riffraff and artists. We were neither the one nor the other. It would never occur to us to patronize prostitutes or cut off our ears or go to Abyssinia. But the cousin who was a dauber, and of whom we rather sadly made fun, bore a good and ancient name: Henri de Toulouse-Lautrec. Everything was going to the dogs.

It was very pleasant around the stone table. Not only did it give off, for each one of us, the perfume of his or her own youth. It also stood for the childhood and adolescence and youth of the oldest among us, of our aged, of our dead. The reader will already have realized that in our family death didn't set up very formidable barriers. A foolish marriage or wrong opinions severed you from the family community much more surely than the narrow streamlet of death, which we skipped across gaily over the footbridges of memory, tradition, ancestor worship, and continuity. No need to repeat the fact that we lived among the dead. We loved God, of course, but he didn't reign alone over our hearts: he had to share the honors with our dead. With their inscriptions and shields and recumbent figures, our tombs were chapels, even churches, and our dead were our gods. We knew their names back to the twelfth generation, and they were nearer to us than many of the living. Why? Because we thought about them. The dead are immortal as long as one living person still carries them in his heart. And our dead lived on because we carried them in our hearts. They all sat there around the stone table, and we were always slightly apprehensive lest they should stand up, in their doublets or jerkins, and retire, in unwontedly solemn protest, against the entry of the Remy-Michaults into the magic circle. We already felt very hostile and mistrustful toward strikes. A strike of ancestors and tradition would have been the most cruel blow to us.

Perhaps all this helps to explain why I have been presenting so familiarly events and people I never actually saw. I've often said "we" and "us," and shall do so again, referring to great-grandfathers and great-grandmothers who were no longer of this world when I came into it. They were no longer of this world in the eyes of ordinary people who see only the present, but they still had their places around the stone table.

When I came to sit there, the world had started to change. The summers were less hot and the winters less cold. There weren't the frosts there used to be in the days when my great-grandmother and her little boy, my grandfather, went skating on the lake in January. Horses were becoming a thing of the past. Machines and motors spluttered along the still-dusty white roads, making the children look up in amazement. The telephone was just learning to ring— not in our house, of course, but at the Remy-Michaults'. And the Remy-Michaults passed on to us speed and noise, agitation and progress, like so many contagious middle-class diseases. The past was less alive, and we sometimes found ourselves discussing the future. Encouraged by science's gradual takeover from history, a craze for change had taken possession of people. Everything was slowly getting beyond us, and the older ones among us were torn between anxiety and indifference. Anxiety because everything was going badly, and indifference because they scarcely belonged any more to the universe of folly and disorder they had abandoned. Everyone around me kept saying that men were without God or king, hope or faith, and were rushing headlong to their ruin. But in the midst of all these perils we still went on leading quite a pleasant life. It was a strict life, but quite pleasant—full of the threats every-one kept dinning into us, but also of the certainties that we still clung to. As far as I can see, looking back, my childhood seems quiet

and happy, bright and sheltered, strewn with its daily meed of
still-living memories and anxieties as yet far off.

At the fortunate epoch when I made my appearance in the world,
there had been a change in our changeless history: the Remy-
Michaults had brought us into fashion. For a long time we had
played the part of exiles in our own country. We'd turned away
from everything to look elsewhere, toward God and the king and
the myths of our origins. But now, through money and fashion, we
found ourselves right up to date. All the rage, as the Remy-
Michaults would say. After so many centuries of grandeur and
pride, we were descending to smartness and vanity.

The shade of Orleanism, of the Citizen King and Philippe Egalité
and the bourgeoisie triumphant, had fallen over our intransigence
and our traditions. The family, together with its castle and its past,
had been taken in hand by Aunt Gabrielle. By one of the ironies of
history, everything my grandfather and grandmother had dreaded
had come to pass. The lucre derived from crime, treason, and parri-
cide put brand-new tiles on the roof and paid for the kennelmen.
Bathrooms and refrigerators loomed in the not-too-distant future.
But my grandfather still put up some resistance. As I've said, it
wasn't until Léon Blum and the Popular Front that we bathed in hot
water. But already we were marked down and encircled by all the
pleasure and all the dangers of easy living.

Aunt Gabrielle, as I think I've mentioned, was extremely beautiful. Before the Great War she reigned at the same time as Madame
Greffulhe and Madame de Chévigné, and in the twenties she was
even more dazzling. She bore our name with peerless style. She'd
introduced into the family a whole series of habits which to outsid-
ers, people who were not members of the family, appeared like old
traditions, but which horrified my grandfather: things such as luxury, fine cooking, travel, soon followed by a craze for cars, a veritable mania for running water, a love of *objets d'art*, an English accent,
and an irresistible attraction, of which more later, for literature and
the arts. With mixed feelings my grandfather watched the castle
escape ruin, grow more beautiful, fill up with friends come from

Paris to stay for two or three days and with furniture that had cost a fortune at Sotheby's or Christie's in London. He watched as the floors that for centuries had been covered only with very old and very lovely rugs were covered with wall-to-wall carpeting, and as the walls and panelings were hung with chintz and cretonne. What Alsace and Lorraine had done to our hearts, Aunt Gabrielle did for the big drawing room and the picture gallery and the conservatory: we became part of our age, and our house with us. Some evenings the Michault guns used to shoot cascades of red lemons and blue and green oranges into the summer sky; they burst out gracefully, to the sound of applause, illuminating like sheafs of lightning the dark roofs and long frontage of the castle, the park and the stone table. It was a hundred years or more since we'd seen such a thing. "Very pretty," said my grandfather. But I'm not sure how enthusiastic he really was about these sumptuous rejoicings: was it right that we should amuse ourselves without the king?

How fast things change! Our tradition still echoed with the struggle against the Remy-Michaults, and Aunt Gabrielle was already, more than anyone else, the supreme incarnation of the family. For all my grandfather's misgivings about the money of regicides, her charm and style and brilliance won over all hearts. And my grandfather himself, by dint of hearing everyone he took any notice of repeating that his wife's son was an ornament to his name, eventually came to believe that the family's destiny might not yet be at an end. If the Spirit of Time to Come had suddenly appeared with a clatter of one-armed bandits and muted trumpets and told him that in his own lifetime there would be dangers and sorrows that would make him forget that the Remy-Michaults had executed the king, I'm sure he wouldn't have believed it. The Remy-Michaults were still evil incarnate. But Aunt Gabrielle did the incarnating with such grace that every day he forgave her a little bit more.

She had plenty of other weapons at her disposal besides her beauty and her millions. She had given Uncle Paul four sons—four grandsons for my grandfather. She'd had five sons actually, but the fourth, of whom we spoke with lowered voices as "little Charles," as if he'd been something to be ashamed of, had died a few days, perhaps a few hours, after a rather difficult birth. With his sons and daughters, sons-in-law and daughters-in-law, and grandchildren, with his height and his already-white hair, my grandfather presented a picture not at all displeasing to himself—the image of a happy patriarch, or as happy a patriarch as the times allowed, surrounded by his offspring.

It was through Gabrielle, it must be admitted, that happiness made its appearance at the stone table. It was a notion with which our tribe was not familiar, a new, individualistic, revolutionary idea. A rather low one. The soldiers and saints in our portrait gallery had had only one idea, and that was to do their duty and remain faithful to it. It would never have occurred to my grandfather to want to be happy. But Aunt Gabrielle thought of nothing else. And happiness was astonished and grateful for her perseverance, and smiled on her.

And even my grandfather himself. . . . Prejudiced as he was against what he scornfully called easy sentiment, there was one sight that could always teach him anew the difficult art of being happy: the sight of the children at play. Never before had laughter and carefree liberty reigned so triumphantly at Plessis-lez-Vaudreuil. The children had everything—wealth and beauty and good health, the past and the future. And of all this they had not the slightest idea. But heedlessness and innocence are the charms of youth. They weren't responsible for the flagrant injustices on which their happiness depended. Can you see them, dressed like little princes and covered with velvet and mud, playing and running around the stone table? You know the scene. All children are alike, for they haven't yet been spoiled and distorted by life and its rigors. They are still in the delightful state when everything is promised but nothing yet given. The world is made in such a way that everything that happens to us—including happiness itself, strength, success, and love— is compromised beforehand by cancer and erosion. But children know nothing of life's ups and downs. They are still on the brink, waiting, holding their breath, conscious of a great impatience growing up in them and eager to be exercised. So they play. Uncle Paul's and Aunt Gabrielle's children played with great zest in the shadow of the ancient towers of Plessis-lez-Vaudreuil. If you looked more closely, there was another youngster playing with them. Me.

Why are we always so fascinated by these pictures of the past? It is because we are like gods when we look backward. God knows all times and all futures. We know but one future: the future in the past, which is what is called history. For us, as we play, five or six years before the first war, with Pierre and Philippe, Jacques and Claude—and with me too—around the garden table where Gabrielle is embroidering roses on trousseaux for the daughters of the poor, while her father-in-law reads *L'Action française,* which has become a daily under Maurras and Daudet, the children's future is already clear. Look, that one who's just fallen down and grazed his knee and is scrambling up, crying—Gabrielle throws her sewing down on the table, and hampered by her long pastel-colored skirt, rushes toward her little boy's tears, already being dried by an extremely correct middle-aged Englishwoman—he will have a much more serious fall one fine May evening between Sedan and Namur, carrying a message to a republican general called André Corap who will be famous for a week. Who would have believed, looking at the three of them, the child soon consoled in his mother's arms and the reader of *L'Action française* already nearly gray-haired, that the grandson would go, in the forests of the Ardennes, before the grandfather? Or that this other one playing with the dog in his big straw hat would twenty years later ... But we mustn't mix up the ages. We must let the children grow up. We shall meet them all again. I have here some photographs taken at that time, showing Uncle Paul and my father wearing boaters and my grandfather looking very different—but changed in the opposite way from the usual one, by the absence of years and trials and sorrows. A young woman in a vast hat is, I think, my mother, but I can't recognize her. With her is Aunt Gabrielle, of whom I say mechanically, gazing at her face under its masses of hair, "How beautiful she is!" though I can make out practically nothing through the dense forest of days and nights which stretch between us. For it isn't only the future which remains closed and inaccessible and impenetrable: even when they are fixed in images, times that are past also elude us forever. How can we judge beauty outside our own period and our own narrow culture? It's often difficult enough to be sure of our own past, of what we were like ourselves twenty years ago, of what we were doing the day before yesterday. Other people's pasts fling us into unknown worlds. I gaze at the photographs and something stirs within me. But what? It's not easy to say. It's as if there were a secret of which they disclose something in spite of themselves, but which they try to preserve behind their yellow paper. But what secret? Their links, of course, with our own world, the world which made us and which in return we kill, in order that we in our turn may also live. But something else too—time, which in its passing hurls into the void the acts, the laughter, the crazes, and the absurd clothes of those doomed ages. Death, too. It is death that calls out to us in these buried images. Dead is my father, my mother, my grandfather, Uncle Paul, Aunt Gabrielle, and four out of the five children (leaving out little Charles, for the fifth now is me). Dead are the English nurses and dead dear old Jules who used to carry us all on his back. When I think of my relations I seem to hear a sepulchral voice calling the roll of the dead. I've never heard anything that spoke to us of the past which didn't at the same time speak of death. And the same is true of the future. Only the present tries, and then almost always in vain, to keep death at a distance. Life can never be anything but a long-drawn-out retreat before death.

And yet how delightful it was, that life so closely mingled with death! I can still see us there, for years and years, sitting around the stone table. The sun is quite hot: it must be spring or summer, or those pleasant autumn days when the year too is getting ready to die. We're not thinking about anything in particular. What would we be thinking about, anyway, when we're so sure of ourselves and so ignorant about everything else? Each one vaguely dreams his own rather trivial dreams. How frivolous happiness is! From time to time there is a word from my grandfather. He still dreams about the white flag, Dreyfus, the comte de Chambord, the old duchesse d'Uzès. He lets fall a phrase or two about Bourget, Barrès, Léon Daudet, of whom he approves, or Mauriac, of whom he does not. Our chief preoccupation is the weather—the sun and rain, the flowers coming up, the trees falling, the deer in the forest. Jules has found the tracks of the great stag whose antlers have thirty-two tines (referred to as horns the other evening by the V.s—the people who, you'll remember, took up the cudgels for America against my grandfather). Like the Remy-Michaults before they got to know us, they also talk about dogs instead of hounds. And Madame V., perhaps to please us and redeem herself in our eyes, said Monsieur Herriot and Monsieur Daladier were "blowing the mort" of society, and took it upon herself to be indignant at the harm they were inflicting on us. We don't mix with Monsieur Daladier anyway, nor with Monsieur Herriot, though apparently the latter is not entirely ignorant of Madame Récamier, Natalie de Noailles, and the duchesse de Duras, and said something quite witty about culture—"Culture's what's left when you've forgotten everything else." We naturally have no intention of ever forgetting anything, nor of exchanging our memories for a culture which is pretty dubious anyway. Moreover, Monsieur Herriot's ideas prevent us from having him in the house. We won't be seeing the V.s again, either. They'll join the rest of the outcasts whom we never invite—the Jews, divorcées, radicals, and socialists. For as well as our ancestors and our castle, good manners, and the Catholic religion, language too forms part of our heritage. Especially the language of hunting, the language relating to animals and nature. Although we are almost completely ignorant, we speak charming French, with a pure accent and some peculiar expressions, often local and sometimes pronounced with a very earthy rolling of the r's. And we don't like anyone meddling with it. We say our language is distinguished, because it distinguishes us from other people, and in order that it should do so. There are a few things like that that we do know something about, things which come from a long way back and are our own particular property: the different kinds of oaks and pears; garden flowers and their English names; the illnesses of dogs and horses; the bell that rings in the courtyard to announce meals; the rites of the Catholic Church; the names of Chateaubriand's mistresses; and the proper use of the imperfect subjunctive.

But since the blood of the Remy-Michaults had made us fashionable, we had drifted away from the nature which for so long had been our refuge against the ills of the ages, and moved closer not only to civilization but also to the culture beloved of Monsieur Herriot, which we laughed at and mistrusted because too often it took on aspects which were secular, republican, and even socialist. But in the end it was to play an important and equivocal part in our life, and one to which I must devote a few words.

Some years before the first war, a section of the family decided to settle in Paris. Uncle Paul and Aunt Gabrielle looked for a house and would take the four children, the tutor, the two nurses, the two chefs and their assistants, the secretary male and female, the butler, the porter, the chauffeur—whom we referred to as the mechanic, but of whom my aunt and grandfather said he "handled" the car well, as if it had been a horse—the footmen, the housemaids, and the three or four more obscure people whose job it was to serve the servants. In those days the choice, for those who had plenty of money, was easy but not very wide: geography had its own hierarchies. The avenue du Bois was a long way out; eighteen or nineteen of the twenty arrondissements were not fashionable, Passy and Auteuil had yet to become so, and the Marais was so no longer, though for two or three hundred years it had contained some of the finest houses in Paris. The Ternes district was swarming with doctors, the Panthéon with students and republican monuments one couldn't possibly mix with even though they were dead, the Champs-Elysées was full of immoral women, and Montparnasse overrun by bohemians and painters no one had ever heard of. That left the faubourg Saint-Germain. My grandfather was inclined to consider it rather frivolous, almost in bad taste, swamped with the money of the imperial and Orleanist dynasties. But Aunt Gabrielle made a beeline for it.

The mansion in the rue de Varenne, a stone's-throw from the rue de Bellechasse and the rue Vaneau, was built as a town house for

the prince de Condé between 1692 and 1707 by Libéral Bruant and
Jules Hardouin-Mansart, but for many years now it has been used
as a government ministry. I went there only the other day to hand
over a file to an efficient and somewhat cynical senior civil servant.
I crossed the main courtyard, a miraculous harmony of enchanting
proportions, and went up the great stone stairway indicated to me
by a porter whose offhand manner, Basque beret, and espadrilles, all
ready for a game of bowls, were but a faint reminder of the stiff
splendors of Monsieur Auguste, Aunt Gabrielle's uniformed door-
keeper. I was surrounded by ghosts: the footmen on the evening
when there was a ball, standing motionless one on every fifth stair
torches in their hands and dressed in eighteenth-century coats with
lace stocks and royal blue breeches; women covered with emeralds
and looking as if they had stepped out of a portrait by Helleu or
Boldini, each with a tiara on her head and in her hand a fan of ivory
and ostrich feathers; the men from Proust or Radiguet or an Alain-
Fournier in which misty schoolyards and Sologne manor houses
were replaced by a setting out of Saint-Simon, with some finishing
touches by Morny or the Prince of Wales. How swiftly the years
go by, how everything changes! I once used to play in these offices
where ambitious young men were drawing production curves and
writing reports full of figures foreshadowing a France as yet un-
born, mingling smoke from factory chimneys with detergents to
counteract them. A head clerk had his office in Uncle Paul's bathroom. The kitchens in the basement were used for storing archives.
Time had caused an upheaval in space. Victor Hugo used to lament
the losses in nature. I contemplated sadly the metamorphoses which
came to pass in culture, so much more fragile than trees and lakes.

It was there, between the Invalides and the boulevard Saint-
Germain, between the chapel of the miraculous Virgin and the rue
Saint-Dominique, between Aristide Boucicault and General de
Gaulle, that Uncle Paul and Aunt Gabrielle reigned over Parisian
life for twenty years in the early part of the twentieth century,
before and after the war. It was there the receptions were held
which were to inspire Marcel Proust, who was fascinated by my
aunt, though she took no notice of him, to write not only the scene

about the princesse de Guermantes' party in *Sodome et Gomorrhe* but
also that of the ball at which the Baron de Charlus ousts "la Pa-
tronne," Madame de Verdurin—later to become first duchesse de
Duras and then princesse de Guermantes—inviting to admire
Charlie Morel a whole crowd of his own friends, including among
many other brilliant names the queen of Naples, the brother of the
king of Bavaria, Madame de Mortemart, and the three most ancient
peers of France. It was there that one or two famous films, of which
more anon, were shown for the first time, much to the scandal of
a lot of other people. Such was the startling evidence of the mixing
of our blood with that of the Remy-Michaults. And so in our turn,
after so much glory and so much silence, so many victories and so
many defeats, we again became acquainted with success. Once more
we had front seats in the theater of the world. We were talked about
in the papers. True, we now appeared on a different page. Our
name, instead of being mentioned in war communiqués and accounts of negotiations beside the names of heads of state and leaders
of the people, had descended among the vanities which brought no
glory, among the gaudy shades of the society news and gossip
column.

   Out of loyalty to my grandfather I rather looked down on these
frivolous parties and pleasures. Paradoxically enough, if I'd been a
bit more frivolous myself and, instead of following Canon Mouchoux's advice and plunging into Plutarch and St. Thomas, had
accepted more of my aunt's invitations, I would have been present,
as an adolescent or later, at evenings which have since taken their
place in history, and met Salvador Dali and Maurice Sachs, Aragon
and Claudel, Georges Auric and Diaghilev, five or six comtes d'Orgel, and all the Swanns and Charluses that were going in Paris.
Everybody except one person. As you may imagine, my grandfather was not invited to the parties where elderly aunts from Brittany, passing through Paris and long since unaccustomed to life
in the raw, might come face to face with denizens of the Bateau-
Lavoir, the rue Fontaine, or the Boeuf sur le Toit. I'm not sure he
ever even suspected what was going on in the rue de Varenne. He
was more likely to be found reading *L'Action française* than avant-

garde or fashion magazines, or even *Le Figaro,* where the youthful Proust gave detailed accounts of the gatherings in the rue de Varenne. He reread Chateaubriand. He went hunting with Jules, and Jules' son, and Jules' grandson, at Plessis-lez-Vaudreuil. He waited for the return of the king as the Jews await the Messiah: he didn't really expect it to happen, but he wouldn't give up believing in it. But behind his back the family had started to change. It was money that had done it.

Uncle Paul, thank God, hadn't lost all sense of family and tradition. He wasn't overburdened with intelligence. I've even heard people he used to invite to his house describe him as a fool. He was fairly attractive physically, rather like a sheep with a big nose stuck on to make it look more distinguished. It was a strange sight to see him in conversation with Paul Poiret, who was Aunt Gabrielle's couturier, or with Cocteau or Nijinsky. He always looked as if he were dying of boredom and only talked with men of talent or genius in order to please his wife. Aunt Gabrielle herself reigned over Raymond Radiguet and Erik Satie in the same way as she reigned over my grandfather. She had applied to the family name the notions of investment and profitability she'd learned at her mother's knee. It wasn't easy to gain political power. As for making money, that had been done already. Sport, crime, and genius all had to be ruled out for obvious reasons. So how was the family, reinforced by the Remy-Michaults, to be made to play its rightful part? Aunt Gabrielle threw herself into poetry and music, painting and ballet, as she once might have into the Fronde or the affair of the Queen's Necklace, the passions of the Girondins, the languors of the Romantics, into either Dreyfusism or anti-Dreyfusism, into Boulangism, or later on into magic or Indian mysticism. The name of Gaby, La Belle Gaby, La Belle Gabrielle, was on everyone's lips in places as far away as Rome and London and New York. And the house in the rue de Varenne came to play a part in the artistic and intellectual life of Paris between 1906 or '07 and 1928 or '30, a part that is reflected in all the memoirs written about the period. Elisabeth de Gramont, first marquise and then duchesse de Clermont-Tonnerre, speaks about it in her *Order the Carriage* and *Chestnuts in*

Bloom; comtesse Jean de Pange refers to it in *My View of the 1900s,
Confessions of a Young Lady,* and *The Ball Before the Storm;* André
Thirion describes it in *Revolutionaries Without a Revolution;* and
various ambassadors and generals and ex-ministers do likewise in the
reminiscences they've published in their attempts to capture the
cupola in the quai de Conti and get into the French Academy.

The rue de Varenne gradually came to rival the other great salons
of the first half of this century—those of Etienne de Beaumont,
Marie-Laure de Noailles, or my aunt's great friend, Misia Sert.
People fought for invitations. But all that was required was a little
wit, boldness, *savoir-faire,* and, if possible, talent. It was an unheard-
of thing to see the family name surrounded by talent. Sometimes
decline is measured in terms of progress. Every stage in the metamorphosis, every step forward by Aunt Gabrielle, every evening in
the rue de Varenne, really needs a paragraph at least, a chapter, a
volume, to do it justice. But I'm not attempting an exercise in
micropsychology. What I aim at is more in the nature of a history
of the passing mood, which tries to catch such elusive things as the
feel of time as it goes by and the perfume of a particular era. What
goes on in people's hearts, only God can know. My grandfather's
pride, egotism, and grandeur; Gabrielle's triviality, skill, and foolishness; Uncle Paul's insignificance and rakish ease—such things I
couldn't begin to evaluate or judge. But in part at least, for nothing
is more difficult to render than everyday life, I do hope to be able
to translate and give expression to these people's way of life, their
opinions, their guests and friends, what made them tick. I am closer,
of course, to the historian than to the novelist, and avoid like the
plague any attempt to assume a godlike omniscience. You could say
I am the family's reporter, the witness of its dreams and follies,
chronicler of the fifty years in which it struggled to survive despite
upheavals. It set itself in the van of these upheavals, applying literally what Cocteau said in *Les Mariés de la tour Eiffel:* "These mysteries are beyond me: I'll pretend I've invented them." So the
family led the way, to preserve the illusion that it was still making
history.

No doubt behind the hectic brilliance of the rue de Varenne there lay ambition, curiosity, fear, a fascination for disorder after long idleness in the fortresses of order, a dread of being left behind, a taste for the avant-garde which might have been inherited from far-off knights who now made a strange reappearance in the wildest masks of excess and experiment. Nor would it be difficult for those who still believe in heredity to distinguish the part played in the events I relate by the blood of the family on the one hand and the blood of the Remy-Michaults on the other. We'd become frivolous through no longer having anyone to sacrifice ourselves for, no longer having anything to die for. We'd put all our eggs in one basket—the basket into which the king's head fell. We were crusaders without a faith, retired believers, faithful servants without a master. We were driven back on cynicism, sneering, despair, and death. From the very beginning the Remy-Michaults had been surrounded by success. They couldn't help being in the front ranks of republican equality. Having killed the king they chopped him up into small change and kept most of it in whatever pockets *sans-culottes* have at their disposal. This mixture of pointless frivolity and success mania was bound to find an outlet in the rue de Varenne.

I can easily imagine there might be many other explanations of the change by which, suddenly and without warning, gamekeepers and parish priests were replaced by the Ballets Russes and Negro art. I'm quite willing to believe that chance, accidents of birth or education, family relationships, the employment of nannies, might all have contributed something. But I am convinced that first and foremost is history itself—that is, society, family, race, environment, and time. Environment and time even more than race. If, to explain our destiny, one had to choose between heredity and society, I'd say that, rather than heredity, it is society—its evolution, the changes in social equilibrium, its irresistible pressures—which has lent our family its predispositions and holds the key to its secrets. So, strange as it may seem, I'm a Marxist—more of a Marxist than a Freudian, at any rate. That means I judge, and perhaps condemn, my family not as a magistrate or a moralist of course, but as a doctor, a biologist, noting the decline of the vital force in terms of great social and economic convulsions deriving from the battles, cathedrals, and crusades of the past, and not in terms of obscure and unseemly influences, masturbation, or the sudden sight, some fine morning, of the primal scene. It's better to be brought down by the rise of the bourgeoisie or the working classes than by nannies' tittle-tattle. We still preferred to be the victims of history rather than of sexuality.

Karl Marx was a German. That didn't matter. But he was also a Jew and a socialist, and that hardly commended him to my grandfather. But there was something about Marx and the Marxists which might have, I don't say attracted, but perhaps vaguely interested my grandfather, if he hadn't made up his mind once and for all to ignore completely the socialist revolution. This something was a mixture of antipathy toward money and industrial capitalism, hatred of the bourgeoisie, sovereign contempt for freedom, subordination of the individual to the community, a sense of necessity, and reverence for history. Confronted with Machiavelli and his prince and their nasty little games, Karl Marx and my grandfather were each in their different ways believers in Providence. History, changeable in Marx, fixed and unmoving for my grandfather, was their concern. Only my grandfather placed moral forces higher than economic ones. And I don't suppose he was wrong. But he didn't choose very well—he sought his moral forces in the past.

A whole world separated the rue de Varenne and Plessis-lez-Vaudreuil. My grandfather, who'd turned sixty during the first war, hardly ever left the country. When he did come to Paris he stayed in his own large apartment near the boulevard Haussmann. Sometimes he'd go to lunch or dinner in the rue de Varenne. And then Aunt Gabrielle put away her sculptors and musicians, hid Proust in a cupboard, gave Cocteau back to the Boeuf sur le Toit, and sent Radiguet to spend a few days in the country or with the Beaumonts. In the rue de Varenne my grandfather would meet no one but country cousins, ladies of the utmost correctness. Transformation scene: the past returned invigorated and drove back the avant-garde, smart society, the discoveries of the season, the sparkling but somewhat dubious froth of talent and wit. The talk was all of hunting, tradition, genealogy, with a sprinkling of history and ethics. The government was abused in the most seemly and platitudinous phrases. Everyone deplored modern goings-on—the very goings-on Aunt Gabrielle did her best to encourage when her father-in-law wasn't there. Everyone reminisced, contrasting the splendors of the past with the horrors of the present. How it would have delighted Proust. Perhaps he would appear, late at night, as Paul Morand describes him, with his hair parted in the middle and his fur coat even in summer, and the humble insolence of young Jews of genius? But no. My grandfather had never heard of him. He knew nothing about music, painting, rebellion, lewd dancing, drugs, or any of the things that excite people and make things move. He knew nothing about literature. He would go back to Plessis-lez-Vaudreuil under the firm impression that family life was going on the same as ever in the rue de Varenne and that Aunt Gabrielle's legendary dinners, which have a permanent place in the history of the arts, fashion, twentieth-century *angst*, and the homosexual and aesthetic revolution, brought together the same ghostly shades as the stone table.

In the summer Uncle Paul, Aunt Gabrielle, the four children, and a few servants came to stay at Plessis-lez-Vaudreuil for three or four months. They left Paris after the Grand Prix, and time would stand still again. Every winter, autumn, and spring of the years between the two wars, as well as of the seven or eight years before the first war, had its own color, its own exploits, its own peculiar discoveries and scandals: it was the year of the "Sacre" or the Russian Ballet, or of Proust's Goncourt; it was the year when Coco Chanel turned down an English duke or a Russian grand duke. But all the summers were alike. In my memory they all merge into the same one long day, endless, motionless, with scorching sun and buzzing insects, scarcely interrupted, for four long years, by the taxis of the Marne and the guns of Verdun: just five or six more dead, wearing caps and muddy blue greatcoats, around the stone table. Every summer, for twenty or thirty years, Aunt Gabrielle would sit in the hooded wicker chair, almost a little hut, which had once been my grandmother's, and in it she just grew slowly old. In the winter, in Paris, she casually mentioned the wicker chair to the delighted Marcel Proust, and you can find its traces in *A la Recherche du temps perdu*. As the years went by, La Belle Gaby came to look like my grandmother, whose image had faded with time. La Belle Gabrielle's arrival in the family may have shortened my grandmother's life, and Providence, chance, the irony of things, the unconscious, or at any rate time, took revenge and made the guilty party take the part of the victim. In Paris, Gabrielle propelled the family toward an unknown future. At Plessis-lez-Vaudreuil, she drew it back toward the past. It wasn't enough to say she imitated my grandmother—she had become my grandmother. She'd adopted her gestures, her turns of phrase, her way of speaking. The same person whose verdict decided the success of an exhibition or play in Paris became in Plessis-lez-Vaudreuil once more a devoted mother, a peaceful needlewoman, a zealous do-gooder, almost a little old lady with white hair, the modest heiress to all the treasures of the past. She replaced Erik Satie with Dean Mouchoux, and the blare of an almost scandalous celebrity with the village harmonium and the litanies to the Virgin, the unchanging repetitions of which were an image in sound of our own priestly tendencies. And I can still hear the hymns through all the mists between.

Yes, I can still hear them—the hymns of my childhood at Plessis-lez-Vaudreuil—and inhale with delight the incense rising in the old church, and despite the tears which dim my eyes I can still see Aunt Gabrielle amid her flock, singing, her big black missal in her hand and strewing from between its pages pictures of members of our family who are already at rest—surrounded by extracts from letters and verses from St. John—in the peace of the Lord.

First and foremost, each one of us is made by others. By changing her surroundings Aunt Gabrielle changed her character, her preoccupations, and her personality. She drowned the avant-garde in children's bumps and bruises, in parish fêtes and all the perfumes of the past. She rediscovered our ancestors, who had been executed by her own, whom she now forgot. She merged into the family. All our dead revived in her whose blood had once helped drive them to the scaffold. A sense of family and tradition came back to her with the summer, and she lost all memory of anything which did not bear our name. She forgot the grand parties in the rue de Varenne, forgot Dada and Surrealism and Negro art and brilliant first nights and musicians of genius. She carried talent so far as to appear not to have any. And in fact she had none. She became foolish again like us, and talked about the neighbors and the weather. She became intelligent again only with the first frosts, the fall of the leaves, the start of the school year, the opening of the theater season, and the resumption of the salons. Then she would take up her role again as Our Lady of the Avant-garde. But the intelligence inhabiting her was the intelligence of others. She freely disclosed her terrible secret, which is everyone's secret: none of us can ever be other than what the world around him decrees.

At Plessis-lez-Vaudreuil our as yet immortal dead had decreed that Aunt Gabrielle should be first and foremost the wife of the eldest son. Later on, people would want to kill our dead so that we might become something more than just the relics of the family. But at the beginning of this secular and republican century, amid the walls and moats of Plessis-lez-Vaudreuil, our dead—by the grace of God, the apostolic and Roman Catholic Church, our victorious army, and our uncompromising memory—were still quite flourishing. In Paris, however, certain subtle and mischievous imps were getting their pitchforks ready.

Until the suicidal folly of people like Lindbergh and Mermoz, until Hitler's tanks, and until television serials, the country, happily, was a long way from Paris. There was a whole world between the two. In my memory Plessis-lez-Vaudreuil, with its stone table, is like a haven, a paradise island lapped against not by the sea but by time. Gradually life in the modern world broke up the family. Work, money, love, and adventure scattered us all over the world. But in the summer we all met again at Plessis-lez-Vaudreuil, coming from London, Paris, and eventually from New York or Tahiti. The ancient park gates closed behind us, and we entered into the summer as into some limitless season without beginning or end. We were cut off from the world, taking refuge in the bosom of the family. We left time that passes behind, to live in time that endures.

The unchanging rules of that time awaited us in Jules, Jules' son, and Jules' grandson, with his gun under his arm, his cap in his hand; in the fifteen or twenty gardeners; in the hunt and the huntsmen; in mass on Sunday and my aunts' parasols. Armies had fought, or were going to fight, on the Marne and on the Somme; millions of men had died or were about to die; more millions still struggled obscurely against hunger and want; the image of the world was changing; poets and physicists were heralding in new ages. We sat around the stone table waiting for the little train, the clockmaker, and the Tour de France.

We had arrived at Plessis-lez-Vaudreuil on horseback. By coach, by carriage, by barouche. In landaus and phaetons, in swift light gigs. We had arrived by train. And now we came by car—great journeys from Paris, Deauville, Forges-les-Eaux, Baden-Baden, in De Dion-Boutons, Rochet-Schneiders, Delaunay-Bellevilles, Dela-hayes, Bugattis, Hispano-Suizas. My cousin Pierre came in a Delage, my cousin Jacques in a Talbot, Aunt Gabrielle in a Rolls-Royce. And then came the era of long American cars and red Italian cars and then the German makes. The last time I was in Plessis-lez-Vaudreuil was in a Peugeot 204, and it was raining hard. But it took me only two or three hours to cover a distance that used to take us seven or eight, on empty roads and with enormous noisy engines. We used to set out in the morning, have lunch on the way, and arrive in the evening. It was the end of the period of real traveling, though our journeys did not take us very far. The day before we left, the car would be taken out for a detailed rehearsal. Everyone would take his seat, with the empty cases and hatboxes stowed neatly in their places. The car held only a tenth or a twentieth of our luggage for the summer. The rest came on by train, the "little train," one of the most sacred myths of my childhood.

I don't really know how it was all managed. Things just took their course all around us without our having to do anything about it, and therefore without our having to understand. It was because we didn't work that we didn't understand anything any more. Financial cycles, the evolution of ideas, technical progress—all these were other people's business, the Remy-Michaults' business, not ours. Aunt Gabrielle was the link between us and machines, the theater, the stock exchange, politics, literature, surrealism, and modern music. She saw to the little train as well. We didn't see to anything. How charming we were! Quite helpless. We just waited for the little train to arrive.

Three or four days after we got there a laundress or gamekeeper or Monsieur Desbois himself would come and tell us that the little train was waiting at the station. A car or cart would be sent, and the contents of the little train would make a somewhat shamefaced triumphal entry into the main courtyard.

The little train happened only once a year in each direction. The clockmaker from Roussette came once a week. Every big house in the world, in Scotland and the Carpathians, Bohemia and the valley of the Loire, has always prided itself on its three hundred and sixty-five bedrooms. Plessis-lez-Vaudreuil too had its three hundred and sixty-five bedrooms. More or less. We'd never actually counted. There was a clock in each bedroom, eight in the drawing rooms, two in the billiard room, and six in the libraries. I'm counting only the real, pendulum clocks, not the others. Monsieur Machavoine used to come from Roussette every Saturday to wind them. Why Saturday? So that all the clocks should strike twelve together at midday on Sunday. Two minutes before midday on Sunday my grandfather, just back from high mass, would sit down in one of the drawing rooms. Soon he would be joined by Dean Mouchoux in his old cassock green with age, invited every Sunday for lunch and dinner, his mouth watering not yet for the fritters—they were served only in the evening—but for the creamed chicken of Sunday lunch. To show he wasn't fanatical, my grandfather used to sit in a different chair on different Sundays, or even in a different drawing room. He would take out the gold watch his great-grandfather had given his grandfather for his twenty-first birthday, and wait. At noon all the clocks in the house would start to strike at the same time. At one minute past twelve, my grandfather would put his grandfather's watch back in his pocket and bury himself in *L'Action française* again, or the duc de Saint-Simon's memoirs, or Monsieur de Chateaubriand's *Congress of Verona*. But sometimes, at three or four minutes past twelve, my grandfather would be interrupted in his reading by the chiming of some clock or other which was slow. Then a footman would be dispatched to Monsieur Desbois to ask him to have a word with Monsieur Machavoine.

The key for each clock was either hidden behind its nymphs or rocks or porphyry columns, or hung up on a ribbon. But it would never have occurred to any of us to use one of these keys ourselves. I can remember clocks which we used to consult every day suddenly running down and stopping, I suppose through an oversight on the part of Monsieur Machavoine. But we'd have to wait until he came again for the clock to start telling the time once more. The explanation was that we lived in an order, a hierarchy, which had to be preserved as it was right down to the last detail, and the maxim "A place for everything and everything in its place" applied also, and perhaps especially, to people. Monsieur Machavoine's role in this vale of tears was to wind our clocks. Ours was to wait for him to come, and to watch. It was a pleasure I never tired of.

Monsieur Machavoine's arrival nearly always brought me inexpressible delight. He didn't say much. He was a small man, a hunchback, who moved about very quietly and did his work with the sureness and precision of an antiquary or a surgeon. He went silently from room to room, always dressed in black, made a brief bow, and then addressed himself to the clock as if it were something alive, stroking it, dusting it with a feather duster, sometimes making so bold as to touch up the paint or glue on some ornament which had come loose. Then he would open up the patient and peer with an eagle eye into its most intimate mechanisms, and finally wind it with exquisite firmness and tact. The music of these magic rites gave me a pleasure which I imagine would strike the eager and subtle ears of our modern psychoanalysts as significant. Its peace and regularity, its simplicity and almost silent gentleness, seemed to transport me somewhere out of time. Inside the refuge of the summer, the castle, and the garden, Monsieur Machavoine's ministrations formed another refuge even more secret and even more profound. By a strange paradox, his winding of the clocks managed to bring time to a standstill—time which had always been unmoving anyway. Every Saturday at about ten o'clock I arranged to be there to watch the magician at work. I did my best to stay in my room, with the blinds down or the curtains drawn against the sun, and there I would take up a book and wait. I used to listen to the little hunchback's footsteps as he went along the corridors, and to the delicious sounds of glass covers being removed, dials touched, clockwork wound, lyres straightened, and little columns tightened up. I imagined I could hear the sound of the feather duster and of the clock hands being adjusted, gently but firmly. I could tell the difference between the chimes from the buhl marquetry, the gilded Louis XV bronze, the rococo in the drawing room, the Chinese case in the blue room, the green horn in the billiard room, and the Greek vase in the room next door to mine. At last the door would open and Monsieur Machavoine would come in. I held my breath and kept quite still so as to appreciate to the full the pure sounds and movements he conjured out of silence and immobility. The tiny thrill would last a few seconds. Sometimes I used to put the hands of the clock back or forward for the pleasure of hearing the hours and the half-hours chime as Monsieur Machavoine, in his own humble sphere, restored the order decreed by God, my grandfather, and himself. He wound up the clock, put back the glass dome, and gave a last whisk of his feather duster or woolen cloth light as silk. That was all. Then he went away. Sometimes I plucked up the courage to follow him, or, better still, precede him. Then he would keep coming across me, sitting in a chair reading and ostentatiously surprised by his unexpected entrance, first in the marquise's room and then in the carnation room and so on. I expect he was a bit surprised too. But he never gave any sign. He just wound the clock, bowed, and went out, and would then come upon me for the fourth time five minutes later in the room in the tower. Then he would greet me again, and again wind up the clock. He was a sage. And though I never said anything, I loved him for the ecstasy he summoned up for me from habit and silence and time.

Monsieur Machavoine lived about five miles from Plessis-lez-Vaudreuil, and he used to come by bicycle. Only three times did a Saturday go by without his appearing. The first time, his little boy had been drowned in a tributary of the Sarthe where he used to play. The water was very shallow, but the child had hit his head against a stone as he fell in. His father was asleep on the riverbank and didn't hear anything. When he woke up, the little boy was already dead. The second time, Madame Machavoine had run away with the butcher's boy. On both these occasions, Monsieur Machavoine came on Monday instead of Saturday. But the third time he didn't come at all. He'd died riding his bicycle on Saturday morning at about a quarter to ten, on the way from Roussette to Plessis-lez-Vaudreuil.

Bicycles played an important part in our lives, no doubt about it. Though you might not have guessed it, every summer since the start of the century had been dominated by the bike and the Tour de France. I suppose the picture I've painted so far of my grandfather doesn't suggest you might find him crouched over the handlebars with his cap on back to front, taking a swig straight out of a bottle proffered by an enthusiast running alongside the contestants. But men are not all of a piece, and for some reason or other my grandfather was mad about the Tour de France. Perhaps he followed it in his imagination as the king once used to watch battles, looking down from a height at the action unfolding below, a telescope in his hand and surrounded by courtiers and plans of fortresses. Perhaps the ancient instinct for strategy and tactics reawakened in him as the Tour approached the mountain passes and the steeps of Alsace. Perhaps he projected his ancestors' love of jousting and duels onto the stars of the cycle race. Anyway, there was a bicycle somewhere in his mind, and by one of the paradoxes which make real life so much stranger than fiction, a large part of the summer at Plessis-lez-Vaudreuil was spent around the stone table, poring over maps and following the snakelike trail of the Tour. Aunt Gabrielle shared this passion. I think that in her case the explanation was simpler than with my grandfather. With her it was just a matter of desiring to be in the popular swim, having already been in the swim of smart society—a hankering after the strong smell of the crowd after the refinements of the few, for sausage and cheap red wine after champagne and caviar. Paris in the spring had given her her fill of those by the time she came to us. I can see us still, sitting around my grandfather and Aunt Gabrielle, discussing the latest news beneath a blazing sun and following all the falls, the spurts, the dropouts, the results of the heats, and the sprints. It wasn't until the First World War that the leader of the race as a whole wore the famous yellow jersey, thus adding a new phrase to the language we loved, a splash of color, bright and shifting, moving over a map of France which had been made so gray and insipid by the departments of the Republic, whose dreary, unremarkable names and abominable elections contrasted so markedly with the gay motley of the old provinces of the monarchy. Now and again we would frown at some eccentricity: a detour into Germany or Italy, a stroll through Luxembourg, leaving out the Massif Central, adding three extra towns, a little jaunt through Spain. Despite such deplorable infringements of tradition, of which, even in the matter of bicycle racing, we quite naturally set ourselves up as guardians, it seems to me, looking back now, that it was the same Tour every year, going through the same summer on the fabulous machines of memory. It seems to me it was all the same superman, the same giant and hero, the same bright archangel of summer, perhaps a little altered by time and age, riding the sun along the roads of Burgundy and Provence, Aquitaine and Roussillon, Brittany and Dauphiné. Meanwhile we sat motionless as ever around the stone table, dreaming of the crowds, the popular triumphs, the competitors arriving in the evening at ancient towns all decorated to welcome them. Perhaps, in a world of machines, the bicycle seemed to us the successor of the horse? Perhaps we saw the bicycle races as a kind of centaur—of course we laughed at them, but even their most ludicrous exploits may have awakened distant echoes of our past greatness. Once upon a time we had been champions, fighting for our ladies and the king, and though we had now forgotten the adoration that was then ours, we were still vaguely haunted by the heady perfumes of victory and glory and applause.

Do you mind if we linger awhile longer in the sweltering summer at Plessis-lez-Vaudreuil? If I listen once more, from behind the half-closed blinds of my room, to the sun blazing down on the flower beds and the gravel path? When I woke in the morning I could tell from what I heard what the sky was like, the mood and the color that would also be mine all that day. I used to listen to the sun. It was already hot and high in the sky, and intermingled with it there was a murmur I can still hear as I write these lines—a sound made up of silence, of water falling on flowers and grass somewhere, of paths being raked, and bees. I would shut my eyes. That was happiness. The king, the Republic, France and freemasons, war and money and morals all paled beside what made up our world. All that was left was the pure happiness of the moment. I could hear footsteps, a horse going by, the voice of my grandfather talking to the gardeners. I couldn't hear the words, just a slow, quiet murmur. I knew it could only be about keeping things as they were. The walls, the trees, habits, nature. No question of building or knocking down, modifying or altering. Just preserving, saving, keeping things the same. There in my room in the morning, lying in wait for the marvelous day as it climbed up into the changeless sky, I could hear my grandfather giving orders, always the same orders, to retainers furnished by God, to ensure that this new day should be like all the rest. I looked out of the window, through the shutters: sunshine and shadow alternated in regular, equal straight lines. Whatever did change in the course of days or seasons—the shadow of the towers, the leaves on the trees, the flowers in the basins and beds—was really but another image of eternity, and perhaps a truer one: the shadow disappeared, but returned; the leaves fell, but grew again; the flowers faded, but only to blossom anew. We loved these cycles which returned, in which what seemed like instability had as its object changelessness. In this threatened world our task was clear: it consisted first and foremost, whether the matter in hand was forests or politics, family or finance, travel or dress, in resisting change. We had but one enemy, and that was time. The Republic, democracy, the bourgeoisie, bad manners, disreputable houses, the cutting down of trees, the rule of money, the deterioration of the stone and slates on the roofs—all these, and anything else we didn't like, was the issue of time. How we hated time! In this case, unlike Marx, we were the adversaries of Heraclitus and his perpetual flow of people and things in the river of years. Without realizing it we were followers of Parmenides, and lived in his indestructible, continuous, immutable, and finite universe. If we'd known his name, we'd have revered Zeno of Elea, for whom the runners in the stadium, the arrow in the air, and even fleet-footed Achilles pursuing his tortoise were really unmoving in a world of illusion. Time brought with it everything we dreaded, everything which destroyed us: attrition, decay, decline, oblivion. We hadn't the strength left to start building, so we'd set up as conservers of what was built in the past by people whose memory we preserved despite the hostility of revolutions and passing ages, and who themselves perhaps—perhaps: it was all so long ago—had changed something in the order which reigned in their own day.

The happiness I felt as I watched the sun rising on the world was very peaceful but rather sad. It was peaceful because history, the accident of my birth, my family, and my grandfather had given me a marvelous yet terrible gift—security. Shut away there out of time at Plessis-lez-Vaudreuil, protected by the clockmaker, the gardeners' rakes, and the champions of the Tour de France, I was safe, nothing could happen to me. But our security was not like that of the Remy-Michaults, which was based on money, and on their talents. Our security had nothing to do with money. Admittedly, it had nothing to do with merit or talent either, which was fortunate, because as I've explained we hadn't any talent, and merit, since it didn't enter into our system, was looked on as not only unnecessary but usually ostentatious and rather dubious. Our security was simply an idea. We claimed, in opposition to the socialists, that the world was preserved by ideas. It was rather funny really, because we had so few. The Marxists, who denied the power of ideas, certainly had more of them than we did, though we were always talking about them. But as a matter of fact it was true that our universe was dominated by an idea, perhaps by one idea only, and one which made us very sure of ourselves. The whole force of the idea derived from its simplicity. The idea was that things are what they are.

As everyone knows, there is a system underlying every self-evident truth. Nothing is more partial than impartiality. When someone says a cent's a cent, what is suggested is a secret truth which goes much farther than the common-sense statement behind which it is hiding: it is not difficult to discover that what it reveals is avarice. When we stoutly maintained that things are what they are, we were proclaiming, under cover of the platitude, that things must be left alone. There was an order, and that order had been decreed by God. God decreed our castle, our gardeners, our family, and our beliefs. God decreed our name. All we had to do was put ourselves in his hands. God always knew his own. And by some incredible chance his own were always we. The family motto, which I've already mentioned, put it all in three words. The gardeners' rakes on the early morning gravel, the sun on the ornamental lake and the forests and the flower beds, the ever-present past, the eternal family: at God's pleasure. The uncertain present: at God's pleasure. The future, which we washed our hands of: at God's pleasure. He would undoubtedly take care of it better than we could, overtaken as we were by time and left on the shelf by history. There was really only one danger which could threaten us, and that was the death of God. Since it was God who sustained us, who sustained our world and history and the sun and our name, he had to be kept alive. The death of God was the end of history, the end of the world, of everything and of us. When we said our prayers in church, or when we sat down at table, or after a meal, or in the morning by our beds, or at family prayers in the evening, our supplications were not only to God, but also for him. Above all we prayed that he shouldn't alter: that he should go on doing his job, that he shouldn't resign and abandon us in the middle of the journey, before the last pages had been written in the book of our life, the life of our children and the life of the great-grandchildren of our great-grandchildren right down to the last generation and the end of time. We prayed for him to go on, in our place and on our behalf, making the world go round. We prayed, like the Aztecs, for the sun to rise, and, like the Romans, for our own success—for good and ourselves to be forever victorious over evil and others. At God's pleasure. Amen.

As you can see, the security which enveloped me was very different from social security, from any reciprocal guarantee concluded between men. I was literally in God's hands. So long as he wasn't dead and still watched over me, I could fall prey to nothing but minor vicissitudes of no serious consequence. I could die, of course. But so what? Merit and talent might not form part of our system, but death certainly did—in our family the dead were more important than the living. And also we were Christians. It seems to me we were less frightened of death than people are nowadays. We didn't worry about it unduly. For a Christian, wasn't death the goal of life? I imagine it was in that spirit that old Eleazar set off for the East with a cross on his breast; that we had got ourselves killed on the battlefield for the king and the Pope; that we had thrown our heads, light in ideas but heavy with faith, at the foot of the scaffold. And it was in that spirit too that my reactionary uncles and monarchist cousins had died in Africa and Asia for the greater glory of a republic which they hated.

The happiness which overwhelmed me as I watched the gardeners raking the courtyard, or Monsieur Machavoine winding the clocks, or read about Antonin Magne winning the Tour de France in *L'Illustration* or the morning paper, was an entirely mystical happiness. As far as large matters went, "What an age!" my grandfather used to say: men had put a spoke in the Almighty's wheel. But at least in small matters God followed out his own plan. He might have abandoned to their deplorable fate the holy places, Jerusalem, Moscow, Constantinople, Baden-Baden, Deauville, Paris, and even Rome, blinded by modernism; but the terrible Lord of Hosts, of battles and ideas, still took pretty good care of Plessis-lez-Vaudreuil, its gardeners and their gardens, its clockmakers and their clocks.

But that peaceful happiness and unshakable certainty were nevertheless rather sad. When I woke up in the morning no one said to me, as Saint-Simon's valet had said to him: "Time to get up, your grace—you have great things to do." What great adventures could

we aspire to, since our ancestors and God had taken care of everything? There was but one thing for us to do, and that was to disturb
what remained of the old days as little as possible. We scarcely liked
to read, speak, breathe, or listen. Who knew if we mightn't further
upset a balance already made precarious by all the dangerous ideas
that were sprouting up like weeds? The thing to do was keep still,
not touch anything, stop up one's eyes and ears, and keep vigilant
watch over the sacred changelessness of the good, the true, and the
beautiful. To put our life at Plessis-lez-Vaudreuil in a nutshell, it was
an iron discipline designed to teach us to do nothing either to the
world or to the future or to ourselves. The dream expressed in all
the precepts handed down from generation to generation like a
sacred heritage was the hope that nothing would happen to us. Hear
no evil. Hear nothing.

All this—in other words, nothing—used to happen in summer at
Plessis-lez-Vaudreuil. But as soon as she got back to Paris, Aunt
Gabrielle would leap onto all the bandwagons of history, boarding
them while they were in motion and making a place for herself
between Dr. Freud and the Boeuf sur le Toit, Dali and Dada, a
Negro pianist and a Surrealist. After three or four months of pious
immobility, between the stone table and Dean Mouchoux's harmonium, she was wild to stir things up. She flung herself into minor
operations of constructing and undermining, the chief effect of
which was to blow up the steps of the thrones on which we sat.
When the weather was warm, she put the brake on history; when
it was cold, she accelerated. There was not much left in the rue de
Varenne of the hymns of Plessis-lez-Vaudreuil. Aunt Gabrielle replaced them with explosives.

Some of the bombs that were hurled at our summers have left
traces in the history of ideas. Probably none caused more commotion than three well-known films about which rumors eventually
reached even Plessis-lez-Vaudreuil, though mercifully toned down
and without any indication of where they'd been shown. You will
already have guessed that it was in the rue de Varenne that Buñuel's
Le Chien Andalou and *L'Age d'Or* were first seen, and there too that
later, on the eve of another catastrophe produced by an age only

too fertile in that respect, Jean Cocteau's *Blood of a Poet* was shown. Aunt Gabrielle couldn't possibly miss such an opportunity to launch her avant-garde on a triple battlefront: a medium which was still new, a revolutionary aesthetic, and a triumphant attack on the shaky idols of the past, common sense, the established order and religion—all the things which had been so dear to us in the days of our greatness, our retirement, and our obscurantism. The harmonium of the summer turned into the infernal piano out of which arose laughing Jesuits who, fifty years before their time, left the religious fashion parades in Fellini's *Roma* far behind. Bleeding statues, hands swarming with red ants, gouged eyes, burlesque, and nightmarish processions—our whole world was mocked, shaken, turned upside down. The rue de Varenne was the negation and death of Plessis-lez-Vaudreuil.

And so we came to be divided against ourselves. It is very hard to keep intact, against the attacks of history, a morality and a rigor which are cut off from action and power. As long as we governed the world, our virtues were recipes for victory. Often they irked us, and then we would decry them and do as we pleased. But we knew our greatness depended on them. Since we had come down in the world they had grown no less demanding, but they were useless. Fidelity, strictness, and tradition, with their airs and their obstinacy, no longer led to success, only to failure. We even came to love failure because we loved the virtues which had once constituted our greatness. And now here was history, that strumpet always won over by money and power and success whatever its form, starting to give us the glad eye again and trying to lure us into the brothels of talent, surprise, and imagination. Blush as we might, and tell her we'd never set foot in such a place and never could, she only laughed at our caution and lack of curiosity, and whispered that there was no reason why we shouldn't have a little fun together. That wasn't how she used to talk to us. In the old days she said we'd do great things which would last forever; there was no mention of fun. Probably we'd have done best to mistrust her wiles. But we'd have had to be saints to say no and turn away. Through Aunt Gabrielle we let ourselves be tempted. There is something narrow-minded about fidelity. We weren't quite foolish enough to remain completely pure. And then, when we looked back on them, the centuries were like so many nights of love we'd already spent with history. How could we fail to be happy at finding ourselves in bed with her again? We knew and loved her, we'd spent so long caressing her. Moreover, she was ours, and we didn't like to see her with other people. So we took up with her again, not without unimportant betrayals and minor scandals. Perhaps we still hoped we'd have the upper hand. But now she'd given herself to everyone, and rolled in all the gutters of the town, the sewers of the crowd and the dejecta of progress, we ought to have known she'd be changed. Where were her big innocent blue eyes, her pure feelings, her fidelity, her docility? Like the weather and the way people went on, like the seasons of the year according to my grandfather—how she'd changed! She'd become avaricious, crafty, and cynical; she looked for comfort to those my grandfather scornfully described as demagogues; she sold herself to the highest bidder, throwing in a touch of sentiment for the riffraff; and you could turn her head just by surprising her. She had left us a princess, who scarcely uttered a word except to us, and now she was a whore who giggled and threw herself around the neck of every Tom, Dick, and Harry. That was our opinion of history, who had betrayed us. But the Remy-Michaults were so fond of success that on the pretext of smartness, amusement, and intellectual liberty, on the manifestly monstrous pretext of intelligence and talent, they forced us to go out with her again. We'd decided to spurn her and not know her any more. We'd shown her the door at Plessis-lez-Vaudreuil. And in she came again through the windows of the rue de Varenne, bright with syncopated music and gleams of ebony.

But it wasn't History with a capital H which came back among us—the history of Rude and Delacroix, Hugo and Jaurès, with her splendid bosom, her Madonna-like face, her head thrown back, her gun in her hand, and her garments torn and covered with dust and gunpowder: the history of liberty and the people's struggle. We knew that history. We were against it, but we understood it. Despite the bad shepherds who according to my grandfather led them astray, there were secret bonds between the people and us. No, in a way it was worse than that. The history that was made welcome in the rue de Varenne was fashionable history in which money played a part, a history full of aesthetes and dubious young men, a history which to us was a mockery and the work of the devil. It was against us, not because it sprang from the people—we were closer to them than the painters and musicians were, the intellectuals and the men-about-town—but because it had set itself up in revolt against tradition. It was in the rue de Varenne that Duchamp, either before or during the war, put a bicycle wheel on a kitchen stool and wrote nonsense on a comb. It was in the rue de Varenne that he painted a mustache on the Mona Lisa, which, like Michelangelo's *Pietà,* the *Winged Victory of Samothrace,* the *Venus de Milo* and the Acropolis, symbolized what we owed to the past. It was from the rue de Varenne that he sent a urinal to the Armory Show in New York. I admit we knew practically no one on the other side of the Atlantic, and that we viewed the New World, with its banks and its mania for liberty, with indifference, if not suspicion. But all the same, a urinal! Even the Americans, democrats and republicans though they nearly all were, didn't deserve that. It was in the attics in the rue de Varenne, which Aunt Gabrielle had turned into a studio, that a Russian painted a black square on a white ground and sold it for a fortune. What would have annoyed us most, if news of these exploits had ever reached Plessis-lez-Vaudreuil, would have been the fact of being beaten on our own ground. We'd always been against the democratic religion of work and merit. One of my great-grandfathers used to say, and he almost meant it, "Thank God there are still some of us in Europe for whom effort, hard work, and personal merit don't count." And now here was a craze for hoaxing that carried this idea even further than we did. But where in all this folly and awfulness were our own traditional good taste, our reverence for the past and for our forebears, our treaties with God, our strictness, our lack of ideas? It was in the toilet in the rue de Varenne that the handle of the lavatory chain was replaced by a Jansenist crucifix which had belonged to my grandmother, until after a few weeks Uncle Paul himself decided to rectify matters. In the old house which now bore our name there were old newspapers stuck on canvas, bits of broken mirrors, trash from the dustbins, soles of old shoes, bits of bootlace, wire, rags, cheese wrappings, trolley tickets, firecrackers, sirens, elephant trumpetings, senseless gibberings, a whole new world without faith or laws, brought into being by people one had never heard of, like Rimbaud and Tzara, Sigmund Freud, a real Jew, and Lautréamont, a fake count. This crowd had neither family nor past nor God, and the only rule they had was to destroy all rules. My grandfather would never have had them in the house. Talent and genius were neither here nor there—they certainly wouldn't have been enough to make him change his mind. On the contrary. This new world was against us, because it was made up of both intelligence and destruction, whereas we were on the side of stupidity and conservation. No—effort and hard work and personal merit were no more in evidence in the rue de Varenne than at Plessis-lez-Vaudreuil: but talent and intelligence blazed away like torches. So when Aunt Gabrielle wanted to revive our name, slowly stifling in the veneration of the past, she hurled it into the furnace of the future, where it too shot forth flames. By a strange paradox our survival and our rank emerged, like new though somewhat moth-eaten phoenixes, out of suicide and abjuration.

After ages of glory, crime, greatness, and lethargy, we had been cornered by history. For a long time we'd played with it, and now it was playing with us. The family name had become a gaudy football, and Cocteau, Dali, Picabia, Maurice Sachs, and Duchamp kicked it around with all the talent that had hitherto so scandalized us.

Jean-Christophe's Revenge

ONE FINE SUMMER MORNING IN 1919 OR 1920, I can't remember which, but anyway a couple of years after the war, there alighted at the station at Roussette, where a car was waiting to take him to Plessis-lez-Vaudreuil, one of the indispensable characters in two and a half thousand years of human comedy, the heir of Socrates, Rabelais, Fénelon, Voltaire, Goethe, Stendhal's Julien Sorel, Paul Bourget's "Disciple," and André Gide's "Isabelle." The tutor. He was a dark young man, not very tall but quite good-looking, with flashing black eyes. He had been born in Pau only a few years before Aunt Gabrielle and Uncle Paul were married. He had a smattering of Latin and Greek, he'd read a few books, he'd gotten "a degree in something or other," as my grandfather said, and he didn't dress very well. The beautiful Gaby and the Jesuits had both, with equal irresponsibility, suggested him for the post. He was the nephew of one of her painters, and a former pupil of the priests in the rue des Postes. He was to do us irreparable damage. But if it hadn't been him I'm quite sure it would have been someone else.

As far as I remember, my grandfather wasn't too hostile toward Monsieur Jean-Christophe Comte. He greeted him with one of the rather awful jokes which made a lot of people, quite wrongly, take him for a fool. Shaking hands with the newcomer, he smiled and made a pun on his name. "My dear Count," he said, "you were simply made for us. Welcome to Plessis-lez-Vaudreuil." As you will soon see, there was something both bitter and comic in the idea that Monsieur Comte was made for us.

His services had been acquired for the benefit of Jacques and Claude, Uncle Paul's youngest sons. They were both nearly old enough to take the school-leaving certificate; despite our contempt for distinctions bestowed by the Republic, these cruel modern times obliged one to be educated. Hitherto we'd been of La Bruyère's opinion: "In France a man needs great firmness and breadth of mind to forgo posts and responsibilities and stay at home and do nothing." But times had changed. Monsieur Comte was charged, as the phrase went, with taking us in hand during the two or three crucial years for which the benighted ministrations of Dean Mouchoux and reactionary parish priests were inadequate. He set to the morning after his arrival, dressed in a brown suit which was too new, with a tie in rather doubtful taste which made us all laugh at lunch and which I can still see to this day. Between cycle rides and dips in the river he began to introduce into the religious silence of Plessis-lez-Vaudreuil the already somewhat disturbing uproar of Spartacus' revolt, the murder of Julius Caesar, the mugging of Voltaire, and the affair of the Queen's Necklace.

Here, despite my reluctance, I must say a few words about myself. This book is not about me but about a strange, various, and multiple entity, at once exceptional and ordinary, which existed in an exemplary yet ambiguous relationship with its time, and whose ideas and collective evolution I attempt to trace through the years and through the individuals which make it up: I mean my old and beloved family. It so happens that for various reasons I was a privileged witness in the matter. I had one sister, but she didn't count— in our family, as you will remember, daughters had no say—and, as in a sentimental novel, I was the only son of a younger son, and orphaned at the age of fourteen. Not only that, but my mother and father had brought me up to have ideas which didn't correspond either to those of my grandfather and Plessis-lez-Vaudreuil or to the more up-to-date ones of Aunt Gabrielle and the rue de Varenne. How amazing life is, and how rapidly complicated its simplicity!

By some unfathomable mystery, my father was a liberal and my mother, as a result of circumstances which I shall try to explain, was inclined to put her faith in man rather than in the God of her childhood. This was a very extraordinary thing at Plessis-lez-Vaudreuil. My mother came from a very old, very poor, and quite unknown Breton family. She'd grown up without any chateau or family portraits, without silver and plate, in an old house in Ille-et-Vilaine where the only article of any value was a big wooden chest unlikely to tempt the most modest burglar: it contained nothing but family papers tracing their descent back to Raymond V, count of Toulouse and son-in-law of Louis VI. But since its early glory the family had only grown poorer and more obscure. However, my grandfather had been very pleased by my father's marriage. My mother was tall and dark, with blue eyes, and after the entry of Aunt Sarah and Aunt Gabrielle into the family, a thoroughbred Breton was greeted by everyone as a welcome breath of fresh air. As I've said, until Aunt Gabrielle's advent we had taken no notice of money, notoriety, or smartness. What counted was a person's name. And my mother's name was excellent. The only trouble was, for a family like ours, and a family like her own, she didn't believe in anything. People have told me, and she told me herself, that when she was a child she believed in everything: in ghosts, goblins, communication with other worlds, all kinds of Christian and other divinities, and, of course, in the return of a king whose memory was still not dead in the Brittany of the end of the last century. Through her two grandmothers, encountered in far-flung places by her Breton grandfathers, intoxicated with adventure and tradition, my mother was of Irish and Spanish descent, and the mixture of these two elements with the Celtic produced in her both violence and dream. She had loved my father, who was just her opposite, almost to madness, and when he died her universe fell to pieces. Just when my grandfather was growing reconciled to the Republic because he'd given it three sons and a brother, my mother started to hate it even more fiercely than before, because, having killed the king and driven out the priests, it had now taken the man she loved. Such is the history of men's hearts, such is history pure and simple: everything has an explanation, but each explanation is different. My grandfather, though he remained a monarchist, made up with France, and almost with the Republic. My mother, locked in her grief and resentment, came to believe in no one and nothing. Her hostility toward victorious democracy did not turn her back again toward her king. She'd stopped believing in the king too, even in the king. Despite her dreams and her passion my mother, probably more intelligent than the rest of the family, asked the only question which could resolve the problem: "The king? But which king?" For it so happened, through the cruelty of history, that the pretender, like the Remy-Michaults, was descended from a regicide. Perhaps it was because my father was killed one morning on the Chemin des Dames, one morning which I was told was rainy and which I tried in vain to imagine, falling asleep in my room at night; but at any rate it was my mother's faith which was affected, her capacity for hope, her love for the values which she'd been brought up in along with the rest. My grandfather and his father and brothers and uncles probably didn't really believe the king would ever come back. But there remained in their hearts a faith which couldn't be put into words, something which for them was what the absolute is to a philosopher or the dark night of the soul to a mystic: something which can't be talked about or described, which can only be loved in silence. My mother had lost this faith. She no longer believed in the king who would never return. It's quite possible she no longer believed in a God who hadn't taken the trouble to raise a finger to divert the bullet which killed my father. She hated authority, governments, war, everything which acted a part in the social comedy that kills fathers and sons, lovers and husbands. Though of old Breton stock, monarchist, legitimist, and Roman Catholic, my mother now believed only in human misery. When she knelt before the ivory crucifix in her room, crowded with souvenirs of my dead father and of her own childhood in Brittany, she was worshipping not Christ but suffering humanity. We—my grandfather, great-grandfather, the whole family in its mythical aspect—loved God, and put him before men. But she loved men, with their cruel and stupid fate, the blood they spilled, the cries of dread they uttered in the face of pain and death.

When I looked at my mother in later years, a kind of living statue of mingled fury and pity, it was hard to summon up the image of joy she used to present when she was with my father. Here again were seen the ravages of time. I was no longer a child when my father died, and I can still see him now, thank God, with his very fair hair, his eyes even bluer than my mother's, the mustache men used to wear in those days, and his cheerful, quizzical air. But now and then he seems to fade and disappear. I say over and over again, "Blue eyes, fair hair, Roman nose, and lips that were . . ." but the life has gone, leaving only words, perhaps shapes and colors and details, elements which fail to make up a face, a look, that mysterious whole to which the soul contributes as much as and more than the body. And then suddenly, perhaps when I'm out for a walk, or in the middle of a conversation, my father suddenly rises up before me again.

For me he was the family. But I realized he wasn't indistinguishable from it. And he wasn't indistinguishable from it because on a number of points, quite important ones—truth, liberty, the Jews, the Dreyfus case, individual worth, even God himself—he had his own independent ideas. Where had he gotten them from? From the age he lived in, from friends I've never heard of, from some silent great-grandmother who never said anything? Perhaps he'd acquired them by chance? I simply don't know. I'm inclined to rule out chance, but to do that one would need to know almost everything, not only about the history of my father but also about the history of the world. A rather formidable undertaking. So I shall merely set down what I do know about my father, without trying to trace causes which may not even exist.

My father was anything but a rebel. But he was also anything but a fanatic. What had been great and admirable, in a way, in my family, what had made some people worship and others hate it, had been fanaticism. My grandfather wasn't a monster—he desired the happiness of the greatest number, of the masses, of everyone. But he had his own ideas about the means of arriving at this happiness. And he stuck to them. He had his own values, loyalties, hatreds, and convictions. In short, with all his virtues and sense of honor and veneration for the past, he was intolerance personified. My father, on the other hand, understood nearly everything. I'm not sure my grandfather attached much importance to intelligence. A good deal of his attraction lay in this blank, or, if you prefer, this virtue. Was my father very intelligent? For a number of reasons, I decline to pronounce on the matter. I couldn't, anyway. But I know he was astonishingly good at understanding people—their ideas and peculiarities and way of life—and at explaining and imitating them. He was at home anywhere. He was one of the few members of the family whom Aunt Gabrielle admitted into the secret of the wild goings-on, metaphysical machinations, and explosive discoveries in the rue de Varenne. Of course he never breathed a word about it at Plessis-lez-Vaudreuil. But while the question of my father's intelligence—if such a word can ever have any meaning—remains a mystery I do not care to probe, I don't think it is impossible for me to weigh his character.

At first glance, character was what he seemed to lack: his charm and humor were what made him talked about in the Paris of 1910. Beside my grandfather, rigid, unbending, cooped up in his beliefs, the first impression my father made was one almost of frivolity. He was uncommitted, he enjoyed himself, whereas my grandfather lived in a closed and complete system. Unfortunately the system no longer connected with the world, but my grandfather didn't bother about that in the least. My father, on the other hand, was marvelously at ease in the world, and very fond of it. Nothing could have been more foreign to him than the spirit of system. And this constituted a kind of revolution at Plessis-lez-Vaudreuil, where the past, morality, the unity of the family, and the mythical power of its name owed their existence to the spirit of system, and used both the gravest events and the most trivial incidents to keep it alive.

Perhaps my grandfather wasn't far wrong in regarding the slightest breach as the opening through which the Barbarian hordes would soon burst in. My father had discovered, all by himself, that the emperor had no clothes, and he no longer believed that the good, the true, and the beautiful had been fixed once and for all by immutable decree. I suppose he could be regarded as a traitor to the cause of the white flag, of the Stuarts, of the laws of primogeniture, and of the sanctity of the temporal possessions of the Holy See. He met with the cruel fate which is the lot of all liberals. But he would have been surprised to hear himself accused of betraying his ancestors and forgetting the lessons they taught. What he was doing was adapting them to modern times. It wasn't easy. From one point of view he was renouncing the family's traditions, but from another he was saving them. My grandfather's eyes were fixed on the pure form of the past; my father tried to distill its spirit. Contemplation, which changing manners had forced to be passive, he replaced with techniques and mental attitudes designed to enable men to share their experience through sympathy and solidarity. Probably one would have to concede a good many of the criticisms the most conservative of his relatives might level at him. I'm not sure he accorded the highest place to our ancestors' ideas and ways of thinking and acting. He thought there was something to be learned from all ages and from all men. In a word, he introduced something shocking and unheard-of into the petrified palace of the Sleeping Beauty: the idea of change.

I might as well admit I loved my father. I admired him too. I loved his ease, his slightly old-fashioned elegance, his fierce loyalty, the way, slightly nervous but smiling, he walked the tightrope between the past and the future. Life and the world amused him, but he tried to understand them. His friends included several of the de Broglies, whose motto delighted him because it united the two forces which almost tore him apart. This motto, emerging from the depths of the de Broglies' illustrious past, was: "For the future." I still seem to hear the discussions the family used to have around the stone table, with me listening fascinated to the mysterious incantations and magic spells being exchanged over my head. My grandfather upheld the device of the Mortemarts—"Before the world was ever there, Rochechouart these arms did bear"—or of the Esterhazys—"Under

Adam Esterhazy the Third, In the Beginning was the Word." But
my father countered with the apparent modesty of the de Broglies,
in which pride gave up trying in vain to penetrate the darkness of
the past, and began instead to progress and construct and if necessary re-create itself. My father thought a past had meaning only in
terms of the future. But he also believed that the future depended
on the past. My father was an admirer of Bossuet, and his favorite
passage was the famous description of the tribe of Judah, which
speaks of "the privilege it had always enjoyed of marching at the
head of all the other tribes." He was an avid reader of Barrès, whom
he considered almost the sole survivor of the shipwreck of modern
literature. "What is it, then, that I love in the past?" Barrès asked in
his *Notebooks*. "Its sadness, its silence, and above all its fixity. Movement bothers me." Movement bothered my grandfather too. And
the acceleration of the modern world often made him sad and silent,
with sudden fits of anger and cruel sarcasm. He loved history because it was immobile and had entered into an irrevocable eternity.
But my father loved history because it was alive and always new,
and because it governed the future. From it he drew strength and
a sort of joy, instead of the dreamy and mythological melancholy
which had haunted our house for more than a century.

Like many men, and most women, in those days and of that class,
my father knew very little. Nor had he read very much. For the last
few years I've heard nothing but lamentations about the ignorance
of modern youth. And yet school, the cinema, television, and travel
have brought them, often with chaos and indifference and even in
an inferior form, more faces and landscapes, truths and follies, certainties and doubts than ever hunting, etiquette, and Dean Mouchoux all put together taught my father. He was very well up in
a few things: the dates in French history, spelling, sermons, claret,
the family trees of leading families. Everything else was more
vague. Philosophy, mathematics, novels, distant civilizations, everything that was more secret or difficult or new his environment cut
him off from. But he had discovered for himself romantic poetry,
which for obvious reasons, moral, aesthetic, and political, was
looked on askance by the family: he even had the temerity to adore

Lamartine and Hugo. I always remember the bits from Hugo which he used to teach me, almost in secret, as we walked in the evening, before dinner, along the main road to Roissy or the tracks which led to the farms and the ponds and the forest. For me it was like listening to the mottoes of the ancient families of Europe: it was a music which remained a mystery. I knew nothing about Villequier, or Charles Vacquerie, or Gautier, or Claude Pradier, or the social and political struggles of the nineteenth century. And he probably knew no more than I did. But I can still see him stopping, half serious and half joking, then striding along again, then stopping again, and almost muttering, as if in self-mockery, looking at me out of the corner of his eye and lifting his arms and his stick heavenward:

> *"O Patrie! O concorde entre les citoyens!"*

And so on. It was as if the lines sprang from the rhythm of his walk —they followed the same beat. He would go on walking, as if in another world, a world which he was opening up to me, brandishing his stick, his head slightly on one side.

> *"Vers ce grand ciel clément où sont tous les dictames,*
> *Les aimés, les absents, les êtres purs et doux,*
> *Les baisers des esprits et les regards des âmes,*
> *Quand nous en irons-nous? Quand nous en irons-nous?"*
> (To heaven, spacious, kind, full of all solaces,
> The loved, the absent, those who are pure and gentle,
> Kisses of the mind and glances of the soul,
> When shall we depart? When shall we depart?)

And he would repeat the last line two or three times, as if he couldn't tear himself away from this vision of departure.

You will remember my grandfather priding himself on not being able to recognize the hated "Marseillaise." It took the deaths of millions of men, and some of our own family among them, to reconcile us to it. And my grandfather lived nearly long enough to

see it transformed into an observance as reactionary as the songs of
our royalist rebels and Monsieur de Charette. Almost the same
course was followed by the lines my father used to recite from the
later works of Hugo, and the pages of Renan which my mother
used to read secretly in the typically Breton decor of her room at
Plessis-lez-Vaudreuil. To my naive astonishment, the boldness, the
novelty, the liberty, the romanticism, perhaps even the Revolution
of 1789 itself—to us the end of everything and as farfetched as
anything could be—were all to find themselves in the rearguard,
amid the retreating forces of a routine solemnity which the younger
generation merely laughed at. Hardly had I thought with gratitude
of how my parents had introduced me to strange beauties, than the
scene had changed and Hugo and Renan, together with many others, were consigned to the dustbins of history. After many long
halts in the shade of its old monuments and monasteries, and a few
straight dashes after its dreams, history for the last century or so has
not minded these hairpin bends, these turns back upon itself. It
doesn't come back to where it began, but reverses its point of view,
destroying what it used to love, rediscovering as if it were new what
it has forgotten, progressing in a spiral which covers the same
ground at different levels, leaning sometimes to one side and sometimes to the other, now to authority and now to liberty, now to
reason and now to feeling, now to the obvious and now to the
obscure, climbing like a mountaineer toward some impossible equilibrium—a mythical culmination of history where everything is in
its right place, looked down upon by gods that are no more.

I am well aware that these accounts of the history of my family,
and incidentally of the history of the time, may often seem banal
and self-evident. That is their avowed intention. Everyone knows
that the Revolution, Bonaparte, radicalism and socialism, Clemenceau, and even Stalin himself all started on the left, in the party of
"contestation"—the better, with monotonous regularity, to end up
on the right in the camp of authority and sometimes of oppression.
Everyone knows romanticism began as an adventure and finished as
an insipidity which makes schoolboys yawn. Everyone knows it
doesn't take long for revolt to harden into establishment, that the

process is unavoidable, it has to if it doesn't want to die out altogether, and that children are the death of their parents. All that is life, part of our long experience. But with so much that was once outrageous already half-dead, amid so much originality now shared by the mob, I should like to make a case for an aesthetic of the obvious. It is everyday things that we need to show, because habit and familiarity make us blind to them. The last thing the prefect of police noticed in Poe's "The Purloined Letter," before the providential intervention of Auguste Dupin, was the crumpled sheet of paper just left lying in the middle of the table. The peculiarities and follies depicted in novels take place against a background which is never mentioned because it is familiar to everyone. Murders are unfolded before us, incest, the most unheard-of and astonishing adventures, and everyone cries, significantly, "Just like a novel!" What no one talks about, what is left to history, though history is quite unable to reconstruct it afterward, is the silent treasure of the general atmosphere, the temperature of life, the laws accepted collectively by the group—the immemorial depths of our way of living and thinking, anchors of the spirit of the age which from their submarine caverns control, with their cables and buoys, the superficial tossings of our daily life, though secretly, for the water is so clear we cannot see them.

A discoverer of the obvious, a conqueror of the everyday, a demonstrator of the ordinary—that's what I'd like to be described as. I tell the story of my family. Not of its crimes, for there were hardly any. Not of its follies, for they were all relatively reasonable. But its everyday life, and what it thought about the world. And I don't even record its clothes, its idiosyncrasies, the anecdotes it exchanged, my grandfather's habit of scratching the back of his neck with just one thumb, my father's boaters and striped jackets, and shoes part yellow and part white, Aunt Gabrielle's hats and gowns from Poiret, or Dean Mouchoux's way of cracking nutshells with his teeth—no, I am going to look farther afield for the mysterious obviousness, the obscure yet radiant reasons governing fundamental choices. I am going to seek them out in the color of the days, in waking dreams, in the first impulses of reason and the heart.

The amazing thing is that if anything is bound to seem obscure and surprising to the generations of the future it is this very banality. Soon nothing will be more mysterious than what is obvious to us today. What we ourselves find hardest to understand about the Incas, the Egyptians, the ancient Greeks and Romans, the Mongols of Genghis Khan or Tamerlane, is not their conquests and pyramids and temples, or the intrigues and political coups which are so like our own, nor even their cruelty and picturesqueness, their sun- or nature-worship, their philosophy or religion—it is their everyday mentality, their attitude toward other people, the way they saw their own situation in the world and in life. In the societies of the future, Uncle Paul's marriage, Aunt Gabrielle's double life, our relationship with history and the state, my grandfather's ideas, my father's efforts at liberation, our image of our task in the world and the purpose of existence, all the things that were so close to me I could scarcely imagine anyone could think or live otherwise, will seem incomprehensible. The fact is that our slightest gesture, our most trivial thought, whatever amuses or concerns us, whatever we do, derives from habits and conventions and myths so deeply and yet so openly rooted in the surface of things that those who live in that same world scarcely suspect their existence.

This only makes me admire all the more, now, my father's attempts to overcome his environment. And I wonder whether his allegedly frivolous character wasn't really just as strong as his charm and humor. It's the most difficult thing in the world to be different from one's own time and surroundings. My father had no example before him that he might lean on, nor any reason for calling into question, however tentatively, the delicious pressures of tradition and order. Religion, morality, aesthetics, what people might say, and self-interest too—all suggested he should cling to the image of himself reflected back by the mirrors of the past, so lovingly preserved at Plessis-lez-Vaudreuil. And yet he struggled free of it. He adored my mother, but I don't think it was she who urged him in this direction. On the contrary, it was the death of my father which threw her back on the tragic love of mankind. At the time of his life when he was happy, my father loved mankind, though he loved it gaily. All this is not really so surprising. Along with its marshals, freethinkers, and much-decorated ministers, the family also has had its small share of saints. I imagine they loved mankind too, and that they too were able to break through the barriers of their caste. My father wasn't a saint. He liked amusement, parties, the good wines of which he was such a connoisseur. He liked comfort and irony. And I'm not altogether sure that his relations with God, which because of the name he bore were very important, were altogether simple. Our saints loved mankind because first and foremost they loved God. They loved men in God, via God. My father loved mankind first and foremost. And this was a turning point in our long history. I might almost say he saw God only as the eternal image of the succession of mankind. But I doubt if he'd have liked such a pretentious way of putting it. He was sufficiently one of us to hate anything which had the slightest suggestion of philosophizing or academic jargon. He loved history and hated philosophy. And, for him, philosophy started early. Naturally I don't even mention Hegel or Marx—no one would have dreamed of uttering their names at Plessis-lez-Vaudreuil. All words of more than three syllables seemed rather suspect to him, and I'm not certain that Anatole France wasn't, in his view, on the borderline of what was tolerable in metaphysics. It wasn't from dialectics or the philosophy of history that he learned to love mankind. Rather, that feeling in him was a combination of natural sympathy and amused courtesy, against a deep-seated background of Christianity. Every member of the family had always shown the same politeness—or rather more—to a Breton fisherman or a Sicilian stonemason as to a notary or a general, not to mention a minister of the Republic or a newly rich oil king. In my father this traditional courtesy went deeper. He felt friendship toward all men. Also respect and esteem. And he hated unhappiness. I am sure that it was in memory of my father, and for love of him, that after he died my mother transferred her worship from him to suffering humanity. But I can't remember my father ever doing anything but smile at life.

Perhaps this shows all that separated him from the infernal machines and somewhat pedantic subtleties organized in the rue de

Varenne. He was even further removed from them than from the outdated traditions of Plessis-lez-Vaudreuil. He was as amused by our rites as by the establishment grandeurs which Pascal had the genius to mock even when their splendor was at its height. But he respected them. And everything combined to make him dislike sacrilege and iconoclasts: his temperament, beliefs, humor, elegance, and sense of morality, which though never irksome was very profound. For he was at once a moralist and an ironist, and even, in his own way, free and bold and almost skeptical though never cynical —a man of integrity like his ancestors, whom, even while he welcomed modernity with open arms, he never dreamed of denying or forgetting.

Perhaps I have now said enough to show what my situation was in the family when Monsieur Jean-Christophe Comte arrived at Plessis-lez-Vaudreuil. My father was quite poor when he died, having always been free with his money; my mother lived almost as a recluse, going out only to pay long visits to all the hospitals and poorhouses and prisons she could find in the neighborhood; my grandfather's reign was not over, but it was Aunt Gabrielle who really ruled, while a crowd of great-uncles and great-aunts, uncles, aunts, and cousins all wove a protective web around the sleeping chateau against any influence from outside. Uncle Paul and Aunt Gabrielle's children had the best of both worlds: from the Remy-Michault connection they had money, and on our side they had the advantage of being sons of the eldest son and future head of the family. I was rather out of things. Monsieur Jean-Christophe Comte's monthly envelope came from Uncle Paul or Aunt Gabrielle, but I was invited into the huge schoolroom on the top floor much as other more or less poor relations were invited to go hunting in the forest, or to come to dinner on Sunday under the gaze of Rigaud's large canvases. Four of us were there to greet Monsieur Jean-Christophe Comte: my cousins Jacques and Claude, myself, and the son of Monsieur Desbois, the steward. We were all between fifteen and seventeen years old and getting ready, in the shelter of Plessis-lez-Vaudreuil's ancient walls, to take our turn at confronting the perils of the world—women, examinations, socialists, adventure,

what the novels called fate and what we saw as a tale which unfolded before our eyes, but far away, beyond the park, beyond the
graveyard at Roussette, beyond our farms and the forest.

From the very first day, Jean-Christophe astonished us. We were
used to being terribly bored by the dronings of our Jesuits and Dean
Mouchoux. At one stroke Jean-Christophe flung open, onto unknown landscapes, windows which had been shut for centuries. On
Monday morning we all waited rather uneasily for him in the
schoolroom, and as soon as he came in he said he thought of teaching as just another word for friendship, and we could all *tutoyer*
him. This wasn't very often done at Plessis-lez-Vaudreuil. We said
vous to our fathers and mothers and to our grandfather, and to Dean
Mouchoux and as a matter of course to all our other teachers.
Jean-Christophe, smiling, went on to say that he wasn't there to
force us but to help us, and he hoped we should be friends. Then,
having dumfounded us by this unexpected declaration, he took
advantage of the opportunity to read us the poem by Verlaine
which begins:

"Souvenir, souvenir, que me veux-tu? L'automne . . ."
(Memory, memory, what do you want of me? Autumn . . .)

The poem, with its melodiousness and its vague outline of a young
woman, is forever linked in my memory with that summer morning
in the schoolroom on the top floor at Plessis-lez-Vaudreuil, and with
the dark, charming, shortish, rather grave yet vivacious figure of
our tutor.

Despite his neckties, Jean-Christophe soon became a kind of indispensable and benevolent demigod for us. We didn't have many
friends. We saw practically no one apart from country cousins
staying at the house, neighbors who came to tea, their names carefully selected from lists kept up to date from year to year, and the
huntsmen on their horses, wearing their horns slung around their
necks and the hunt insignia on their lapels. I was very close to my
father, but it would never have occurred to me to think of him as
a friend. I loved and respected him. But perhaps because he was

killed when I was still a child, I didn't think of myself as his equal.
I was his subordinate. He knew about people and what things
meant, and I did not, and it was for him, as a father, to impart his
knowledge to his son. But Jean-Christophe, as a true disciple of
Socrates, didn't set out to teach us anything, but just to reveal to
us what was already in us. We had a whole universe inside us,
though we didn't yet know it.

The instrument of this revelation, which might well be said to
have caused a complete upheaval in our lives, was books. It may be
that Monsieur Comte did only one thing, but that one thing was
decisive: he taught us to read. Plessis-lez-Vaudreuil contained not
only drawing rooms and bedrooms, dining rooms and a chapel, but
also, of course, a huge library in which bearded scholars with eye-
glasses, and girls already nearsighted, sometimes came to work. The
Plessis-lez-Vaudreuil library, with its light wood shelves and oak
and leather stepladders, was known to all the specialists and connois-
seurs. It contained about thirty or thirty-five thousand books, including many incunabula, rare or original editions, books that were
out of print and sometimes quite forgotten, together with some
outstandingly fine prints and engravings, legal documents and accounts which none of us ever so much as looked at, and one of the
best private collections of autographs in France, perhaps in the
world. Experts wild with wonder and envy had come across letters
written by Sylvius Aeneas Piccolomini, otherwise Pope Pius II; St.
Ignatius Loyola and St. John of the Cross; Du Guesclin and Joan
of Arc; Leonardo da Vinci, St. Louis, François I, and Charles V.
One precious, indeed unique, item was the bull in which Pope
Alexander VI, a Borgia, proclaimed the canonization of the emperor Alexis. We ourselves used the library very little. In a corner
of one of its five huge rooms there was a wooden chest full of rather
undistinguished novels, and above it a dozen shelves containing the
memoirs of Saint-Simon and Madame de Boigne, historical works
on people like Marie Antoinette and Richelieu, Rostand's *Cyrano de
Bergerac*, various pious tomes, volumes of *L'Illustration* in their red
marbled half-leather bindings or else in unwieldy half-vellum, to-

gether with the theater supplement, which if I remember rightly was called *La Petite Illustration.* We rarely strayed beyond these familiar works: the rest of the enormous library was like a huge field lying fallow. But Monsieur Comte led us there on marvelous excursions which always remained dazzling in our memories. We discovered Corneille and Racine in sumptuous bindings, La Fontaine in the edition of the Fermiers-Généraux, even some rare Romantics illustrated by Gustave Doré, which by some aberration, perhaps by stealth, had been smuggled into Plessis-lez-Vaudreuil. To our surprise, we even found a copy of Maupassant's *Contes de la bécasse* ("Woodcock Tales"), which my great-grandfather or some great-great-uncle must have taken to be a manual on shooting.

Perhaps my grandfather and the rest were right to be suspicious of reading. For no sooner had we set foot in that enchanted kingdom than the world around us crumbled away into nothing. A properly organized narrative would no doubt show the diverging destinies of Monsieur Comte's four pupils, bringing out the difference between the fates of those who liked and those who disliked books. But truth forces me to say that all four of us flung ourselves simultaneously and with the same eagerness into the discovery of religion, jealousy, ambition, love of nature, war, and provincial life whether under the Restoration, at Versailles during Louis XIV's reign, or in Paris at the time of Voltaire. It would of course be an exaggeration to say that up till then we had never heard of Villon, Diderot, Balzac, or Jean-Jacques Rousseau. And we were more familiar than most people with the smell of the forest after rain, stags drinking at moonlit pools, how people lived in the old days before machines, and popular culture—all that is repeated over and over by history and by the countryside itself during the long evenings of summer and autumn or in winter in front of great log fires. We were already accustomed to reading about them in books we might pick up on a rainy day or at night when we couldn't get to sleep. They were an amusement, they called up dreams or memories, they moved us—but we could take them or leave them. But the secret world of books had remained quite closed to us. The scenes in "Polyeucte" and "Athalie," Lamartine's poems, Fénelon's descriptions, Voltaire's letters, and George Sand's pastorals meant hardly anything to us. They didn't enter into our life, they said nothing to us about ourselves. What we had to learn by heart we learned by heart, but scarcely ever was this formidable task interrupted by some word or feeling, some thought or description, which might just for an instant make us close our eyes in one of those sudden illuminations in which pain and pleasure play an equal part.

In a few months, a few weeks, Monsieur Jean-Christophe Comte made us love books. He taught us to choose and understand them, to seek out what we liked, to explain to ourselves what we disliked. The first thing he taught us in regard to books and their authors and their ideas was familiarity. We weren't obliged to like the whole majestic range of French literature from the *Chanson de Roland* to Péguy. We were allowed to stroll about and pluck what suited us. We dropped *Horace* and concentrated on *Le Cid*: long before Brasillach, Jean-Christophe showed him to us as a young, handsome, brave cloak-and-dagger hero, but with a rather wild and disturbing side to him, a combination of feudal lord and highwayman, intoxicated with love and adventure. "One of your ancestors, perhaps," he said, smiling. And Jacques put his hand up and said yes, quite right—through the mother of one of our great-grandmothers we were descendants of the Carrions, who themselves were descendants of the Bivars. We tended to neglect the adventures of Télémaque for the more exciting exploits of young Julien Sorel. Leaving castles behind us at last, we set out on the highroads for the first time in our lives, in search of strange lands; we entered into shops, into secret societies, into hovels and into prisons. We learned about crime stories from *Zadig* and Balzac, about the opposition between our family and parliament from Saint-Simon's memoirs, about the rise of the bourgeoisie everywhere, and about the Revolution from Michelet and Hugo. "Michelet?" my grandfather used to mutter. "Michelet!" Finally, with Zola, we came to suspect the existence of a social class of which we knew almost nothing, and whose very name seemed part of some dreadful mythology—the working class, and the industrial proletariat.

We spent three or four delightful, agonizing years steeping ourselves in books. As you may imagine, it took more than three months, more than six or eight, for world literature to yield up its secrets to us. But we learned very quickly to read and judge a text —I don't mean to decide irrevocably whether it was good or bad, but to know whether we liked it or not. It is a decisive step, and not only in the matter of literature, to know what one likes. Monsieur Jean-Christophe Comte had the right to be satisfied with the bunch of "reader's apprentices" he had conjured up out of thin air, and which moved two or three times to the rue de Varenne in Paris from autumn to spring, and then came back for the summer to Plessis-lez-Vaudreuil. A poison had entered our veins. We needed the drug now. Every new book, every new author, led us to other books and other authors. A world of imagination grew up around us, a kind of giant jigsaw puzzle which existed only on paper and of which, by some fortunate or unfortunate paradox, the more pieces we succeeded in fitting together the more were still missing. We were doomed to an endless pursuit of the fragments of our dream. After some months, perhaps a year, perhaps more, Jean-Christophe no longer confined himself to writers of the past. Every so often—on Sunday, for Christmas, or when we were ill—he would bring us books which had just been published—a mere glimpse of their covers as he approached made our hearts beat faster. To say we were looking for new solutions would not be quite accurate. It was the problems themselves we were ignorant of. And every time we saw one of Grasset's green or yellow covers, or the white covers with black and red lines of the formidable *Nouvelle Revue française*, we thought that perhaps they contained the problems we hadn't been able to formulate to ourselves, and perhaps their solutions into the bargain. But we didn't really want or need solutions: we had centuries of those behind us. What we longed for was the thrill of problems. One day Jean-Christophe would present us with an artilleryman with a bandaged head who had fixed his dreams not only in time like other poets, but also in space, like a painter or a sculptor. The next day it would be a young Jew of genius, who curiously enough led us back into a more familiar world, yet whose trivial stories of kisses bestowed or denied, of middle-class life in the provinces, and of dinner parties in Paris among people like our cousins the Chevignés or Montesquious, were to become—perhaps we already guessed it?—one of our Bibles. I remember Jacques had influenza at the time, or perhaps it was scarlet fever. He seized the book and read the first few lines aloud to me: "For a long while, I used to go to bed early. Sometimes, almost as soon as the candle was out, my eyes shut so fast I hadn't time to think, 'I'm falling asleep.' Then, half an hour later, the thought that it was time to try to go to sleep would wake me up. I would try to put down the book I thought was still in my hands, and make as if to blow out the candle . . ." Not until much later did we learn that Marcel Proust had lived for a long while in the boulevard Haussmann, in one of the houses that belonged to my grandfather.

And so Rimbaud and Apollinaire, Lautréamont and Gide, entered into our lives. We found out that the world had many different faces all contradicting one another, that it was nothing but an aggregate of reciprocal glances continually swallowing one another up. Each book destroyed the one we'd just finished reading and offered new roads to truth and beauty along which we plunged headlong. This alternation of deep despair and wild hope did a certain amount of damage. We hadn't discarded the old family favorites. We read Maurras and Chateaubriand at the same time as Jarry and the Surrealists. The arrival of the latter among us—at about the same time as some of them had started going to dinner in the rue de Varenne, though we had no suspicion of it—caused a great upheaval. All these disparate elements swirled around in our heads, unable of course to organize themselves systematically— anyway, we'd had enough of systems—and causing us considerable suffering as well as unspeakable happiness. Sometimes in the summer, drunk with reading and weariness, we would let two weeks go by without opening a book, to get our breath back and learn to live again. Then we would fling ourselves back again into our habitual vice. Everything around us succumbed to the merciless blows of words and phrases, commas and periods, enchanting nouns and verbs and adjectives as rare as they could be. We were a little dizzy. Through books, we were feeling the world go round.

When I think nowadays of those years of our youth, in which there grew up between the four of us, who'd always known each other, a new and intense friendship born during evenings at the Guermantes' and the Verdurins', at balls at the d'Orgels', on voyages with Urien and Lafcadio, in the palm groves of Algeria and at fancy-dress parties in a dream version of Sologne, I am struck by two or three things. First, I imagine it cannot be a very common thing for four lads to fling themselves simultaneously into a love of books. If you examine our situation more closely, the motives which urged us all in the same direction were in fact very different. To begin with, of course, there was the blood of the Remy-Michaults. The Remy-Michaults had always—that is, for the last hundred years, as my grandfather used to say—loved studying and books and the clash of ideas. According to my grandfather, they preferred it to the clash of swords. I can afford to admit it, because unfortunately or otherwise I haven't a drop of their blood in my veins— the Remy-Michaults were very intelligent. Aunt Gabrielle might have any number of faults, but she also had some heaven-blessed gifts which probably came down to her from the member of the Convention and the statesman, the ambassadors and businessmen: curiosity, dissatisfaction, a need to go farther afield and find new territory, a desire to do something different, and perhaps to do it better than everyone else. All this was handed on to her children, and it was this soil that Monsieur Jean-Christophe Comte had culti-vated.

I think the same features, but in quite a different form, were to be found in the second son, who was nineteen or twenty when we were fifteen or sixteen, and so was not with us in the schoolroom. What mysterious influences had presided over the metamorphosis? Philippe put the same insatiable eagerness into collecting women as the other Remy-Michaults had hitherto put into accumulating dip-lomatic missions, ministerial portfolios, and seats on boards of direc-tors, and as his two younger brothers had transferred to books. It was no use offering him Horace or Ovid or *Phèdre*, the passions of

the Romantics or the loves of Baudelaire. He despised literature
both with the military scorn of my family and with the administrative and commercial contempt of his mother's kin. It wasn't in
books that he looked for life and love, the agony of waiting, the
delights of surprise, or women. He didn't *read* life, as we did all day
long with Monsieur Comte, and by lamplight in bed, at dawn or in
the night. He lived it. And I admired him too, in secret. He was an
irresistibly charming good-for-nothing. Perhaps, if one insisted on
applying to him the laws of heredity which were so dear to us, one
might see him as a true great-great-nephew of the uncle in Argentina who was too fond of girls and their dowries. But Philippe,
though fabulously frivolous, did not dissipate his energies. His only
interest in money was spending it. All that really interested him was
women—their distracting smiles, their hair, their hands, their teeth,
their bodies: he could talk about them for hours. A taste for women,
like atheism, was not entirely forbidden by the family code. Our
ranks had included famous libertines, and on the female side we
were descended from the celebrated maréchal-duc de Richelieu,
grandfather of the Richelieu whom several of our family had followed to Russia. Some princess or other having closed her door to
him, she said to him tearfully as he continued to tap at the portal:
"No, monsieur, leave me be—I don't want to see you again." "Ah,
madame!" he sighed, "if only you knew what I was knocking with."
But for several generations, perhaps in token of mourning after the
death of the king, the fashion had changed with us to the strictest
morality. Philippe, however, with the help of maids, actresses,
friends of his mother's, flower girls, and professional courtesans, had
flung convention and the old ideas to the winds. He amused himself,
staying out till all hours among the gypsies and the broken bottles.
It was fascinating, and at the same time rather gruesome. Watching
him, I came to see how much time and effort a ruling passion can
demand. He never did anything else. He spent all day and every day
getting hold of women, making a fuss over them, quarreling with
them, consoling them. If he'd spent a quarter of the same energy on
painting or oil-prospecting or military strategy, he would have been
a formidable rival of Fautrier or Staël, Gulbenkian or Onassis,

Guderian or Rommel. But no. His models were Casanova, Valentino, and the bold Lothario.

Claude, the youngest, the one who was the same age as I and to whom I was closest, had an additional reason for rushing with us into the reading-trap set by Monsieur Comte. He was very good-looking, but ever since childhood he had been slightly different from the others. His left arm didn't develop quite normally. We were so accustomed to it that we came not to notice it any more. But other people were not like us, and their attitude toward him was affected. This in turn prevented Claude himself from forgetting. Families can be so secretive, and ours was particularly so, that I've never known whether the defect in him was due to an accident at birth, to some later mishap, to illness, or to the fact that he had to pay the price for so many intermarriages between cousins, even though he was the son of a Remy-Michault. I wonder whether he suspected as much himself. But I never wanted to ask him. In any case, his infirmity, though it caused him practically no physical inconvenience, made him suffer because it isolated him and separated him from other people. He was on the lookout for compensations. And books were for him a dream, a consolation, a victory over adversity.

Monsieur Comte also provided another of us with the material to fill in gaps. Monsieur Desbois' son was called Michel, and I swear that we loved him like a brother. But he was the son of the steward, and in a society as hierarchical as ours the difference in status definitely made itself felt. Where and how? When we went riding; at table on Sunday evening with Dean Mouchoux; in the drawing rooms, where every morning at ten and every evening at six there took place an amazing ceremony which was partly parade and partly prayers, and which the steward attended wearing a hat and gloves; in church, where we sat in red plush stalls and they sat on straw-bottomed chairs; in processions, where they walked always behind us; but above all, in our minds. It was all pure myth, but what is more real than that which we imagine? There is something mythical, too, about the equality of today. I mentioned the incredible courtesy and affability the family used to possess: their manners nowadays would be hard put to it, I fear, to give any idea of what I mean. And I stick to what I said. It wouldn't have been possible to be simpler, kinder, more truly cordial than we were toward the Desbois. But everyone was aware of the gulf that separated us. One might say that nowadays there is equality between cads. Then, courtesy and affection and real friendship separated the inferiors from the superiors in our family. Everyone knew that both existed —everyone admitted it and accepted it. Affability and good manners were then in vogue in the relationship between masters and servants, and the latter did not yet call themselves employees or minor personnel. They were part of the same system as the hierarchy itself: they were a corrective and an expression of it.

I think Michel Desbois was the cleverest of the four of us. He had an incalculable advantage over us three, the two brothers and the cousin: he had a distance to cover and a backlog to make up. Later on I shall tell how he covered that distance and made up that backlog. It may be merely hindsight, but I think a close observer would have noticed that he tended to leave poetry and novels to the others, and throw himself on Montesquieu and Saint-Simon (the other one, not the family version), Auguste Comte and Durkheim, economics and the nascent science of sociology.

One winter day when Claude and I were in the schoolroom in the rue de Varenne, almost as fine and spacious as the one at Plessis-lez-Vaudreuil, reading something by Claudel—*Tête d'or,* I think it was, or *Partage de Midi*—Michel came in, gravely enthusiastic over a book he was holding which we'd never seen before, though we'd heard of the title: Karl Marx's *Das Kapital.* But kindly do not jump to conclusions. It was another of us who was one day to call himself a Marxist, whether this development was due to predestination, chance, some shortcoming on the part of Monsieur Comte, true conviction, the mysteries of heredity, or the pressure of the times.

I've talked of Jacques, and Claude, and Michel Desbois, and even, incidentally, of the rollicking Philippe. And now I must say a little more about myself. It seems to me that even then I used to play the marvelous and modest role which was to remain mine through all a life by now long and perhaps almost over: the role of witness.

When I look back at the five of us, at Plessis-lez-Vaudreuil or in the rue de Varenne, there between the blackboard covered with figures and the shelves groaning under all the books selected by Monsieur Comte, how can I avoid the conclusion that my fate—and I don't complain—was to look on and listen? I was probably sufficiently aware of it at the time to understand and follow the efforts of Jacques and Claude, and even those of Michel, the eldest among us, who in three or four years blossomed into a promising student of political economy. At the same time as Jacques he took one of the most difficult exams in the French civil service, the entrance to the administrative grade of the Treasury. Jacques failed but Michel passed. I was at any rate sufficiently aware to admire my companions passionately. Claude wrote poems which seemed to me as fine as anything by Péguy or Apollinaire—I was fortunate enough to get them published two or three years ago. Jacques was writing a novel, and used in the evenings to treat us to ardent descriptions of his successive approaches to the material, and to his characters, the issue of a terrifying conjunction between Claudel and Radiguet. Michel used to explain Sismondi and Pareto to the rest of us, and was later to launch into Keynes in the same way as Claude and I plunged into Giraudoux and Malraux, Montherlant and Aragon. I was just a mirror to the rest of the group. On a laughably small scale, I was a reincarnation of one of the family's most constant traditions—social responsibility and service to the community. To this I added the peculiar characteristics bequeathed me by my father: wondering amusement at the spectacle presented by the world, and friendship toward the universe. I told myself I would be the witness of great things, things which would change the course of history. Because we were young, we thought not of ourselves but of history. And not of our own history, but of that of the past. We thought of history in the making, the history of the future. Malraux says somewhere that the difference between himself and his teachers when he was twenty was that history was present to him. We were twenty too, and geniuses like everyone else. We had lost our memories, exchanged them for hero-worship and for the memories of others which seemed to us greater than our own.

It didn't take my grandfather long to realize that books might well finish what had been begun by the Revolution, the abolition of the laws of primogeniture, and the introduction of compulsory military service and mass education. And that they might well lead to the famous death of God, about which sinister rumors were beginning to spread even in our part of the world. In one sense Monsieur Comte and the schoolroom at Plessis-lez-Vaudreuil marked the reawakening of the family. In another, they sounded its knell. It doesn't do traditions any good to be too well explained. They only lose the rigor and obstinate narrowness which contributes to their beauty. The new world we saw from the mansard windows of our lofty schoolroom spread far beyond all the familiar horizons. We had a better understanding of men, of life, of passing time, of others and their needs. That was the trouble: we understood. Whereas for centuries the greatness of the family had consisted in not understanding, in obeying and especially giving orders, in acting, and in marching straight ahead for as long as necessary without asking too many questions. My grandfather believed questions produced weakness, and from generation to generation we had mistrusted them. And from time immemorial and with all our hearts we had preferred answers without questions to questions without answers.

But the books were attacking our habits and our ancient beliefs. They may have destroyed one another, but they also destroyed us. They did nothing but deride the insignificance or stupidity of all we had held dear: order, changelessness, silence, blind faith. They were so many engines of war fighting against our unexpressed system. They talked away, piling up against us all the battering-rams of criticism, all the towers of wrath, all the mines and trenches of satire and ridicule. They laid waste our ancient estates, our silent churches, our palaces and museums, our chateaus and cloisters. To the list of the family's enemies, which already included Galileo and Darwin, Karl Marx and Dr. Freud, Gutenberg had to be added, for he had made silence speak. When we looked back with regret on the past, it was silence we thought of first and foremost. Cover our

ears as we might, the noise of the world came at us from all sides
—from books, newspapers, engines, even from machines in the sky,
from what we called the wireless and the cinematograph, and this
only pending TV—making our heads spin. We were like old animals harassed by the din, the racket of one world in the process of
being swallowed up and another in the process of being born and
crushing us out of existence. Our enemies said we were deaf to the
mounting tide of science and progress. We only wished we were.
They said we were blind to the changes taking place around us in
a universe that had lived too long. If only we had been. Blind and
deaf. Deaf so as not to hear, and blind so as not to read. My grandfather predicted—it came back to me recently, when the Left was
denouncing publicity and the Right pornography in a hullabaloo of
mass cultures clashing one against the other—that one day one
would have to be deaf in the name of culture and give up reading
in the name of intelligence. And that was why he placed Gutenberg
on the green-and-black list—he said they were the colors of disappointed hopes—of criminal breakers of the peace.

But what we chiefly learned from books—and what could be
more natural?—was that we were no longer alone. Our greatness
and our poverty derived from the same source. Love of family,
carried to the degree of passion we experienced every day, proved
only one thing, and that was that in our own estimation we were
better than other people. That was why we didn't like speeches,
lectures, discussions, dissertations, or any other form of expression
or contestation. We had nothing but mistrust for competitive and
other examinations: we had passed them once and for all, and on the
battlefield rather than in reading rooms, and we had been awarded
first-class degrees. There was no point in reopening the matter in
the name of wild schemes and projects for perpetual peace. The
order of the world depended on us and was organized around us.
To put it bluntly, our marriages, our precedence at table, our place
in the Almanach de Gotha proved there was no one else like us in
the world. The others didn't count. They were there only for our
convenience, to serve us and our designs. We were like so many

Robinson Crusoes, startlingly elegant, forever marooned on the desert island of Plessis-lez-Vaudreuil, surrounded by devoted Fridays and menaced by storm.

That was what the waves of books had to batter against. Even when they didn't attack us—though did not even the best of them do so?—they looked at the world from a point of view different from ours, and reflected back from it different echoes. All I've been able to say, for good or ill, in praise or with reservations—doing my best, against obstacles and forgetfulness, to bring out all I can of the treasure of truth which probably doesn't actually exist anywhere, yet flickers for us through the darkness with a thousand intermittent gleams—all I've been able to say about the ancient family which will always be mine and which I love and admire, can probably be summed up in a few words: the world was our way of looking at it. I believe, nowadays, that it's the way everyone looks at it. But thanks to I know not what economic and social, historical and psychological, and above all mythical spectacles, our way of looking at things, even through all the mists of modern life, was still very piercing. It reduced all those who came into our vision to dust and ashes. Books simply smashed our magic spectacles and miraculously revived the voices and points of view of other people. The greater mass of mankind had for a long time belonged to our own history. Like women and younger sons in the family itself, they made up the numbers. And they obeyed our orders. And now we ourselves belonged to the history of slaves and the poor and those who had rebelled against us—to the history of the masses. Talent, passion, love of humanity and its hopes and weaknesses—in the pages we devoured, another victory than our own arose before us. There was the marquis de la Mole, but there was also Julien Sorel. There was Count Mosca, but there was also Fabrice; Almaviva, and Figaro; Prince André and the Russian earth. The king, and the people. We discovered with astonishment that other people's eyes were on us, and not only to admire, but to judge us as we judged them. Books showed us that we too had to appear before the tribunals of history, on which, despite '93 and the Dreyfus affair and the taking of the royal family at Versailles in 1789, we had still imagined we were the judges. A terrible alchemy was going on every day under the roof of the chateau in those postwar summers, with the four young apprentices studying late into the night by the light of lamps scarcely brighter than candles in fairy tales. But they weren't, as in fairy tales, to light us up the cold and solitary ladders of social climbing. Our lamps were there to light us toward others, toward a little more friendship, toward a little more life and passion. In a way we too were emerging from a ghetto. A luxurious ghetto, but none the easier to escape from for all that. And since books had taught us to know and love the world, it was there beckoning to us from beyond the bars.

Many years later, I met our tutor again, in less agreeable surroundings than at Plessis-lez-Vaudreuil. It was in Auschwitz, where he died of typhus and exhaustion in April 1944. Two or three days before he died, talking together in our wooden hut which showed scant sign of spring, we recalled how he had arrived among us one bright summer day. We spoke of his brown suit and the awful tie which glimmered at dinner in the light of the candles, and made us choke with laughter during the first two or three days. I asked him if he'd noticed, and he told me he had, and that on his very first evening, going up to his room after a last goodnight pun on his name by my grandfather, he swore he'd get his own back by overturning the universe of the silly little idiots who made fun of him because they lived in a world which had centuries of good taste and stern habit behind it. He told me he'd thought about running off with my sister Anne, who had blue eyes and black hair like my mother; or leading us into vice and debauchery and thus shattering our courteous insolence and hateful elegance. And then he too had been won over by the spirit of the family, that mysterious combination of blindness and charm. And instead of sweeping through the house like a train of gunpowder, like the heroes of Paul Bourget's *Le Disciple* or Pasolini's *Teorema*, he just did the best he could to perform his mission as our awakener. "And you know," he said, with a little smile and in a voice already very weak, "you know how I took my revenge. I made the little idiots read good books. I led those rich and elegant imbeciles toward curiosity and pity and

passion for life—in other words, toward love of humanity." But I
in my turn, with our family's famous mixture of arrogance and
fidelity, I was already having my revenge on him who had tried to
change us. For like all those who had entered the family never to
leave it, he was dying in my arms, there in that faraway corner of
Poland where history had thrown us and where even in April it was
still cold. And in accordance with our musty, hypocritical, almost
insulting old traditions which he more than anyone had helped to
undermine, even though he hadn't run away with my sister, I was
holding his hand.

TWO

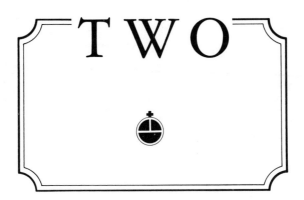

1

From the Teutonic Knights
to the Sister of the Vice-Consul

◉ THE WORLD WAS MOVING, AND SO WERE WE.
We flung ourselves into the Orient Express, into big black-and-
white yachts, into communications and transatlantic telegrams, into
weekends in London and Salzburg, and into the endless cars which
for more than thirty years were to occupy an enormous place in our
lives and which embodied all the things we had hated just as much
as we hated talent and intelligence: speed, change, machines. We left
our lime trees for Wall Street, for Mediterranean cruises, for safaris
in Kenya, for West End tailors, and later on for the ecstatic discovery of erotic temples in India, pyramids in Mexico, sandy beaches
by the sea, and fields of snow in the sun. For we were becoming
reconciled with the sun too. It played no part in family tradition.
Neither my grandmother nor Aunt Yvonne nor Uncle Anatole
would ever have basked in the blazing heat the way my sister Anne
or my cousin Claude did. To protect ourselves against the sun we
had long lived in the shelter of hats and parasols, closed shutters and
enormously thick walls. Perhaps, like the eagle and the globe and
the fleur-de-lys, it was a symbol of power and royalty. But like all
symbols it was to us something abstract. As soon as it actually
started to shine we were afraid of its rays. We had always favored

cool gardens, pale complexions, the shade of the trees which grew up around us to satisfy our pride, our belief in our own durability, and our sense of greatness. Even the Remy-Michaults didn't quite trust the sun. Even more than we, they preferred fruitful shade to its aggressive brightness. And now it took its revenge and burned us. Some of us had blue or green eyes, some brown or gray; our hair might be either brown or fair. But we all had very pale skin. And what with Cannes and St. Moritz, Capri and Biarritz, we all started to get brown. "Blacks!" my grandfather would say when we came back in September, our eyes shining and our teeth white in our dusky faces. And in his vocabulary that was not a compliment.

At all times and in all weathers, clothes had always played an important part in our lives. The Remy-Michaults were crazy about bootmakers and tailors and custom-made shirts, and the beauty and elegance of their clothes often had something exaggerated, *recherché*, and showy about it. But with us clothes were not so much an attraction as a matter of morality. Rather paradoxically, they brought us into the world of ethics rather than that of aesthetics and vanity. They were rarely new, but by their quality, their good taste, their worn splendor, even by their very age, they always demonstrated our own idea of ourselves, our rank, and the duties incumbent on us in a world threatened by vulgarity. Now, for the first time, we were abandoning them. One after the other we renounced morning coats and frock coats, top hats and bowlers. We even went so far as to take our clothes off altogether on the trivial pretext that it was hot, ending up quite naked on the decks of boats and by luxurious swimming pools. Once we'd changed clothes there was no reason why we shouldn't change climates: we left the Haute-Sarthe to go swimming in warm seas. Perhaps because we were trapped between history and society, we fell back on nature. But a different nature, not the one where we used to be protected by our good breeding and our traditions, our horses and hounds, and the deep shade of our forests. No, we turned to the nature that belonged to everyone, and in it we sought to lose rather than find ourselves. By the same token we started to take an interest in the savages and snows of Africa, in African sculpture and music. Aunt Gabrielle had gotten there before us. Despite the admonitions of Maurras and Renan, whose love of the Acropolis had imperceptibly transferred him from the rebel camp to that of tradition, we were no longer satisfied with the Parthenon and the *Venus de Milo.* We started to worship unknown gods consumed by the sun, the temples at Angkor and the Valley of the Kings. After our long fidelity we were turning away at last from our own. Our only concession was an obstinate preference for vanished civilizations, the old parts of modern cities, memories of conquerors, and echoes of forgotten history. We might accept yesterday, perhaps, out of habit. But in any case it had to be far away. The world was becoming our adventure.

Originally we hadn't been afraid of adventure. Our name didn't just happen. We made our name ourselves, but afterward we didn't do much else. To make our name, we'd had terrific adventures which had made us rich and strong and famous. And then suddenly we didn't care for adventures any more. Whether in the singular or the plural, we dreaded them like the plague after the beginning of the eighteenth century. When my grandfather mentioned adventures, in relation to a woman, the government of the Republic, a bank or a businessman, or even the hero of a novel, the word took on a sinister implication. The family name, the chateau, the orchard, the forest, and even hunting—stags and partridges didn't involve much risk—were at the opposite pole from loathed adventure. But the world now in motion suddenly gave us back our taste for it. During the second quarter of the century, just as in the days of conquering Islam or of the wars against the buccaneers, Plessis-lez-Vaudreuil grew every day more insufficient for our huge appetite. There were no more Crusades, no more new worlds to conquer, no more corsairs, no more Barbary pirates to teach a lesson, no more Turks to repel. But there was still travel. So we traveled. And about our travels, far from the horses and carriages, the crush hats, the flunkeys and wigs and frock coats, all the fantastic social paraphernalia from which we'd derived our greatness, and under the hot sun which at last made us like everyone else, there fluttered money, women, business, politics, all the small change of God and our vanished past.

Of course, it mustn't be supposed that all these romantic follies lay in wait for us in the woods of democracy, to fall on us just at the beginning of the twentieth century. We'd already had our share of intrigues and forbidden loves, rages, excommunications, and sometimes murders. Gilles de Rais was a rather distant great-great-uncle, but the Sades and the Choiseul-Praslins were quite close cousins. My grandmother and great-grandmother weren't eager to summon up the memory of the duc de Praslin, who murdered his wife, nor that of the marquis de Sade, with his peculiar imaginings. But when they did have to refer to them, they could only call them "Uncle Charles" and "Uncle Donatien." In other words, bloodshed and sex, soon to be spread all over the front pages of the newspapers, were not altogether unknown to us. The difference between the order of the old days and the disorder of modern times derived more from the society around us than from our own passions and instincts, which remained unchanged. We had been wild and cruel before, but we had been strong too, and everything had always been arranged satisfactorily. Things didn't get out so easily, and we had more control over them. Even when we were suspected, caught, arrested, sentenced, and executed, we left behind memories of fire and brimstone which had a certain grandeur. Children still read about Bluebeard; Uncle Charles did contribute, unwittingly but effectively, to the fall of Louis Philippe and Orleanist usurpation; and intellectuals, even and perhaps especially those of the Left, still showed a loyalty, affection, and even passion for Uncle Donatien which, though quite incomprehensible to us, was after all very touching and flattering. But for the last fifty or sixty years we had been tossed to and fro by winds and waves, and everything had turned against us. In the days of our strength we had had a great advantage: we'd had chateaus in which to entertain little boys and girls, pretty young governesses, marchionesses, and wives of the bourgeoisie. We'd had lands and horses and money—a great deal of money. We'd had valets and chambermaids to look after our guests and attend to our pleasures. We'd even had thugs at our disposal, if necessary, to see that people kept quiet. And we hadn't had any journalists. There was a whispered tradition that my great-grand-

mother had not been altogether insensible to the charms of the duc
d'Aumale, and that a door which can still be seen in the moat at
Plessis-lez-Vaudreuil was opened more than once during the warm
summer nights to let that nobleman pass through. Some people even
suggest that if there is no mention of the duc d'Aumale for two or
three weeks in contemporary records it is because he mysteriously
disappeared to recover from a sword wound inflicted by my great-
grandfather, who had been secretly warned and had lain in wait for
him. But of course there were neither photographers nor gossip
columnists to spread all these rumors. For hundreds of years there
were only two possible sources of information, and it is those which
are still consulted today by historians and archivists: lawsuits
brought against us by the king or the Church, and what we imprudently or out of vanity committed to paper ourselves in the form
of letters, memoirs, confessions, or novels.

But at the period I am now speaking of there seemed to be a vast
network of amateur reporters with nothing better to do than scruti-
nize everything we did. Rumors began to be repeated endlessly
between Vienna and New York, London and Corfu, by dowagers
sipping their tea, youngsters on holiday, press agencies, and society
journalists hard up for copy. At the very moment when we no
longer had any part to play, the most trivial of our pleasures were
reported to the whole world. They filled whole pages of illustrated
magazines, and began to provide material for after-dinner conversation not only in the exclusive clubs of London and at White's or the
Jockey Club in Paris, but also among a bourgeoisie anxious to be in
the swim, steeped in printer's ink, and in whom our name rang a
faint bell. Any historians of the future who take it into their heads
to interest themselves in the history of the family during the first
or second quarter of this century will have plenty of material to
choose from. Though we didn't do much any more, we were talked
about everywhere: in *A la Recherche du temps perdu* and in the social
columns of *Le Figaro,* which had taken over from *Le Gaulois;* in the
correspondence of Cocteau and Maritain; in Maurice Sachs' *Sabbat*
and *Chasse à courre;* and in the letters exchanged during the summer
by elderly people separated by the holidays and for various reasons

still unwilling to use the telephone. In this way my grandfather
more than once, through the most roundabout channels, received
news of his grandson Philippe and the handsome collection of
young women he was accumulating: less than two or three days
after the event, Plessis-lez-Vaudreuil might be informed of a supper
in London or New York, a trip to Venice with a young actress, or
a cruise among the Greek islands with the daughter of an oil millionaire. But it was above all the story of Pierre, Aunt Gabrielle's
oldest child, that we followed with bated breath for five or six years
between the wars—we together with a few hundred other people
scattered about the world (in other words between London and
Vienna), who all kept up with it as if it were some sort of serial,
depicting brilliantly and ironically the family's irresistible decline.

I can't remember now where my cousin Pierre met Ursula. And
who is there left to ask? Increasing age expresses itself not only in
the weakening and general deterioration of the body, but also in the
memories which when your nearest and dearest are dead you alone
possess, and of which every day you let a little more slip into
oblivion. The sickle time brandishes over our heads not only threat-
ens our future, but also fiercely obliterates our past. When an old
man dies a bit of the past, a bit of history, vanishes forever. What
I myself don't know about the secrets of my grandfather and grandmother, my uncles and cousins, no one after me will ever know.
Those who are interested enough, archivists and historians, will still
be able to find the certificate recording the marriage between Pierre
and Ursula von Wittgenstein zu Wittgenstein; they will be able to
follow their honeymoon trip to Rome and Florence, Ravenna and
Florence; they will read of the months of receptions given in their
honor by the privileged of Europe. But if I cannot remember myself, who else will remember what we said among ourselves about
the first meeting between Pierre and Ursula, the first looks and
words exchanged between them? Those chance encounters, those
acts and words and looks, have all tumbled into the strange abyss
which has fascinated me all through a long life which itself will soon
follow them—the void of that which has been and will never be
again, and which no one, anywhere, remembers.

With her pretty, echoing name, which Giraudoux was to use, almost to the letter, for the knight who fell in love with Ondine, Ursula von Wittgenstein zu Wittgenstein belonged to one of the old families, as old as our own, which all through history, in blood and flame, helped to spread eastward the Germanic influence resisted by the Slavs. Two Wittgensteins in succession had borne the illustrious title of grand master of the Order of Teutonic Knights. A Wittgenstein was killed at the battle of Tannenberg in 1410. Another fell at the battle of Tannenberg in 1914. Throughout the ages, Wittgensteins were to be found from the Baltic countries in the north to Sicily in the south, just as we were to be found from Flanders to the Po. They were with Frederick II at Palermo, the emperor Rudolph in Prague, Queen Louise of Prussia at Tilsit, and Bismarck at Versailles. They managed to send one of their number to Rome just in time to act as host to the wild young poet Goethe. In one way or another they were involved in Gutenberg's invention of printing and the introduction of postal service by the Tours and the Taxis; in their castles in East Prussia and on the Rhine they gathered up the best part of the Fuggers' and Pirchenheimers' fabulous collections. Ursula's father, a younger brother, had married a Krupp. The Hohenzollerns and the Prussian monarchy were at their zenith at the time when royalty was collapsing in France. Active before in Palermo, Prague, and Vienna, the Wittgensteins' evergreen ambition found a new springboard in Berlin. When we were taking refuge in exile within our own country and in agonizing withdrawal, they gathered together in one brilliant bouquet the army, society, culture, patriotism, and tradition. They were only putting off the evil day. For the Wittgensteins the fall of the German empire was the beginning of the same end as had started for us a century before.

The Weimar Republic, democracy, inflation, the humiliation of Germany—all these were so many sinister blows at the Wittgensteins' pride. Perhaps you still remember the German cousin who bore our name—Julius Otto, the son of Ruprecht. Two or three Wittgensteins fought beside him under Ludendorff and Ernst von Salomon. Perhaps, I don't really know, it was in these brilliant but obscure circles, eaten up with resentment, that Pierre, who had distant and indirect connections with her through the Krupps, first met Ursula. The Wittgensteins' castle, crammed with relics of the Teutonic Knights and the Knights of the Sword, was between Königsberg and Vilna, almost exactly where the new frontiers between East Prussia, Poland, and Lithuania met. Two years after the treaty of Brest-Litovsk and the Rethondes armistice, war still raged in those parts between social democrats and Spartakists, Bolsheviks and nationalists, regular armies and bands of partisans, Russians and Poles, Poles and Lithuanians. Ursula was born a few years after the turn of the century, in about 1902 or 1903. When the great upheaval took place she would have been about fifteen or sixteen, and her memories of that time must have been vivid and awful. After Hindenburg's victory at Tannenberg and the collapse of the Russian front in 1918, and after the rebirth of Poland, came the Russian offensive of June 1920 and General Tukhachevsky's famous order of the day: "The path to world conflagration lies over Poland's dead body." The front moved back and forth a few kilometers from the German frontier, first from west to east, then the reverse, then from west to east again, and then came the struggle for Vilna and the attacks of the Freikorps. Every night fugitives and deserters crossed the border—now Russians, now Poles, now Lithuanians, now communists, now nationalists. The same men would reappear in different uniforms. Double agents changed sides. The man who sat next to you at breakfast might come back at night to die between the embroidered sheets of the castle. Ursula grew up among armed attacks and the rape of laundrymaids, among rising hatred and fear, between the twin specters of Bolshevism and the Freikorps.

A few years later the burning question was the price of bread, of a toothbrush, of a ticket to Königsberg. Germany was ravaged by inflation. At the age when girls are usually thinking about dancing and getting engaged, Ursula was carrying suitcases full of banknotes to and fro so that the cook who had once prepared dinner for the Kaiser could pay the butcher. Ursula had two brothers a couple of years older than she. Naturally, like the rest of the family, they belonged to extreme right-wing groups, and I've always understood that they were involved in the murder of Rathenau. Later, when Ursula was in the limelight in Paris, there was another, vaguer rumor. One version had it that as a girl she'd been raped by a Lithuanian cavalryman, another that she'd fallen in love with a communist officer and that her family had only kept her from eloping with him by locking her up. In the torpor of Plessis-lez-Vaudreuil and the effervescence of the rue de Varenne, it was hard for us to imagine the flames that were burning in the east. We were stuck in the grooves of routine. They were shattered by one shock after another. It was at about this time that Pierre and Ursula met.

She had very blue eyes and very black hair, and what we used to call great style. Beside her, Aunt Gabrielle looked like a candidate —a successful one, mark you—in some prewar seaside beauty contest in Brittany or Normandy. Ursula had features, bones, and a bearing that were made to last. She had a full, high forehead that was never ruffled, a slightly scornful mouth, a nose that might almost be called big, and vague eyes that could suddenly become very hard. She didn't talk much. She gave orders. But above all, and all the time, she was unpredictable. In the end Aunt Gabrielle had settled down quite quickly into her dual role of patroness of the avant-garde and do-gooder. What fascinated us about Ursula as soon as she came among us was her calm which at any moment might change into the most terrifying storm. Perhaps she had been affected by her disturbed youth. Perhaps—I don't know—she was indifferent to people and things. Whatever the explanation, she passed through life, especially ours, like some quiet torrent.

Unlike his father, Uncle Paul, my cousin Pierre was not a kind of elegant puppet. He was a strapping young man as tall as his mother, with plenty of nerve. He treated Monsieur Comte, with whom he didn't have much to do, with a mixture of irony and candor which caused him entirely to escape being impressed, as we were, by the tutor's charm and distinction. You didn't have to be a genius to see that my grandfather had invested all the family hopes in him. I scarcely counted, Jacques and Claude were lost for the moment in the distractions I mentioned earlier on, and Philippe was

occupied with buying earrings by the dozen at Cartier's to hide in
the table napkins of the ladies sitting next to him at Maxim's or the
Pré Catelan. Pierre was not only the eldest: he went stag-hunting
in Austria and had adopted the new line of national reconciliation.
He'd joined up at the end of 1917, fought for a bit with the Spahis,
won the Croix de Guerre, become an officer in the reserve, and
entered the diplomatic service. So now we were serving the Republic as once we had served our kings.

It took some courage and broadmindedness to marry a German
just after the war. But Pierre didn't hesitate, and neither did my
grandfather. It was a family tradition to get together with the
enemy once the battle was over. The diplomats, on the other hand,
started to make a great fuss. Perhaps this Prussian princess—or was
she from the Baltic?—was a spy. How awful! But whom would she
be spying for? Well . . . no one quite knew . . . perhaps the Germans,
or the Bolsheviks, or the social democrats, or the extreme right-wing
nationalists. Pierre made up his mind in forty-eight hours. He sent
in his resignation and asked Ursula to marry him.

When Pierre talked about those spring days later on, he used to
say he had no regrets. The family was carried away on a breeze of
adventure. The Wittgensteins' castle stood on the heaths of Prussia,
in Masuria, between a little wood of firs and a group of quiet lakes,
under a threatening sky. By some incredible chance the Wittgensteins, because of Bavarian and Polish connections, were half Catholic and half Protestant. But still, they were very far away from us.
Listening to Pierre tell of his journeys over the dreary eastern plains,
we suddenly understood to what extent the Republic had rubbed
off on us. We still thought about the king and the Vendée uprisings,
papal troops, hunting and horses—but we'd become French.
Through Aunt Gabrielle and her Russian and Spanish painters,
through Dean Mouchoux, Monsieur Jean-Christophe Comte, the
Tour de France, the taxis of the Marne, and Sunday dinner, we had
come to absorb all the ideas of the day. The family had been seized
with a desire for happiness and friendship, with a thirst for understanding. We were closer to Antonin Magne and Monsieur Machavoine than to the Krupps and the Wittgensteins. We still saw our-

selves as noblemen who had come down in the world slightly, antiquated feudal lords, characters out of Joseph de Maistre or Barbey d'Aurevilly. But in fact we were already middle-class types out of Henri Becque or Curel, Labiche or Paul Bourget. Ursula von Wittgenstein zu Wittgenstein, cold, stiff, impenetrable, and disturbing, with her Teutonic legends and shattered youth, arrived just in time to restore some tone to our passive decline.

There was a fairy-tale quality about Pierre and Ursula. They seemed to skim along high above our everyday existence. Unlike my grandfather, they were no longer preoccupied with the past. Nor were they, like Aunt Gabrielle, on the alert for a future they were afraid they might miss, as one just misses a train or a taxi. They moved in a world apart, a world in which they themselves were supreme. Ursula's family had lived for years in a style whose luxury and sumptuousness we could scarcely imagine. It was said that one of her great-great-uncles, Prince Leopold, a friend of Brummell and of Metternich, wore gloves of which each finger was specially cut out for him from the rarest leathers, and that when he went to a ball or supper there was always a row of five or six footmen stationed one at the door of each drawing room to add the necessary touch of powder to his old-fashioned wig. There was a strain of madness in the Wittgenstein family. Nothing could have been better for us. Edmond About refers to them, noting with a touch of malice that the Wittgensteins often end up with some affection of the brain, if there's any brain there to be afflicted. An uncle of Ursula's had lost his wife during a trip to Venice, and, wishing to bring the body back to Germany and bury it in the family tomb, had it stowed in the carriage behind him. On the way home he stopped at all the castles he knew, and he knew a lot. And when, after the usual polite exchanges, the host who was going to put him up for the night or for a couple of hours asked him where the princess was, he said she was down there, of course, in the carriage waiting in the courtyard or put away in the stables. Then there would be a cry of: "But what's she doing there? Tell her to come up and join us!" "She can't," said the prince, sipping his tea or puffing his cigar. "She can't. She's dead."

It will be clear by now that the Wittgensteins, with all their misfortunes and their incomparable style, were very different from us. Clearly, they weren't interested in bicycles. Our passion for the Tour de France simply dumfounded them. They fought duels with sabers, went tiger hunting, and assassinated the socialists whom we, like timid shopkeepers, were content to exclude from our drawing rooms. They were haughty, curt, irresistibly stiff and elegant, sometimes witty and sometimes quite stupid. Ursula introduced something new to Plessis-lez-Vaudreuil—a sort of dreamy grimness, a wall behind which there were ghosts. But we weren't too much put out by her silence. It's always correct to say nothing. And she said hardly anything.

Pierre was one of the few people who could cross the bare and icy spaces which cut her off from our everyday world. I think that was why she fell in love with him. She loved him, and he loved her. On the evening of the wedding at Plessis-lez-Vaudreuil, when once again the guests from Paris had been entranced by the sound of the trumpets echoing among the vaulting of the ancient chapel, Pierre and Ursula drove off for a secret destination, secret especially for Ursula. And this is what Pierre had arranged.

In his youth Ursula's great-grandfather had been Prussian ambassador in Paris for a few years toward the end of the July monarchy. There he'd led the sort of life all young diplomats lived, dining in the boulevard restaurants and going to the theater, though with his good looks and famous name he outshone the rest. One night, passing behind the recently completed Madeleine on his way home from a lively evening during which he had lost quite a bit of money, he came upon a carriage with a broken wheel. He asked if he could help, and then saw that inside the carriage was a pale and very beautiful young woman who couldn't have been more than twenty-one or twenty-two. She wore white flowers on her gown and in her hair. The carriage was full of their scent. It was Marie Duplessis, the Lady of the Camellias.

The young German saw her home. He persuaded her to dine with him the next day, and the next, and the next. This was the beginning of a love affair which was to inspire Alexandre Dumas' most famous play and Verdi's *La Traviata*.

Prince Ludwig von Wittgenstein fell madly in love with the girl, and showered her with gowns and furs, jewels and knickknacks, and of course with camellias. But the life Marie led and the anxiety of her lover's family sometimes led to terrible quarrels, which always ended in fits of coughing and delirious reconciliations. One evening, after an argument more violent than usual which had ended in the usual way, Marie said she was tired of that unsettled existence, and would like to go and live a pastoral life outside Paris, and devote herself exclusively to her passion for him. Wittgenstein was enchanted at the idea of having her all to himself, and took her at her word. After two weeks' search, he gave the Lady of the Camellias the most splendid present he had ever lavished on her— a beautiful Renaissance chateau in the department of the Lot, not too large and not too small, which he had bought without even going to see it. And it was there, a few years later, that the last breath left the famous bosom of the real Marie Duplessis. When she died of consumption, she bequeathed Cabrinhac to Prince von Wittgenstein, from whom she had received it.

Cabrinhac was handed down from father to son, and remained in the Wittgenstein family despite the Franco-Prussian War. Ursula went and stayed there several times early in the century, and with a northerner's typical love of the sun and the heat, of the southern accent and southern cooking, she had wonderful memories of the long months she had spent there. But in about 1910 or 1911, despite his daughter's entreaties, her father, who never went near the place now and was afraid of war, decided to sell the house to a local notary. It was from this man's son that Pierre had secretly bought Cabrinhac back.

The sun was setting when Pierre and Ursula set off from Plessis-lez-Vaudreuil—in a black-and-red Delage, if I remember rightly. They drove through part of the night in the direction of Italy, Ursula sleeping trustfully and unknowingly on her husband's shoulder. She scarcely woke when the car stopped. Pierre carried her up to bed, and in the morning she awoke to find herself in the chateau of her childhood.

We were very fond of that story. It catered to some of our dearest myths: the myths of earth and stone, of permanence and the resurrection of the past, of time's unending cycle. The tale surrounded the couple in all the mists of poetry.

It didn't take Pierre and Ursula in their turn long to conquer Paris a quarter of a century after their parents had. But their style was very different from that of the rue de Varenne—stiffer, more correct, in many ways more conservative, and steeped in music, especially Wagner. From his brief period at the Quai d'Orsay, Pierre had retained quite cordial relations with politicians, foreign ambassadors, and French diplomats. It gave him pleasure to see them, but he also felt a sort of melancholy made up of thwarted ambitions and abandoned dreams—abandoned voluntarily, but abandoned all the same—and even perhaps, some evenings, there was also a touch of jealousy and friendly envy. The dinners in the rue de Presbourg weren't particularly famous for their gaiety. But when the sultan of Morocco or Monsieur Titulesco came to France on a private visit they were glad enough to come and spend a few hours at Ursula's dinner table, sitting beside ladies who were often beautiful, under a Watteau or a Rigaud presented by my grandfather. The dinner itself, served by dozens of liveried footmen, would be one of the most elegant to be found in a Paris still unrivaled for its cuisine. Ten years after the war, which had brought about so many changes in this as in other spheres, the entertainment Ursula provided still had the lavishness typical of the early years of the century. While the avant-garde was triumphant with the parents, the children, though still quite young, used the combined wealth of the Krupps and the Remy-Michaults to revive the sumptuousness of a Belle Epoque which they themselves had scarcely known. Such are the paradoxes, jolts, and hesitations of the march of time, now speeding up and now slowing down. We shall encounter plenty of examples of abrupt acceleration. So let us pause for a moment and savor an instance of time's turning back. Among the old papers I've been dragging around with me for the past fifty years I came across the menu of one of the dinner parties in the rue de Presbourg. I must have been there myself, at the lower end of the table, but I can't remember anything about it. I reproduce the menu here by way of illustration, or perhaps rather as a historical and sociological document:

MENU

Consommé florentine
Croustades à la Régence
Esturgeon à la ravigote
Turbot sauce cardinal
Selle de Béhague à la Renaissance
Suprême de volaille à la Maintenon
Salmis de bécasse à la Cambacérès
Turban de foie gras en gelée
Ortolans rôtis sur canapé
Salade sicilienne
Asperges en branches
Bombe Johannisburg
Tuiles dentelles
Biscuits au parmesan

A very nineteen-hundredish menu. My monarchist grandfather would have passed the *croustades à la Régence* and the *turbot cardinal,* but he would never have tolerated the woodcock *à la Cambacérès,* named after a notorious figure in the Revolution, who helped to draw up the Code Civile. The menu was written by hand, of course, in mauve ink, in an elaborate Italian hand with a touch of Gothic, on thick gilt-edged cardboard with a ducal coronet embossed above the family motto in small but very distinct lettering. Needless to say, the wines were not shown as they are nowadays to make sure no one fails to notice the vast amount of money that has been spent on them, and also perhaps because butlers nowadays no longer know how to whisper the sacred names of the vintages and their dates of

birth into a guest's ear: "Château Margaux 1895 . . . Château Latour
1899 . . ." Between mouthfuls, between swigs of Haut-Brion and
Château Lafite, radical ministers and ambassadors of the Republic
would raise the shiny white card to their often nearsighted eyes to
try to make out the ancient, sacred formula: "At God's pleasure."
I imagine the dinner in question must have been in about 1928.
Perhaps nearer 1926. Or nearer 1929. I think it must have been
1926. The spirit of the old and the spirit of the new were both
hovering over the table. Though the settings were very different,
in the rue de Presbourg as in the rue de Varenne the king was well
and truly dead, together with all he had stood for. No one bothered
about all that any more. The lights, the warmth of the wine and of
the human bodies, the perfumes, the spirit of the age—everything
combined to stifle the very memory of it all, though it still lived on
in the tall, silent, chilly rooms at Plessis-lez-Vaudreuil. Luxury—a
luxury which though it was oppressive was also bare, in the sense
that it was devoid of anything that might surround and sustain and
justify it—was the sole heritage of a vanished past.

One day a rumor spread through the clubs and the drawing
rooms and the race courses that Pierre had a mistress. This was a
staggering piece of news to those who knew him. By an apparent
paradox which contradicted all the usual clichés, the eldest sons of
the family had always married for love, as far as I have been able
to trace the matter. My grandparents had been passionately in love
with each other. Uncle Paul defied his parents to marry Aunt
Gabrielle. And Pierre had given up a good deal for the sake of his
love for Ursula. It's not impossible that these marriages for love
were also marriages of convenience—that it was some subterranean
principle so strong as to be almost an instinct which enabled love
to manifest itself and come to fruition. I've already mentioned this
possibility in the case of Uncle Paul. But in any case Pierre and
Ursula had presented "all Paris"—a mixture of literary people, businessmen, politicians, beautiful and fashionable women, and relics of
the old aristocracy who had managed to survive—with a spectacle
not only of happiness but also of equilibrium and strength, into
which it was difficult to see how the alleged mistress could fit. But

slowly, from chance encounters in unfashionable restaurants, from idle conversations, there arose the image of a small, fair young woman or girl, insignificant according to some, pretty and interesting according to others. Pierre was seen at the cinema, at Formentor, and in the Pinakothek in Munich with a young person of whom little was known except that she was fair and rather slight and insignificant and quite pretty, and so on. From time to time she would be described as Titian-haired or a brunette. Were these variations mere mistakes, or were they deliberate red herrings placed by Pierre, who was an experienced huntsman? Whichever they were, they did not prevent a more and more real figure from emerging gradually through the maze of clues and gossip, and the object of all this curiosity and speculation finally appeared in the full light of first nights and the race course at Longchamp. A classic story like that of all the mistresses sprung from obscurity to become haughty duchesses or inhabit vast and dreary villas on the Riviera. They all ended between the palms and the casinos a long life strewn with obstacles and dangers, with sudden disappearances which no one noticed, or with white mink coats and diamond necklaces.

The most astonishing thing about this surprising affair was the little blonde's name: Mirette. No member of the family had ever pronounced such an appellation: they'd have thought it more appropriate for an operetta, a kennel full of hounds, or a porter's lodge. And where had she sprung from? Rumor had it that she had been born somewhere in the south of Finland or perhaps the north of the Baltic states. Her family's claim to fame resided in a probably apocryphal brother whom she talked about with such enthusiasm that people shook their heads and had to stifle their mirth. Did he really exist, this elegant, rather fearsome brother possessed of every talent and grace, who was first Finnish consul in São Paulo and then vice-consul in Hamburg? Once she was fairly firmly established in Paris, Mirette used to vanish every so often for a week or two. She came back radiant, saying she'd been staying with her brother in Sicily or Norway. People laughed and didn't believe a word of it. And there was Mirette back again at the races, holding Pierre's arm at the Prix de Diane.

She wasn't really beautiful. Her looks were a sort of living compendium of all the conventional expressions to be found in the fashion magazines. But she was attractive, with her irregular but pleasing features and her shapely, plump little figure just asking to be caressed. She wore big capes and daring narrow gowns shown in *Femina* and *L'Illustration*. She babbled a good deal of nonsense with a cheerfulness that would suddenly be submerged by waves of sadness which Pierre's friends found very charming. Her nonsense was uttered with a throaty laugh and a Scandinavian accent which soon transformed her from an insignificant foreigner into the darling of Paris. She was to be seen everywhere. But her status was not clear. Did she really belong to Pierre? It was a question pondered by many a rich and smart young man who'd given up pursuing unattainable academic laurels, as he came home from Maxim's or a restaurant in the Bois de Boulogne where she'd gone wild and smashed all the glasses. She vaguely took up hunting, and in the summer sailed around in big white yachts with Italian industrialists and American newspapermen. Often, in the spring, she would drive to Bagatelle or the Pré Catelan with a greyhound on a leash, or a leopard cub whose fur matched that of the coat she was wearing.

In the end, Mirette also appeared at the dinner parties in the rue de Presbourg. And transformed them. At one stroke she introduced a slightly uneasy element of gaiety and animation. Everyone watched Ursula's reactions and wondered how she would behave. But she too lived up to her reputation. She greeted the little blonde with a calm, lofty, almost protective air, not at all as if she were a rival, a boisterous stranger, or an undesirable intriguer. One of Mirette's young gentlemen, the son of an important Jewish picture dealer who was making his way in Paris society, put it rather picturesquely: it was as if Ursula were treating Mirette like a little sister who had gone astray.

The fact that Mirette was the protégée of both Ursula and Pierre led to some curious consequences. It's fascinating to watch the spectacle presented by people and events and societies as they change. The world is full of hints and rumors that often lead to nothing. It takes talent, genius sometimes, to tell which of all the premonitory signs really do predict something, to distinguish, among all the thousands of living creatures and their mysterious relationships, when it is that history is being made. The history may be of the most humble kind, that of individual loves, individual careers, or it may be the history of peoples and nations and the great religions, which decide the future. I'm not trying to make out that Mirette was a sort of miniature Ignatius Loyola or Hegel or Joan of Arc—nor even a Madame de Staël or a Lady of the Camellias. No. She wasn't a harbinger of socialism or romanticism or a new wave of mysticism. She didn't even alter the history of the emotions. She marked neither the end of one era nor the beginning of another. It's even odd to think about history at all in connection with Mirette, who was insignificance personified. But the fact is that she, like Monsieur Comte, like Monsieur Machavoine, like Garin or Petit-Breton, had a part, perhaps even a major part, to play in the history of my family, the history I am trying to retrace so as to understand a little more about the times I've lived in, and about my own life. If she appeared in our family history it was because something else was about to disappear. What a vast area is touched on by even the most trivial existence! I have to make an effort to remember that Mirette was with Pierre in Morocco, at Cannes with Ursula, and dining with them both in the rue de Presbourg, at the same time as Cocteau, at the soirées in the rue de Varenne, was introducing Stravinsky in all his glory, the rising Dali and Max Ernst, and the still unknown Maurice Sachs to an aging Uncle Paul and an Aunt Gabrielle who had finally combined her two careers to become the benefactress of the avant-garde. Most surprising of all, Mirette was also contemporary with my grandfather as he sat unmoving by one generation of Juleses after another, his age a better protection than any enjoyed by his children, already past their prime, or by his grandchildren, now quite well on in life. In the photographs of that period or a little earlier, which I leaf through as I write, the only person who hasn't changed much, the only one who is recognizable despite the ravages of time, is my grandfather: he was already too old to change much. Is that really Pierre, that child in rompers, that little boy in a sailor suit, that youth in an Eton jacket and an enormous collar spreading over his lapels, that young man in Spahi uniform during the war, then dressed as a diplomat and standing behind Briand, then wearing a white alpaca suit and cruising along the Turkish coast? And then, suddenly, in another photograph, I find Mirette's fair hair, while Plessis-lez-Vaudreuil remains just as it was before, with its everlasting trees and interchangeable hunting prints. I look at Mirette's fair hair, and even after all these years I find it as striking as I did the very first day. How modern she is, that little sister who'd gone astray! I mean, how modern she seems now, even in that bizarre get-up, perhaps even more old-fashioned and strange than my grandmother in 1898 with her chemisettes, or great-great-uncle Anatole with his wing collar and timeless frock coat. And she came from somewhere else, not from our own immemorial estates and our own innumerable years, to lead us to places other than our great forest rides where we had always walked before through sun and snow. This little girl from Finland, or perhaps the Baltic, will, in the course of melancholy evenings, have helped to construct, or to destroy, our family history. How strange it is. How sad and comic at the same time. Now that time has passed over her as over all the rest of us, I almost find it difficult to be surprised at the upheaval she caused among us. But as I look again at that half-turned head, as she laughs in the sunshine, her hair in her eyes, I remember all the reasons why, if someone should take it into his head, fifty or a hundred years hence, to take our family as the subject of a detailed history of one small fragment of French society in the first half of the twentieth century, she should have, in that unfurling, or perhaps I should say in that collapse, a role to play and a chapter to haunt.

Ursula and Mirette became inseparable. You met them both everywhere with Pierre, and sometimes even without him. I myself came upon the three or the two of them, quite apart from the dinner parties in the rue de Presbourg. Sometimes we spent a few days together at Plessis-lez-Vaudreuil, or at some friend's house near Paris, or staying with some Italian cousins at Vallombrosa, near Florence. I must say it was an astonishing sight. Pierre very affable and at ease—very well bred, as the family would say. Ursula as rigid as Death on Judgment Day. Mirette exuberant, whimsical, and all smiles. Other people started to talk about the three of them with exaggerated familiarity, as of a somewhat shocking thing which had come to be accepted. What astonished our small world most was the friendly relationship between Ursula and Mirette. The fact that Pierre had a mistress was very surprising, because he was what he was, because Ursula was what she was, and because Mirette was what she was. It was rather awkward. But after all, even with us, it wasn't of great importance and didn't require comment. And that the wife and the mistress should be the best of friends—that too was in the best traditions of boulevard comedy. It may have been that from our point of view there was something a bit odd about having such a note of burlesque introduced into the family. But the most upsetting aspect of the affair was what was then called the climate, the rather oppressive atmosphere that surrounded my cousin and his wife and mistress. Strangers were all struck by it. In the end it even struck my grandfather, who as a rule never noticed anything. There was an air of starchy tragedy hanging about them, in strange contrast with Pierre's nonchalance and the sparkling insignificance of the little sister who'd gone astray. On the other hand, it went very well with Ursula's silent grandeur. It was she who imposed on that typically bourgeois triangle the cold, haughty, almost sinister atmosphere which was always present with Ursula herself. The most subtle observers—and I admit that I was too close and too familiar with the people concerned to be one of them—soon saw that the nub of the affair was neither Pierre nor Mirette, but Ursula. Pierre, whom she loved dearly, might have deceived her; she might, to use the words that had been familiar on the stage for the last thirty years, have been betrayed under her own roof. It didn't matter. She was still supreme. Kind hearts might weep for her, but there was no need. If they'd looked a little closer they'd have seen that Ursula was not suffering. No, it wasn't Ursula who was suffering. Was it Pierre, then? Or perhaps Mirette, trivial, and no doubt stupid, as she was? Even the most insensitive onlookers finally scented a mystery. You couldn't spend a few days or even hours with Pierre and Ursula and Mirette without thinking that there must be something hidden among the three of them. But as often happens when people contemplate one another, even the most mysterious, it suddenly struck you that the secret was really quite simple: once you had the key to the combination, all would be explained. A number of friends told me later that more than once they felt themselves right on the brink of the solution when they saw Ursula accompany Mirette up to the room she now occupied in the rue de Presbourg, then come down again to the drawing room and treat Pierre with the gruff affection she could put on so well, because with her it wasn't put on at all. And then, once more, it would all become incomprehensible again. Pierre would go off almost openly to spend ten days with Mirette in the Balearics or the Canaries. Mirette would come back, and Ursula would greet her with a calm generosity which combined protectiveness, a love of domination, perhaps a shade of cruelty, and real affection. Some people began to suspect that perhaps Ursula had allowed someone else to enter her life, and that Mirette was useful to her in distracting Pierre's attention and keeping him occupied. Ursula was surrounded by a spontaneous and discreet surveillance. But the voluntary observers discovered nothing. Ursula was irreproachable. She had many friends, but no one of them was more important than the others. The only people she was intimate with were Pierre and Mirette.

How did the truth emerge from appearances which at once constituted that truth and hid it? Did it suddenly burst forth one evening? Did it slowly forge its way through people's minds? Again I can't say. All I know is that one fine morning everyone—in other words, the couple of thousand people who decided success and reputation in Paris—felt they'd known all along what you, less blind than those who were regular visitors to the rue de Presbourg, have probably guessed ages ago: it wasn't Pierre who loved Mirette—it was Ursula.

People get used so quickly to sudden reversals of expectation that hardly are they amazed at some revelation than they are vexed and astonished at themselves for not realizing earlier what now seems so obvious. And in their haste to align themselves on the recent discovery, in their eagerness to come to the aid of a truth they never even suspected before, they neglect anything which might contradict the faith they have just been converted to. Everything was now explained. Ursula's calm, her self-control, her imperious ways. Good Lord, it was all because she loved Mirette, and it was she who ran everything. How was it that her affection for the little sister who'd gone astray hadn't leaped to everyone's eyes? Those long walks, those tête-à-têtes in the evening? Mirette stood still, but around her Pierre and Ursula exchanged positions: it was Ursula that Mirette belonged to, and Pierre was the victim.

Everyone suddenly remembered Ursula's smallest gestures, her glances at Mirette, and Pierre's uneasiness even in his triumph. All the rest was forgotten. No one thought any more of how the whole business had started with Mirette and Pierre's secret meetings, their absences, and the trips they took together. Pierre ended up cast in the role of the complaisant or fooled husband who supports his rival. Only the rival now was another woman. All Paris was ready to swear that for some obscure reason Pierre had never felt anything for Mirette but friendship or fatherly affection. He became the little sister's big brother. But those who, like myself, knew Pierre quite well were not taken in for long. I didn't guess anything when it was Ursula who was the mystery, but I soon realized that Pierre wasn't —or wasn't only—the victim and blind instrument other people now took him for. I'm afraid I was actually among the first to discover all the figures of the secret combination of which others suspected only a digit or two, and which at last opened wide the hidden safe in which Pierre and Ursula had shut up the drama behind their brilliant public existence. I came back to the self-evident fact camouflaged by the scandal: Pierre and Mirette loved one another. But the scandal remained—it didn't displace the self-evident fact, it was merely superimposed on it. Mirette didn't belong just to Pierre. She belonged to Ursula too.

For a long while I hesitated to recount these family adventures which hardly redounded to our credit and which caused my grandfather much pain. I decided to do so for various reasons. In the first place, all the people involved have been dead for a long time, from the oldest among them, like my grandfather, to the youngest, like Mirette herself. And I, who was only a witness, am not very long for this world. But there is another reason. The affair, though probably quite forgotten by now, was at the time the talk of Paris for several months, and there was nothing any of us could do about it. But today, after all the economic crises, the rise of Nazism, the Popular Front, the Spanish Civil War, and the Second World War, so many huge events have reduced my family's emotional and social troubles to insignificance that it's impossible to understand or explain it without probing the wounds and lancing the abscess, without revealing secrets which anyhow many people have known. In human history there are private revolutions just as profound and disturbing as public ones. In the history of my relatives and their decline, Mirette played a role comparable to that of Robespierre, Darwin, Karl Marx, the Black Thursdays on Wall Street, Freud, Rimbaud, Tzara, and Picasso: she undermined a little further the columns of our worm-eaten temple.

My grandfather never breathed a word to me, nor, I think, to anyone else, about the vicissitudes of his grandson's generation. I even wonder sometimes if he really quite understood what was going on. I'm not sure. But he sensed that the order of things had suffered a blow, and the knowledge spoiled his last years. Let me repeat that the family had produced in the past, and was to produce in the future, many other examples of audacity or vice, call it what you like—of mental or physical freedom, or of depravity. Debauchery, drink, homosexuality, bestiality, incest—we've always been acquainted with deviant behavior in both its grossest and its most subtle forms. As you have already seen and will see again, we had plenty of cheek. You have only to read what Brantôme, Saint-Simon, or Restif de La Bretonne have to say about the scandalous doings of members of our family. They are full of verses about knights who were pederasts, fathers who made love to their daughters, countesses surprised in the arms of their coachmen, their confessors, or their chambermaids. What was new about what happened with Pierre and Ursula and Mirette was that somehow libertarianism had taken on an aspect of devastation and destruction. In the old days dissipation had been joyful. It was an image and an expression of the life force. And now it was gradually going over to the camp of death and despair. Perhaps because we were just emerging from the age of Victorian, bourgeois puritanism, there was now something somber and wild about our excesses. Under all the gaiety and agitation it wasn't hard to detect a desire for escape, for thrills, a fascination with risk and a thirst for excitement. It was as if we were always trying to forget something. Perhaps the famous death of God, or war, or ruin, or the irresistible rise of democracy, or the population explosion, or the vague possibility that human life might end altogether? We weren't healthy any more. It wasn't lust we abandoned ourselves to now, but the abysses of annihilation. Our jaded follies, our forbidden pleasures, were like suicide. They were irrevocably linked to a certain economic and social situation, to political and moral decadence. We were the nervous cases of a weary civilization—weary of itself and weary of us. And while we flung ourselves into our dubious explorations of every kind of liberty, others started to dance in the streets, to ride in the sunshine on tandem bicycles, to go camping in the forest or on the beach, to discover the innocent world whose simple vigor and hackneyed charms we were trying to run away from. Those others were the people. The Popular Front was already looming on the horizon. But we were using up our last strength flouting all the rules which, before they finally suffocated us, were the source of our greatness. We had a vague feeling that somewhere a new and different morality was going to arise, and that we would no longer be the masters of it. So we threw ourselves into our own negation. And my grandfather, all alone, weighed down by the years, by the past and even more by the future, sat there upright and motionless like the statue of the Commander, stripped of his glamour, a monument to an outmoded system of ethics.

No history ever ends. The bourgeois Paris in which we ourselves now lived, and into which we had been flung by the rush of history, the revolution in morals, the cult of the avant-garde, and the wealth of the Remy-Michaults, gradually got used to what I am obliged to call, though the words stick in my throat, the threesome formed by

Ursula, Mirette, and Pierre. Whenever there was some fashionable and rather farfetched reception for some Italian princess passing through Paris, or in aid of orphan chimneysweeps with tuberculosis —there was no Biafra or Bangladesh in those days—no one dreamed of inviting one of the three without the other two, or two of them without the third. Mussolini, Stalin, Roosevelt, Hitler, Blum, and Franco appeared one after the other on the stage of history. The trio, every year a little less surprising and a little more sinister, grew older, but still in a blaze of glory, in the front row of the stalls. Dénouements always come like bolts from the blue—not in history, for it has no dénouements, but in life. One evening the telephone rang in the rue de Presbourg, where there was an important dinner party with Paul Reynaud, Cécile Sorel, Giraudoux, and the Princess Colonna. Some of the guests were already suggesting going to meet Paul Morand and Aunt Gabrielle at the Six Jours. For once, Mirette wasn't there: as always in such cases, Ursula had announced calmly that she had gone to spend a couple of days with her brother, the vice-consul in Hamburg. As he was pouring the Château Lafite the butler—I can still see him now: his name was Albert and he had long white hair and a very chilly manner, inspired perhaps by his mistress —bent over Ursula's shoulder just long enough to whisper. Between the Rigauds and the Watteaus, the conversation of the two or three dozen guests kept up a continuous chatter. Ursula didn't move or show any sign of surprise. She just picked up the little reticule of fine gold and silver chain that she always carried about with her, took out her lipstick, and wrote three words on the gilt-edged menu bearing the family arms which lay by her plate. Then, between the Dresden épergne and the silver candlesticks, she tossed it lightly across to her husband opposite. Pierre was talking to the Princess Colonna. Laughing. He picked up the menu carelessly, took out his glasses, and went on talking as he peered at the three fateful words. Then he stood up, very pale. There was a sudden terrible silence. The minister, the actress, the homosexuals, the financiers, the ambitious young men at the lower end of the table, watched Pierre stagger and fall. Later on, in the confusion that followed, some bold or impertinent or perhaps merely tactless guest picked up the menu, which had fallen on the floor. It had three words written on it in red greasy letters: "Mirette is dead."

How had she died, Mirette, the little sister who'd gone astray, my pseudo-cousin twice over? The first thing that emerged was that she hadn't set foot in Hamburg. The know-alls crowed: "But of course! What did you think? It was as plain as the nose on your face!" She'd been killed in a car crash near Biarritz. She was with a man, and he was killed too. There was a police inquiry, which left no doubt on the subject. Mirette and her unknown companion had left Paris on the previous Friday. The first night they'd stayed in the Loire valley, the second night near Angoulême, the next at Biarritz, where the weather was very fine. At each stop they'd taken a room with a double bed. "They must have been in love!" the manageress of the Aigle Noir, between Blois and Amboise, told a reporter from *Paris-Soir*. "They spent all their time kissing and cuddling." It didn't take long to establish who it was that the little sister who'd gone astray went to meet at Le Bourget that Friday. He came from Hamburg, where he was vice-consul. He was Mirette's brother.

The road was quite straight at the place where the accident happened. There were a few trees in the fields, but not many. The car had been going at a very high speed for those days, and had hit the only tree that was anywhere near the road. Some police official told Pierre that in his opinion, though he hadn't any proof, it was a case of suicide, or perhaps murder and suicide combined. Mirette was driving.

Ursula remained very stiff and dignified. But after a year or two she started to sleep around. Pierre no longer even tried to conceal that other people and life in general became more unbearable for him every day. But it was hard to tell whether his suffering was due to Mirette's absence or Ursula's presence. Perhaps it was both. Ursula's beauty and her incomparable style rapidly faded. At the time of the Popular Front and the Spanish Civil War she was only just thirty, but she looked forty-five or fifty. She aged fifteen years in six months. She used to spend whole weeks at Cabrinhac with dazzled South American attachés, motor mechanics from Rodez, lady interior decorators or manicurists, or unrecognized painters, delighted with their good luck, whom she'd pinched from her mother-in-law. You remember who her mother-in-law was, of course? Aunt Gabrielle.

One evening just before Munich, Jacques and Claude and I had met as we often did, despite the separation imposed by life and our different opinions, to have dinner or go to the cinema together, and we were listening to the latest news on Radio Paris. I believe we'd just been to see Léontine Sagan's marvelous *Mädchen in Uniform* for the second time. It had first been shown in Paris five or six years before. Our heads were still full of the scene of the royal visit, which reminded us of our grandfather and Plessis-lez-Vaudreuil. We could still see the pretty French governess who laughed too much and was of course much more attractive than our friend Jean-Christophe, still remember the radiant schoolgirls dressed as monks and acting Schiller, still hear the frightened young voices crying "Manuela! Manuela!" through the empty house to try to stop the little German girl, going up the stairs reciting the Lord's Prayer, from throwing herself to her death for love of her teacher. What mysterious associations did those images of melancholy and of forbidden love set up in our minds? As we listened to the hysterical voice once again addressing his troops and demanding the repeal of the Treaty of Versailles and the restoration of all former German territory, I heard Claude in his corner whisper: "Why don't we give them back Ursula?"

We didn't have the chance to carry out that inspired suggestion. On May 9, 1940, Ursula swallowed three vials of barbiturates. No, she hadn't been warned, either by sudden intuition or by her own secret agents, that the Panzer divisions and the Stuka bombers were about to attack. But a novice bullfighter she'd picked up at Saragossa or Pamplona had just left her for the daughter of a hotel-keeper in Marseilles. The young couple lived together for a year or two, then they also separated. But they had time to produce a little girl who is now familiar to all of you. With her southern accent and her snub nose and her black hair, she's one of the most popular singing stars on television. I wonder if she has the slightest idea of how she's connected with us through Ursula. I doubt it.

2

The Whore of Capri

WHEN I LOOK BACK, AS I DO MORE AND more often now that I'm getting older, it seems to me—am I wrong? —that the ages of happiness haven't lasted very long. I was practically in at the birth of the idea of happiness, of indefinite progress, of individualism triumphant, between the reserve of my grandfather and the enthusiasm of my Aunt Gabrielle. Monsieur Jean-Christophe Comte had not only introduced us into the magic world of books: he had also taught us that books were nothing if they did not herald a new age. And they did herald a new age. Their humor, profundity, adventure, subtlety, genius, and beauty all came together in great hopes. You had only to wait for time to go by, and man would be better, life grander and finer. As you may imagine, this attitude to history was far removed from the beliefs of my grandfather. When I try to understand my own and my cousins' youth, it appears to me as a kind of conversion. We went from the ideas of my grandfather to those of Monsieur Comte. We emerged from a world that did not move into a world that was on the march toward a glowing future. The 1914 war had dealt a blow to the great wave of optimism on which Monsieur Comte was still borne along. But for several years it seemed as if the war were only an unfortunate interruption of the move toward progress, or, better still, that it was the end rather than the beginning of an era. It was the revenge of injustice, the last act of violence. The trenches, the shells, the suffering, the dawn attacks on the edge of a wood, all these were themselves part of the struggle for happiness. This was the war to end wars—a promise of peace. Jean-Christophe, who believed in progress and the dignity of man and a form of socialism inherited from Michelet and Hugo, took as much pride in victory as my grandfather, though for fundamentally different reasons. It seemed to me, at that time, that people and events and history were always ambiguous, and that agreement was rarely anything more than heaven-blessed misunderstanding. For my grandfather, the victory of 1918 stood for the triumph of the army, of the hierarchy, of discipline, and all the other virtues of tradition. For Jean-Christophe it represented the end of armies and hierarchies, the replacement of discipline by solidarity, and the triumph of freedom. Victory appeared in the image of the past for those who loved the past, in the image of the future for those whose hopes lay in what was to come. To cover up their differences, my grandfather and Jean-Christophe managed to agree on certain all-purpose phrases whose meanings were of course left as vague as possible: phrases like national unity, national honor, justice, and law.

Leaving aside the troubles of the war, the idea of happiness never shone more brightly than it did when I was a child. There was a half-century or so, around 1900, when men thought they were going to be able to be happy. Shall we dwell again for a little on the happiness that appeared among us in the wake of Aunt Gabrielle? It's a subject quite pleasant enough to be worth reverting to.

I was brought up on two or three contradictory ideas which were in fact commonplaces. For my grandfather and the family as a whole, happiness was identified with the past. But as we advanced in time, the age limit of happiness was surreptitiously brought forward. We hated Talleyrand, but we loved to quote the famous phrase in which of course, in our view, he condemned himself out of his own mouth: "Anyone who hasn't lived before 1789 doesn't know the joy of living." The year 1789 was replaced first by 1830, then by 1848, 1870, 1900, 1914, 1929 and 1939. And nowadays it seems to me that we were remarkably happy still between 1945 and 1965 or '70. It's little things like this that make me realize I've grown old.

In his peaceful offensive against my grandfather's ideas, Monsieur Jean-Christophe Comte had taught me two things, among others: that the past only meant the joy of living for a privileged few, and that happiness, true happiness, happiness for everyone lay not behind but before us. For a long time I had believed my grandfather. For another long time I believed Monsieur Comte. But today I wonder if, in the difficult area of the history of feeling, the truth isn't much more complicated. Has anyone ever written a history of feeling? We've had histories of battles, dynasties, painting and music, literature and philosophy, economic doctrines and social movements, the price of corn and meat, the means of communication, costume and manners. But we need a history of feeling. I'm afraid, though, that it would be impossible to write. How, without figures, graphs, statistics, almost without any evidence at all, can we form any idea of what was felt and experienced by a Roman living at the time of the decline of the Empire, or by a medieval peasant, a *condottiere* of the Renaissance, a citizen of Paris during the Enlightenment, or our own great-grandparents in 1848 or under the Second Empire? We can just about manage to reconstruct and understand what they thought. But how can we know what happiness, pleasure, suffering, tenderness, resignation, or despair meant to them? Above all, how can we compare their feelings and our own? To do that we'd have to be able to put ourselves in their place, and we can't. The most we can do is try to learn from what they said and wrote—books, letters, speeches—what sort of picture they had of the future. That alone would be something. Like many another, I've sometimes thought of attempting something of the kind. The title was ready and waiting: "A History of the Future from the Remotest Past." But even a valuable piece of research like that wouldn't really tell us much of what people have actually felt throughout history. No one will ever know if people were happier or less happy without cars or television, without news, money, needs, ambitions, without great hopes but without illusions, under the eye of a God who bade them be silent, amid an immutable order and in the absence of all change.

Jean-Christophe would never have allowed me to ask myself such questions. For him, happiness and progress were one. If I ask myself these questions now, it's because having lived for three-quarters of a century I see on all sides that progress is suspect. Monsieur Comte's optimism has become as open to doubt as my grandfather's pessimism. I myself have remained loyal enough to Monsieur Comte's teachings not to deny progress. But what surprises me, and what would have surprised my grandfather even more, is that the notion of progress itself has gradually become reactionary. Science, that old enemy of my grandfather's which Jean-Christophe admired so much, is once more considered an enemy by the younger people I come across. And even those who don't deny the triumphs of progress have the strongest possible doubts about its connection with happiness. For many people nowadays, happiness consists in damning and escaping from progress. I'm often sorry my grandfather isn't still here. I wonder if he mightn't have seen this tendency as a bitter, paradoxical, (dare I say it?) dialectical form of victory over the ideas of Jean-Christophe.

If one may venture an opinion on so mysterious a subject, I'd say people were never happier than they were at the end of the nineteenth and the beginning of the twentieth centuries, not because they actually were happy then, amid the spread of industrialization, but because at last, after thousands of years, they hoped to become so. For centuries they hadn't even hoped. The marvelous achievement of socialism was to give the great mass of mankind a hope of happiness. Whether the fruits of socialism and communism and Stalinism have fulfilled the promise of the dreams and hopes and flowers, that's another question, and the answer is doubtful. I wonder if mankind hasn't been rather like those fiancés, madly in love, who dream fondly of the blissful life in store for them with their beloved. But the marriage never lives up to the engagement. Socialism has been rather like a century-long engagement between humanity and happiness.

I don't think even we, who had been among the privileged for centuries, were ever happier than at the end of the nineteenth, when power had already deserted us. Saint-Just said that happiness was a new idea in Europe. And that was true even for us. Our dukes and cardinals and marshals of France and presidents hadn't put happiness first. Oh, I know they had a much easier time of it than their peasants and soldiers. But I still think that, with certain exceptions who didn't get much credit for it, they thought not so much in terms of happiness as in terms of greatness and power and faith and justice. They may well have been acquainted with pleasure. Pleasure—rough, rapid, with no thought for the future or spirit of habit —was just an episode in lives dominated by the duties of office. My grandfather, who was a man of the past, would never have dreamed of organizing his life around the idea of happiness. You may say that's all very well—he had everything he wanted. I admit it. But comfort, amusement, the surprise of novelty, love of leisure and travel, everything which lends charm to our passage through the world—all these were quite foreign to him. He was born to a certain place and condition, and there was no question, for him, of taking advantage of it to obtain enjoyment or easy options. It was neither good luck nor chance. Come, now—you know very well what it was! It was the will of God. And that conferred only duties. Yes, happiness was a child of the great Revolution. That was why it came among us at the same time as the bourgeois values of intelligence and self-destruction, with Aunt Gabrielle.

What mattered to Jacques and Claude and me, under the dual influence of Aunt Gabrielle and Monsieur Jean-Christophe Comte, was liberty, being on good terms with the universe, other people's happiness, and our own. Thanks to Jean-Christophe's teaching, our own happiness had become inseparable from that of all. Gradually racism, intolerance, dictatorship, privilege, and violence had become unbearable to us. We wanted a world of fraternity. We would hate fascism, which was already growing up in various places. We flung ourselves with abandon into the spirit of modern times, and found things which were halfway to all that my grandfather loathed: humanism, socialism, the cult of the individual, and the search for happiness. And we started to think that history wasn't a motionless sphere suspended in the ether, but an arrow aimed at a future always higher than the past.

I think that was what made our childhood and youth so happy, on either side, in time, of the firing line of the Great War. We came from a privileged class which still retained much of its privilege and charm. We were moving toward a world in which everyone would have more happiness than before, and Jean-Christophe had made us capable of rejoicing with him in that fact. History was at a turning point. We were balanced between past and future, on the point of equilibrium between still and already. Unlike the young people of today, we were full of yesterday. But I fear we still rushed headlong into all the traps of sincerity and its opposite.

We were very happy for a few years still after Monsieur Comte left us. He went to teach first in Germany and then in the United States, and came back to France in about 1930. Perhaps we were happy just because we were young. While my cousin Jacques and Michel Desbois went on studying law and economics in Paris, Claude and I went and spent two or three years in Spain and Greece and Italy, on those Mediterranean shores which had always been dear to us and which my grandfather and Jean-Christophe, each for different reasons, had taught us to love and admire. We were twenty, a little more or a little less, and they were, if we had only known it, the happiest days of our lives.

Aunt Gabrielle, who was always very generous, offered us a lot of money so that we could live for a while without any material worries. But we were still under the influence of Monsieur Jean-Christophe Comte, and we declined the suggestion, which would have enabled us to exist like a couple of miniature Rockefellers. But we did accept enough for us to be able to live simply, and for quite a long time, in country inns or family pensions in Athens or Rome. Other than our wandering hippies of recent times, I don't think many people have spent such years and months as we did, and right at the beginning of our lives. The demands of life, a career, the claims of family, and the need for money usually throw all their weight on the scale against such delightful freedom. But a whole combination of circumstances made things easy for us: Aunt Gabrielle's wealth was one of them, of course, but above all there was our own lack of vocation. We didn't know what to do, and that was a blessing. Jacques and Michel were preparing to take the entrance examination for the ministry of finance, Philippe devoting himself entirely to his adventures with ministers' wives and girls from flowershops. Pierre was the eldest son, and that was a career in itself. And he also had first the diplomatic service and then Ursula. But Claude and I were free. We had nothing in our lives—no women, no ministry, no responsibilities, nothing, not even plans. We had time to waste, or in other words to save. We were midway between the young men of 1830 who went about Venice with hearts divided between Byron and George Sand, and the long-haired guitarists of today who indefatigably parade their boisterous bitterness on the Spanish Steps or beneath the Acropolis.

Nothing is more unfair or misleading than books or films which depict a world that is unrelievedly dreary. Even in the most somber lives there are sunny days, strolls by the river, and hopes of happiness. It must be admitted, and we did admit it, that Claude and I held all the trumps. Without lifting a finger we'd won first prize in the lottery. The gods had smiled on us. They'd given us money, freedom, leisure. Throughout our Mediterranean adventure they didn't let any of our relations die or even fall seriously ill. Above all they'd spared us those passions which, though they may have their compensating virtues, prevent people from giving themselves up freely to the delights of existence—passions such as envy, jealousy, avarice, and ambition. We didn't desire anything except to be happy. And so we were. It was because we had no thought for our future as adults, because we abandoned ourselves to the happiness of the moment, that our honeymoon with the world was so radiant.

We set out for Italy as for an unknown continent. Mussolini had just made his first appearance on the balcony in the Piazza Venezia. The highways, the modern hotels—the ineffable Jolly Stendhal in Parma and the Hilton in Monte Mario, the site where after their long journey on foot the medieval pilgrims could look out at last on the whole of Rome, with its legendary Capitol and fabulous treasures—gas coupons for tourists, and huge airports, all were still hidden in the future. The Forum had emerged only recently into the daylight. St. Peter's was still shut in on all sides by a tangle of old houses and narrow streets, soon to be swept away to make way for the majestic but somewhat tedious vistas of the via della Conciliazione. Most of the roads were not surfaced. We used to walk or cycle with our packs on our backs along the little white lanes, where the occasional car left a cloud of dust in its wake.

To start with, we explored Tuscany and Umbria, flinging ourselves with rapture into Florence and Siena, San Gimignano and Volterra, Urbino and Spoleto. We stayed for three weeks in a balconied pension in Fiesole, and for ten days we had Room 17 in the little hotel in Montepulciano, whence we used to go down to the plain and spend hours contemplating the golden church in the old town of Sangallo—San Biagio, I think it's called. In the evening, looking down from our windows, we discovered beauty—a different beauty from that of our childhood and the familiar forests of Plessis-lez-Vaudreuil. We were filled with a kind of fervor. Sometimes we could hardly breathe for happiness. We were carried away by the light, the combination of loveliness and nobility, the reminders of past grandeur, the intoxications of the moment. For months we lived in a state of grace. The reason: we were young and the world was new.

We often used to get up and set off at dawn. A few months ago I went back to Italy, perhaps for the last time—ah, how hard it will be to die and leave the world behind, though it has left us behind long ago! Here and there, behind the highways and the lopped-down trees, I could still glimpse the ghost of our youth—a recollection of a halt among the olive groves beneath Assisi or Gubbio; traces, as much in myself as in the buildings or the fields, of our enchantment at the sight of Todi or Piacenza. In the end, we got to know every bend of the road between Florence and Rome, every ancient pine on the hills. At night, having walked about thirty kilometers or ridden on our ancient bicycles for eight hours, we'd stop at some tiny inn and collapse with fatigue after a hearty meal of *pasta e fagioli,* mozzarella, and Orvieto.

After Tuscany and Umbria we made for Venice, Rome, Apulia, and Sicily. Everything in the world that was beautiful was ours. And in books we encountered the same dazzling images recorded by others. We read Barrès on St. Mark's Square: "With its Eastern palaces, its vast radiance, its alleys and squares, its mooring posts and sudden ferries, its domes, its ship-filled quays and mast-filled skies, Venice, caressed by listless waves, sings the Adriatic an eternal opera." We read Chateaubriand at the seaside, Stendhal, Regnier, Byron, and that delightful old fool, President de Brosses, who loathed everything that we admired: "I found the painting in Florence very much inferior to what I expected ... Cimabue, Giotto, Lippi: very poor pieces of work for the most part. The pictures are not up to much here." Or the same author on Siena and its Palazzo Publico and marvelous Piazza del Campo: "The palace is an old building with nothing notable or even interesting about it except a few pictures even more antique and ugly than itself." And on Spoleto: "It was too dark for us to see it. And anyway it isn't worth the effort. Assisi isn't far away, but I was careful not to go there: I have a mortal terror of stigmata." And on St. Mark's: "You imagine it's a wonderful place, but you're much mistaken: it's a church in the Greek style, low, admitting no light, and in wretched taste both inside and out ... You've never seen anything so lamentable as the mosaics ... the whole floor is made of them. They're joined together so well that although the floor has subsided in some places and been pushed up in others, not the smallest piece has come unstuck or out of place. In short, there's no denying it's the best place in the world for spinning a top." It didn't take much to amuse us. We learned to be disrespectful ourselves about the things we loved. The ancient stones of Italy, like Monsieur Comte's books, had become so familiar that we enjoyed making affectionate fun of them. We hated compulsory veneration, routine admiration, lip service. Tourists got on our nerves, with their mixture of indifference and passive acceptance. Claude defined them simply and perfectly: tourists were other people. We ourselves delighted in the snipers and nonconformists who at least had the courage of their shocking convictions. We read a lot of Maupassant, who in 1886

wrote to his mother: "I find Rome horrible . . . 'The Last Judgment'
is like an awning for a wrestlers' booth at a fair, painted by an
ignorant carpenter . . . St. Peter's is without doubt the biggest monument to bad taste that was ever built." And there was a lesser-
known traveler called Louis Simond who expressed himself even
more freely, if that was possible, on the subject of our Florentine
and Venetian demigods: "Very poor pieces of work in the style of
the ninth and tenth centuries." Of Raphael he said: "The drawing
is incorrect, the expression mean, the color cold and lacking in
harmony." Of Michelangelo's "Last Judgment" he had as low an
opinion as Guy de Maupassant: "A mixture of arms and legs, faces
and backs—a veritable pudding of resuscitated corpses." How
bright and refreshing this was in comparison with the textbooks
and guides all repeating one another! Louis Simond was surprised
Michelangelo had produced so little: "There are very few pictures
by him, and even fewer statues. What did he do with himself for
all those eighty years?" We reveled in his dreams of grandeur and
his plans for works of art: "If I were the Pope, I think I'd show my
good taste by having all the gilt and different-colored marble in St.
Peter's covered with a coat of gray paint." "If I were the Pope"
became a catchword between Claude and me. Whenever someone
annoyed us or something went wrong, we used to remember Louis
Simond and say, "If I were the Pope . . ." Claude said it to me the
day he died, and it brought back the perfume of those enchanted
days.

Here too, no doubt, you can see all we owed at once to the
traditions of the family and to the lessons of Monsieur Comte. We
were at home in Pisa and Bari, Verona and Syracuse. We discovered
little towns scarcely mentioned in the guidebooks and completely
unknown to tourists in those days: Ascoli Piceno, where we wandered amazed through a series of squares each more beautiful than
the last; Todi; Bevagna, with its Romanesque churches; the baroque
splendors of Noto; Cosenza, deathplace of Alaric, who was beginning to fascinate us because he was a barbarian; Benevento; l'Aquila;
little villages in the Sabine country with magical names like Fara in
Sabina, l'Abbazia di Farfa, and Poggio Mirteto. In the winter we

used to take refuge in libraries, among our beloved books. In the summer we'd set off again. For Salamanca or Segovia. For Patmos and Mistra. What a marvelous life it was! Sometimes, on the road, in a temple, at Delphi or Olympia or Bassae, on a hill, under a blazing sun, Claude would turn to me. Perhaps we'd be in sight of the sea, white houses, olive trees, an ass braying, a windmill or a ruined aqueduct. And he'd say: "Aren't we lucky?" Ah yes, we were lucky! Sometimes it would flash through our minds that we were too lucky, and that it was unfair that other people were not so fortunate.

And what about Granada from the top of the Vela tower, looking down over the Alhambra, the Generalife, the Darro ravine, the Alcazaba Cadima, the Albaicin quarter and the plain where the Catholic monarchs knelt on January 2, 1492, as the trumpets sounded and their flag was slowly hoisted to the top of Boabdil's tallest tower? What about Ithaca and Paxos, and Zanthe with its arcades? And Trogir, and Bodrum, once called Halicarnassus? We used to make up little counting rhymes out of the names of our treasures:

> Skiathos, Skyros, Skopelos,
> Tinos, Patmos, Kalymnos,
> Paxos, Symi, Parga, Mistra,
> Alcazaba Cadima.

Or:

> Gubbio, Pylos, Rhonda,
> Levkas, Orta, Todi,
> Borgo Pace, Borgo Pace
> Ascoli Piceno.

We used to sing them as we went along. On foot, cycling, swimming, we covered the whole Mediterranean, intoxicating ourselves as we did so with the names of its bays and islands.

There were other things to thrill us besides ancient monuments, libraries, and the Crucifixions in Romanesque churches. The sun, the sea, the great red or black cliffs rising steeply from the sands, the cypresses on the hills, often white with dust from the road, the great groves of olives, the umbrella pines mounting guard, sinister yet soothing, along the deserted beaches—all these filled us with joy during the still evenings when the wind had ceased. For a long time we'd lived in the past. Later we were to live in the future, watching history in the making according to the preachings and predictions of the great sages of modern times, the Jewish geniuses who so alarmed my grandfather—Marx, Freud, and Einstein. But now, between the hills and the sea, looking down from the great Arab and Venetian forts, looking up at frescoes and temples, we surrendered up everything to the present.

We were happy. We swam in caves. We wandered about among gods, painters, architects, philosophers. For nearly three years we did nothing but be happy in beautiful surroundings. Now and then we'd think about the family at Plessis-lez-Vaudreuil. There, as here, we still owed a lot to the past. Slowly, through century after century, by patience and genius, it had prepared all these splendors for us. The past of the Haute-Sarthe, where we'd been brought up, suddenly seemed small in comparison with Ravenna, Granada, Palermo, Mistra, and all the fabulous deeds connected with them. We were finding out about the Barbarians, the Turks, the death of civilizations, Boabdil's tears, Galla Placidia's mausoleum, the monuments of Theodoric. Everything crumbled away, but everything was born again in a different form and in another place. We too were going to die. We were already dead. But history, whose very salt and savor we'd thought we were, carried on without us. For a long time Plessis-lez-Vaudreuil had been the center of the world. But now the world was growing bigger. For us it still didn't include the Forbidden City or the pyramids of Yucatan or the temples at Angkor or Machu-Picchu. But already Asia was invading our dreams, with the Persians at Salamis, the Turks in Athens, and above all the Barbarian hordes attacking the Roman Empire. We had always seen ourselves, if not as victors, at least as men of power, like Caesar and Sulla, Alcibiades and the Catos. But perhaps we were forever among the vanquished, with people like Honorius and

Romulus Augustulus, relegated to the twilight chapters in the textbooks where a school year and a civilization perish together, overtaken by summer and decadence.

These thoughts about the history of societies may have been
lurking somewhere among our inner corridors, our secret attics. But
they didn't stop us from throwing ourselves joyfully and without
the slightest reserve into the delights of church frescoes, of marble
staircases in ruined palaces, and of the sun shining on the rocks or
the white houses around the harbors. Ruins and decline acted rather
as an invitation to take advantage of the passing moment and its
uncomplicated charms. There were other things to attract us even
more than buildings, color, and the beach. There were men. And
sometimes women. Among all the figures which accompanied
Claude and me on our excursions among the islands and the temples
there were two in particular we would not forget. On Skyros we
met an old sailor, and in Rome we met a young woman who spent
the summer in Capri and the winter on the café terraces of the via
Vittorio Veneto. The sailor of Skyros and the girl from Capri
entered our portable mythology while they were still alive. They
too opened up an unknown world to us.

It was a world in which everything which had hitherto mattered
to us was wiped out. The past, the family, tradition, the moral code,
language, the hierarchy of people and things were all overthrown.
Monsieur Comte had taught us to widen our lives by opening them
onto books. The sailor from Skyros, and the girl whom, as a joke,
and above all to make *her* laugh, we called the whore of Capri,
suggested a completely different picture of life. We knew, of
course, that Eskimos, Aztecs, the descendants of slaves in the United
States, and the people my grandfather called "savages" in Africa or
New Guinea led lives quite different from ours. But they inhabited
other planets. In our own world there were rich and poor, but we
saw them all as based on the same model, just as Jules at Plessis-lez-
Vaudreuil was an exact copy of Uncle Anatole, and Michel Desbois
a slightly younger brother of my cousins Jacques and Claude. But
the lives and memories of the sailor from Skyros and the whore of
Capri projected us into landscapes we had never seen before.

Skyros is a greenish island with tortuous streets lined with white houses. The old sailor lay in wait for us between ouzo and tavli, with his white beard and tales of adventure. He'd never had any family —neither father nor mother, uncle nor aunt, grandfather nor grandmother. When he looked back, all he saw was himself. We talked to him about Uncle Anatole and Aunt Yvonne and the whole family system, about Aunt Gabrielle and Uncle Paul, and of course about my grandfather. How odd it was! If we'd been telling him about Merlin and Morgan le Fay he couldn't have been more astonished. Our descriptions of hunting, of the vast kitchens at Plessis-lez-Vaudreuil, of all the setting that seemed to us familiar and natural, so flabbergasted him that he laughed and shook his head. He himself had never had any family ties or connection with the past. The only thing he knew was nature. He'd never been taught anything. All he knew he'd gotten from the sky, the wind, the perfumes of the night. He'd managed all on his own between his beloved sea and his beloved islands. He didn't even know where or when he had been born. Perhaps in Greece, perhaps in Turkey. The only thing he knew was that he spoke Greek. And therefore hated the Turks. When the metaphysical fit took him, he would attempt, with some difficulty, to think, and then he would tell us that the Turks probably hated him as much as he hated them, both him and all those belonging to him, who had slaughtered the Turks just as the Turks had slaughtered them. He seemed to recall a lot of bloodshed in his childhood, and sometimes in the early hours he woke from nightmares about it. Ever since he could remember, he'd gone from island to island in the Ionian Sea and the Aegean, but never farther than Corfu in one direction and the Turkish coast in the other. He lived among temples and memories of the gods, but it never occurred to him to start philosophizing about history. He loved the sea, horses, everything that was simple and rather primitive. At the age of seven he was a cabin boy; when he was fourteen he had cut the throats of a couple of Turks. At the time we met him he must have been about sixty-five or getting on to seventy. The thing that mattered to him was friendship—he protected his friends; he stole from other people and sometimes killed them. Once, for a few months, he'd had

a job in a canning factory, but what he'd chiefly preserved from
that was a horrible memory. He loathed the army, industry, offices,
houses. For a long while his one aim in life had been to own a gun,
and he'd managed to get a very fine one from some Turks. He'd
never submitted to any restraint, never been anything but free,
never served in the regular army or navy. On the sea he'd been a
buccaneer, and on land a bandit, one of the honorable kind descended from those who fought against the Turks in the War of
Independence. He lived out of time, in an eternal present of violence
and joy. Meanness, fear, and ambition seemed unknown to him. He
lived according to no rules, but in obedience to secret laws which
came to him from the sea, the ancient trees, the caves, and the
evening air. Every so often he would suddenly remind me of my
grandfather, but a grandfather who instead of hearing ancestral
voices heard the even more muted tones of earth and water. But it
was impossible not to see the gulf which separated him from us. We
represented lassitude, he represented strength and youth. We had
set up morality to defend an order bequeathed to us by the past. He
knew nothing of principles or rules or laws, and acted in accordance
with his nature and as the fancy took him. He loved life. It so
happened—and this was fortunate—that money, security, treach-
ery, and honors didn't appeal to him. He preferred taking risks and
enjoying himself. He'd never done anything but survive, and enjoy
himself in the process. Did he invent the adventures in Crete and the
storms at sea he used to tell us about in the harbor in the evening,
eating pistachio nuts and drinking his ouzo, while we in return told
him about hunting collations and family dinners at Plessis-lez-Vaudreuil? Very possibly. But his tales were good ones, and gave us
something to muse about.

Our friend from Capri hadn't suffered from not having a family.
On the contrary. Before she was fifteen she'd been raped by her
father. Her father was a stonemason, and they lived in a village in
Calabria which Claude and I had passed through on our way to
Sicily. Marina's beauty and her family's poverty impelled her irresistibly toward the big cities of the north. She worked in a small
hairdresser's shop, and then in a larger one, first sweeping up the

customers' shorn locks and then being allowed to shampoo them. Then she went out and washed well-to-do ladies' hair in their homes, where she met their husbands and sons, their secretaries and lovers. Eventually she started to go out with one or another of them, to a cinema or a soccer match. They invited her out, gave her a scarf or a necklace of imitation pearls. Someone took her to Portofino; she went on a cruise to Capri. Capri in May was for her a foretaste of paradise. It was full of women much less young and beautiful than she, and men looked at her, made a fuss of her, tried to please her and impress her. Everything was wonderful, most of all the fact that other people thought she was wonderful. Before, in Calabria, the sun, the sea, and money had been enemies—you couldn't win against them. But there they were at her disposal, and turned into sources of pleasure. When, sitting on the terrace of some café in the via Vittorio Veneto opposite the Hotel Excelsior—Doney's, or Carpano's or Rosati's if they existed then—she used to tell us about her discoveries, we were overwhelmed by the ardor with which she lived through such commonplace adventures. Our fictional heroes, with their elegance and fine phrases, paled before her. It wasn't until she was twenty and went to Capri that she realized she was beautiful. She found it out when she saw men fight over her, and make sacrifices just in order to lie beside her on the sand or on the rocks. Oil millionaires, film celebrities, members of ancient Roman families all swarmed around her. She still hadn't a penny to her name, but she lived in luxury, surrounded by the warmth of restaurant music in the cool silence of the best hotels. Several times she managed to tear herself away from Capri and go back to Milan and her curlers and beauty creams. Then, one fine warm autumn day, she decided not to go back. She dreaded the cold and fog of Milan. She gave in, decided to live on the wealth of the men who desired her. Already, for a long time, they'd paid for her vacations, and she'd given herself to them on the beach, at night, in ships' cabins, during the siesta, in hotel rooms listening to youngsters outside playing tennis in the sun and calling out the score in English. But she always took with her her hairdresser's or manicurist's equipment as a symbol of independence; she had a boss and a job in Milan, which paradoxically meant that she wasn't subject to anyone else. It was by getting richer that she lost her freedom. She raised her prices. She was kept. She was passed from one yacht to another, one cruise to another, like some priceless cook or marvelous lady's maid.

She loved this world of dim lights, allusions, sudden dislikes, crazy competition. Loved and hated it at the same time. She felt she was living, getting her own back, that now she had the upper hand over men who had once despised her. She was a prisoner, but she thought she was free. She spread her nets as she pleased, but sometimes it was she who was caught. She didn't really know how she was living. But it was too late. She'd made her choice.

Three or four times, she didn't quite know why, she'd become fond of someone. Because they were weak, because they were strong, because they were good at making love, because she was frightened of them, or because she wanted to protect them. Some were poor, some were rich. One of them she married. Not the richest. He died. Of course, some people said she'd killed him. How were we to know? Eventually she acquired a certain celebrity within a limited circle. She used to go on trips to New York, to castles in Scotland, and to hunting parties in Austria. Some of the things she said gave Claude and me the impression that her life was about to intersect with ours. And indeed, despite the vast distance between her father the stonemason and Plessis-lez-Vaudreuil, our two worlds did come together. She'd spent a few days among the Lipari Islands on the boat of one of our Italian cousins, and one of our English cousins had proposed to her. She hesitated for a week, and then refused him. Perhaps she was slightly crazy. Perhaps she was too fond of her freedom. Perhaps she set too much store by vice, or by virtue.

Like the sailor from Skyros, but in another key, she told us stories of emeralds thrown into the sea, and of people committing suicide with harpoons, which we only half-believed. Perhaps we were wrong. The same stories were to be found in literary masterpieces and bookstall romances. It was impossible to say whether she'd read them, or inspired them, or if the history of love and manners was so unimaginative that it repeated itself.

And did Claude and I . . . ? Yes, of course. We were only twenty, and she was still beautiful. I think we were even in love with her. And she was very fond of us. Both of us. Both at once. There was no jealousy or rivalry between us. We didn't even share her. We all lived together. We would all go to Ostia to bathe together, or to little inns in the Sabine Hills where we ate cheese and drank wine and took siestas. On the days she wasn't free we used to be furious with her. One morning she had to appear as a witness in court over some fight or car accident. Some official asked her for her name and address and profession, and when she scornfully gave the latter as "Prostitute!" we were enchanted. We were thinking of our grandfather, Aunt Yvonne, and Uncle Anatole.

As far as I know, at least at the time I'm speaking of, she didn't have a protector. At any rate, she was very free. One unforgettable hot summer we took her to Greece. Perhaps, dimly, we wanted to get her away from the cafés and big hotels of the via Vittorio Veneto for a few weeks. The evenings on Skyros when Marina and the old sailor and Claude and I used to dine outdoors on squid and stuffed tomatoes, under the faintly interested gaze of tourists and fishermen, are still for me, after so many years, so many trials, magic memories full of light and affection. It was peaceful, the weather was fine, the world was ours, and we were learning to live.

We were learning that things pass away, and one can only live in the moment. We were learning about the present, about happiness. We knew very well that our foursome wouldn't last forever, probably couldn't last very long. The sailor would die. Marina would go back to Rome and her *avvocati* and *commendatori*. That was her life, and we had ours. We'd go back to Paris and Plessis-lez-Vaudreuil. Just a little different, perhaps, a little changed. Back to our grandfather and his grandfathers, to the family portraits, our old myths, the punctual meals, funerals, and weddings where the line and the breed indefatigably emerged from the fleeting fate of individuals. Sometimes at night, after we'd had dinner in the harbor and were walking by the sea or toward the windmills on the hills, we'd think one ought to be able to change one's life. And still we went bathing, watched the ships sail in and out, talked to the tall

Swedish girls who came down from the north, and took them to dance, handkerchief in hand, the *syrtaki* and the *hassapiko,* all the old dances of our new country. One morning when I got up, a surprise awaited me: Claude had gone, and so had Marina. They'd left me a note, between the figs and the cheese, to say they'd be back. I went sea-fishing with the old sailor. I don't remember what I thought. I'm rather afraid I tried to forget. But I must have felt some sadness, tinged perhaps with anger. The sailor said nothing. He never did say much before sunset and a few glasses of ouzo. But there were two of us instead of four. The weather was suddenly less fine than it had been, and I didn't love life so much.

Claude and Marina came back after four or five to me interminable days. What a relief! When they told me, with a mixture of mystery and mock solemnity, that they'd found they were fonder of each other than they'd thought, I was almost surprised not to feel more unhappy. But what I couldn't bear was simply our being separated, and their having secrets. If we all went on living together as before, I was quite ready to look on the relationship between Claude and Marina as a special one. So it all started up again, with very little change, except that the love between my cousin and the whore from Capri was an understood thing. I didn't get on too badly with the sailor from Skyros.

I'm not going to enter into detail here about the affair between Claude and Marina. Nor am I going to tell you about my own love affairs. As I've said, what I'm trying to write is a collective history —the history of my family over three-quarters of a century. Claude's passion for Marina—or his crush, or fancy, or affection, as you choose—is only one small episode in that long adventure. Small, and yet more important than it seems at first glance. That's why, together with Mirette, Jean-Christophe Comte, Antonin Magne, and Monsieur Machavoine, the dark and charming form of the whore from Capri flits through these pages. As you may well imagine, the affair didn't last six months. Soon after we got back to Rome, Marina went away again—to London, Munich, and by a supreme irony to Paris. She went without Claude. She came back to see us, and she was still marvelous, but life isn't easy. Claude was writing a short story, obviously based on life, about a young American from Boston in love with a prostitute from Venice. He tried to hold out through one whole autumn, in competition with industrialists and film directors who would never have been allowed into Plessis-lez-Vaudreuil. But the winter and spring, with their trips to Mexico and dances in New York, got the better of the great love affair. The funny thing was that Marina eventually had entrée into all the most elegant salons in Europe, or what was left of them. During the war she married a scion of the highest nobility in Rome, and after a divorce and two or three other marriages she ended up as a genuine English duchess. Among the photographs which lie scattered about my desk and the floor as I write, I can see the letter she wrote to me before she died, two or three years ago. In it she still spoke of Claude, Skyros, the via Vittorio Veneto, and of me and our walks on the beach and in the Sabine Hills. She signed herself "Marina, Principessa R———, Duchess of T———, whore of Capri." And it's all so far away and so strange, after so much time and hope and destruction, that I start to laugh to myself. And tears come into my eyes.

I really think Claude did love Marina. Anyway, it was as if he did. There were consolations, other pleasures and other girls, but I won't say much about them—they weren't up to Marina. And there were more books, more journeys. When we had come to Florence, we had been scarcely more than children, and now the time was near when we should be going home. We were almost men. And we were seized by a certain dread: we were going back to our own life, real life, the life we'd escaped from with the sailor from Skyros and the whore from Capri, on the pebbly beaches and the little squares sweltering in the sun, between on one side the church, with its faded frescoes and carved doors and its handful of flowers in the cloister, and on the other side the *palazzo pubblico*, or town hall.

It was one evening in Assisi that Claude first told me he wasn't satisfied with his life any more (we always talked in the evening, after spending the day walking or with our noses buried in books). As far as I can trace it back, the family's strength has always resided in being in constant harmony with itself. I am ready to believe that this hereditary inability to doubt ourselves was our weakness—but it was also our strength. Perhaps—no, certainly—we were mistaken. We followed paths which were absurd, we got ourselves stuck in blind alleys. But we never doubted. My grandfather put it in a nutshell: we had principles. But Claude started to doubt. The conflict between these principles and their collapse made him have to fight against himself. It was a belated adolescent identity crisis. Everything had contributed to bring it on: the lack of any definite profession, being so far away from the family, Monsieur Comte's teachings, the advent of Marina, the prospect of going back home. We suddenly realized, with a sort of holy terror, that one could live happily outside the family. We had seen that other lives, very different from our own, were just as worthwhile. After centuries of past, discipline, strictness, and hierarchy, we were discovering the moment, liberty, pleasure, and fraternity. We were uncertain. We were the first bearers of our name who had allowed themselves to be uncertain.

I think now it was because he doubted that Claude started to talk to me about the Church and his wish to become a priest. Throughout history our family had taken religious orders. When, with our grandfather, we looked at the family's holy books—that is, its genealogical tables and the interminable lists of consanguinities and marriages—it almost seemed as if throughout the centuries we'd done nothing else. From father to son we were priests, bishops, cardinals. And we were descended from several Popes. And it wasn't because we doubted that we'd entered the Church, but because we believed. Not always in God, I might say. But in the Church and its ceremonies and its works, in its power, and above all in ourselves. We went into the Church because we had faith— and quite often Faith with a capital *F*. Claude was the first to want to become a priest because he had doubts. He had doubts about us, about our rules, about a life that seemed suddenly empty. When we talked—always in the evening—on the beaches or in the squares, drinking the local wine or strong black coffee, we agreed that whatever we did we belonged to the past. The past! It started to haunt us. It stuck to us body and soul, like glue. If we buried

ourselves in books, it was the past. If we went to museums and
ancient monuments—the past. In the waters of the sea, in the sun,
on the roads between the hills—the past, the past. Even when we
were happy and living for the moment, the past didn't weaken its
grip on us. When we tried to escape it among the islands with the
sailor from Skyros, or in Marina's arms, it still pursued us. We were
the sons of the past, we resembled it. And the happiness of the
moment wasn't strong enough to fight against it and against the
huge shadow cast by my grandfather. So, to escape the past, Claude
threw himself into the arms of the eternal.

Two or three years after we'd left France and the family portraits
and the forests of Plessis-lez-Vaudreuil, we were vanquished by the
past. How we longed to catch up with the world which books and
the sands had taught us to desire! Several times—in Rome, Calabria,
Segovia—we'd come across men who attracted us less than the
sailor from Skyros or the whore from Capri, but who embodied a
world that was unknown to us, and who surprised and intrigued us.
Socialists, communists, anarchists. They'd told us about their struggles, strikes in the factories, the Red Flag, union meetings, police
charges, and working-class solidarity. Yet another unknown universe. We remembered Michel and his discovery of Karl Marx. We
hadn't read as much of Marx as we had of Proust, Barrès, Stendhal,
Henry James, or Chateaubriand. But we sensed something stirring
in that direction, a world yet to be born and from which we were
excluded. My parents had talked a lot to me about love. But that
was something else. We didn't really understand. In that world we
knew nothing about, the world of the workers, the socialists, the
Red Flag, there was a combination of violence and fraternity that
was quite foreign to us. Although, through the Christianity in
which we were steeped, through Aunt Gabrielle and her craze for
change, my father and his friendship for mankind, and my mother
and her love of suffering, we had some inkling of a future which
might be very different from anything in our experience, it was
very hard for us to fit all this together and see how Christ, books,
abstract painting, freedom, violence, unearned increments, and love
for prisoners and the poor could somehow present an image of

things to come. But all those things were seething about inside us. We couldn't actually express it, but suddenly our rarefied existence among the ruins of ancient cultures and the white houses of Mediterranean harbors struck us as composed of rather empty delights. We were no more in touch with reality than my grandfather, with his huntsmen and his memories—perhaps even less in touch, because for him bygone ages were still present. We hungered and thirsted after a life which eluded us. Perhaps happiness, like the past, was a dead end. We were still exiles, perhaps emigrants, banished from history in the making. Claude turned to God because he doubted the world which had been handed down to us.

All these somewhat vague elements combined, of course, with what we jokingly called Claude's mystical crisis on coming of age. I suspected that the memory of the whore from Capri had something to do with it. Every so often we used to draw up what we called our balance sheets—a survival of the self-examinations which Dean Mouchoux and the priests had taught us to go in for. But it didn't take long to balance our accounts: we hadn't done anything at all. And the future was unknown. Of course we had everything, and we knew it. But sometimes everything doesn't amount to much. We were on the decline. We were like the ruins we so admired. We were twenty. Our friends were the sailor from Skyros, the whore from Capri, people who'd struggled ceaselessly for love of a life that had been handed to us for nothing. They were more alive than we were. What was it we hoped for? At twenty, you can't be content with hoping there won't be any change. The only thing that could reconcile us with ourselves was God.

I remember the last few months of our exile as having quite a different atmosphere from those ardent mornings when we were first discovering beauty. Half a century later, their fervor seems tinged with impatience and melancholy. We were looking for something to hope for. In Rome we'd come across some friends of the family or distant cousins who also gave an impression of doomed survival. We tended to avoid them. Their dreary great palaces with their antique marbles and dozens of footmen in sumptuous liveries, designed by Michelangelo at about the same time as those of the Swiss Guards, delighted and depressed us at the same time. They offered yet another image of the splendors of the past, mingled with agitations of pleasure, passion, eccentricity, and gambling into which, it seemed to us, many plunged just in search of oblivion. There was also an element there which was new to us, and which simultaneously attracted and repelled us: fascism. We knew several young men and women who had tried to find a new faith in obedience to passwords, in the collective will, and in the establishment of a new order. I'm not sure if we too mightn't have been tempted by the passionate accounts of our Italian cousins, Mario and Umberto, if it hadn't been for the thought of Monsieur Jean-Christophe's teachings, the wrath of the sailor from Skyros, and the indignation of the whore from Capri. We had acquired a taste for liberty, and that taste proved stronger in us than the doctrine of Maurras, a love of uniforms, or the attraction of a call to arms. We realized that like socialism, but in a different way, fascism offered some kind of answer to the problem we were struggling with. In a way, it reconciled the spirit of tradition with the need for hope. But in fascism, fraternity and power took on aspects of brutality and vulgarity which were now intolerable to us. Of course we didn't suspect then what fascism was going to become ten years later, in Hitler's Germany. But even at the time we shrank from it instinctively, out of a love of books, a sense of humor, and having enjoyed a whiff of liberty.

I can see Claude and me now, as we strolled around Rome a few days before taking the train back to Paris. In the Palatine Gardens, between the Forum and the great amphitheater, he told me how, amid so much trouble and folly, only God could give life any meaning. Things moved too fast, changed too rapidly. Only God offered a refuge, a haven of grace, an anchor of salvation. He gave an order to things. It wasn't too much to say that Claude abandoned himself to God, clung to him as to a raft of eternity in the shipwreck of time. The family had long believed in a God of plenitude and perfection, but Claude's God arose out of collapse, and belonged not so much to reason as to the absence of reason. He was the God of all the questions and small anguishes which had slowly started to sap our certainties, a God of the void, of doubt, of insecurity and perplexity. But of course he was still God. Anguish and scandal had been part of his domain for a whole line of his sons and daughters, from the Mount of Olives down to Pascal's tears, from Kierkegaard's rejection of a history *à la* Hegel, all smoothed out and justified in advance, without any roughness or remorse, down to Max Jacob and Cocteau. For a long time we'd unwittingly been on the side of Hegel because we were on the side of history. We'd been for Hegel minus the Revolution—at any rate, for Bossuet, and for the iron hand of God ruling a world and a history that were well defined and self-justified, and in which we dwelt on the heights between the tribe of Judah and the Sacred College, between the Pope and the king. But after Monsieur Comte and Aunt Gabrielle, after Skyros and Capri, those days of order and plenitude and the heights were over. After so much quiet, a God of disquiet; after so much sufficiency, a God of insufficiency; after flawless splendor and glory, a rift in the lute, a fly in the ointment, a sort of God in reverse.

Our excursions often brought us back to the chapel of San Giovanni in Oleo, where the family motto is carved on the lintel: be sure not to miss it if you're in Rome—as I've said, it's only a couple of minutes' walk from the charming San Giovanni a Porta Latina. We looked up and read: "At God's pleasure." No, cardinals, marshals, princes of this world and the next, dukes and peers and donors, we sat no longer, lords beside the Lord, on the right hand of God, with a crozier or a baton or a sword in one hand and Plessis-lez-Vaudreuil in the other. We had emerged forever out of the company of God and into the company of man. God's pleasures are not easy to understand. Claude bowed to them in advance. He was still sufficiently one of the family to bow before a God who abandoned the family, or the image we had made of it, with its excess and its pride. I said to Claude, laughing—though our grandfather wouldn't have laughed—that his Remy-Michault blood undoubtedly helped him to follow in the path of the Lord, since a Remy-Michault hadn't waited for God to doom our family name. The time had come; God's pleasure had turned against us. Ah well, we'd had our turn, and now we passed it on to others. Perhaps it was God's pleasure to see the family who had adopted him for its motto simply fade out decently. We had always done our best to die without complaining. And now not only individuals but the whole family, our name itself, were threatened by the sands of insignificance and oblivion. We must do all we could not to disappoint the Lord. We were at the watershed between the time of the family and the time of its absence. Twenty or thirty years later, we, together with everyone else, would witness the sometimes bloody upheavals of decolonization. But we, as we walked through Rome, were already in the last stages of an inner decolonization which had started during six hours of a summer night in 1789. We were rendering back to man the lands and the powers which God had given us. And because nothing in this world was done without his consent, we were still carrying out his orders. For some thousand years those orders had caused us to march at the head of all the tribes, and now they were making us return to the ranks. To say that we were obeying them was putting it mildly: it was perhaps actually because of them that Claude was giving himself to God. We were rather fed up with being princes and captains. We wanted to be ordinary soldiers at last. Soldiers of God, of course, but still ordinary soldiers. We were like Job on the dungheap of history. God had given us the world, and now he was taking it away. But the world had been a heavy burden, and we blessed the holy name of him who lifted from our shoulders the weight of a history made unbearable by accumulated time. And decadence, too, is part of history, and has its own charms, just like ascent and violence and success. And perhaps it has its own duties too. At God's pleasure. And may his pleasure be our law.

It was raining in Rome when we boarded the train to come home. A storm had just broken. Claude talked to me about God. He hardly talked about anything else now. God had replaced the family, the past, books, Marina. It was a sort of exchange. For a long time we had been God's chosen and now God was Claude's God. We were quits.

"This bargain between equals just goes to show our family's ineradicable pride," I said to Claude, laughing.

"It's a pride that leads to humility—the pride of descending," he said. "And when we're down we shall stay down. Pride, if you like, but tragic pride."

"Some humility!"

"Yes," said Claude. "There's never been anyone to touch us for humility!"

"The thing that's going to be difficult," I went on, after a pause, "is working out your salvation alone."

"Alone?" He stared at me.

"I mean without the family."

"And what about God's help?" he asked.

I sighed.

"God's such a long way away," I said.

"But there are men," said Claude. "And their love."

3

A Hard Day

AND SO WE WENT BACK TO OUR FAMILY, and money, and the history of every day. For almost three years we'd lived to ourselves. Now we stepped back into our frame, into our natural setting. The after-the-war period was over—now it was the period between the two wars. We didn't know then how short it would be. Soon, in the eyes of the future, it would be our own prewar period. Now not only Pierre and Philippe but also Jacques and Claude and myself were grown up. Henceforward, when I say "us" it will no longer mean just the family, together with its reverberations through history and its memories, but also Pierre and Philippe and Michel, Jacques and Claude and me, and the men and women among whom we lived. Space, a larger and larger space, had taken the place of the time which for centuries had been ranged in ever-thicker stretches behind every one of our actions. But what happened now at Plessis-lez-Vaudreuil had to do not with the Bourbons or St. Louis or the Crusades, but with London, New York, Berlin, Moscow, and Leningrad, which only my grandfather still referred to as St. Petersburg. New words made their appearance in conversation around the family table. Less was heard about cousins and great-uncles and the traditions of the *ancien régime*, and much more about the stock exchange, interest rates, domestic and foreign policy, strikes and revolution. The next war was approaching so fast that no one had time to remember the last. Mussolini, whom we'd seen addressing the Blackshirts from the balcony in the Piazza Venezia in Rome, was soon joined, and then overtaken, by a little friend for whom my grandfather had no time at all. I've often heard him write Hitler off in a phrase as cutting and decisive as the guillotine: he wasn't at all the thing. Oddly enough, the man my grandfather regarded as most distinguished in the years leading up to the Second World War was Léon Blum. What a pity he was a Jew and a socialist and an atheist, and that he'd written that essay on marriage! But at least he was elegant.

Anyone who wants to understand anything about my grandfather's opinions, or about what still, after a fashion, constituted the family, must remember that for some twenty years, and increasingly with each year, my grandfather used to spend most of his time prophesying disaster. I think he would have been amazed, and even rather disappointed, if his prophecies hadn't come true. Disaster itself didn't surprise him. Maurras talked about "divine surprise," but for my grandfather the collapse of the Republic was far from being that. It was divine, perhaps, because everything that happened was that, even the worst catastrophes. But it certainly was no surprise. It was a divine judgment which my grandfather had always predicted, a decision of the Almighty which was all the more natural because my grandfather had long since come to the same conclusion himself.

But let us stop leaping over the years like this. When we came back from Italy, or a year or so later, what mattered was not so much fascism and clenched fists and red flags, or, as yet, Adolf Hitler, or national socialism, or even socialism pure and simple, but the economic crisis. I don't know if capitalism has learned how to get over its crises yet, but then, toward the end of the twenties and the beginning of the thirties, it seemed as if the crisis, the famous crisis that was on everyone's lips, was going to carry all before it.

My grandfather had about as much patience with capitalism as he had with democracy—he lumped them both together. But I don't want to give the impression that he was really modern. In fact,

he was far from being ahead of his time. He was behind it, in that
he still believed in the long-defunct hierarchies of feudalism. But,
paradoxically, the young leftists of today might understand him
better than he was understood by the left-wingers at the time, who
declared themselves for democracy and against capitalism. He was
against both. But capitalism had come into the family with the
Remy-Michaults. And so, in a way, had democracy. Uncle Paul
stood as a candidate for the Haute-Sarthe in the general elections
—I can't remember whether he stood for the moderates, or the
center Right, or the National Union Party—and was elected. He
wasn't the first deputy in the family. My grandfather had once sat,
for a few months, at the extreme right of the extreme Right in the
chamber of deputies, where he acquired a certain notoriety by
interrupting a member of the extreme Left, who was just expound-
ing his policy, and asking, through the speaker, if the right honorable gentleman would accept an invitation to come and amuse the
children. Public opinion and his own soon made him retire from
political activity, and he went back to his reading at Plessis-lez-
Vaudreuil. But Uncle Paul, urged on by Aunt Gabrielle, thought
that the family ought to emerge once and for all from its self-
imposed exile from public affairs. He had disapproved of Pierre's
opting out, and was by no means reluctant to play a part which for
different reasons in each case neither his father nor his eldest son had
been able to undertake. My grandfather was then approaching
eighty, and Uncle Paul was sixty. His ambition was to bring the
family back into politics just as his wife, Aunt Gabrielle, had made
its name famous again in the sphere of Cocteau and Nijinsky. Albert
Remy-Michault, Aunt Gabrielle's father, had helped Uncle Paul
immeasurably before he died, not only financially, which was important, but above all by giving him entrée among the upper middle
classes who then ran France. No need to explain again how for more
than a century we'd held aloof from every form of public life. Of
course we had no part in the "three glorious days"—July 27, 28, and
29—of the 1830 revolution, nor the February nor the June days of
the 1848 revolution, nor the coup d'état of December 2, 1851, nor
the defeat at Sedan in 1870, nor the uprising of the Commune in

1871, nor its repression by the Army of Versailles. Memorial plaques in streets or squares had long ceased to have any reference to us. Our only contribution to victory in 1918 had been to have half a dozen of our number killed or wounded in defense of their country. After its lengthy absence from the annals of the Republic, our name reappeared only in the social columns of the newspapers or on the war memorial in Plessis-lez-Vaudreuil. Uncle Paul and Aunt Gabrielle considered the time had come for us, as for a courtier long absent from court, to return and make our official reappearance in the corridors of power.

Uncle Paul knew nothing. His ignorance was encyclopedic. He'd read even less than my grandfather, much less than my father. I don't remember whether I've mentioned it before, but my grandfather spoke Latin fluently and could read Greek easily. One day Aunt Gabrielle brought a well-known academic, a former minister and a member of the French Academy of Sciences, to Plessis-lez-Vaudreuil: no doubt she'd told him to expect to find the place a very den of ignorance, which in a way it was. So what was the ex-minister's surprise when my grandfather talked to him about Tacitus and Thucydides as if they were old and familiar friends. Uncle Paul didn't converse in Latin with his wife's friends, Salvador Dali or Maurice Sachs. But although he was probably less intelligent than my grandfather and than his own sons, there was one thing he did understand. Perhaps under the influence of the Remy-Michaults, he'd realized that history was no longer governed by history, if I may put it like that, but by economics. While his wife was sponsoring Russian ballets and avant-garde films, he set about studying, if not Pareto and Keynes, at least the rudiments of their subject. His knowledge may have been rather shaky, but he'd come to the conclusion that economic and social developments were the key to the future. This was a turning point in the family, which had hitherto considered social change the work of the devil, and for which money had been of no importance.

It seems to me that with Uncle Paul, so long regarded as a mere man-about-town, a featherbrain, an elegant puppet, in short a fool, the family entered a new stage in its reconciliation with the modern world. It's strange that the change should have come about through one of the least intelligent among us. Perhaps it was just another instance of the insignificance of the part played by men, and the irresistibility of that played by events and the spirit of the age. Perhaps it was another proof of the relativeness of intelligence, a notion we have already seen to be very open to question. Or perhaps the whole thing was simply due to the influence of the most remarkable member of the family during the first half of the century— Aunt Gabrielle, to whom I fear I may have been rather unfair. I really can't say. What is certain is that ten years after the war and more than a quarter of a century after Uncle Paul and Aunt Gabrielle were married, the family fleet left our private docks and sailed triumphantly into the territorial waters of the upper middle class. If some of the crew experienced certain qualms, they were careful not to show it, and even did their best to fight the feeling down.

For centuries we had been separate from the bourgeoisie and opposed to it. We felt closer to soldiers, to craftsmen, and above all to country people than to the citizens of the big towns. We were separated from them by an almost obsessional love of nature, a fear of change, obedience to the Church, distrust of machines, and hostility toward money, buying and selling, and ideas. But now we were going to live and think and respond like them: all the barriers between them and us were going to be broken down. At the same time, the upper middle class was going through a parallel evolution in regard to us. We and they, under the pressure of the rise of new social classes—engineers, technicians, workers, the masses—finally coalesced into a more or less homogeneous bloc, with the same values, the same fears, the same mannerisms. They, the upper middle classes, started to hunt, to have the archbishop to dine and to kiss his hand, to talk about the past, to be particular about whom they married, and to become attached to the land, to their forests and their country estates. We, on the other hand, went into business, married money, entered wholeheartedly into the modern system. Before the end of the nineteenth century we'd known nothing of bourgeois attitudes. But now the merger was complete, and we too in a way were now Remy-Michaults. If we took on their faults, we also took on their virtues—their admiration for hard work and their desire for success. And they for their part came to think they'd always had a family motto, and that it was the same as ours: "At God's pleasure." And perhaps, by becoming like us, they started to decline.

These were at least some of the reasons why the famous crisis of 1929–30 worried us so much. A few decades earlier, a financial and economic crisis would have left us cold. We'd even have been pleased, because it would have weakened our opponents. But now it came too late to confirm our hostility to democracy and the Republic: we were already reconciled with them. Indeed, with Uncle Paul and Aunt Gabrielle, with cousin Pierre before the catastrophe of the vice-consul from Hamburg, and even with Jacques, who'd changed greatly since the days of Jean-Christophe, we'd been trying to take the lead. Scarcely five or six years before, my grandfather had been lamenting that an aristocrat like Monsieur Blum was not a Catholic and a monarchist—if he'd dared, he'd have asked him to Plessis-lez-Vaudreuil to discuss the opinions of the Pope, the denunciation of Action Française, and the future of the Christian family—Uncle Paul, his son, had revealed himself to be a republican. A moderate republican, he said, but not moderately republican. He mixed in financial and political circles, and to the astonishment of his sons, especially Jacques and Claude, and of course to my surprise also, he eventually emerged as an important influence in what was called the center-right. He thought of acquiring a newspaper to disseminate his ideas. We knew he had horses, but we didn't know he had ideas. He wouldn't have dared to boast of them, anyway, twenty or thirty years earlier, under the limes at Plessis-lez-Vaudreuil. Another astounded witness of all this was Jean-Christophe Comte, who on his return from America found himself sitting a couple of seats away from Uncle Paul at one of the radical or radical-socialist banquets where the guests included bankers, writers, and politicians. Anyhow, all these developments made Uncle Paul very aware of all the crises hanging over us halfway between the two wars. It was a cruel irony that we should have

thrown our lot in with money, business, and industrial democracy
just at the moment when they were about to collapse. It was hardly
worth the trouble of having gone over to the system on the eve of
a breakdown that we'd been hoping for and expecting for the
previous hundred and fifty years.

When I think back now to what Plessis-lez-Vaudreuil was like
between 1926 or '27 and 1936 or '37, it seems at one and the same
time very like and very unlike what it was in my childhood. In one
sense, nothing had changed: the lime trees, the stone table, the
ancient portraits on the walls, the atmosphere of the Tour de France
—all those were still there. But what had changed was the spirit of
the age. Plessis-lez-Vaudreuil was slowly catching up with the rue
de Varenne and the rue de Presbourg. The king and his return,
unquestioning loyalty, and willful blindness were no longer the
dominating elements in the conversation. We'd caught up with the
times. Of course, the past still exercised a powerful influence over
our hearts and minds, but instead of being monarchic and mythical,
the past was now bourgeois, national, and collective. It was full of
memories of the war, public ceremonies, the mayor and the dean
brandishing flags at one another, full of common suffering, full of
blood. Although my cousin Ursula sometimes appeared at table
between my grandfather and cousin Philippe, Germany was no
longer just the country where some of our cousins lived, but a
danger and a threat. It was the vanquished enemy which always
revived to do battle again. Nationalism had gotten the better of the
old feudal and cosmopolitan traditions which had still been opera-
tive at the time of Pierre's marriage. Oddly enough, our patriotism
made us throw our lot in with France just when Action Française
was anathematizing its government.

Some thirty-five or forty years after Cardinal Lavigerie, in his
famous toast in Algiers, called for the "rallying" of the monarchists
to the Third Republic, and some ten years after the war, and despite
the fact that Pierre had left the diplomatic service because he was
in love with a Prussian, we became once and for all nationalists,
patriots, almost republicans. Of course my grandfather still called
himself a monarchist. But you could bring tears to his eyes with a

well-timed "Marseillaise," a tricolor flapping in the desert breeze, or by conjuring up France's finest hours. He was a monarchist who was grateful to the Republic for having acquired an empire. Whether we liked it or not, in the last hundred and fifty years France had become a parliamentary republic and a liberal democracy. New layers of memories began to rise to the surface of the family consciousness, or unconsciousness. Now that we were reconciled with the nation as a whole, we began to realize, and even to say, that the king would not return, and that tomorrow would be different from yesterday. My grandfather, like thousands of other old men in France, used to start a sentence by saying, "In my day . . ." But the past was no longer present. It might have become the same for everyone, but it had fallen into the abyss. Even my grandfather spoke of it as if it were dead, and people lamented over it more than ever. In the old days, my grandfather and his father hadn't lamented over the past, because it was still alive. But now we had buried it, now we made plans for the future from which the past was excluded. We spoke of it as one speaks of the dead, praising its vanished virtues. The beginning of the century and the years before the war seemed like some golden age: there was no king, certainly, but also there was no income tax and no bolshevik menace. And now income tax and communism mattered more than the king. We were starting to feel nostalgic about a period when there wasn't any king: we knew that the happy days when Caillaux and Lenin didn't exist were gone, never to return.

My grandfather, who never set foot outside Plessis-lez-Vaudreuil, delighted in repeating how, before the war, Turkey and Russia were the places in Europe where one needed a passport. He forgot his views about theocratic monarchies, and described the Russians and the Turks as savages. He would recall, with all the melancholy proper to that which is no more, how, for the citizens of all other European countries, a visiting card was enough for them to travel all over the Continent, from Madrid to Bucharest, from Oslo to Athens. The peace and tranquillity that reigned in the world before 1914 was one of the major themes of our conversation. Another theme was how easy and comfortable everything used to be. There were far fewer gardeners, scullions, and footmen nowadays. Something new was spreading through the world in the shadow of socialism: men cost a lot of money. In the old days they were dirt-cheap. They still weren't worth much in the forests of the Argonne and among the potholes of the Chemin des Dames. But ever since, their price had been soaring. We often talked about the wages coachmen or carters used to get in the 1900s. When they were paid no more than a few pence a day there was nothing surprising about their number, or even their loyalty, for they couldn't have found anything better elsewhere. And so money became one of our preoccupations. And through Uncle Paul we came to take an interest in the stock market too. Every morning before he went out, he used to consult two scales to find out what the day had in store for him: the barometer, which he used to tap with his finger, and the share prices on Wall Street, which he would examine anxiously. Yes, there's something else that's new. One fine day, without anyone really knowing how or why, we woke up to find ourselves linked with America. A regular rhythm was established in our lives, which were still very different from life on the other side of the Atlantic —we were told, though we scarcely believed it, that the Americans didn't have servants any more, but used machines instead—and yet already parallel: anything that happened beyond the Atlantic Ocean, which could now be flown over in a flash, reached us after ten or twenty years, and sometimes after just a few weeks. For machines were taking over with us too. My grandfather gazed sadly and disapprovingly at the rows of cars drawn up in the courtyard. He couldn't stand it when the young people discussed their average and top speeds. He didn't like speed. "In my day . . ." he would say, and tell us for the hundredth time how my great-grandfather, Aunt Yvonne, Uncle Anatole, and he used to go to Paris by coach. We used not to listen to him. But now I think with regret, almost with grief, of all the questions I never asked, and which will remain forever unanswered.

Speed insinuated itself everywhere, in travel, in morals, in the course of history (everyone said history was moving much faster), in fashion, and even in literature. We used to read Péguy, Apollinaire, Maurras, Gide, Claudel, the Surrealists, and Giraudoux and Valéry. And then came Morand. He hadn't yet written *The Man in a Hurry,* but already he was everywhere at once, skillfully making use of the wonderful new instruments unknown to my grandfather but hymned by Valéry Larbaud—the "means of communication." The face of life was changing around us like the fleeting landscapes glimpsed through the windows of the great European trains—the Harmonika-Zug or the Orient Express. We knew now that every new day would bring its own contribution of irreversible changes, in time and space. Do you still remember my grandfather, giving orders every morning to ensure that each day exactly reproduced the day before? But now we had entered an era when nothing was repeated. Whenever my grandfather glanced behind him, he saw nothing but corpses. It was as if, after 1914, things, like men, did nothing but die. And, of course, be born. It wasn't only oil lamps and sailing ships that disappeared. It wasn't only electricity and the telephone, divorce and socialism, that were new. The appearance of the countryside and the streets, clothes, women's hats, cooking, the ordinary implements of everyday life, cars and airplanes of course, dancing, music and painting, language, ideas, and manners—all grew old every few months, and were transformed and reborn. I know the dinner parties Pierre and Ursula used to give in the rue de Presbourg just after the war were anachronisms, a bizarre survival from the early years of the century. But when tragedy struck there—at about the same time as the effects of the economic crisis, which we shall examine in more detail later—the style of living in the rue de Presbourg changed overnight. The ten or twelve servants became three or four, the colossal menus melted like snow in the sun. The next stage of the culinary revolution—to remain for a moment on this humble but important subject—occurred during the Second World War. As late as 1939 the news that Hitler's Germans were reduced to one dish per meal was a piece of propaganda which filled Frenchmen with a mixture of consternation, horror, sadistic pleasure, and real compassion. A single dish was a kind of Loch Ness monster in the eyes of liberal abundance. But a year later, and perhaps forever, the ordinary dinner of a French family of the upper middle classes rarely included more than one dish apart from soup and cheese.

Change did more than separate past from future. Even within the present it tended to destroy the homogeneity of the family. Some people said we were entering an era when everybody would be alike. That was possible. But within the family, differences were growing rather than decreasing. In the old days the family had been first and foremost a whole, an entity. We were all like one another, from great-grandmother to great-grandchild. We had what others called, and indeed what we ourselves with satisfaction and triumph referred to as, a family resemblance. One of the great amusements of the adults when I was a child was detecting this famous family resemblance in third cousins and great-great-nieces of a great-great-grandmother. We never had any difficulty in finding it. One day a distant cousin visited Plessis-lez-Vaudreuil, accompanied by two young men. My grandfather rushed up to the handsomer of the two youngsters and cried:

"No mistaking the family resemblance here!"

"He's my chauffeur's son," said the cousin humbly.

My grandfather, without batting an eye, turned to the other lad and said:

"Well, my boy, there's no denying where you come from!"

And it must be admitted that Uncle Anatole, Aunt Yvonne, my grandfather, and my great-grandfather definitely had many characteristics in common—their stature, their opinions, their likes and dislikes, their reactions to things. Of course there were exceptions —natural and cultural aberrations, like my uncle in Argentina. But they were looked on as monsters, and even, despite their cynicism or love of pleasure, regarded themselves as such. They always repented before they died, and, as I've said, came to end their days at Plessis-lez-Vaudreuil. But now every member of the family seemed to lead his or her own life. We still hadn't reached the stage of rampant individualism that marked the second after-the-war period. But within the group the life-styles began to be different. The community, the organism, the totality that used to be called the family no longer existed. There was So-and-so, and another, and yet another. They all had the same name, and that was all. "At God's pleasure"—the family motto itself gradually came to have a different meaning. A vague suggestion of insolence and fatalism imperceptibly prevailed over the idea of exultation in submission.

On one side there was God, on the other, money, and, in between, women, cars, travel, and pleasure. In the old days God had supplied the money, and everything, including pleasure and women, formed part of the same system. And what was shattered in the middle 1920s was the notion of system. If I had to summarize what happened between 1925 and 1933, between the end of the First World War and the rise of Nazism, not only in Plessis-lez-Vaudreuil but also in France and the West as a whole, I wouldn't talk about the tango, or jazz, or cloche hats, or the end of Poiret, or the beginnings and then the triumph of Chanel, nor the craze for amusement, nor of perfumes called Love and Delight, nor of the exhibits at the Arts Décoratifs. All those things existed, but they take on their real meaning only in a wider context. I'd put it simply like this: in spite of, or perhaps because of, machines, speed, and progress, the system didn't work any more. In literature and painting, as in politics and affairs (the word used to mean politics, but now referred merely to money), something had stuck. The machine had jammed. There was a crisis.

The world's already eventful career had always consisted in staggering from one crisis to the next. Were not the Barbarians a crisis, and the Hundred Years War, and the Wars of Religion, and the Thirty Years War, and the French Revolution, and the beginnings of the industrial revolution? What was new now was that it was no longer a matter of fighting, slaughter, or even upheavals, but first and foremost of uncertainty. It was as if the world no longer knew where it was. The crisis consisted in the fact that everyone felt they were in a crisis. There was uncertainty and hesitation around the family table. Everyone started to play a part of his own, and to do the best he could for himself. Uncle Paul gradually came to represent a mixture of money and politics which was fundamentally at odds with the family tradition, though he still claimed to respect it; Claude gave himself to God, not within and for and through the family, but, in a way, against it. If you looked at us assembled for dinner in the old dining room at Plessis-lez-Vaudreuil (still at half-past seven, but soon at a quarter to eight), you would see religion and business sitting side by side. In the old days cardinals, marshals, courtiers, and freethinkers all formed part of the same universe. But in the modern world, relations between God and money became very difficult, not to mention love of pleasure, the thirst for novelty which was the very opposite of tradition, and all the other pressures of a liberty which everywhere lured and beckoned. The family had fallen to pieces. The Dreyfus affair, the separation of Church and state, the war against Germany, and the rallying of the monarchists to the Republic had created only a few chinks in the edifice of the family. But time had now done its work. We didn't actually hate each other, but now each of us lived in his own separate world. Our different beliefs (in any case less fervent than before), our different ways of life, and hopes, and ulterior motives, all made us like Montagues and Capulets who managed to rub along together. We had emerged at last from the Middle Ages. Individualism had triumphed over family spirit.

Albert Remy-Michault was dead. He left Uncle Paul, his son-in-law, his factories and his industrial empire. Uncle Paul went to and fro between the chamber of deputies and his enormous business interests. Yes, he was in business, and his business was enormous. "My son is in business," my grandfather used to say to people who asked after Uncle Paul. And the words nearly choked him.

Uncle Paul in his turn relied on two of his sons—Pierre and Jacques, of course. Pierre was the eldest, but his period in the diplomatic service and his subsequent to-ing and fro-ing between Ursula and Mirette had rather separated him from Plessis-lez-Vaudreuil and the hub of the family. Jacques worked in insurance, ships, oil. Unlike Michel, he hadn't passed the examination for the ministry of finance, so he'd become an American. Twice a year he went and spent five weeks in New York, and came back with projects which he suggested to his father. Philippe was no longer in his first youth. He was nearly thirty. But he still thought of nothing but women. Over the years he'd become a professional philanderer.

When the Second World War came he would touch up his prematurely graying temples and be as attractive to nurses as he used to be to his mother's friends. For different, opposite reasons, both Philippe and Claude were out of the running, the one because of his passion for women, the other because of his passion for God. But already, in the small dining room attached to the large one (in those days, the children of the family didn't eat with the adults), something new was sprouting, a strange repetition of what could have been seen twenty years before, or forty, or sixty, around the stone table under the limes: a new generation, the fourth—or could it be the fifth?—that you've seen arising at Plessis-lez-Vaudreuil. Perhaps, at the beginning of this book, toward the end of the nineteenth century, you caught a vague glimpse of my great-grandmother. You know my grandfather, his son Paul, and his grandchildren Pierre, Philippe, Jacques, and Claude, not to mention me. And now here are Jean-Claude, Anne-Marie, Bernard, Véronique, and Hubert. Véronique and Hubert are scarcely out of the cradle, but Jean-Claude and Anne-Marie are almost grown-up. I don't remember if I told you that Jacques got married, and that Pierre and Ursula, during the time they loved each other, at Cabrinhac, had time to produce a son and a daughter. So many things happen in a family that it's as if life were slipping between my fingers, carrying away with it nursemaids, governesses, childhood love affairs, engagements and deaths, parties and examinations, military service and games. Sport had begun to play an important part in our lives, replacing the nature we were in the process of losing but which we need if we are to be able to breathe. I know I ought to tell you about people's encounters, about the life of every day; I ought to reproduce the letters still lurking in my trunks and chests of drawers, record conversations, quarrels, dealings with servants and tradespeople, business discussions. But I'm afraid I have neither the space nor the time nor, unfortunately, the skill to do all that. All I can do is show the family in the rue de Varenne and the rue de Presbourg, and at Plessis-lez-Vaudreuil around the stone table or in the dining room, beneath the portraits of the marshals, and hope that in the process some fragment of passing time may be caught.

Some of the changes in the family which I have ascribed to the crisis may in fact have been only the result of the passage of time and the new perspectives that passage brings. When I was a child the family seemed to me an entity in which I had a place between my mother and my grandfather. Of course I knew that its members were not interchangeable. My father's ideas were not always the same as my grandfather's, and my mother was clearly very different from Aunt Gabrielle. But when I was young, the family came first, and the individuals that made it up came afterward. But now it was difficult to see any likeness whatsoever between Uncle Paul and his son Claude, for example—perhaps just because I understood them better than I'd ever understood my grandfather and my mother. They seemed, my uncle and my cousin, to belong to two different worlds, each equally foreign to the spirit of the family itself. Uncle Paul had chosen money, politics, all the powers of the modern world which we could see rising before our eyes. And as we have already seen, Claude had chosen God, perhaps only as a protest against his father.

Claude was at a seminary, at some place like Maredsous or Pierre-qui-Vire, when one of those two worlds began to collapse. When his father-in-law died, Uncle Paul, perhaps on the advice of his son Jacques, thought he had discovered the American miracle. He was dazzled by the exploits of Wall Street: its name rang in his ears like a modern El Dorado, and he transferred the greater part of his fortune into "blue-chips." The name delighted the children of the family. I thought, with already a tinge of melancholy, that twenty years earlier I too would have built castles in Spain on blue-chips. Uncle Paul wasn't a child, but he let himself believe in fairy tales. All the old factories of the Remy-Michaults came to be dependent on New York, Detroit, and Chicago. Michel Desbois warned him of the danger. Jacques and Michel had remained friends and brothers in the same way as Claude and I. You remember the three musketeers of Monsieur Jean-Christophe Comte, drunk on Proust and Stendhal? Well, with the months and the years, they had divided up into two groups—on the one hand Jacques and Michel, with their files and their factories, and on the other Claude and I, between Romanesque cloisters and an undying love of literature, between the call of God and the whore of Capri. Jacques at once admired and made fun of Michel. He criticized him for being too timid and for letting himself be worn down by the everlasting routine of the ministry of finance. Jacques himself, perhaps by way of revenge because he had failed to get into the ministry, urged his father on to all kinds of risks. Only a few years after he went into the ministry, Michel, thanks to the friendship of Uncle Paul and Jacques, was appointed to the board of all the Remy-Michault interests. But he couldn't prevent the Remy-Michault empire from becoming dependent on the fate of Wall Street. All he could do was openly voice his disagreement. At the end of the spring of 1930, and more and more with every month that passed, it was evident that Uncle Paul and the American depression between them had made a clean sweep of the Remy-Michault inheritance. The years leading up to 1914, and the war itself, had brought about great expansion in the arms factories: now they had to be hastily closed. All the other branches of the business were affected. Bankruptcy loomed ahead, perhaps total ruin. On September 3, 1929, the Dow Jones index beat all records and closed at 381.17. The only question was when it would pass 400. But on October 24, the famous Black Thursday, the myth of American prosperity was exploded. In less than twelve hours some fifteen million shares were thrown on the market, share prices plummeted, panic swept huge companies and small investors alike, eleven speculators jumped off skyscrapers in Wall Street, and in a few days mass hysteria broke over three hundred and fifty banks. On July 8, 1932, the Dow Jones average was down to 41.22—the same as in 1896.

I have a vivid memory of the summers of 1931 and 1932 at Plessis-lez-Vaudreuil. My grandfather was not unduly worried by the specter of ruin—relative ruin, of course: the upper middle class always have reserves, and the Krupp connection made things less drastic than they might have been. I wonder if, in a way, my grandfather wasn't rather pleased. It would have been quite natural. One section of the family—you could trace the line from my grand-father, through my father and mother, down to Claude—had al-

ways despised money. And Uncle Paul's failure might be regarded
as the end of an experiment, a sort of liberation. The disagreeable
thing about it was the bankruptcy. Failure, bankruptcy, official
receivers, suspended payments—all these were quite new in the
family's vocabulary, and very unpleasant. And this for two or three
reasons. They marked not only the family's entrance into the world
of affairs which we held in such low esteem, but also its failure—
we hadn't even been able to succeed in doing what we despised. And
the proceedings involved lent a further painful significance to the
failure. Thirty years earlier, we wouldn't have minded appearing in
the lawcourts of the Republic, for political or religious reasons. But
now that we were reconciled with the state and had adopted the
views and way of life of the ruling bourgeoisie, there were few
things more unbearable than being suspected of malpractice or
financial unscrupulousness by the press and public opinion. Of
course it was only a matter of ineptness or imprudence. But we'd
stuck our finger into the system, and the system wasn't going to split
hairs about it. It pained my grandfather to see the family honor
measured in terms of finance. In his view, one shouldn't have anything to do with such matters. But since the modern world had
induced us to engage in them, we must find a way of disengaging
ourselves decently. Even in these decadent days the family was still
good for something. Hélène, Jacques' wife, hadn't any money. But
most of Ursula's dowry went to repair the damage.

There are advantages in having connections with the Krupps.
And there are advantages in having connections with the Wittgensteins: Ursula wasn't even tempted to object. She thought it quite
natural that her money should be used to tide things over. How
difficult it is to judge people: some took their hats off to her, others
thought—and said—that she'd still have enough left to satisfy her
taste for manicurists and garagemen.

For me, the most interesting aspect of it all was the repercussions
of the crisis on two boys I loved, and who were now men—Claude,
and Michel Desbois. Though in aspiring to the priesthood Claude
had obeyed our most ancient traditions, he had moved farther than
any of us away from the family's attitudes about things. But he was

with my grandfather in hoping that the crisis would loosen and perhaps even destroy the links we'd contracted, through the Remy-Michaults, with business and money. I did think, not long ago, of writing a few pages about the life of my cousin Claude. I would have tried to show that his vocation could be explained in two different ways. You could say, and there was certainly some truth in it, that God had called him and he had answered the call. You could also say that there were three decisive experiences which predisposed him to do so: the influence of Jean-Christophe, his meeting with Marina, and his rejection of the modern world of business and money. Scorn and hatred of money, love of God and men, love of God through men and men through God—and he had endless conversations with my mother on the subject, at which I wasn't always present—the rejection of a dead past and an all-too-living present: all these things had shaped a life which for a long time was very close to mine, and of which I think I still understood the secret development better than anyone else.

While the crisis and everything to do with it helped to drive Claude still further away from the modern and perhaps already aging world, it drew Michel Desbois deeper into it. A lot of nonsense has been talked about his success. Just before, or perhaps it was just after, the Second World War, someone wrote a novel, using very transparent pseudonyms, in which he was represented as acting a very dubious role between Jacques and Uncle Paul. It must be admitted that the appearances were somewhat strange: in less than six weeks the son of our steward, as yet scarcely thirty years old, practically took over control of all the Remy-Michault concerns, or what was left of them. And a year or so later, he married my sister Anne.

You can easily imagine the comments this gave rise to in the early thirties. Some talked of conspiracy and blackmail. Others added sentimental considerations, some seeing the marriage as an additional insult to the family, others, on the contrary, interpreting it as an attempt on the part of the family to salvage what they could, by one means or another, of the Remy-Michault loot. All these theories are equally absurd. Michel Desbois hadn't intrigued in any

way against Uncle Paul and Jacques. All he'd done was see things
more clearly than everybody else. If his advice had been taken,
Black Thursday on Wall Street wouldn't have had such disastrous
consequences for us. Michel's strength lay in the accuracy of his
predictions. And in the upheavals which followed the crisis, it was
quite natural that the financial bodies who took over from the
family should look for someone to help them who was familiar with
our affairs but who hadn't contributed in any way to our disaster.
Uncle Paul and his son were only too glad to be able to count on
Michel, and he behaved to us as we had always behaved to him and
his family: perfectly. The difference was that in the old days it was
we who had the upper hand, and now it was he. He conveyed the
situation with the same tact we had once prided ourselves on at
Plessis-lez-Vaudreuil, when we'd almost apologized for being the
masters of our servants. Now he was almost apologizing for becoming, and so swiftly, the master of his masters. There was nothing he
could do to save Uncle Paul, but he managed to have quite an
important job kept for Jacques in the business that used to be ours.
As for his marrying Anne, which the novel I mentioned presented
as a modernized version of that nineteenth-century tear-jerker *Le
Maître de forges* ("The Ironmaster"), there was no question of its
being an extra revenge on his part or a financial maneuver on ours.
Michel loved Anne, that was all. And he'd loved her for a very long
time, perhaps always. Perhaps since the days when, first as a little
boy and then as a young man, he'd accompanied his father the
steward to six-o'clock prayers in the drawing room at the chateau,
where Monsieur Desbois appeared in a frock coat, wearing a hat
and carrying his gloves in his hand. But now Michel was in a
position to ask for Anne's hand in marriage. All one can say is that
the crisis was at least a help to them. I'm rather doubtful about what
my grandfather's answer might have been five or six years earlier.
The only solution for Anne would have been to elope with Michel.
That would have made an interesting page in these recollections of
days gone by. But never mind. As it was, they just had a middle-class
wedding in the old chapel at Plessis-lez-Vaudreuil, which so many
of our family had already entered in order to begin life, or to pass

out of it. Their story was to end happily enough. After various
adventures which we shall deal with in due course, Michel and
Anne were very happy for some forty years. I am godfather to their
eldest son, who is doing research in atomic energy at the University
of California. He already has a daughter himself—Elisabeth. She
wants to go on the stage. Anne wrote to me only a few days ago
to ask my advice. Her anxieties reminded me of my grandfather:
Elisabeth, her granddaughter, has been going out for the last few
months with a Moslem ethnologist who's a member of the Black
Panthers.

When I think about all that business, one small strand mixed up
with the terrible events which were to change the family's whole
destiny, there's one detail I'd like to say a few words about. Michel
was my best friend and Anne was my sister. They both told me
they'd loved each other for years. They saw each other every day
at Plessis-lez-Vaudreuil, at least in the summer, when he was about
twenty-one and she was about eighteen. And yet I never suspected
what they felt for each other. It's terrifying to think one can be so
blind. I thought at the time that my sister was taken with Jean-
Christophe. And I learned later that this was so, and that Michel had
hated Jean-Christophe. And I'd thought Michel admired Jean-
Christophe and had a sort of passion for him. And this was true too.
He both loved and hated him. What reasons did Michel really have
for this hatred? Things were certainly more complicated than I had
thought. I realized my little sister was no longer a child, though we
still thought of her as one. But I wonder if perhaps, in some way,
what with Michel and what with Jean-Christophe, she mightn't
have . . . But she was my sister. And before the Second World War
we didn't talk much among ourselves about what we called our
private lives. We preferred to turn a blind eye. Sometimes, when I
think of the vanished paradise of our childhood long ago, I suddenly
remember Anne and Jean-Christophe and Michel engaged in games
less innocent than the calm and austere setting of Plessis-lez-Vaudreuil might suggest. Goodness, now I come to think of it, I remember one summer evening in 1922 or '23 when Jean-Christophe and
Anne . . . But it's all such a long time ago, and it's all over and done

with. Anne's a grandmother. She might be the great-grandmother
of a little Moslem in two or three years' time. Or even in six months.

A great-grandmother! My goodness, we *are* getting on. I can still
see that early autumn of 1932, when my little sister got married. All
Plessis-lez-Vaudreuil was there, and all Roissy and Saint-Paulin and
Villeneuve and Roussette—everyone we loved, and everyone who
loved us. The upholsterer, the painter, the radical schoolmaster, the
nuns from the old people's home, the owner of the local bar (said
to be a communist), the fire brigade and the gamekeepers, the old
aunts from Brittany who'd come by train from Finistère, the notary
and the farmers, my grandfather's gymnasts and the poachers all
dressed up in their Sunday best, the drunkards and the religious old
ladies, the lady who kept the dry-goods shop in the place de l'Hor-
loge, and the neighboring landowners—everyone was blinking back
tears, and everyone was happy.

The only one who wasn't there was Uncle Paul. He'd shot himself at the end of the previous summer. He was the first of our
family who, despite our motto, despite not being ordered to do so,
voluntarily handed in his notice to God.

4

Pauline the Bareback Rider, and the Rival Brothers

🔹 SO THERE WE WERE, RUINED. IT WAS OF no importance. In the first place, of course, because money didn't matter. And also because, as often in middle-class families, ruin left us plenty to keep going on, enough to live quite comfortably in the manner to which we were accustomed. Michel Desbois, wonderfully ingenious, one of the cleverest financiers of his day, saved all that could be saved from the disaster. But the main thing was that it was only the Remy-Michaults who had really lost a packet—though it's true it was they who'd had the most in the first place. Anyway, whether it was a triumph or a catastrophe, business didn't interest us. Aunt Gabrielle and her money had done a lot for the roof of the chateau and the gamekeepers' liveries. But even without the luxury provided by the Remy-Michaults, Plessis-lez-Vaudreuil could still get along quite decently on the income from our estates in the Haute-Sarthe and the houses in Paris which Monsieur Desbois senior still went on managing with unswerving strictness and methodical care. His son's marriage to Anne had presented him with a few minor problems of etiquette. He was now my sister's father-in-law, and relations between him and the family were bound to be affected by this unusual rise in the world. Several confabulations were held among us, and it was decided that Monsieur Desbois

should be offered a more intimate association—that he should have
a large bedroom close by that of my grandfather, that naturally he
should take his meals with us, under the somewhat astonished gaze
of our bewigged marshals, and that he should go on running our
affairs from within. Monsieur Desbois was very grateful, but flatly
declined. He came to see my grandfather, even more solemn than
usual and dressed in clothes which went back at least to the turn of
the century or the beginning of the Great War, and he told him
what he thought. It was only with reluctance that he'd agreed to
his son's marriage. He wasn't in favor of leveling or mixing up the
different social classes. Like my grandfather, only even more so, he
believed in hierarchy, distinction, order, and the permanent classifi-
cation both of people and of things. He used the same arguments
as Cardinal Mazarin, pleading with Louis XIV against his niece
Mancini. It must have been an astonishing sight—my grandfather
putting his hands on Monsieur Desbois' shoulders and preaching the
cause of historical progress and human equality. But Monsieur Desbois wouldn't listen. He was in our service and intended to remain
so.

"Come now, Desbois," said my grandfather, "you're my oldest
friend, and we're all very fond of you. Your son has married my
granddaughter—you're one of the family."

"Your grace," answered Desbois, "my father was steward to the
late duke, your grandfather, and to the late duke, your father, and
so was I. Now I am your steward, and I mean to go on being your
steward—unless, of course, you were no longer to have confidence
in me."

"But my dear Desbois, do you really appreciate the situation?
Your son is my grandson. In the same generation but one, we have
the same connection with you as with Albert Remy-Michault. And
it's no secret that I have much more affection and respect for you
than I ever had for him."

"Your grace . . ." said Desbois.

"Call me Sosthène," said my grandfather.

"Your grace," went on Desbois, "the trust and affection the family is good enough to repose in me is the greatest conceivable

happiness for me. But I shall die in the condition to which God thought fit to call me."

"Well, my dear Robert," said my grandfather, "let's say nothing has changed. But you will know I love you more than I've ever loved anyone outside the family, and as much as I love my own kith and kin."

And they fell on each other's neck and wept. As age weighed more and more heavily on his stout shoulders, my grandfather could be moved to tears by noble sentiments, the national anthem, the once hated flag, the past, the family, and, now, within the family, the conferring of democracy.

When my brother-in-law Michel came to spend a few days at Plessis-lez-Vaudreuil, Monsieur Desbois senior used to sit with us around the stone table, like one of the ancestors who were more and more rarely in our thoughts. But his whole attitude made it plain that *he* thought of them, though his only link with them was through his daughter-in-law. And his best reward for his fidelity was in the way my grandfather looked at him.

Uncle Paul's death was of course a terrible blow for my grandfather. I'm not sure they were ever very close. I'm inclined to suspect that despite their differences my father was my grandfather's favorite. Perhaps that was just because he'd been dead so long, and belonged to the past. But Uncle Paul was the eldest, and his death was an awful shock. Fortunately he left four sons. Pierre, naturally, took over from his father, and all the hopes of the family were vested in him.

At that time he was divided between Ursula and Mirette. A few more years, and the drama that was brewing between them would burst forth. There's a good deal of awkwardness about the way I've chosen to tell this story, but I don't really see what I could have done so as to present simultaneously all the different threads which I'm endeavoring to disentangle. What has to be remembered, of course, is that many of the different events which have been described in different chapters actually happened at the same time. While Claude and I were sailing to Skyros, Mirette was arriving in Paris, Aunt Gabrielle was leaving Poiret for Chanel, Jacques met

Hélène at a dinner party in the rue de Bellechasse or the rue de l'Université, and Michel resigned from the ministry of finance to take up an important post with the Remy-Michaults. My grandfather was the only one who hardly budged: he was over seventy, and age, conviction, and a long habit of idleness made him almost immobile.

One *could* try to capture what the life of the family was like by just freezing it at some arbitrarily chosen date—for example, the evening Mirette died, or the celebrated Thursday, October 24, 1929, when at what seemed the height of prosperity the fifteen million shares that were to kill Uncle Paul were thrown on the market and the New York stock exchange suddenly collapsed. But every facet of that suddenly arrested world would involve a past and a future; each separate factor would proliferate under the pressure of all the events that had helped to create it, and all the others that were to derive from it. Whether the narrator likes it or not, and however fragmentary the effect, he finds himself following continuity in time rather than attempting to knit everything together at once as it happens. That is why we have seen Mirette, Uncle Paul, Jean-Christophe, Michel Desbois, and Claude live and die separately. But they all knew each other, and their separate lives went on simultaneously and intersected.

They were intermingled with rumors from every side. Our barricades were crumbling on all fronts. They had long protected us from barbarian invasion, epidemics, merchants, dangerous ideas, all the winds sweeping up from the plain. But with newspapers, the wireless, the perpetual movement of people and ideas, the world was rushing right into Plessis-lez-Vaudreuil. Not long ago we had lived almost alone with Aunt Yvonne and Uncle Anatole, but now our family intimacy was intruded upon by what my grandfather called frightful riffraff or funny customers, according to the mood he was in. Karl Marx had come into our midst; we looked under the beds at night to see that Lenin wasn't lurking there with a knife between his teeth; Freud sat at our table, introduced by rich American ladies who'd married our cousins and who lay on a couch in New York three times a week and told of all sorts of dreadful things and of childhood memories closer to the pranks of Uncle Donatien than to those of Aunt Ségur, née Sophie Rostopchine. We didn't suspect then that even she would one day be subtly interpreted as a pervert in disguise. The ladies from across the Atlantic had fallen under the wicked spell of the worthy doctor from Vienna, who, crossing to America from Europe in the summer of 1909 and seeing the lights of Manhattan appear in the distance, turned to his traveling companion—Dr. Jung, perhaps, or the faithful Ferenczi—and said: "Little do they know that we're bringing them the plague."

The stone table hadn't stirred, there under the limes of the chateau. But there were newcomers around it whom my grandfather regarded with a distaste which easily got the better of his curiosity. The most ridiculous was the little man with the raincoat and the mustache who has already been mentioned, and who in three years' time was going to make those who made fun of him laugh out of the other side of their faces. The ex-corporal's cowlick—we were certainly unlucky with corporals—was not to be amusing for long. The cabaret singers were still joking about him when Nuremberg echoed to the tramp of thousands of boots under forests of torch-lit banners. Goering, Goebbels, and Himmler became household words, together with Lenin and Roosevelt, Stalin and Freud, Lindbergh and Stavisky, Ford and Renault, Mauriac and Jules Romains. When I search my memories and try to define, through the perfumes of the summer and the echoes from the world, the image of the years between the crisis and the war, the "climate of the thirties," to use the sort of modish expression which my grandfather, despite Aunt Gabrielle, forbade the children to utter, what I see arising on the horizon, beyond the stone table and the lake and the trees, is anxiety, fear, the famous modern *angst* about which everyone, from Keynes to Freud, from Picasso to Charlie Chaplin, all had something to say in their own particular manner. The echo of the "Roaring Twenties" had reached us, usually through La Belle Gaby, laden with jazz and the tango. The thirties echoed—but is this hindsight?—with the sound of boots and the clank of arms. The twenties were the Indian summer of the Belle Epoque: 1925, despite the rupture of the war, was still like 1900, with frenzy added and

the dead taken away—a golden age over which had passed Verdun,
the Dada movement, the October Revolution, and the split at Tours
between the Second and the Third International. But still, a golden
age. The thirties brought the Stavisky scandal and the "suicide" of
Albert Prince, the assassination of King Alexander of Yugoslavia in
Marseilles, and of Louis Barthou on the pont de la Concorde. It
brought the Popular Front, the Moscow trials, the Spanish Civil
War, the Nuremberg rally, and the night of the long knives, whose
internecine complexities we were to understand only much later.
The blood of the Chemin des Dames and the mud of the Argonne
didn't take long to come back into fashion. They crept back into
daily life, into families and villages, into politics and city streets.
Meanwhile everyone went indefatigably on performing his exploits, riding along under the summer sun, between fascism and
communism, scandals and the Spanish war, riots and strikes.

There was one word especially which entered into our conversation and our ordinary life for the next fifty years—perhaps more,
perhaps for a couple of centuries, perhaps for a couple of thousand
years: communism. Everything revolved around it, as once everything had revolved around God and the king. It already had a long
past, going back to Babeuf, Campanella, the Incas, and Plato. But
now it no longer represented just an abstract idea, a risk, a danger,
a beautiful philosophical dream, and temporary upheavals. It was
coming to be merged more and more with the inevitable future
vouched for by its apostles. The stone table seemed gradually to be
changing into a bastion of the past, a besieged fortress, a fragment
of vanished time held back from the future. It was in the thirties that
we began to suspect that God's pleasure had turned aside from us
forever, and that all the values to which we'd linked our name went
against the tide of history.

There is no hiding the fact that for some of us it was plain that
we were heading for a trial of strength, and that the only thing to
be done was prepare for it. When women left him time for it,
Philippe was not indifferent to the great nocturnal celebrations held
in Prussia and Bavaria, and to the huge, marvelously disciplined

crowds in which youth and order strangely combined. For him, then between thirty and forty, and for Pierre's son, Philippe's nephew, then in his early teens, our age produced a fascinating violence which had a promising future before it. Philippe started to read *L'Action française* when it fell from the disillusioned and Catholic hands of my grandfather. Seven or eight years before, the denunciation of the movement, first by the archbishop of Bordeaux and then by the Pope, had confronted my grandfather with one of those moral and intellectual dilemmas which it is hard for people nowadays even to imagine. You could, I suppose, compare it with the world repercussions caused by the twentieth congress of the Soviet Communist Party. To have to choose between God and the king meant that a whole universe was collapsing. But there wasn't a king any more, and God still ruled the world. So my grandfather yielded. And sank a little deeper into his bitter solitude. Philippe no longer had any belief in the monarchist cause. But once he had believed in women, and now he believed in manly friendship, sport, and a moral soundness which showed itself chiefly through force and the exercise of force. All this had brought him around to Action Française, to the loaded sticks of the "Patriotic Youth" or of the "Newsvendors of the king," of whom he was one of the leaders and who used to sell the Action Française's paper outside the churches on Sunday. In short, it brought him to the brink of fascism.

So far, I've said far more about Pierre and Jacques and Claude than about my cousin Philippe. Philippe was by far the best-looking of us all. My grandfather and great-uncles and Uncle Paul were all, as we said, "frightfully smart," but they weren't really handsome. It wasn't impossible, with them, to detect that tinge of the ridiculous in their get-up which I've mentioned before. The Remy-Michault blood had at once corrected and spoiled this rather eccentric originality, which had its own touch of grandeur. There was nothing ridiculous about Pierre or Jacques or Charles. Nothing surprising, either. Even in the case of Claude, it wouldn't have occurred to anyone, except perhaps himself, to laugh at his crippled arm. All Uncle Paul's sons had gotten back into line. But Philippe stood out above them all by the elegance and fineness of his features, his excellently proportioned body, and by a wonderful sort of ease which owed nothing to intellect and everything to a kind of harmony inherent in all his person, and which, as we know, brought him success with all sorts of women of every age. When he was about thirty or thirty-five, a short time after Uncle Paul, his father, started to go in for politics, with views that though recently acquired were steadfastly republican and democratic, Philippe discovered the nationalist extreme Right. You will naturally point out that this was completely in the family tradition. And in a way you'd be right. But, here again, it's a bit more complicated than that.

If, with all the differences, all the variety of opinions which now flourish among us, one can still speak of the family spirit, I'd say that in the previous ten or twenty years it had steadily been evolving toward a defense of liberty. With a time-lag of a hundred years, as usual, we'd all become followers of Chateaubriand. We were still, out of habit, on the side of God and the king; we were naturally also on the side of tradition; but we were also for liberty, for a certain idea of man, almost for the rights of the spirit. How had this surprising mutation come about? In the simplest possible manner: through the irresistible influence—my grandfather called it contamination—of the ideas of the Remy-Michaults; as a result of the Great War and the victory of democracy over the Central Powers; and by an instinct of self-preservation which made us dimly perceive that in the future it was people like Hitler and Lenin who would probably wield the power we had revered for so long, and that those we had admired, like Sully, Louis XIV, Colbert, Louvois, Villèle, MacMahon, Polignac, and Metternich were gone, never to return. No doubt our motives were not absolutely disinterested— show me any motives in history that are. But at any rate they ranged us on the side of the defenders of that liberty which for centuries we'd fought against. You've heard what my grandfather once thought about liberty. And now here he was, respecting and defending it. The reason was that whereas it used to consist in rejecting our ideas, it now consisted in rejecting other people's. There was something both comical and profound in this intellectual evolution

of ours. Socialism's leading wing was in favor of liberty insofar as
it needed it in the struggle against us. We were in favor of authority
insofar as we hoped to preserve it against the depredations of the
socialists. The extreme Left, coming to power in Soviet Russia,
renounced liberty and aspired to dictatorship in the name of values
as totalitarian and exclusive as our own values had once been. And
we, vanquished and thrown on the defensive, trying as hard as we
could to hold back the rise of new beliefs, set up as defenders of the
individual freedom which was now our only salvation. Such were
the contradictions of the modern world, and of our family.

Dear Philippe had his contradictions and inconsistencies too. And
he certainly wasn't intelligent enough to resolve them—different as
he was from his father, he was very like him from the physical and
intellectual point of view. Nationalism was a fairly new tradition in
the family. It may be objected that tradition has to start somewhere.
Yes, but the question is, was the mixture of Action Française and
fascism, to which our Philippe had gone over, fatigued perhaps by
his amorous successes, was this doctrine a suitable vehicle for these
recently adopted beliefs? It was a doctrine that itself contained a
fundamental inconsistency that it would find impossible to throw
off, and from which all the woes of the extreme Right in France
were to derive: although it was nationalist in attitude, it went
abroad, indeed it went to the enemy, for the model and ideal of its
nationalism. Like Claude, Philippe wanted to show his independence of the family, of my grandfather, and of Pierre, who'd married a Prussian. He hated the peaceful, traditional Germany,
because he read *L'Action française*, the organ of "integral nationalism." But in 1933 or 1934 he started to admire the worst side of it,
its hysterical excitement, its *Zusammenmarschieren*, its wild anthems
in the darkness, its appeals to murder and for the purity of the race.
Which race? The race against which, through blind tradition and
despite our sympathies and even our family relationships, we'd
always fought. Perhaps you will remember that we'd always looked
in the direction of Greece and Rome and the Mediterranean. But
Philippe never spoke of anyone but the barbarians who had become
Germans, the blond, Aryan races who had held aloof from Mediter-

ranean wickedness, bastardized culture, mixed civilizations (in which he included Christianity, born in the East, the Jews, the Freemasons, the radical-socialists, American democracy, and parliamentary democracy, though the Norman and Anglo-Saxon origins of the latter were well known). So you see how Philippe, confusedly, saw himself as the one who was right in the line of the family and its traditions. And how at the same time he departed from it, from its obedience to the Church, from its Roman Catholicism, its long rejection of nationalism, its close links with artisans and peasants, and from what, through all our follies and errors, was the real heart of the matter: a certain idea of God and man and the universe, inseparable from one another, and also, though such a claim may make people laugh, a certain simple but strong idea, to which we were unswervingly attached, of individual and collective morality.

He'd never read a line of Racine or Stendhal, but he plunged headlong into translations of Nietzsche, of which he didn't understand a word, and the complete works of Chamberlain and Gobineau. He despised the Italians, though he admired fascism for making the trains which served indolence or whim arrive on time. He couldn't stand Aunt Gabrielle and the homosexuals she liked to surround herself with. That being the case—the life of a family is like high politics, where alliances are reversed and new balances of power replace the old—*we* immediately saw Aunt Gabrielle as clever and out of the ordinary, which she was. She was completely open-minded, and Philippe shut himself up in his vague and brutal myths, which were completely foreign to my grandfather and from which Philippe excommunicated all the rest of us. By the middle of the thirties the stone table had become a kind of debating society, and we sat up around it late into the night, arguing. Looking back on them now after all this time, despite some of the terrible things that happened, those endless discussions under the summer limes, beneath the moon and stars and the pink and black glow of the ancient house, still seem delightful! The rise of fascism, the Popular Front, the Spanish Civil War, and the Moscow trials, all, together with the Tour de France and the sailor from Skyros and the whore from Capri, still retain in my memory the incomparable fragrance not of youth—that was, alas, long gone—but of a vanished past. I remember two or three instances in which the confusion of ideas and feelings which was so characteristic of our age—or perhaps we just have an oversimplified view of other ages because we haven't actually known them—reached the heights of complication and paradox. For example, Claude and I almost worshipped a young man ten years younger than ourselves, one whom I think I've already mentioned. Robert Brasillach had done what Claude and I would have liked to be able to do: he'd gone to the Ecole Normale in the rue d'Ulm. Its very name sent us into ecstasies. We still retained something of the idea of an élite with which my grandfather had inculcated us, and which was to disappear so completely some thirty or forty years later, toward the end of my life, when I'm writing this very history. We'd simply shifted the notion forward, imagining that, as always, we were the spearhead of a progressive process which in a few years would be outdated. We thought the only élite was that of science and culture, and we read Martin du Gard's *Les Thibault* and Jules Romains' *Hommes de bonne volonté*, and dreamed of the roofs of the Ecole Normale and its famous competitive entrance examination.

Another writer also caused some uproar around the stone table. Claude and I admired André Gide, just as we admired Brasillach. Philippe, of course, hated him. By a strange chance, Aunt Gabrielle couldn't bear him either. She always used to repeat what one of her friends—Picabia, I think—had said: "If you read Gide aloud for ten minutes, you get a nasty taste in your mouth." So Aunt Gabrielle forgot Philippe's fascism, Philippe forgot Aunt Gabrielle's misunderstood poets, abstract paintings, already almost concrete music, and what he called her love of Surrealist decadence and pederasty —well might he forget that, for you had to know nothing at all about Surrealism to see it, as Sartre did later, as the triumph of homosexuality—and, by a truly surprising coalition, they were reconciled at our expense. It must be admitted that Gide, with his hairsplitting, his immoral scruples, his puritan sensuality, and his oblique intelligence, was better suited than anyone to sow disorder in the bosom of a traditionalist family that had been overtaken by events. And highly delighted he would have been at the trouble he'd caused.

Philippe had made his decision as early as 1934, when, with some friends of similar persuasion, he was invited by some young Wittgensteins that he knew to go to the first National Socialist Party rally at Nuremberg. He came back fascinated and dazzled, and it's not difficult to know why. Since the end of the eighteenth century we'd been devoted to an order that was irremediably cut off from the people, the masses. What secretly obsessed us and drove us to bitterness, and to a solitude grotesquely relieved by the fanfares of my father's gymnasts and by the excitements of the Tour de France, was a need for communion with the people, who had revered and followed us until they cut off our heads. Without realizing it, we dreamed of a reconciliation between law and order and the mob, between action and tradition, between the past and the future. And Philippe thought he had found that reconciliation in the impressive operatics at Nuremberg. He used to see red when newspapermen or cabaret singers ridiculed the little man with the cowlick. He'd seen only the grandeur, the laughing faces, the young men's enthusiasm, the faith and unanimity. When, alone, followed by two dignitaries of the new regime, the Führer walked in, in an overwhelming silence across the huge empty space between the dense ranks of the S.S. and S.A. in their black uniforms and brown shirts, something seemed to stir in the crowd—something more to do with love and religion than with politics and ceremony. While liberal and democratic France watched an endless succession of presidents doffing their top hats, Hitler's Germany was taming and mastering the savage instincts of man, pressing into its own service all the magic of night and silence and blood brotherhood. Hitler walked slowly past the flags of the ancient provinces of Germany—of Saxony, the Rhine, the Danube, and the Black Forest; of the Saar, Holstein, and Silesia; of all the lost territories dispersed by the lottery of history and scattered by the winds of history, and not yet gathered back into the Fatherland. With one hand Hitler touched these flags, and in the other he held the standard red with the blood of the victims of the failed putsch in the *Feldherrenhalle* in 1923. And so, between heroes and soldiers, the earth and the leader, there was sealed a mystic bond of history and sworn allegiance, sexuality and religion. Women swooned with joy—and with sensual pleasure; children offered themselves up to the savior and vowed to die for him. Everyone knew already that the promise would be kept. Philippe watched the young S.S. from Bremen and Friedrichshaven, Konstanz and Cologne; the Japanese in wing collars and the plump Italians; and the old generals of the traditional Wehrmacht trussed up in their uniforms, impassive yet vaguely contemptuous with their monocles—all watching the Führer. He didn't think that these tens of thousands of men standing there singing, shovel or gun in hand, would one day hurl themselves on his own countrymen. He just thought that history and the future of the world were being made before his eyes in the surge of swastika banners and standards, in the fabulous chiaroscuro of a cathedral of light.

The universe might be crumbling around him, but my grandfather didn't budge. Amid troubles and yawning chasms, he was imperturbable. Imperturbable, and perhaps, gradually, rather indifferent to men's agitations and their wild hopes. He'd known the Empire and its fall, Sedan, the Commune, the unsuccessful attempt to bring back the king, the third foundation of the Republic, first the triumph of the industrial bourgeoisie and now its decline, scandals and the Dreyfus case; the swing of the pendulum between clericalism and anticlericalism, hatred of Kitchener and the craze for the Prince of Wales, Anglo-French rivalry and the Entente Cordiale, and the alliance with Russia and anti-bolshevism; and the rise of democracy, socialism, American power, and what he was sufficiently behind—or in advance of—the times to call the "yellow peril." He didn't believe in much of anything but the eternal, but he did believe in that, or what he took to be that. He already had about him something of the stillness of eternity. Amid all that was changing so fast around him, before his eyes, he at least tried not to change. He succeeded marvelously. Time had no more effect on him than on the stone table. It made him stoop a little, it whitened his hair, but it never managed to change his convictions or his

impossible dreams, it never affected his inner universe. Time
avenged itself through the people and events that surrounded him.
The death of three of his sons and a brother in a war fought by the
republicans for the victory of democracy; the suicide of his eldest
son after failing in business; the amorous adventures—he never
mentioned them—of his eldest grandson; another grandson who
was a fascist; a granddaughter whose maiden name had been that of
the family steward—all these things were blows to him. But no
doubt they weren't enough to assuage the thirst for vengeance of
some new, sarcastic god, greedy for blood and humiliation, who,
though unknown to the mythology of the Greeks and the Romans,
played an incalculable part in ours: the god of irresistible, cruel, and
brutal change. What else did this god want of the period we were
living through? A great deal, and to begin with, he wanted the
abandoning of our beliefs and traditions, the denial of our past, the
reversal of everything which for centuries had constituted our
reason for living. And what he demanded, with all the arrogance of
a recently born faith and new and popular ideas, he was soon to get.

Claude came back fairly regularly to spend a few days with us
at Plessis-lez-Vaudreuil. I was always happy to see him. But I could
see that he too was changing, from one visit to the next. He became
more gloomy, more violent. Although he was very fond of Philippe,
he would often get so angry with him that relations between the
brothers were strained. Claude didn't get on much better with
Pierre and Jacques. What he held against Pierre, and this was natural
enough on the part of one who intended to become a priest, was the
frivolous life he lived and the sort of people he mixed with. Jacques,
whom for a long time he'd been as close to as he was to me, was
reproached with thinking of nothing but factories, the bank, and
money. Claude had real affection and even admiration for Michel,
who thanks to Jean-Christophe had come to be an even greater
reader than Claude himself. But now he criticized him for his job
in what used to be the family business. It was impossible not to
notice Claude's moods, and my grandfather and I used to wonder
about them. Perhaps Claude was taking his religious vocation too
seriously? Or perhaps, on the contrary, now that he was about to

take his final vows he had a few twinges of envy toward those who
were going to enjoy a life whose pleasures he was going to reject?
I remember the walks my grandfather and I used to take around
Plessis-lez-Vaudreuil, on the road to Roussette or along the unmade
roads, now surfaced, which led to the farms and the forest. The
unity of the family was very precious to him. We used to consider
Claude's strange attitude from every point of view, trying to make
it out. "But you," my grandfather would say—he used the familiar
tu to me, though he addressed his sons with the formal *vous*—
"you're Claude's friend, you're closer to him than his own brothers.
Doesn't he say anything to you? Hasn't he given you any explanation?" No, Claude hardly said anything to me, and he hadn't explained anything.

But one day he wrote me a letter. For a long time I kept it, but
it was swept away in the storms of war and occupation. But I read
and reread it so often that I think I remember every word, which
seemed to have been set down in the heat of passion and emotion.
The letter was to tell me that Claude had decided not to become
a priest. It was not that the fire that used to consume him had gone
out. But new landscapes had opened up before him. The love of
men and the love of God had finally come into conflict. "I used to
think," he said, "that one couldn't serve God and Mammon. But I
did believe that one could love both God and man. That you had
to love God to be able to love men—that you loved God through
men and men through God. But I don't believe that any more. I
believe you have to choose between God and man, and that you
have to love man for himself." And he asked me to tell our grandfather that he'd given up the idea of going into the Church.

In 1934, the very year Philippe went to Nuremberg, Claude went
to Moscow. I stayed behind with my grandfather. My wretched
iron constitution, which I'd sworn not to mention in these pages,
and which despite one threat after another has finally brought me
to the age of seventy, that year obliged me to remain at home,
sharing the solitude of one who had become an old man. He seemed
very old to me. In fact he was scarcely ten years older than I am
now. I can still see us, walking in the cool of the evening along the

changeless paths which led past the kennels, the sheds where young pheasants were tended, the two gamekeepers' cottages, and the ponds. Or, a little later, hunting across the plains between the woods at Bailly and the woods at Saint Hubert, between the pond at Quatre-Vents and the ride that used to be called after the trees but which my grandfather had renamed the "allée Gabrielle" after my aunt. Or at the beginning of winter, by the huge hearth in the drawing room hung with the pictures of the marshals, with my grandfather sitting gazing for hours at the flames creeping up from the crackling tinder and consuming the great dry logs brought five or six years earlier to the huge cellars under the kitchen and the chapel, on creaking carts which I used to hear going by under my window. We didn't say much. I didn't like to ask my grandfather, nor even to ask myself, what he was thinking. Things, events, and other men had gone on swiftly changing. But we others had got used again in the end to anxiety and change. We might even have missed it if life had suddenly stopped changing. But my grandfather had scarcely emerged from centuries of immobility. The upheavals of modern times seized him by the throat. Just as others had once scarcely been able to breathe for silence and slowness, so he was literally choked by change. The perpetual progress of the world gave him pain. As far as he could, he fled from it, taking refuge in his memories. As for me, in my pocket were letters from Claude and Philippe, full of the great dreams of modern man, the springtime of life, the dawn of the new age sweeping through Europe.

"The twentieth century," Philippe wrote to me, "will be the century of fascism and friendship between nations." He described the dark wonder of the processions, of the martyrs struck down in the struggle, the red immensity of fascism. And Claude talked to me about brotherhood between peoples, the iron rule of profit, and the Soviet cinema. He told me about all the things that had been unknown to us and that he was now finding out about with horror: hunger, unemployment, infants and old people dying, the despair of the enormous mass which our world was crushing.

Had we any idea of this awfulness? Did we know what was going on around our Edens enclosed in the past? In a few months, a few

weeks, I could see him getting farther and farther away from the
complex structure of habits and beliefs I've been trying to describe
as fairly and accurately as I could. Everything which made up our
family, our class, and our religion he rejected irrevocably. The same
passion which had urged him toward God now urged him toward
a history which meant our death. History, even modern history,
especially modern history, was not the tissue of foolishness my
grandfather lamented over. It had a meaning and an aim: revolution.
And my cousin had gone over to it. Revolution was inevitable, yet
one had to fight for it at the side of the proletariat and the working
class, which stood for something like God made history. And in
Claude there was a new sort of feeling—a feeling of shame at
belonging to us, at being connected with a class condemned by this
new kind of history for injustice and stupidity. Love and hatred,
pity and violence all united in him now in a combination which at
the time struck me as extraordinary. We brandished the specter of
Uncle Constantine, and reminded Claude how he and his wife and
children and servants had been murdered in the Crimea. Claude
replied that history could only advance across spilled blood, that we
ourselves hadn't scrupled to shed it or cause to be shed or allow it
to be shed in floods, and that the only reason we'd become so careful
about it was that we were afraid our own, far from innocent, blood
might be going to flow. He talked to me about Russia and about the
communists' faith in the future of their cause, and his own contempt
for frivolity, bourgeois decadence, and the worship of money
which was gradually taking the place of our fallen idols. "Look
around you," he said. "Where there was once God and the king,
whom our family used to die for, all I see is money and yet more
money. If there's anything else, tell me—I can't see it." He also
wrote: "I'm not leaving anything behind, or abandoning or betraying anything. The fact is that all the big words we used to believe
in have vanished into the void." As far back as I remember, Claude
had always been the one of us who most needed to believe in
something. The day he didn't believe in the Church any more, he
was an orphan. So he chose himself another father whom he had had
to go further to seek: the people.

Claude had been even more passionately attached to books than his brothers and myself. He didn't really discard them now, but many of those we'd liked best he denounced as art for art's sake or because he regarded them as instruments of the ruling bourgeoisie. He replaced them with new gods whom he taught me in my turn to read and admire: Zola, Jaurès, Barbusse, Eisenstein, Essenin and Mayakovsky, Aragon and Nizan. One of his letters from Moscow ended with a quotation I didn't recognize:

> And in the red six-o'clock sky
> Was a great red banner—
> "Greetings to the Bolshevik Party"
> V K P
> And to its leader Comrade Stalin.

It wasn't until later that I learned the name of the author, who was to play an important role in my cousin's life. It was Aragon.

In the months and years which led up to the war, I saw through Claude's eyes what the picture I've painted for you of the family looked like to other people, and how the world and humanity can change their meaning. Loyalty, tradition, love of the past were only the expression, for the most part unconscious, of class politics. We didn't even belong to the age of industrial bourgeoisie now in the process of collapse. We were pale fleshless ghosts of a raving feudalism which had passed out of history two or three hundred years earlier. The great eighteenth century, when we were still quite brilliant, also marked the beginning of our decline. Louis XIV, with his courtiers in bondage at Versailles and his shopkeepers in charge of the state, with his personal dictatorship and the abasement of the great, in a way foreshadowed the Revolution. Anyhow, he indicated the end of the feudal world to which we were now bound only by our illusions. The bourgeoisie had overthrown us, but reluctantly, with a bad grace, yet with a secret satisfaction which we concealed from ourselves, we'd allied ourselves with it in order, somehow, to survive. It wasn't by chance that Uncle Paul married Aunt Gabrielle, at the turn of the century. Claude hated his mother's blood even more than that of his father. The rise of the Remy-Michaults, their successful effort to stem for their own advantage a revolution which they'd helped to unleash, their links with industry, their contempt for the masses from whom they themselves had recently emerged—Claude spurned all these with a violence that frightened me. "I hate them!" he would say. "I hate them—all of them!" For him, this hatred was a sudden revelation of the universe, of its evident folly, of its real meaning. He'd found an image of the world in which events fell into a consistent order, in which all the contradictions we used to argue about seemed at last to be resolved. He clung to this image, and forced the slightest details of our common existence to square with it. It offered an explanation for everything. There was a place for everything in a system which was even more rigid than the one that had ruled our destiny for centuries before. God, our own old history, our own old morality, and the king—they were all dead and buried. But they had revived again in strange guises in the system of Hegel, concealed behind Marx's long beard and under Lenin's cap. Philippe didn't understand Claude, but Claude understood Philippe: after liberalism and traditionalism, violent nationalism was a last line of defense against the new and rising forces of the international proletariat. Claude's position with relation to his mother was rather ambiguous. Of course he disapproved of her love of amusement, dressing up, aestheticism, and oversubtlety. But he didn't underestimate the revolutionary aspect of her attitude—in Paris, at least, for, as we know, no one could be more conservative than she was at Plessis-lez-Vaudreuil. Maybe she was only destructive. Others would construct.

Perhaps, though not necessarily, there was something surprising about Claude's becoming a socialist and a Marxist. But what struck the family itself as really astonishing was that he was ashamed of bearing our name. A long time ago, about 1900 I think, a distant cousin of ours had exhibited herself in the music hall. Such things do happen. Do you remember the uncle in Argentina? Well, he had a son in rather obscure circumstances, and that son had a rather good-looking daughter—"common, though," my grandfather said—who sang and danced and dragged our name through low-class

vaudevilles and did an equestrian act in a circus. My grandfather,
with Uncle Anatole in support, solemnly went to see her. As far as
I could discover, the interview didn't go off too badly. I'd have
given a lot to be there. They all drank absinthe and talked, accompanied by a tightrope walker and a trainer of performing seals—
both artistes were our cousin's lovers. Before leaving, my grandfather said to Pauline—for she was called Pauline, like our Tonnay-
Charente great-grandmother and a Rohan-Soubise great-aunt—that
of course she was free to live as she pleased, but that it mightn't be
a bad thing to change her name and put something else on her
posters. "Change my name?" said Pauline, putting out, in her glass,
one of the little cigars she chain-smoked. "Why? I'm not ashamed
of it." This reply remained famous among us, and in the end, after
the fury it provoked at the time had been calmed by time, the war,
new attitudes, and death, including that of Pauline herself, it even
made us laugh, gathered around the stone table some twenty or
thirty years afterward. Claude's feelings were nothing like so naive.
His name seemed to cling to him, and made him suffer as if it were
some physical or moral defect. He told me later that once, in a fit
of anger or despair, he'd burned all his papers, his passport, the
bookplates with the family arms, and all the Doucet or Hilditch
shirts with his initials on. For him the name that was our pride was
the sign that he was accursed in this world, and there was no other,
since his God was dead. But the family name, his name, was enough
to mark him off forever from the people he longed to be part of,
the anonymous mass of workers and peasants who constituted the
history of the future as against that of the past. Even the family
motto meant nothing to him: God's pleasure had become the will
of the people, embodied in the Party and expressed by revolution.

I fear my grandfather must have guessed a lot of the things that
were going on around him at the end of the inter-war years. Aunt
Gabrielle's audacities, the adventures of Pierre and Ursula, Philippe's fascism, Claude's atheism—all of them must have done something to embitter his old age. But I don't think he ever knew that
Claude regretted his own name. He couldn't have guessed or under-

stood, he couldn't even have conceived of such an inversion of all our values. If he'd found out about it he'd have died on the spot.

Claude deserted us. He scarcely ever came to Plessis-lez-Vaudreuil. I still saw him often, but usually in Paris—not really in secret, but not as one of the family. Mostly I saw him alone, but sometimes with Jacques. I was still very fond of him, and now my affection was somehow mingled with surprise and admiration. He worked for a few months on the shop floor of a steel plant in the northeast, in a car factory, where an engineer we knew was amazed to come across his name on the staff list. He took part in strikes, and sometimes organized them in various places. He also used to write for *L'Humanité,* but we didn't know this until later, as his fiery articles were signed with a pseudonym. He mercilessly cast aside everything that connected him with us. Everything to do with our clothes, our cars, our social habits, the setting in which we lived, even our cast of mind, he rejected with horror. He lived in another world, where all that we thought and were, our self-interested loyalty, our haughty simplicity, our hypocritical gentlemanliness, were weighed in the balance and found wanting. But he still felt a sort of desperate tenderness toward us. He loved and hated us at the same time, as we used to love and hate the black sheep who ignored the true God and the king and followed the slippery slope to destruction. I think he still loved us as I loved him. But he could only hope for the death of our selfish blindness.

Meanwhile the world was like the family. Or perhaps the family modeled itself on the world. We went on with our betrothals and births and family tea parties; we wondered what future could lie before the youngsters at Franklin or Stanislas high school, who were left way behind in class by Samuel Silberstein, the son of a rich Jewish furrier, and by the nephew of a Catholic novelist whom my grandfather regarded as the incarnation of the extreme Left. For us as for everyone else, all this combined with the assassination of King Alexander and Louis Barthou, with the Popular Front and the war in Spain. Europe was divided up between fascism and anti-fascism. Apart from Philippe and Claude, who had chosen their sides, we no longer knew what to believe or which way to turn. It seems to me that our chief occupation during the five or six years leading up to the war was simply waiting for a catastrophe which we could do nothing to avert and before which we were defenseless. "I told you so," my grandfather used to say, reading of fresh disasters in the newspaper and shaking his head.

Socialism on the one hand, and nationalism on the other, we found equally alien and repugnant. And National Socialism was every kind of disaster rolled into one. But did the word "we" have any meaning left now? Several members of the family had become nationalists or ultranationalists, and Claude was more socialist than the socialists. What the family in general regarded as terrible misfortunes were wished for by some of its individual members. On February 6, Philippe took part in the young royalists' demonstration on the pont de la Concorde; on February 9, Claude marched in the communists' counterdemonstration from the place de la Bastille to the place de la Nation and along the main boulevards. Philippe was a passionate defender of the entry of German troops into the Rhineland—"Good gracious!" he announced, laughing, "the Germans are invading Germany!"—and Claude represented the Popular Front as some sort of gigantic fête. Listening to them, you'd have thought the masses were overwhelmed with happiness, though according to different methods and dogmas. Of course, each regarded the other's doctrines as illusions or deliberate deceptions. Claude adopted the tandem bicycle of the working classes, scattered about the highways and byways by Léon Blum and Léo Lagrange, and vaunted holidays with pay and the forty-hour week with raised fist and to the tune of the "Internationale." Meanwhile Philippe, with shovel and gun, under the aegis of the swastika and the fascist emblem, celebrated the virtues of strength through joy. Were people and things as divided as this in the past? Did the world change as fast? Was history so various—so somber for some, so full of contradictory hopes and promises for others? I think the answer is plain. Alexander, Charlemagne, Genghis Khan, and Napoleon all conquered a large part of the world in only a few years. Barbarians and Romans, Moslems and Christians, Catholics and Protestants had spent their time cutting one another's throats, and seas of human blood had been shed in aid of glowing futures depicted by prophets, martyrs, and revolutionaries. But we at Plessis-lez-Vaudreuil, just emerging from an almost stationary world and limited by our own image of the past, had the impression that history had suddenly gone mad, and we pitied the generations that would come after us. This time, once and for all, gracious living, with its great fancy-dress balls, its armies of servants, its leisure and culture, its silver plate and piles of linen handed down from generation to generation in great fragrant cupboards, had gone with the wind sweeping up from Bavaria and the Rhine, from besieged Toledo, the ruins of Guernica, and the dreary plains of Siberia.

The younger generation, as we'd started to call it, adapted itself quite well to the world we lamented over so bitterly. We pitied them for their fate, and they remained perfectly calm. Like his Uncle Philippe, Jean-Claude was a fascist. The decision was not much effort for him. He was preparing to take his school-leaving certificate, he played tennis, he was already fond of the girls. His sister Anne-Marie, Pierre and Ursula's daughter, was sixteen or seventeen when war broke out. She promised to be very pretty, and in this difficult world her beauty was a consolation. It even tamed Claude. The militant with raised fist had a soft spot for this Prussian's daughter, this niece and sister of fascists, bearing a royalist name that had distinguished itself by the sword and the censer. When I told him she'd been a great success at the end-of-term party at her convent, at a private dance at the Brissacs or the Harcourts, and later at her first real dance, with photographs in *Vogue*, Claude would smile. He used to sell *L'Humanité* outside the subway on Sunday, but he was proud of his niece and her successes in the drawing rooms of the ruling class to which he too belonged but which he had rejected. Anne-Marie was very fond of her uncles. Of course, her mother hadn't much time for her. Sometimes, on Sundays, Philippe or Claude or I would take her to see an elderly aunt at Versailles, or to a cinema in town or in the Latin Quarter. Because it was young and awkward and unusual, the cinema was still a treat in those days. We went to see *Quai des brumes, Le Jour se lève, Snow*

White and the Seven Dwarfs, Hôtel du Nord, La Grande Illusion, La Règle du jeu, Stage Coach, and *The Lives of a Bengal Lancer.* Anne-Marie adored the cinema. She loved life. She seemed to us such a simple creature, in her budding beauty. Anne too had seemed simple to me, and so had Ursula, twenty years before. Everything is simple in men, and in women, if you look at them from the outside, and watch them, hesitating and laughing on the brink of the world. And everything is simple too, long afterward, when life is over and done with and you explain them after their death, looking back on lives which are now only history. It is while it is unfolding and still taking place that fate is obscure and sometimes mysterious. I remember, more than once, among the still well-kept paths at Plessis-lez-Vaudreuil or amid the Sunday crowds in the Champs-Elysées, listening to Anne-Marie talking, being amused or excited by a trifle, and suddenly stopping and wondering what would become of her.

At Plessis-lez-Vaudreuil the children began to lead a very different life from what ours had been at their age. What struck us most, and even aroused our indignation, was their need of amusement, perhaps merely love of change in another guise. I think there was a bit of envy, and perhaps jealousy, mingled with our astonishment. Had we had tennis courts and swimming pools and friends to stay for the weekend and skiing in the winter and motorcycles when we were seventeen? The more difficult things were, the more demanding the children seemed to become. The family's financial situation had grown steadily worse since the turn of the century, since the war, since the crisis. Yet there were two kinds of people of whom we said, day in day out, that they were always asking for more: the children and the servants. It was beginning to be rather difficult to find cooks and butlers for Plessis-lez-Vaudreuil, where there was no movie theater, and the Saturday-night dance was a poor substitute for the pleasures of the big city. And the children complained as bitterly as the exiled chambermaids pining for Paris: already they longed for the mountains, travel, the sea. We sometimes had the monstrous (to us) impression that the children were bored here in the old house. Instead of the great old myths, now vanished forever, we used to spend a lot of time discussing family problems. The children's holidays and the kitchenmaids' wages had taken the place of the king. It was mainly to please the children, whom he loved deeply, that my grandfather had had a tennis court built in part of the kitchen garden, and, as I've already said, had had two bathrooms installed in the chateau right at the time of the Popular Front. Despite the help provided by Michel and Aunt Gabrielle, they nearly ruined him. And it seemed to him that the children never expressed, and probably never even felt, anything faintly resembling gratitude. One began to hear a phrase which had a great future before it: "Children are never satisfied. They think the world owes them a living." And indeed a slight breeze of rebellion had begun to sweep these fifteen-year-olds. On the eve of the Second World War, as always somewhat behind everyone else, behind literature, behind Gide's *Counterfeiters* and Martin du Gard's *Les Thibault*, the specter of the generation gap arose, bright though veiled, in the constellation of the family.

How difficult it is to say everything there is to be said, to describe a whole era, to depict as I should like to do the color and flavor of a particular social group in a particular age! What I should like to bring to life is only a limited environment, and yet do I convey anything more of it than superficial anecdotes, a veneer, an appearance? Still practically nothing actually happened at Plessis-lez-Vaudreuil, and yet the whole world passed through it. There were letters from Jacques in New York, from Ursula in St. Tropez or the Lot, an occasional postcard from Claude in Russia or China, one from Philippe in Nuremberg or Rome. In the evening, before dinner, the family used to gather around the wireless set. We heard of ministerial changes, the triumph of the Popular Front, then the fall of Léon Blum, the changing fortunes of the Spanish Civil War, the annexation of Austria and the Sudetenland to Hitler's Germany, just as once we had learned of the occupation of the Rhineland and the assassination of the king of Yugoslavia.

There was a constant coming and going to and from Paris: as one lot came, another went. We talked not only about politics but also about dances—the latest dances, as we called them. For another thirty years, perhaps more, we were to sing the same old tune every spring and autumn: theater, literature, sport, and society gossip. Michel Desbois and Jacques used to tell us about America and the fantastic fortunes people made there. The crisis was a thing of the past. Roosevelt and the New Deal had rebuilt capitalism on liberal ideas which my grandfather regarded as next door to socialism. All I've described before about the Tour de France and the regular Saturday visits of the clockmaker remained the same. In 1936, Sylvère Maës. In 1937, Lapébie. In 1938, Bartali. And in 1939 Sylvère Maës again. But Monsieur Machavoine was dead. His place had been taken by his son, the brother of the little boy who was drowned in a tributary of the Sarthe. He was a tall, rather subdued-looking young man, but bolder than he seemed, in fact as forward as his father had been retiring. He got Jacqueline, the cook's daughter, a pretty blonde who thought of nothing but Paris, into trouble. This affair preoccupied us a good deal, and is inseparable in my mind from the Munich agreement, because on one and the same day we learned that the war had been put off for a while and that Jacqueline was pregnant.

As always, important matters were all mixed up with trifles. Little bothers and vexations and successes mattered as much to us, often more, than great catastrophes and events that would be set down in books in the form of dates, dispatches, meetings, or statistics in which we scarcely recognized the slow evolution of our everyday life. I've often referred to the Spanish Civil War and the Popular Front, because although I am not writing History with a capital H, our family chronicle does overlap with the upheavals of the age, it expresses and reflects them, in a way it contains them, and is contained by them. What Malraux said about the omnipresence of history was truer than ever. If I've dwelt on Philippe and Claude it's because, as we shall see, in their different ways they showed the modern world entering into the traditions and routines of the family. When the Spanish war broke out, it had already been brewing for a long time in the family. As soon as the first shot was fired, Claude and Philippe knew which side they were on. Philippe was for the Christ-king, the fascist order, tradition and the army, Sanjurjo and Franco. Claude was for fraternity, the people, social justice and equality. In the mediocre age they lived in, without grandeur, decadent, dedicated to comfort and the radical socialism they both hated, both had found something to die for. For communism, or against it. On the one hand, priests buried alive and nuns raped, and on the other, Hitler's and Mussolini's planes bombing towns and villages. Claude wrote to Malraux and Hemingway, to Mauriac and Bernanos, who was already thinking of his *Moonlit Graveyards.* He joined the Communist Party. Philippe cried, *"Viva la muerte!"* An attempt at greatness even in the void was one solution for someone who stood where the family and the modern world intersected. It struck me later that certain pages in Montherlant about useless service and the knights of nothingness might have served as Philippe's motto. He also reconciled, more or less consciously, Christianity and paganism, indifference and values, the cult of death and the love of life. One fine morning in 1936 we learned that Claude and Philippe had both gone. Together. They crossed France, and dined together in a little restaurant in Toulouse, where they sent a joint postcard to my grandfather telling us what they were going to do. Above his signature, Claude had written, *"No pasarán."* Above his, Philippe had written, *"Pasaremos."* Then they went their separate ways into Spain to join their respective sides. Philippe shut himself up with Colonel Moscardo in the Alcazar in Toledo—even in the besieged fortress he managed to find and seduce a few girls. Claude fought with the international brigades in the Sierra of Teruel. He spent a few days in the house of the Duke of Alba, which had been requisitioned by the Madrid militia. Pierre and Ursula had spent a week or two there as the duke's guests in 1926. Claude found the same furniture, the same fine pictures that his brother had told him about, the same huge stuffed bear holding the same tray—now empty—for visiting cards, and the old cook from Andalusia who wouldn't run away. After all the marriage announcements in *Le Gaulois* and *Le Figaro,* after accounts of Aunt Gabrielle's parties, after—and before—all the photographs of dances in *Vogue* and *Harper's Bazaar,* the family name caused a stir by appearing in accounts of the fighting. *Paris-Soir* had a big article on the front page, headlined "The Rival Brothers."

The most surprising thing in all this was the attitude of my grandfather. The role of head of the family prevailed over the partisan in him. If anyone asked after Claude or Philippe, he would answer calmly, as if he were talking about one of our hunting parties, a kind of safari, or some rather dangerous riding contest, "Yes, two of my grandsons are in Spain. But not in the same place." My grandfather, naturally, was not on the side of the republicans. When Philippe wrote and told him that the Carlists used the traditional battle cry, "For God and the king," how could an old monarchist, brought up to despise the Republic, fail to be moved? But what he liked and admired most, what he had missed since his childhood under the Second Empire, was the fact of fighting for one's faith. He realized that Claude had at least one thing in common with the dead he denied: he was a man of faith. A different faith, but still a faith. Though he didn't care for the republicans, my grandfather didn't like the excesses of the Francoists, either. He had fought, as far as lay within his power, against godless schools and liberal and parliamentary democracy, and now he found it quite natural that his two grandsons should fight one on each side. Time had gone by for him too. He thought, and said, that we were no longer at the end of the last century, nor even at the beginning of this one. He held the balance as evenly as possible between Claude and Philippe. It never occurred to him to reject or criticize Claude. He saw his grandsons as the modern counterparts of the Burgundians and the Armagnacs, the Catholics and the Protestants, of his great-great-uncle François who fought with the Russians under Suvorov and Kutuzov, with the Austrians under Mack, and with the Prussians under Hohenlohe, while his great-uncle Armand was a colonel in the Imperial Guard.

Philippe was wounded in the arm, but both of them came back from Spain, in time to change wars and concentrate on our own. Meanwhile, Aunt Gabrielle's hair had gone gray, and was soon to go white. She no longer took any interest in parties and dressing up and the now almost nonexistent avant-garde salons. In 1936 she entered upon ten years of anxiety, from which she didn't emerge until 1945. The rest of the family took the view that her two sons had merely had a rather special education, a sort of practical staff college, perhaps a bit rough, with internal rivalries and serious risks, but of no great consequence, rather like the Oxford and Cambridge Boat Race, or medieval tournaments. They had fought for their convictions, for the sake of what they believed in. In my grandfather's opinion, after a hundred and fifty years when there had been nothing to arouse enthusiasm, they had done quite right. I think, as he gaily entered upon his ninth decade, he really envied them for having found, in this broken-down age, something to fight for, even against each other. Our rather untalented family had a genius for being able to go on living decently through cataclysms, to come to terms with them without baseness or cowardice, and make them conform to good taste. Claude and Philippe, in their own way, had revived something of the hopes and passions that had led their ancestors to the Rhine, Lombardy, and the Holy Land. Very good. Excellent. It was a sign that the family was in good health.

Claude and Philippe hadn't had much chance to meet since their dinner in Toulouse, of course. So my grandfather invited them both to a family gathering at Plessis-lez-Vaudreuil. And the best of it was, they came. And after all the death and hatred, there they sat drinking tea together at the stone table, under the limes. Neither had changed in his fundamental beliefs. Philippe still believed in the leader, blood, the land, and one's native country, and Claude believed in a proletariat without frontiers that was being impoverished by the profit motive. But it didn't matter. Anne-Marie was there, and Jean-Claude, and Bernard, and Aunt Gabrielle, and Jules, rather alarmed. Naturally, Pierre and Jacques were there too. And so was I. And cousin Ursula, who'd left the Lot and come with Pierre to be at the party. I think it was that day that I first had the idea of writing something about the history of my family, my poor dear old family. I can still hear my grandfather saying, standing there with his hands resting on the stone table, "Well, children, welcome back. Things aren't going very well. I hear that Monsieur Hitler, who seems to take himself for Bismarck and the Imperial General Staff all rolled into one, though he hasn't either the talent or the looks, wants to do us another Sedan, another Belgium. So you were right to get some practice in. But now you must settle your differences." He spoke truer than he knew. Because he was always behind the times, he sometimes ended up being ahead of them. I'm sure I remember hearing him say, when the Maginot Line was all the rage, that the whole thing would be settled, as always, between Belgium and the Ardennes. Philippe was a bit taken aback, but he shook hands all around as he'd seen people do in emotional scenes in old engravings in the billiard room and the library. The contradictions of history had caught up with him fast. He'd just been fighting side by side with the Germans, and now he was going to have to fight against them. But still, for centuries reversal of alliances had been a specialty of the royal house and of our own. Philippe was a fascist, true, but he was a nationalist too, and he was going to fight better than anyone against the Germans he admired. Claude himself, gloomier than ever, appalled at the news from Spain, standing with arms folded a little apart from the rest, still vaguely contemptuous but reconciled to us by Hitler's ravings and my grandfather's attitude, nodded his head approvingly. He was still living in the age of heroism. For him too, later, there would be a time of conflicting loyalties and contradictions. The champagne circulated to celebrate the return of the two prodigal warriors, the rival brothers brought together at last because their country was in danger—a phrase which we had long detested, and which now, by an irony of history, we were adopting. It was getting dark. It was a fine, mild evening, and we fell silent to watch night falling over the old house.

The Respite

I EXPECT YOU STILL REMEMBER THE anguished autumns when Monsieur Daladier and Mr. Chamberlain were doing the best they could—in other words, not much. They disembarked from their planes after having exchanged some thousands of men and square kilometers for a shaky peace, and to their own amazement they were acclaimed. France entered singing into the era of respite. It covered its eyes, stopped its ears, and gave itself up to cowardly relief. But Daladier's trilby and Chamberlain's umbrella, which both became so familiar, scarcely counterbalanced the armored cars and planes which four years of fanaticism, aided by the Krupp cousins, had brought forth from the void guaranteed by treaties. There was something new in the world: force. We may have been right but we weren't strong, and right without might . . . While the Popular Front offered the delighted French happiness and holidays with pay, Hitler offered the Germans dive bombers and tank thrusts.

The children enjoyed those Septembers. At the end of the vacation, the soldiers came out of their barracks to keep them from going back to school. There was a general atmosphere of agitation and still very comfortable danger—very appealing to the imagination of the young. Everyone's head was spinning. The huge headlines of *Paris-Soir*, the Saturday coups anticipating the sacrosanct British weekend, were our drugs, our pep pills. One had the impression of being drawn into a vortex already set down in history, and this made life seem abnormally vast. It was like some huge and rather risky game.

Like millions of other Frenchmen, we were much preoccupied by one particular danger, about the only one that never actually happened—gas. Do you remember? We've made so much progress since those far-off days that no one's frightened of gas now. But then it loomed large in our picture of the future. The future is always different from the gloomiest predictions. Sometimes it's worse. But without partiality one can safely say that all the series of governments which ruled France took only one precaution, and that precaution was to turn out useless: they did provide us with gas masks. We each had one in a little gray oblong box which hung at our sides. Where are they now, those millions of gas masks which were as much a part of their age as the tango and parasols were part of theirs? Disappeared, vanished, not only like things of the past but like things of a future which never happened. As we were fortunate enough to have a refuge a fair distance from Paris, most of the family—except Ursula, who continued to bury herself in her place in the Lot for a few more months, until the offensive, the bullfighter's betrayal, and the barbiturates—withdrew, as we said in those days, to Plessis-lez-Vaudreuil. There wasn't much chance of the Haute-Sarthe being ravaged by gas. Never had the family, divided by the gay twenties, divided by the troubled thirties, been so united. The autumn of '38 and the summer of '39, between the prewar period and the war itself, formed one of those brief remissions where fate hesitates before suddenly making up its mind and falling into the abyss.

The children worked in the same schoolroom where, twenty years before, Jacques and Claude and Michel and I had listened passionately to Jean-Christophe and to the lessons that turned our world upside down. There was no Jean-Christophe now. We couldn't afford a tutor, and anyway the children wouldn't have wanted one. With their Quicherats and their Baillys, the spitting image of our own tattered textbooks, they managed on their own, and very well too, doing the same Greek compositions and Latin translations, the same arithmetic problems and letters from Corneille to Racine and from Voltaire to Rousseau that we used to do. When we looked at the way life was organized at Plessis-lez-Vaudreuil, it was still possible to think things had hardly changed at all. We were older, that was all. We'd gradually taken the places of our parents and grandparents, we'd become our parents, and the children had taken our places and were now playing the parts we once played under the masks of childhood and adolescence. We'd all gone up, or perhaps down, a notch in our world, and what we were once, others were today. For what moves most, even when nothing moves, is motionless time, which shifts nothing but eats up from within, inserting our parents and their age and their weariness into us, and infusing into others our youth, our strength, our thirst for knowledge, and everything that we used to be.

But time does not limit itself to these linear transfers, this ever-changing biology. It also confuses structures and constellations, modifies relationships, transforms perspectives and balances. The world is always changing because it is getting older. But above all it changes because life's equilibria are always being upset. They are upset, but they are kept artificially in place by the force of law and habit, tradition and will. And then suddenly, its nerves and strength exhausted, the whole edifice collapses in a revolution or a war, some social cataclysm out of which survive, if anything, only memories and myths. The kaleidoscope falls into new patterns, and a new age begins which in its turn will crumble away after much glory and bloodshed. Atlantis, Crete, Carthage, Rome, Samarkand and the Inca Empire, the *ancien régime* and the Belle Epoque all finished in convulsions and surprises, quite easy to foresee for that godlike observer, the historian. Everything was still quite peaceful at Plessis-lez-Vaudreuil. But the precipice was already yawning at our feet.

What's false and sometimes foolish in films, plays, novels, histories, and even the sort of memoirs you have in your hand now, is the perspective, the partiality, the narrowness of the point of view. It's as if the author were just taking an arbitrary glance at a situation or a problem that was fashionable for a few months. But what meaning can there be in a novel that tells a love story without placing the characters in the context of the historical events which as we all know play an enormous part in our everyday preoccupations? Or without giving the details of their economic situation, which, as we knew before Marx and know still better since, plays a leading part in their reactions and their way of life? Conversely, how can a book on political or military history explain any decision without first showing its biological, emotional and—after Marx, here comes Freud!—sexual background? At any moment in a life everything is essential at the same time: geography, history, climate, family, money, perhaps cooking, religion, and memories of being bathed as children by the Breton nursemaid or the German governess. Balzac's genius consists in putting all the cards on the table. And if *Holy Week* and *Men of Goodwill* and *Hadrian's Memoirs* and *The Leopard,* to take a few titles at random, are books one remembers, it's because they bring to life a world together with its setting. Of course, the world isn't always the same. Some periods accord the first place to money, others to sex, others to art or force. Anyone can see at a glance which, of all these, is the characteristic sign of the Renaissance, the end of the nineteenth century, and our own age. Can one really present a true image if one treats of life today without mentioning the enormous importance of physical love and sex in our preoccupation, or of the Belle Epoque without speaking of money? In the long, yet in a way short, interval from 1938–9 to May 1940, and, in another way, amid the fury and the hope, right up to 1945, what stood out, underlined in red in everyone's life, was of course the political and military situation. Things had reached the point where no one could have imagined any play or novel set in the West in that period which didn't say something about the war and Hitlerism and the struggle between democracy and National Socialism. The most important character everywhere, in a family in Poland or a village in the South of France, in a factory in Wales or at Plessis-lez-Vaudreuil, was Adolf Hitler. For just under ten years, though those years left their mark on the whole century, he was the familiar figure of three or four generations, the companion of our maturity, the strange god of a whole universe of pyres burning in the darkness, of delirious youth, and banners. Like Charlie Chaplin's Great Dictator, he held the globe in his hands, and before dropping it and passing the ball to Comrade Stalin, he played terrible and fascinating games with it which might have put an end to thousands of years of history, of battles, bugles at dawn, and classical victories. France in 1939 was nothing but a stronghold— not very strong, alas!—besieged by the enemy. We were awaiting the attack. Did we hope that perhaps it would never come? Just wait a little, it would come. At Plessis-lez-Vaudreuil, as everywhere else, a siege mentality prevailed. We were shut up by an Austrian corporal who tried his hand at painting, more famous for us—listen, children!—than all your Marilyn Monroes and Brigitte Bardots, your Dayans and Nassers and Fidel Castros, in two sets of time and space which fitted inside each other like Russian dolls: Plessis-lez-Vaudreuil, with the mass of traditions and memories I've been trying to depict, and radical-socialist France at the end of the third prewar period my grandfather had lived through. Such is history and the fate of men.

There were still—*in illo tempore*—some marvelous times at Plessis-lez-Vaudreuil. It was the autumn of a world. People often spoke in low voices, as if someone were dead. We were waiting. The town crier's drum rang out over the square. Between announcements by the mayor about the next pig fair or the felling of the three elms near La Gâtine-Saint-Martin, the crier announced the call-up of certain categories of reservists. One wiped away a tear—La France! My grandfather went out of his own way to make a gesture, and shook hands with the socialist schoolmaster. What was more natural, since his own grandson now openly professed to be a communist? The amusing thing was that thirty years later, i.e., the other day, the schoolteacher's son was to become one of the leaders of the French Right. But of course my grandfather could have no idea of that. Before the great "general post" of social upheaval, there was this somewhat sinister togetherness, the short-lived reconciliation of those condemned to death. There was a general atmosphere of reconciliation. Claude used to come and spend a few days with us

occasionally. Dean Mouchoux wasn't there—he'd been dead for
years. But his young successor also held out his hand to the Republic. And the Republic took it: the prefect, invited for a hunting
expedition, went to mass. For a long time, out of consideration for
my grandfather, the "Salvam fac Rem publicam" which had succeeded the "Salvam fac Regem" had been delicately left out of the
ordinary of the mass. But now the Republic was in the place of
honor again, and my grandfather prayed for it. In the summer of
1914 we'd seen nationalism prevail over traditionalism, and now
once more we saw it prevail, in Philippe, over fascism. He too,
according to an ancient tradition, would fight for a regime he hated
against the companions in arms in whose songs he had once joined.
As against this, Maurice Chevalier used to sing an ironical song
which depicted the French army as made up of anglers and family
men, determined individualists who had nothing in common. Maurice Chevalier's worthy Frenchmen against the Teutonic Knights
and the death's head SS—before the tragedy, the bloody farce, the
sinister buffoonery was begun, the issue was decided in advance. But
at least there was national unity at Plessis-lez-Vaudreuil, as in the
rolling r's of the author of *Ma Pomme*. The man in the boater had
had a kind of genius. It was true—my grandfather was a monarchist, my cousin Philippe a fascist, my cousin Claude a communist.
And the whole of this little world, which had always made fun of
the regime, was getting ready, with a comic mixture of consternation and insouciance, to go and hang out its washing on the Sieg-
fried Line. It takes great misfortune to unite the French. People
were almost ready to thank Hitler for having restored at least a
semblance of unanimity among them. A little more bloodshed and
a little more misfortune, and the holy alliance of the people, in
which poets and ministers had raised antimilitarism to the height of
a national institution, would re-form around first a marshal and then
a general, who didn't at all agree with one another. Come! All the
newspapers on sale in the streets, all the posters on the walls, all the
radios on the air persuaded us: for this nation of humorists, all was
going to be for the best in the worst of all possible worlds. And the
cream of the jest was that it was true. The way we laughed at Paul

Reynaud and his "We shall conquer because we are the strongest."
We were the strongest. There was nothing stronger, in those days,
than industrial democracy. It was only going to take four years to
wake up. But the world, our English cousins, the Ukrainians, the
Jews in Poland, Hitler himself, and us—we were going to feel the
passage of those four years, those fifty months, those fifteen hundred days and fifteen hundred nights.

Of course, international politics weren't the only thing we ever
thought about. They were the framework within which the trivial
episodes of our family serial went on unfolding. Anne-Marie had
begun to take an interest in young men. Did she have lovers? I don't
think so. Not yet. But she was always on the telephone, thus exas-
perating my grandfather, who was still not used to the lightning
speed of modern communication. When she was in Paris she began
to come home late at night. She made up outrageously. She spent
a lot of time listening to jazz records, so succeeding in the difficult
feat of causing equal annoyance to her uncles Claude and Philippe
and to her great-grandfather. Instead of being concentrated on
diplomacy and strategy, in which, following Henri Bidou and
Geneviève Tabouis, twenty or thirty million Frenchmen had
become expert, not counting the superannuated and babes in the
cradle, family tension gladly switched its attention to morals.

Philippe had been very fond of women. You know the sort of life
Pierre and Ursula had led, first together, then apart. The uncle in
the Argentine and cousin Pauline still provided material for family
conversation around the table in the evening. But, come hell or high
water, marriage had remained for us an institution which had something sacred about it. The marvelous thing about it was that it stood
at the intersection of passion and self-interest, tenderness and power,
flesh and spirit, money and God. It was at one and the same time
very useful and very holy. What luck! There could be no question
of tampering with such a state of affairs. Marriage was not immune
from tension and crises, but in our family they remained as hidden
as possible. For a long time we'd preferred secrecy to scandal.
Instead of boasting of our extravagances and inconsistencies we
concealed them. No doubt that's why some of our enemies accused

us of hypocrisy. Of course, on the eve of the Second World War, we no longer subscribed to the immutable notions which reigned unchallenged at the end of the nineteenth century. We'd forgotten the singers and dancers and high-class courtesans, the Lady of the Camellias and Emilienne d'Alençon. The courtesans were dead, and we'd married Jewesses, women from the middle class, foreigners. But for a number of reasons—social, religious, traditional of course, and perhaps also economic—divorce hadn't been accepted among us. We didn't get divorced. It was forbidden. Even Pierre and Ursula hadn't been divorced. No, our family didn't believe in divorce. Up to the beginning of the century, up to the 1914 war and perhaps up to the end of the first third of the century and Uncle Paul's new political orientation, my grandfather, as a matter of principle, didn't receive either Jews or militant republicans, either Freemasons or divorcees. Certainly my grandmother never had them in her house. But after her death, exceptions of course rapidly multiplied. In the first place, one had to meet those members of the family who'd taken a wrong turning. And then, life soon became impossible without the republicans and the Jews. We ourselves were converted, if not really to Israel, at least to the Republic. But on the subject of divorce we remained inflexible. God, society, the family, morals, and tradition all came together in marriage. To give way about marriage was to give way about everything. We were fiercely attached to it. But as the Republic, the Jews, socialism, love of change had all one after the other attacked the solidarity of the family and opened yawning breaches in it, there was really no reason why divorce shouldn't have a go. It was to effect its thrust in the wake of the upheavals which had afflicted us ever since the death of the king and the rise of such scourges—for so we thought of them—as individualism and the rights of man. And it was to find an active ally in Anne-Marie.

There was a romantic air about those days before the war; everyone felt expectant, powerless, and ominously excited. The die was cast. It could be heard rolling along the Rhine, the Danzig corridor, the roads of Silesia, in the rumble of tanks and in the shrill of fifes or the thunder of swastika-covered drums. Our fate was beyond our own control. It was in the hands of an amateur painter, an unemployed corporal. We were once more experiencing the end of our world. Of course we were beginning to get used to it: it was exactly a hundred and fifty years since everything had crumbled around us before.

Perhaps you vaguely recall those country neighbors of ours who approved of Christopher Columbus, and whose slightly defective French both amused and annoyed my grandfather. Several of their children and grandchildren are still alive today, so I can't give their real name. The V.s were excellent folk, slightly ridiculous, even more conservative than we were, if that isn't a contradiction in terms, who'd gotten rich in the most respectable manner, through making socks and knitwear. They were snobs. We had plenty of faults, many defects, a few vices and repugnant aspects of our character. But of course we weren't snobs. Why not? Because, under our simplicity, our kindness, our economic collapse, and our ideological and social vicissitudes, we still had a vague idea that we were superior. Money didn't impress us, nor did worldly position or title or elegance: as to all those, history had given us as much as we wanted, thank God. Nor were we affected by intellectual snobbery: whether we were reactionaries like my grandfather or socialists like my cousin, we still stuck without self-consciousness to our convictions and our dreams. We didn't live for show or appearances, we really had no ulterior motives, we liked people and things for themselves, and we were quite comfortable about ourselves. Even Claude, who'd resented bearing our name, hadn't remained long between two political and social stools, in the no-man's-land of ideology. He'd soon settled down in *L'Humanité* and among his comrades in the international brigades, and he'd become friends with Malraux. There was nothing between our likes and dislikes and ourselves. What we wanted to have we had, and what we didn't have we despised. We had a slight contempt for money which had been earned. And it was precisely that kind of money which we'd lost. The other kind, the sort that remained to us, was not and never had been earned: it had always come to us from our lands and forests. We didn't suffer from the dreadful fever of envying what

we didn't have. You could say we had more pride than vanity; that
we tended to be self-satisfied and good-naturedly superior. Perhaps,
in that way, we offered history rods for our own backs. I don't claim
that the picture we gave of ourselves was altogether delightful. But
we weren't snobs. And the V.s were.

They came from a very humble background. The grandfather
was a wine merchant in Quimper or Vannes. The father had married the daughter of a tradesman in Quimper and had gradually
begun to acquire shops, warehouses, and factories which in less than
thirty or forty years founded the family fortunes. So long as we
didn't marry them, it would never have occurred to us to criticize
them for their humble origins. I believe I've already explained how,
in our folly or perhaps our wisdom, we made no distinction between a Breton sailor and a French ambassador, a prime minister and
a wine merchant. There were us and ours—the family, the cousins,
the dean, Jules and Jules' sons—and then there were all the rest: the
Rothschilds, the Rockefellers, the Einsteins, the schoolteacher at
Roussette, the policemen at Villeneuve, the ministers and deputies,
criminals, and the V.s. And all these were neither more nor less than
an appeals-court judge, an accountant in the audit office, or a gar-
bage collector. The grocer and the saddler and all the rest of the
little world of tradesmen at Plessis-lez-Vaudreuil were about midway between these two unequal parts of society and the universe.
But something drew the V.s toward us—a kind of fascination, our
reserve, our kindness, the no doubt irresistible combination of our
pride and our courtesy. As the irony of history would have it, the
V.s were on the way up and we were on the way down. We got
poorer every year, our role grew less important, we didn't count
any more, we were divided among ourselves. But the V.s were the
image of success and good luck. You might say that they were now
what the Remy-Michaults had been a hundred years before in all
their glory—but without their dark and disturbing side, without
their betrayals, without their great torments. The funny thing was
that the V.s were attracted because, for them, we stood for tradition
and rigor, at the very moment when we ourselves were abandoning
this heritage. Robert V., the eldest son, began to appear at horse

shows and fashionable dances and to be friendly with the Noailles and the Montesquiou-Fezenzacs at the exact time Pierre withdrew from the society he had once ornamented, the time when Uncle Paul committed suicide and Claude was converted to Marxism. The V.s were running after the very illusions which we were turning away from. But that was only one more reason for them to admire our ease and style and indifference to the vicissitudes of history— all that remained to us, in fact, of a vanished past.

Robert V. was a tall, good-looking young man not yet thirty, with black brilliantined hair, athletic and rather nice. He rode well, shot partridges according to all the rules of the art, drove his Talbot at record speed, and, unlike his parents, never made mistakes in pronunciation. But his real trump was that he entered into our lives in the shadow of Adolf Hitler and his equinoctial ravings. The best way to describe 1938 and 1939 is to say they were like a period of time outside time. Other years led somewhere, formed part of a continuous pattern, and you could make plans in them. But 1938 and 1939 were just an interval, a blind alley. One just knuckled under and let the days and weeks and months go by, hoping for a miracle—that Hitler and Goering and Goebbels and Himmler might die or be converted to liberalism, or that Nazism in Germany and Bolshevism in Russia would both simultaneously collapse. How did we think things were going to end? Perhaps by some prodigy: my mother and grandfather still had some hopes of Nostradamus' prophecies and Our Lady of Fatima. I think everyone dimly expected some catastrophe. At any rate, even as we were living through them, we ruled the twenty or thirty months leading up to the war out of history, out of our lives, out of the real sequence of time. They didn't count. They were a nightmare, a reprieve, an imaginary stretch of time, an error, an exception, a night in which we were like condemned men dreading the dawn. Even Philippe, and we know what his notions were, longed to emerge from this long pass between the cliffs and steeps of history, though for a French nationalist the outlook was obscure. But throughout the interval, the reprieve, the running of the gauntlet of axes and arrows, Anne-Marie, at Plessis-lez-Vaudreuil, where we were taking

refuge from the Nazi gas, went riding in the forest with her brother
Jean-Claude, her cousin Bernard, and Robert V.

As you may imagine, from earliest childhood to quite recently,
when she started to use makeup, Anne-Marie had been brought up
very strictly. In those days, passion could still find clear skies in
which to burst forth. Despite their own morals, Pierre and Ursula
had brought their daughter up with a combination of Prussian and
French rigor. When Ursula started to live her own life, Anne-Marie
was entrusted chiefly to the charge of her uncles, and I wonder
whether there wasn't a tinge of jealousy in the way Jacques, Philippe, Claude, and I applied the family rules. It was especially delightful to see Claude performing prodigies of subtlety in order to
reconcile his convictions with the most traditional and conventional
principles of female education. It was only because of the Sudetenland, the threat of war, the unusually long vacation in the Haute-
Sarthe, the interval and the respite, that Anne-Marie managed to see
Robert every day for months. My grandfather and the rest of us
were all the more unsuspecting because Robert was already married. Unhappily married, but married. He had married the daughter
of an extreme-Right deputy when she was very young, and they'd
separated after eighteen months. The deputy had once crossed
swords with Uncle Paul, criticizing him for compromising with the
Republic. All that—Hitler, the impossibility of making plans, the
fact that Robert was married, the fact that his father-in-law had the
right opinions, the peaceful, healthy life everyone led at Plessis-lez-
Vaudreuil, without the shadow of a nightclub or even a movie
theater—all these things made it possible for the young couple to
gallop through the family forests, followed at a distance by Jean-
Claude or Bernard, laughing or indifferent. They had to get some
fresh air, and what could be healthier than riding among the pines
and the oaks? Before the summer of 1939 was over, Plessis-lez-
Vaudreuil was struck by three simultaneous catastrophes: the declaration of war; our cook Marthe's daughter being abandoned by her
lover with a baby; and Anne-Marie announcing to all and sundry
that she was going to marry Robert V.

Marry Robert V.! The uncle in Argentina's swindling, cousin
Pauline's loose living, the trio of Pierre and Ursula and Mirette,
Philippe's fascism, Claude's conversion to the Communist Party, and
Uncle Paul's suicide had all caused less consternation than this outrageous news. We almost forgot his name, his social standing and
his insignificance. The thing was that he was married. "My dear
child, he's married. Don't you understand? Married." They kept on
repeating it to her as if she were deaf or mentally defective, as if
they were trying to find some language which might reach someone
who'd suddenly been struck with madness. But she wouldn't be
moved. "All right," she said. "He'll get a divorce." Another thunderbolt. Divorce? She must be crazy. Where had she gotten such monstrous ideas? Her mother? Her Uncle Claude? Perhaps from talking
to me? My grandfather, who'd faced up bravely to the Republic and
democracy, to scandal and sorrow, to ruin and decline, to the Popular Front and the death of God, was almost speechless with indignation. Divorce! So he was to be spared nothing! People had had the
effrontery to tell him that the Dreyfus affair was the search for
truth, and that socialism was the passion for justice. Well, here were
the fruits of these modern times: his great-granddaughter wanted
to marry a divorcé. His argument, the links between cause and
effect, were not evident to other people, but they were perfectly
clear to my grandfather. And poor Robert, who did his best to
flaunt his anti-Semitism and who loathed socialism, strutted about
naively in the midst of an uproar which called in question a whole
fifty years of evolution. As for Claude, he didn't know which way
to turn: it really was an awful shame to make the great principle
of liberation and progress serve the purposes of a bourgeois idiot
belonging to the extreme Right.

The arguments provoked by this crisis brought to light family
secrets which might have been thought buried forever under the
silences of the past. We learned with astonishment that Aunt Marguerite, though she hadn't actually asked for a divorce, would in the
natural course of things have had every reason to resort to this
frightful extremity. Why "in the natural course of things"? She had

been married to Uncle Odon, one of the members of the family who'd died a hero's death in 1916 or 1917. Well ... he ... she ... well, to put it plainly, Uncle Odon was a homosexual. And his father and brothers and uncles had made it clear to him that the war was an almost unique opportunity for a man who was dishonored to disappear, to fail to come back. He didn't come back, and his name was inscribed proudly on the war memorial at Roussette where my grandfather paid his respects among the tricolors—not, needless to say, on the Fourteenth of July, but on All Souls' Day, sanctified and purified by following All Saints'. Uncle Odon was dead, the honor of the family had been entrusted to German machine guns and shrapnel, but Aunt Marguerite hadn't divorced him; she was a widow, which was a much better solution. We didn't go so far as to ask Anne-Marie to urge Robert to kill himself, to send him to the Sahara or suggest that he should assassinate Hitler or Stalin, though this would have had the advantage of killing several birds with one stone. All we asked was that she shouldn't marry him. She hesitated. She struggled. But when you're divided between several worries, at least you're not obsessed by one, and the woes of Marthe's daughter and the problems of Anne-Marie did much to cushion the family from the shock of the declaration of war. Robert went off to join his tank regiment, leaving a rather vague arrangement. Perhaps they were engaged? At any rate, Anne-Marie hadn't married him. And everyone breathed a secret sigh of relief and thanked Heaven that she wasn't expecting a child, like the cook's daughter. But the shadow of divorce had fallen over the family at the same time as the shadow of war. And I don't know which of these two specters frightened us more.

There was another member of the family for whom the summer of 1939 wasn't very gay—I mean, for whom it was even gloomier than for most people in France: Claude. At the end of August 1939, right in the middle of the Anne-Marie business, we heard the astonishing news of the nonaggression pact between Stalin and Hitler. Two or three months before, Pierre had told us rather uneasily that Litvinov was being replaced by Molotov as Soviet foreign minister, a piece of news which, like many another, we couldn't make head or tail of. Pierre, who'd met the charming Joachim von Ribbentrop several times when the future German foreign minister was in the champagne business, didn't know either Litvinov or Molotov. But he still had enough friends among diplomats and politicians to know more than the rest of the family—that wasn't difficult—about what was going on in the world. As soon as he heard about the change of Russian foreign minister he'd scented danger, and when the signature of the pact between Molotov and Ribbentrop was announced he told us that the red curtain was going up and war was inevitable. And wasn't the curtain coming down a little further on the family destiny? God's pleasure moved in a mysterious way, moving our fate further every day from the memory of Eleazar, and bringing it ever closer to Molotov and Hitler and Stalin. A lot Anne-Marie cared for Stalin and Molotov. Or for Eleazar. She went riding with Robert around the pools in the forest at Plessis-lez-Vaudreuil. For her it was the Bay of Naples, Lake Maggiore, the view of the Grand Canal from the Rialto, the meeting of the White and Blue Nile: amid the follies of history, despite a past that meant nothing to her, she was having her first love affair. Love doesn't love the past. It upsets and overturns things, it only looks forward, it is the enemy of tradition. Have you noticed how small a part it plays, really, in the family's history? We sensed vaguely that it, together with socialism and modern manners, threatened to destroy the work of centuries. Love is democratic. It's on the side of revolution. It is revolution. Riding with Robert through the forest which still echoed with hunting horns and all the memories of the past, Anne-Marie did as much as Captain Dreyfus or Jaurès or Joseph Caillaux to bring down the crumbling walls of our ancient house and open up to the future that fortress of the past. At almost the same time, Jacqueline, the cook's daughter, was struggling desperately to see that Monsieur Machavoine's grandson should have a father, and Hitler at last brought the name of Danzig into world history.

Claude was suffering. The German-Soviet pact which heralded the war was welcomed at Plessis-lez-Vaudreuil with a kind of enthusiasm. The world was beautiful and straightforward. Perhaps we were to be beaten and crushed and trampled underfoot by this unnatural alliance, but at least all our enemies were in the same camp, that of ignominy and reprobation. Philippe was relieved. Claude was in despair. Our hearts were about to beat faster for Finland perhaps than for France—Finland, attacked, thank God, by the friends of our enemies. In Marshal Mannerheim we were to find the first hero we had had for a long time, the heir of Joan of Arc, the Grand Condé, the maréchal de Saxe and younger brother to Doge Morosini and Jean Sobieski. Finland wasn't big enough to take on the red bear of the steppes. But it didn't matter. She was holding out against history. Everything was going well for us. Everything was going badly for Claude. Stalin Hitler's ally! Claude's new world collapsed before our old one.

Claude's troubles brought me closer to him. I could understand passion if I looked around me in the peaceful corridors of Plessis-lez-Vaudreuil: there was Jacqueline's anguish, Claude's despair, Anne-Marie's bliss. The undistinguished Robert and Machavoine junior, the tumult of history, all produced the same effect: hearts turned upside down in the struggle with men. I could see Claude literally bite his fingers and go around in circles. The proletarian revolution allying itself with fascism. What was the use of having broken with so much, only to find oneself smiling and shaking hands with the invaders of Prague and the butchers of Guernica?

Later, Claude would pull himself together. He would explain to me that the Moscow pact was the outcome of Munich and the weakness of the democracies. It was a wise, anticipatory move, a marking time, a parenthesis within a parenthesis, a respite within the respite. But the harm was done. The heads of Machiavelli and Talleyrand were rising up behind Marx and Lenin. In socialism too, the end, as always, justified the means. From then onward, in the tall shadow of Stalin, it was to be dragged through the mud of the trials, the snow of Siberia, the blood of Prague and Budapest.

And that was more or less how, through the still heated corridors of Plessis-lez-Vaudreuil, the greatest war of all time arrived. I'm writing thirty or more years afterward. How far away it seems, this war of yesterday or the day before! As far away as the Fronde or the Seven Years War, as far away as Austerlitz or Jena. Many of those who played a part in it are still here, and yet the play itself is already retreating into the past, seized in the grip of history. It's not yet fixed and petrified and motionless, like the fall of Rome or the Hundred Years War. It is still occasionally moved, by memory, anger, hatred, or remorse. But young people look on it as Uncle Paul looked on the Commune or Sedan at the beginning of this century, or as Anne-Marie looked at the Great War as she rode with Robert through the forest. Time takes strange forms in the eyes of memory. It can expand or shrink, multiply or diminish. Men of fifty often are surprised nowadays at young people's vagueness when they hear the name of Churchill or Hitler or Stalingrad. But think what the veterans of 1914 meant to you, when you were twenty, in 1939 or 1940. Their war was twenty years old too. And ours is thirty. I remember that in the fifties the gay twenties seemed very far away to me. And in 1925 itself, the turn of the century seemed like another world. But now 1950 seems quite near, within hand's reach. And yet there's as long between 1925 and 1950 as between 1950 and now, and between 1900 and 1925. Days, weeks, and months don't all pass at the same rate before they fall into the abyss of the past. Time is like the sea: it's very difficult to measure distances in it. In the second it takes to turn one's head, everything may vanish. And yet a whole lifetime isn't long enough for our past to take its place in the chilly eternity of passionless history. History is intermingled with our life, and we die too fast for it to be disentangled. And yet our own lives are almost history to those who are born after us. They have only to grow a little colder and they will be motionless forever.

I still walked about Plessis-lez-Vaudreuil, but uneasily. The boys made themselves useful, trying to imitate the prodigious efforts of the Hitler Youth on the other side of the Rhine. Working with Jules the Third, still proudly reigning, and Jules' nephew, they sawed up branches to make firewood for the old people's home. Every day, in the morning, at noon, and in the evening, we used to gather in the drawing room to listen to the news. For the rest of our lives, now, we would listen to the news. Soon we would watch it. First there had been Daladier and Reynaud, then it would be Pétain and his speeches, de Gaulle and his calls to the nation, voices in the darkness that belonged to unknown faces. *"Honneur et patrie,"* *"Voici la France libre"*—to listen to these free voices, we shut the doors and windows and put out the lights. Almost in the dark, we would sit there as my grandfather hunted for Stalingrad on the map by the glow of the radio. Then there would be the liberation of Paris, the snipers at Notre-Dame, the departure of the general, Queen Elizabeth's coronation, Dien Bien Phu, Churchill's funeral, May 13, de Gaulle again, the generals' *putsch*, de Gaulle again, his extraordinary press conferences with him standing on a chair and waving his arms, his elections and referendums, the excitement of May '68—"I shall not retire. The people will come to their senses" —the French people's "No" to what was called dictatorship, the general's departure and death. In 1939 we entered into the immediate communication of history, what it sounded and looked like, and we entered into it for good.

I still walked about Plessis-lez-Vaudreuil, but uneasily. I looked at the walls and painted ceilings, the old portraits in the drawing room, the books in the library. What they had survived in the past! The fury of flames, of men, of war and revolution. Would it hold out now? Our solid universe, anchored in eternity, suddenly seemed very fragile to me. I went back to the drawing room. My grandfather had obviously been listening to the news on Radio Paris. He was sitting in the Louis Quinze armchair which was upholstered in rather worn mauve silk, dozing over *Le Temps, Le Journal des débats, Le Figaro,* and *L'Action française.* From the big wooden box, with its dark dial and three round knobs, came a low murmur: perhaps Jean Sablon or Rina Ketty or, if one was lucky, Charles Trenet. I used not to listen much in those days. A few more years and Edith Piaf, with her accordionists and her lovers for a day, would join General de Gaulle and Brigitte Bardot in our imaginary waxworks. I went upstairs to ask Anne-Marie to send someone to tell the young dean that we were expecting him to dinner. I found her in the attic, in Robert's arms. They blushed to the roots of their hair and told

me they were hunting for some old clothes in a trunk, to dress up
Véronique. Old clothes . . . dressing up? I see. I suggested they go
downstairs, if possible separately. I called in at the kitchen and went
back to the drawing room. I'd walked a couple of kilometers inside
the chateau that day. I took up my Mauriac, my Malraux, Aragon's
Beaux Quartiers, the last Morand. A world was ending. Tomorrow
it would be war.

THREE

1

Charles V's Letter

ON JUNE 18, AT TEATIME, A GERMAN colonel came into the main drawing room at Plessis-lez-Vaudreuil. My grandfather stood waiting for him, very pale, his hands resting on the back of the chair where my mother or Aunt Gabrielle often sat knitting or reading. Old Jules opened the door and the colonel halted on the threshold. He clicked his heels and saluted. My grandfather bowed his head.

It was the second time that the Prussians, to use my grandfather's expression, had occupied the chateau. In 1815, after Waterloo, we had been hosts to the Russians. In January 1871 my grandfather, then aged fourteen, had seen the Uhlans come. Now, I suspected, his stiffness and the restraint of his greeting imitated the attitude of his own grandfather in 1871, and it struck me that that same grandfather had perhaps modeled his actions on those of his own father after the downfall of the emperor. The interesting thing was that on each occasion the regime which had fallen to the invader was alien to us, and sometimes hostile. Ah well! In all our country's troubles, something at least—and something essential—remained unchanged: the family.

The colonel spoke French with quite a good accent. We discovered later that he had written a thesis on the military spirit in the work of Alfred de Vigny. I stood a little behind my grandfather:

no doubt I was trying in my turn to learn how I should behave in
the presence of some future invader. The army had rejected Claude
because of his arm, and me because of my health. But we had both
managed to insinuate ourselves into its ranks and see a little action
between the Sambre and the Escaut, and then between Amiens and
Beauvais. I had had no news of Claude. Jacques and Robert V. were
already dead, but we did not know it. I myself, after having been
caught in the collapse of General Altmayer's Tenth Army, had
come under the orders of General Weygand on about the 10th or
12th of June, and on the morning of June 18 I found myself about
ten kilometers from Plessis-lez-Vaudreuil. So I decided to go there
for a few hours' sleep before continuing my desperate attempt to
reach the Loire. I collapsed onto my bed at about eleven in the
morning. Just after four o'clock Anne-Marie came into my room.
I had heard her running along the corridor, just as she used to do
when the only telephone in the chateau rang in my grandfather's
room, and she would rush to answer it because she knew that it
would be for her, and that it was Robert. But this time it was not
Robert: from what heaven, from what underworld, could he have
called us, his mouth full of earth and his face covered with blood?
Anne-Marie did not knock, but flung open the door and cried, "The
Germans!"

The Germans! So they were here. They had come from Pomerania and Lower Saxony, from the Black Forest and the lakes of
Bavaria, from the peak of Brocken in the Harz Mountains and from
the Walpurgisnacht, from old university towns with peaceful little
squares and names steeped in legend. They had crossed the Rhine
and the Meuse, the Ardennes, the Marne and the Seine, and they
were making for the Loire and the two seas of which the Barbarians
have always dreamed. And now they were descending upon our
house and its sacred memories. Telling myself that history was
about to be enacted before my eyes, I ran my hand through my hair,
did up a few buttons, ineffectually smoothed my crumpled uniform,
and rushed down to the drawing room where my grandfather was
waiting. He put his hands on my shoulders and drew me to him. A
few seconds later, Colonel von Witzleben entered the room where

Henri IV was said to have wooed a beautiful ancestress of mine called Catherine, and where men armed with pikes and axes had come to arrest two of our family a hundred and fifty years before. Collaboration and resistance both entered Plessis-lez-Vaudreuil with the same stiff, smooth step.

Amid the slow progress of history, with its meanderings, its hesitations, its marshes and its pauses, there suddenly appear, often with pain and bloodshed, great blocks of violence and comparative simplicity: the capture of Constantinople in 1453, the discovery of America in 1492, Marignon in 1515, the great Revolution, Trafalgar in 1805 and Waterloo in 1815. From June 1940 up to the liberation of Paris, German France is like a gray-and-brown stain on history. Things happened so rapidly it was like one of those films where everybody suddenly starts to run and everything that moves seems to have gone mad. And yet memory dwells on them without too much pain, and much more easily than on those peaceful years when every day is like another. This is because the Armistice, Mers el-Kebir and Dakar, the invasion of Russia, Pearl Harbor, America's entry into the war, and the various landings in Europe are so many bearings to which we can attach our memories. Throughout all those dark years the life of the family continued to be intermingled with history. Jacques and Robert V. were killed in 1940, Philippe set off for Spain again in 1942, Claude was arrested in 1943, I was arrested in 1944, and Michel was sentenced to death in 1945: so many white or black milestones in the baleful pleasures of the God of our family and of Hosts.

From 1940 to 1944, one lot of German troops succeeded another at Plessis-lez-Vaudreuil, with intervals when we were left to ourselves. There were airmen, infantrymen, parachutists, mechanized cavalry, S.S. men with their death's heads, Ukrainians, Vlasov's Georgians, and even, for a few days, sailors on their way to one of our ports in Brittany. But people and places tend to be fixed in the memory in terms of one face which combines all their various features and aspects: Victor Hugo with his beard, Verlaine with his glass of absinthe, and the aging Pétain. And my mental image of Plessis-lez-Vaudreuil during the war consists of tanks, trucks, enormous motorcycles in the courtyard of the chateau, on the paths, and on the grass around the stone table. When the troops were about to leave or to go on an exercise and all the engines started to rev up, heaven and earth were filled with a terrible thudding, and all the windows in the chateau began to tremble

My grandfather managed to keep his own room in the tower, together with two little antechambers which were crammed with some of our most precious souvenirs. He had two hideous stoves installed, and all the members of the family used to come in turn to visit him amid the unwonted clatter of gas engines. He scarcely left his tiny kingdom except to go for an hour's walk, morning and evening, in the grounds of the chateau. With exemplary self-discipline, he led the life of a voluntary recluse, a prisoner de luxe. Several times, headquarters staffs decked with Iron Crosses and oak leaves established themselves at Plessis-lez-Vaudreuil. Various generals and colonels wrote to my grandfather—in one instance, on a crested family card, discovered in one of the drawers of a commode in the big drawing room—inviting him to dine with them. Each time my grandfather replied, with punctilious yet ironical courtesy, that circumstances forbade the master of the house to enter his own dining room and that he himself had vowed not to go outside the limits of the area where he was still at home. Inevitably, there were a certain number of farcical, trivial, and tragic incidents. Whenever a German officer or soldier saluted him, my grandfather always replied by silently raising his hat and staring into space. General von Stülpnagel, on a tour of inspection, came to spend a couple of days at Plessis-lez-Vaudreuil. My grandfather came across him between the house and the stone table. The general looked at this very respectable old gentleman, rendered more majestic and impressive than ever by sorrow and age. My grandfather just glanced at the general as he stood there motionless. The general made no sign: He was commander of all the German troops in occupied France. My grandfather kept walking, leaning on his stick. That evening after dinner a sergeant came and told my grandfather that the general was waiting for him.

"An invitation?" asked my grandfather.

The sergeant nodded.

"Well, please tell the general I don't go out in the evening."

Ten minutes later, the sergeant was back.

"An order?" said my grandfather.

The sergeant nodded. My grandfather followed him out of the room. The general was sitting behind a big desk which had replaced the billiard table. Several officers were with him. My grandfather gazed around him disapprovingly—he did not like the new arrangements and the taste that they betrayed. An officer began to explain in indifferent French that the general had been surprised when he had not been saluted.

"So was I," said my grandfather.

Then the general got on his high horse. He started shouting that it was for the vanquished to salute the victors, and through an interpreter he asked my grandfather what rank he had held in the French army.

"A humble one," said my grandfather, who had never been even a private nor ever received the slightest distinction or decoration from the Republic. "But I am in my own house."

This didn't go down very well, and the general started to storm again. My grandfather, twice a Grandee of Spain, a Knight of the Golden Fleece, of the Annonciada, of the Black Eagle, and of the Order of St. Andrew and St. George, Grand Bailiff or Prior of various supreme military and equestrian orders somewhat forgotten by modern historians, dimly sensed that this was a marvelous occasion for him to express at last what had been on his mind for a hundred and fifty years, and what was impossible to mention in the piping times of peace without sounding ridiculous. He settled down in the chair which a soldier had placed for him and calmly and firmly declared that while it was always possible to set aside the rules of the game, since they were now being appealed to, his individual position permitted him to expect to be greeted first by everybody, no matter who they might be, with the possible exception of cardinals, princes of the blood, heads of state, and field marshals. He couldn't think of anybody else in the world to whom he was obliged to show deference. For good measure, he added that if by any chance the general was a field marshal he was very ready to offer him his apologies. But if this was not the case, he expected the general to apologize to him.

By a trick of history, it was our faults, our pride, what others called our arrogance, which drove us into resistance and lent my grandfather a kind of national and popular halo. It was the winter of 1940–41. It was cold. World history had already encountered many surprises. But the ad hoc jury set up by the general was stupefied by my grandfather. The Germans were prepared for anything, from a nationalist declaration of faith to a terrified climbing down. But this diatribe à la Saint-Simon dumfounded them. As he delivered it, my grandfather bore a somewhat ludicrous resemblance to the comte d'Orgel, the prince de Guermantes or the duc de Maulévrier in Robert de Flers' and Armand de Caillavet's *L'Habit vert.* But he was speaking before the occupying power, sitting in judgment. The accused had ceased to be a joke and become a hero. I think he would have quite liked to get himself shot for making fun of the Germans in such a fundamental cause as the reputation of our name and the respect due the family. But the cream of the jest is that the old gentleman had succeeded in impressing the Germans. He received no apologies, but he was seen back to his room by a colonel and a captain who stood at attention and saluted him at his door.

He stood motionless for a moment on the threshold of his room, and looked at the colonel. He did not look at the captain, nor did he hold out his hand or bow. He simply said, "Thank you, my friend," in the inimitable tone which constituted our only talent, and vanished into his room.

A year or more later, during the winter of 1941–42, a rather strange story put our national feelings to the test once more. The house was occupied at the time by the German Luftwaffe. My grandfather was still a refugee in the tower, in what he called his pillbox or personal prison. One evening when he was out for a walk with Anne-Marie, they noticed a German of about forty, tall, almost gray-haired, and wearing an Iron Cross, whose manner and demeanor had something both impressive and charming about them.

Next day and on the days that followed they came across him several times in the house or in the garden. The German officer saluted without saying anything. According to the now-unchanging ritual, my grandfather stared into space and touched his hat, and Anne-Marie proudly threw back her head and drew close to his side.

I was still at Plessis-lez-Vaudreuil at the time of poor Robert V.'s transfiguration. The news of his death took a long time to reach us. We heard about it around the end of August or the beginning of September 1940. The news that Jacques had been killed in the Ardennes trying to rejoin General Corap had reached us very quickly, but Robert had been listed as missing for two or three months. At last, one of those sinister salmon-pink field postcards, with blanks to be filled in, which never announced anything but disaster, arrived at Plessis-lez-Vaudreuil.

This card is strictly reserved for family correspondence. Strike out what does not apply. Do not write anything except in the spaces provided.

N.B. Any card which treats of anything but family matters will not be delivered. It may be destroyed.

NAME:...................... DATE: ....
is
Well..........
Tired..........
Slightly/seriously ill/wounded..........
Dead..........
Prisoner..........
Would like news of ....
Would like supplies of ....
Is back at .... *Works at*....................
Is due to take up a course at ....
Has passed an examination in ....
Is due to go to .... *on*.................

Affectionately/With Love

SIGNATURE:

The card bore the name Robert V., and the word "Dead" was perfunctorily underlined.

As soon as we knew how he had met his end, the *bête noire* was transformed into a knight in armor, a figure from a stained-glass window, a model for children to admire and imitate. He had, moreover, been recommended for a decoration: singlehanded, for six hours, he had defended a broken-down tank and two machine guns against a hundred Waffen S.S. on the approaches to a bridge over the Meuse. I was quite sure of the significance of his death: as if in obedience to our secret thoughts, he had deliberately set out to be killed. We never talked about it. But we knew, deep down, that the spirit of the family was not altogether innocent of the death of him whom we had now turned into a hero. I am not going to dwell here on Anne-Marie's sorrow. Human strength is limited. She had already had to struggle too much against the structure of our ancient family, still so rigid despite all the upheavals which had beset it. Robert's death was a tragedy for Anne-Marie, heartrending, shattering. And yet at the same time, in the cruelty of life and its terrible reversals, I think it was a kind of relief. Rebel as she might against the rules of the family, it was still too soon to throw them off completely. Now that he was dead, praise mounted on all sides to the memory of the beloved Robert, who had been such a good rider. But I'm not sure that in everyday life, far away from the banks of the Meuse and his machine guns, he would have been substantial enough to fill Anne-Marie's life. It is always very strange to see the fates of our nearest and dearest working themselves out: we were amazed to see all the impatience and the ardor there really was in Anne-Marie. No, Robert was not the man to fulfill all those expectations. And the cruel thing was that Anne-Marie herself, it seems to me, gradually came to realize that, in its pitiless unfolding, history was right and she was wrong. In the end she came to reproach herself for not lamenting her dead love more passionately. Her tears were all the more bitter because they were not unquenchable.

Meanwhile the rest of us, who had rejected Robert when he was alive, adopted him now that he was dead. Jacques' death had been a deep sorrow to all of us—to his brothers, his mother, his grandfather, and, if I may say so, to myself. And we associated the memory of Robert V. with the memory of Jacques, who was so very dear to us. The grave sorted everything out. We had always gotten along better with the dead than with the living.

You see what I'm driving at, a year or eighteen months after Robert's death. The German airman was the first man Anne-Marie looked at after the tragic end to her first love affair. Of course she didn't actually look at him, but she saw him immediately. He was more than attractive, marvelously tactful, and extremely distinguished. As for him, how could he have failed to notice, in the grounds of that ancient chateau, gloomy amid the gloominess of the time, that dazzling girl walking beside the old man? One morning my grandfather received a letter written in excellent French. Of course it came from our airman. It was signed Karl-Friedrich von Wittgenstein. The German of Plessis-lez-Vaudreuil was Ursula's cousin.

The signature was not the only thing that was remarkable about the letter. It enclosed what seemed to be a very ancient document. The letter explained that these were instructions signed by Charles V, asking a Wittgenstein of the period to meet an envoy of the king of France, who bore our own name, at Trier. In memory of his visit to France, he said, the German would like to offer this rare manuscript to my grandfather for the archives of Plessis-lez-Vaudreuil. He had remembered seeing it among his family papers, and had sent to Prussia for it.

As you know, my grandfather took a passionate interest in every kind of family souvenir. He hesitated for a whole week. He consulted Anne-Marie and every other member of the family he was able to contact in those difficult days. At last he gave his answer. I still have the draft of his letter, addressed, in French, naturally, "To Major von Wittgenstein, Plessis-lez-Vaudreuil." The letter expresses his grateful thanks: he was touched by the major's thought and by his gesture. But circumstances and history forbade him to accept. "We are all subject to events and laws which prevail over our private lives and sometimes over our wishes. I shall never forget the bonds which have grown up between us across frontiers and centuries. If I could have done so, I would gladly have accepted your friendly gesture. But history forbids. Later, perhaps, when there is peace between our two countries, you will come back one day to Plessis-lez-Vaudreuil, and then you will be greeted by us all with esteem and affection which can at last be unhidden and freely expressed. And then you will give me, or my grandchildren, if I am no longer in this world, this fine letter from Charles V which contains our two names."

But Charles V's letter did not come back to us. Colonel von Wittgenstein, then serving in Russia under General von Paulus, was killed at Stalingrad. The news reached us from Switzerland, via some cousins of Ursula's, toward the beginning of spring 1943. It was one of the rare occasions on which I saw my grandfather weep. I had seen him weep for the deaths of his sons and grandsons. And now I saw him weep for the death of this stranger, this enemy, who had, in the silence of history, perhaps without knowing it, become his friend. I don't know if the colonel left any brothers or nephews. I don't even know if he was married. I never tried to find out. Charles V's letter will not enter into the family. And I wonder if either the family or the letter still exists.

The German airmen stayed quite a long while. Wittgenstein went away three times, but managed to come back twice. He seemed to have grown fond of Plessis-lez-Vaudreuil. Every morning when they came down, Anne-Marie and my grandfather used to find a single flower in a vase on the little table at the foot of the stairs, where since time immemorial we had left our letters. Thence, under the surveillance of Jules or Estelle, his wife, they were mysteriously conveyed to the post. There was no more gasoline and no more heating, and my grandfather's table was frugal, to say the least. But in the evening, or early in the morning, Anne-Marie still went out riding in the forest on the only horse we had left, which by daily efforts we somehow managed to provide with oats. He was called Avenger, a very good name. Robert was no longer there, nor Bernard—he was away at school—and Jean-Claude was absorbed in other occupations, which we shall refer to later. But there was a silent horseman who galloped through the forest on a beautiful white horse: Major von Wittgenstein. One couldn't say that Anne-Marie went riding in the forest of Plessis-lez-Vaudreuil accompanied by a German officer. No—she went riding alone, and allowed no one to accompany her or talk to her. But the rider of the white horse followed her like a distant, silent shadow. Anne-Marie would leave the stable and ride across the park into the ancient forest where she knew every tree, every wind in the path, every copse and clearing. After a few moments she would see, standing out against the sky at the end of a path, the familiar silhouette. She would ride on. The horseman would pass her, greet her without a word, and gallop off; then he would reappear a little farther off and follow her at a distance of a few yards, the whole length of one of the rides. It was not to be a long love story. But it was a love story. Many years later, in Rome perhaps or Cannes, Anne-Marie, still beautiful, famous throughout almost the whole world, and both blessed and bruised by life, would tell me that perhaps no one had ever loved her more than the taciturn cavalier in the forests of the war.

One morning, as she was going out with my grandfather for a walk in what remained of the orchard, Anne-Marie found, in place of the usual rose or jasmine, a beautiful mixed bunch of twenty or thirty flowers. They bore a card which read: "With respectful greetings from Wittgenstein." Underneath, in small letters—a touch of bad taste amid all the delicacy: after all, this suitor did belong to the occupying forces—was written "p.p.c." This stood for *pour prendre congé*, to take leave or say goodbye. It was like a cry for help.

That evening, as usual, Anne-Marie rode out on Avenger in the direction of the Arbres-Verts. The phantom horseman was waiting for her near the lake. The evening is often very beautiful in that part of the Haute-Sarthe where our house stood, between its ancient forest, the heath, the woods and fields, and the rather melancholy lakes. It was a bright, mild evening. Anne-Marie urged her horse into a trot. The German came closer to her than he had ever allowed

himself to do before in all their strange rides together. But no more
than on previous occasions did they exchange a word. After about
a quarter of an hour, the horses of their own accord fell into a
walking pace. And the girl and the German went slowly and still
silently through the fields, the clearings, the intersections in the
paths, where a few years earlier a lively crowd of grooms and
pink-coated huntsmen disported themselves among the hounds,
now either dead or dispersed. From time to time, Wittgenstein
turned toward Anne-Marie. She felt his look imploring her. I can
easily imagine the German's feelings. I too had often looked at my
young niece and admired the purity of her profile, the simplicity
and beauty of her features, the lively contours of her open countenance. And then I would feel proud: this lithe body, this face, this
eagerness for life, was still a bit of us, a bit of this pleasure of God
which we embodied on earth. I can imagine the despair that enemy
officer must have felt, divided by history from what he admired.
Everything that for us was pride and gratitude was for him but
absence. They ambled through the silent forest. The oaks, the birds,
the cloudless sky, the mild air, knew nothing of the war dividing
men. Perhaps there is nothing stronger than the great melancholy
happiness to which he was a prey. Night fell. Afterward, Anne-
Marie couldn't remember very well what happened next. They
passed a cross which had been put up in the sixteenth century on
the site of a battle in which several members of branches of our
family, Catholics and Protestants, had brutally slaughtered each
other. Its local name was La Croix des Quatre Chemins—the crossroads cross. By it they dismounted and, still without saying a word,
kissed.

"There was a man I might have loved," Anne-Marie told me. But
how precarious are things, our poor lives, our frail hearts, history.
The night we received the news of Wittgenstein's death, the night
I saw my grandfather weep, I think Anne-Marie already had a soft
spot for the tall, dark, curly-haired fellow who led a Resistance
group near La Flèche.

Anne-Marie was not the only one with passions. In 1940, and for
many years afterward, long after the Liberation and victory, there

were two men in our lives. Two men, two soldiers: Marshal Pétain and General de Gaulle. The marshal, if one may put it like that, had fired the first shot by laying down his arms. Even before the Germans arrived at Plessis-lez-Vaudreuil, my grandfather, sitting with the dean in the big drawing room, had listened to the speech I myself had heard some fifty kilometers to the north, through the open windows of the inn of a village we were passing through:

"Frenchmen!

"At the request of the president of the Republic, I today assume the leadership of the government of France . . . Sure in the trust of the whole nation, I offer myself to France to lessen its sorrow."

When Marshal Pétain paid us his second visit I had joined my grandfather, and Colonel von Witzleben was already our guest.

"The spirit of pleasure has prevailed over the spirit of sacrifice. People have demanded rather than served. They have wished to save themselves effort; and now they encounter sorrow."

And again, a few days later: *"I hate the lies which have done us so much harm. The earth does not lie. It is still our refuge. It is France itself. A field which is allowed to fall fallow is a part of France which is dying. A field newly sown is a part of France which is reborn. Our defeat has sprung out of our slackness. The spirit of pleasure destroys what the spirit of sacrifice built. I summon you first and foremost to an intellectual and moral revival."*

My older readers will still recall that tremulous voice rising out of anguish and the whirlwind. My grandfather listened, stricken, standing among the family gathered together in the drawing room. What he heard pierced him to the heart. The references to family, land, agriculture and the country, morality; the denunciation of error and easy ways out; the exaltation of the spirit of sacrifice in contrast to the spirit of pleasure—all these expressed what my grandfather himself felt in the depths of his soul. The voice of Barrès and Péguy, which he had so often contrasted with the wickedness of Gide and the complications of Proust, echoed in the background behind the voice of the marshal. From the first moment of the expected defeat, my grandfather ranged himself unhesitatingly behind the victor of Verdun.

Perhaps you have already realized that throughout the German occupation my grandfather was always to be at one and the same time, and with one and the same heart, favorable to Vichy and hostile to the Germans? In his view, Marshal Pétain, transformed into a political Janus, was really two people, one good and one bad. The bad side was expressed in President Laval; in the meeting in Montoire, in which, by an ultimate paradox, there still survived the subtle and lethal trickery of the defunct Republic; in shaking hands with Hitler; in the measures against the Jews. The Jews were suddenly back again in my grandfather's good graces. He even went so far as to hide several of them in the gamekeepers' cottages in the forest, and for one moment, perhaps out of solidarity with the memory of Aunt Sarah, contemplated wearing the Star of David himself. The good side of Pétain embodied that which was sacred, safeguarded the highest values of fidelity and patriotism, and sacrificed to them not only the marshal's own person, but also his place in history, leaving Frenchmen's scorn and hatred to concentrate upon the bad side.

While Pétain's handsome countenance, radiating military glory and rustic nobility, was, through papers, posters, stamps, and children's exercise books, being engraved on everybody's mind, there suddenly arose a murmur like thunder—another voice, the voice of refusal and perseverance, coming to us from across the sea. The legend had begun. Perhaps never in the course of history had there been a symmetry so amazingly well adapted for textbooks and schoolchildren's memories. On one side there was the native land, the soil, peasant good sense, the eye and what the eye could see, realism, the past, the immediate, obedience, and saying "Yes": that was the marshal, in Vichy. On the other side was the sea, exile, adventure, the voice and what the ear could hear, reflection piercing as a thunderbolt, the future, challenge, revolt, and saying "No": that was the general, in London. A new and extraordinary page was being written in the history of France. Its two elementary principles —in which the dim memory of men would see, a couple of thousand years hence, a mythical struggle, a legendary epic whose protagonists intellectuals would say had never existed—were now fighting to the death, rending each other, excommunicating one another, condemning one another to death, drawing along behind them thousands upon thousands of fanatical supporters who had entrusted their existence and their honor to the one or the other. Everything combined to lend the conflict a dramatic character, not only on the political, but also on the sociological and metaphysical planes: the bonds which united the two men, their friendship within the military caste, their common origin, their common love of words, their common yet contrasted love of glory and of France. France's situation was never more terrible than in those years of disaster. And yet never did it offer so many opportunities for every kind of dream, every kind of greatness. Those whose task it was to foster the dreams of men and to celebrate their actions were for many years to find inexhaustible sources of inspiration, fury and faith in the struggle of the general against the marshal. Some would die of it.

The name of the man in London meant almost nothing to my grandfather and me. I think we'd heard it twice before: once on the occasion of an armored counteroffensive at the end of May, near Abbeville or Montcornet, and once during a government reshuffle by Paul Reynaud during the last ministry of the Third Republic, when an acting brigadier was made undersecretary of state for war —a specialty for which he was better qualified than anyone else in the world, not from the point of view of administration and military regulations, but from the point of view of ideas, the management of men, and the meaning of history.

Alone, a rebel, in exile, in one of the greatest catastrophes in history, apparently irremediable, the acting brigadier was soon to show that amid bloodshed and tragedy, setback and hatred, he was a genius at explaining war and understanding history: *"But has the last word been said? Must hope disappear? Is the defeat final? No!... The same means which have conquered us may one day bring us victory ... This is a world war. Struck down today by mechanical force, we may in the future conquer by superior mechanical force. The fate of the world lies in that. I, General de Gaulle ..."*

My grandfather and I, at Plessis-lez-Vaudreuil, did not hear this
first appeal of General de Gaulle, launched just after Marshal Pétain's first message. But fragments of it reached at least two of our
family, lost, like the rest, in France's troubles. Claude in a café in
Clermont-Ferrand in the heart of the Massif Central, and Philippe
in Bordeaux, on the lookout for everything that was happening in
a world on the point of collapse, both heard for the first time this
echoing voice, faltering, distant, grandiloquent and simple, unknown and yet immediately recognizable above all others, staccato,
profound, with unexpected intonations and accents which were to
make the world hold its breath for a quarter of a century.

On the very first day, June 18, 1940, one single word struck
Claude: resistance. He had been horrified at everything Pétain said,
though my grandfather agreed with it because it was what he
himself had always thought. For years Claude had bracketed honor
with rejection. Pétain was the embodiment of the army, tradition,
perhaps reaction, at all events hostility toward democracy on the
march, and he had also represented France *vis à vis* Franco's Spain.
Claude threw himself behind de Gaulle. He wouldn't even admit
that Pétain had common sense on his side. Claude believed that
realism was on the same side as duty. And three or four days later,
Claude heard de Gaulle's voice speaking again from London:

*"Many Frenchmen do not accept capitulation or servitude for reasons
whose names are honor, common sense, national interest.*

*"I say honor, for France undertook not to lay down arms except with
the agreement of her Allies ...*

*"I say common sense, for it is absurd to consider the struggle as lost.
Yes, we have suffered a great defeat ... But the same conditions of war
which have caused us to be beaten by five thousand aircraft and six
thousand tanks may tomorrow give us victory with twenty thousand
tanks and twenty thousand aircraft.*

*"I say national interest, for this is not a Franco-German war to be
decided by one battle. This is a world war ...*

*"Honor, common sense, national interest all demand that all free
Frenchmen continue the fight wherever they are and by whatever means
they can ...*

"I, General de Gaulle, undertake here, in England, this national task . . .

"I appeal to all Frenchmen who are still free to hear me and to follow me."

Claude had already chosen: he would follow de Gaulle. His decision was sealed by the appeal of June 22; by the appeal of June 24, the day after the signing of the Armistice ("There must be an ideal. There must be a hope. There must somewhere shine and burn the flame of French resistance"); by the appeal of June 26, in which the general, after having referred to the German jackboot and the dancing pump of Italy, openly attacked Marshal Pétain ("Monsieur le Maréchal, in these hours of shame and anger for our country, there must be a voice to reply to you") and referred to victory as if it were inevitable and perhaps already imminent. Claude went to London on a commercial aircraft piloted by a comrade who elegantly waggled his wings as he passed over the towers of Plessis-lez-Vaudreuil. In London, Claude was among the first to present himself to General de Gaulle, who had just left Seymour Place for the country, and St. Stephen's House for Carlton Gardens, where he set up his offices. In those days there were not many people around the general, and after just a few days, de Gaulle saw Claude for a whole ten minutes.

"I'm told you're a communist," said de Gaulle, at the end of the conversation.

"I am," answered Claude. "Or rather I was."

"Well," said the general, flinging out his arms, "now you're going to be a Gaullist. There's no one like a traditionalist for loving adventure. There's no one like a revolutionary for loving his country. You are both—all the better to lead the way for us. I take my hat off to you."

He stood up.

"Good," he said. "I am happy to welcome you among my companions."

Claude, wearing a strange uniform that was half British and half French, stood at attention and saluted, opened the door, and went out. One word among the few the general had uttered had struck

him: the strange word "Gaullist," destined to become so famous. I
think that was the first time it was ever used. Claude went through
the little antechamber which the general's aides used as an office,
and just as he was about to leave heard one of the officers, who was
reading a paper or talking to someone, say in a rather loud voice,
"Death to all asses!"

Claude started to laugh, but his smile froze on his lips: in the
mirror opposite him he saw the general, who had just opened the
door, put his head through to say something or call someone. The
officer's exclamation echoed in a chilly silence. Then Claude heard
the general say calmly: "An ambitious program, gentlemen, an ambitious program."

Claude saw General de Gaulle a few more times before he left on
a secret mission in occupied France. A few days after their first
meeting the leader of Free France reviewed a small detachment in
which Claude's companions were all soldiers and sailors who seemed
to be from the Île de Sein. After the review, the general sent for
Claude. He seemed at once confident and depressed. Confident,
because he did not doubt that he was right. Despite bombs and fires,
despite threats of German landings, England was going to stand
firm. The United States would come into the war one day. The
factories of the free world would mass-produce aircraft and tanks
that would impose on Germany the same suffering she had imposed
on France, only ten times, a hundred times worse. But what surprised the general and made him downcast and bitter was the very
small number of Frenchmen who had joined him. He asked himself
whether France were not Pétainist. And he was not wrong to ask
that question. For in fact France was Pétainist. He asked Claude
how his first appeal had been received in France by those who had
heard it. Could Claude answer that most of those around him had
merely shrugged their shoulders, sometimes in anger? That his "I,
General de Gaulle" carried no weight against the glorious memories
of the victor of Verdun, the father figure? He hesitated. But the
general knew the answer already. With a few exceptions, he felt he
was surrounded by mere adventurers and hotheads—"scrapings of

the barrel," as he called them. The Free French consisted at that time of scarcely more than four hundred men.

"You are here," he said to Claude and five or six officers and civilians who were listening to him in silence. "You are here. That's fine. But where are so-and-so, and so-and-so, and so-and-so?"

And he cited the names of famous politicians, generals, and diplomats. Claude had the feeling that nothing would ever make this touchy giant swerve from the steep path mapped out once and for all through the jungle of history and its terrible obstacles, but that he was sorry he could not rely, in his patriotic struggle, on those he considered his natural allies. He looked around him.

"Where do these men come from?" he asked a tall young officer, a cavalry lieutenant who seemed to be acting as his aide-de-camp and whom his comrades called Geoffroy.

"From the Île de Sein, sir."

"And those?"

"From the Île de Sein, sir."

"And those over there?"

"From the same place, sir."

"How many inhabitants are there on the Île de Sein?"

"Well, sir . . . I don't know exactly . . . six hundred? Perhaps eight hundred. Anyway, there are about a hundred of them here. They came in small ships and rowboats."

"Well," said the general, "a hundred out of less than four hundred men—that makes our Île de Sein contingent a quarter of France."

All this seemed to belong to another world of heroism and heroic folly, and Claude told me about it during the winter of 1940–41, in a gamekeeper's cottage in the forest at Plessis-lez-Vaudreuil. He was unrecognizable in those days with his beard and his dyed hair, dressed up as a postman or a railwayman—once even, in 1941, as a priest. In just under three years he made the perilous journey between England and France seven or eight times—by train across Spain, by motor launch, and by plane, sometimes landing by parachute. In September 1940, with the general and Admiral Cunningham, he took part in the unsuccessful expedition against Dakar, defended by Boisson. He saw the bodies of the first Frenchmen killed by other Frenchmen brought back on board his ship. He fought in Syria in June and July 1941, but, back in France more or less definitively at the end of the summer of 1941, he became one of the organizers of the Resistance. Two or three times, between periods when the house was occupied by the Germans, he was bold enough to come and spend a few hours at Plessis-lez-Vaudreuil. He would appear at night like a thief, like one of those magnanimous highwaymen whose mysterious, benevolent, and cruel role he delighted to play. My grandfather, overcome with emotion, welcomed him with open arms. Claude threw himself into them, as if he were still ten years old, and they began to talk.

The war had brought considerable changes to Plessis-lez-Vaudreuil. The series of requisitionings, lack of resources and maintenance, looting, secret departures, outbreaks of fire, had combined to empty the drawing rooms, the billiard room, the dining room, and most of the bedrooms. The stables too were empty; only Avenger remained amid the deserted stalls and silent kennels. Guns, saddles, hunting horns, cars, and many of the books and pictures had disappeared. The flowerbeds at the front of the house now grew potatoes. Family life, made chaotic and uncertain by transport difficulties and public events, no longer centered on the stone table beneath the astonished lime trees, but on the wireless set which had some years ago replaced the cat's whisker, and which in ten or fifteen years would be transformed first into a radio, then into a transistor, and finally into a television set. We listened alternately to Radio Paris and the radio from London; to the marshal and to the general; to the communiqués of the Wehrmacht and those of the B.B.C., its coded messages scarcely audible through the atmospherics. Some voices vanished, like that of the traitor Ferdonnet, soon forgotten. Others appeared and became familiar and famous, like that of Philippe Henriot, Jean-Hérold Paquis, or that of an unknown spokesman of fighting France, whose unforgettable accents took over from those of de Gaulle, and every day, after the first four notes of Beethoven's Fifth Symphony, instilled a little hope and clandestine enthusiasm into its evening listeners.

As time went by, my grandfather felt more and more sympathy for General de Gaulle. Of course, the general appealed to Carnot and Gambetta a little too much for my grandfather's taste. But he also invoked Louis XIV, Joan of Arc and de Tourville, Richelieu and Suffren. He spoke above all of the honor and the soul of France —"The soul of France! It is with those who continue the struggle by all possible means, with those who do not give up, with those who will one day be present at victory"—and he gradually came to embody, for my grandfather, the sword of France militant. But at the same time the old man clung obstinately to his belief that Marshal Pétain, for his part, represented the shield of a crushed and suffering France. His discussions with Claude bore chiefly on this point. Very soon, at the beginning of 1941 and still more in 1942, there was no longer any question of any of us condemning or rejecting de Gaulle. The only problem was whether a dual allegiance to Pétain and de Gaulle was still possible: Claude was certain that it wasn't, and my grandfather thought that it was. What my grandfather could neither accept nor understand was that the general had any right to rule out the marshal. He admired the general's courage, energy, sense of duty, and ideals, his gifts as a seer and a leader, but for him the origin of de Gaulle's powers was tainted with rebellion and illegality. All this led to some astonishing paradoxes. My grandfather, who all his life had decried democracy and the Republic, saw the votes of July 9 and 10, 1940, in the Casino at Vichy as decisive proof of the marshal's legitimacy. And Claude, who in 1936 had greeted with joy the creation of the chamber of the so-called Popular Front, could not stomach the members of that same chamber and the senate when, with the slender exception of 80 against 649, they voted plenary powers to Marshal Pétain. What my grandfather hoped for was a reconciliation of the sword and the shield. Claude didn't see it like this at all. For him Pétain, perhaps unconsciously, was an ideal instrument in the hands of the Germans. A German proconsul, protector, or *Gauleiter* would have been unable to lead the French as far along the road of submission and collaboration as the senile marshal. I can still see Claude, come to Plessis-lez-Vaudreuil to pass a night or two when the Germans were away, sitting down in front of the radio with pencil and paper and noting down passionately the names of those whose ignominy seemed to him to have gone beyond all bounds. "Laval: To be shot. Darlan: To be shot. Pucheu: To be shot. Philippe Henriot: To be shot. Brasillach: ..." He hesitated a moment. "To be shot. Henri Béraud: To be shot. Doriot: To be shot. Déat: To be shot ... And Pétain: To be shot."

My grandfather started. Shoot Pétain! Of course, said Claude. Pétain was the guiltiest of all, the ideal disguised, the Tartuffe of treason, the masochist of defeat, whose paternal air and guilty authority covered every kind of crime and every kind of cowardice. "I prefer Laval," said Claude. "He does less harm." My grandfather defended the marshal, tried to get Claude to substitute Pierre Laval, painted a dreadful picture of what France would be like without Pétain. Claude denied that the marshal's régime was really preferable to direct control by Hitler's occupying army. He cited the examples of Belgium and Holland, and ended by wishing that France had had even worse troubles: that might have brought her more rapidly to the side of de Gaulle, the side of resistance against an invader who was disguised as a partner, as a somewhat unceremonious friend, and sometimes almost as an ally, by the hypocritical ambiguity and the tergiversations of Vichy.

It was not very difficult to see what made my grandfather incline toward Pétain: age, of course, but also the collapse of democracy and the fact that no one any longer expected the monarchy ever to return. There was one man who had remained if not in the shadow, at least in the background, and who was in a way at the center, paradoxically, of the new situation created by the simultaneous collapse of the country and the Republic: this was Maurras. The two enemy chiefs, Marshal Pétain and General de Gaulle, both had special relationships with Maurras' thought. Claude told Philippe that when General de Gaulle arrived in London in June 1940, the English, naturally trying to find out what they could about this French officer who had suddenly come among them surrounded by strangers and abandoned by all his compatriots whose names were familiar, found nothing in their archives but a dithyrambic though already rather old article by Maurras in *L'Action française*.

The reversal of values and positions lent the catastrophe a paradoxical aspect: nationalism came to terms with collaboration because it was the price that had to be paid for the collapse of the Republic. And liberals, pacifists, socialists, all those whom Vichy lumped together, somewhat exaggeratedly, under the collective term of Judeo-Communists, prepared to fight for their country at the side of a traditionalist and terribly obstinate general, because the path of the fight against fascism lay through military strength and devotion to the national cause. Philippe naturally found in Vichy and the doctrine of the marshal many ideas that were dear to him. And he was not surprised by the German victory. Fascism's conquest of Europe had been achieved very swiftly, at the rate of about two purges, two crises, and two offensives a year. For six or seven years, Philippe had witnessed nothing but the triumphs of the swastika. Like *L'Action française* and many of the militants of the extreme Right, he told himself that out of extreme misfortune good might come. The creation of the French state, the cult of hierarchy, the abolition of parliament, the Legion, the young people's work camps, the system of national relief, the replacing of trade unions with corporatism, all these corresponded to hopes which he had almost abandoned but which were now suddenly embodied in the National Revolution. But although he had been a fascist and admired Mussolini and Hitler, he was first and foremost a nationalist. I have already explained that nationalism was far from being always identical with the family tradition. Anyhow, Philippe was a nationalist. Fascism for him was merely an instrument of national greatness. At a moment when so many democrats and republicans, socialists and communists, were drawing near, at least temporarily, to National Socialism, Philippe was drawing away from it. Why? Because Germany was the enemy. Philippe, as they say, had a splendid war. While Claude and I were tossed by the troubles of 1940 from one end of France to the other, Philippe, like Robert V.,

was among the few who held firm, retreated in good order, and
sometimes even managed to reply to the enemy. The policy of
collaboration seemed to him unbearable. He accepted it with difficulty, telling himself that, after all, Pétain and Weygand knew what
they were doing. He supported the new regime, but with ever-
mounting doubts about the legitimacy of the state and the reality
of the national renaissance. The invasion of the unoccupied zone
and the scuttling of the fleet at Toulon under the orders of Admiral
de Laborde, a distant cousin, drove him first to Spain, then to North
Africa, where he was at the center of the extraordinary intrigues
that grew up around Admiral Darlan, who, assured by Auphan of
the "secret approval of the marshal," proclaimed himself high com-
missioner and the repository of French sovereignty in North Africa
"in the name of Marshal Pétain, unable to be present." After the
death of Darlan and in the absence of Weygand, arrested by the
Germans, everything that happened ought, logically, to have
brought Philippe to the support of Giraud. But a political and
emotional *coup de foudre* placed him under the orders of de Gaulle.
To the former fascist, the supporter of Pétain, the admirer of Weygand, it suddenly became clear that the French nation was de
Gaulle. He never went back on that decision. So by radically different paths, and with a couple of years between them, Philippe and
Claude both found themselves in the early days of 1943 behind
General de Gaulle, who embodied for each of them, in different
ways, France and freedom.

Perhaps one day I'll tell what I know, thanks to Philippe, about
the assassination of Darlan by Bonnier de la Chapelle. Philippe had
known Bonnier de la Chapelle for several years, and was himself
fairly deeply involved in the end of Admiral Darlan, last heir of the
admirals of France. But as I have said, I am not trying to write a
history of the Republic, nor even a history of contemporary manners. Nor am I trying to tell the history of the war or of the
short-lived French State. My only object is to give an account of
the evolution of a family—perhaps, also, of its end. It is true that
the family was deeply involved, after its long years of withdrawal
into itself, in the great upheavals of the Second World War. But I

propose to limit myself to the points at which history and the family decisively intersected.

Another of the points of intersection during those somber years was provided by Michel Desbois. Since our studious years under Jean-Christophe Comte and since his marriage to my sister Anne, Michel had pursued two apparently divergent paths. While playing an increasingly important part in the long-standing family business, he grew closer and closer to the socialists. I remember that he had always been interested in social and economic problems, and already under Jean-Christophe he had made a study of French socialism. As the years went by, though he never engaged in active politics, he felt more attracted by the sort of socialism inspired by Proudhon and Jules Guesde, a kind closer to Sorel and Péguy than to Marx or Lenin, and intermingled with a comparatively advanced Christianity. Michel's situation at the end of the thirties was almost unique. Very close to certain Catholic and trade-union movements, very hostile of course to Stalin's brand of communism, at the same time he played a considerable role in the world of finance and business. Toward the end of his life Uncle Paul often made use of him to cover himself on the Left, while making use of his father and the memory of his grandfather to cover himself on the Right. On several occasions it was rumored that Michel was about to enter active politics. He was offered parliamentary seats, with the assurance that he would soon be given a portfolio under the Third Republic, already on the decline and seriously threatened. He always refused these offers, preferring to devote himself to business, which occupied all his time and in which he was a dazzling success. But after the dismissal of Laval, Marshal Pétain summoned him, and then, either as principal private secretary to various ministers, or as direct adviser to the head of state, he began to play a discreet but important part in the Vichy government.

I won't go into detail here about discussions which have already caused much ink to flow and inspired much passion. For whole evenings, whole nights, Claude and Philippe and I, and sometimes even my grandfather, looked at the case of Michel Desbois from every possible point of view. Michel never denounced Jews or

members of the Resistance. On several occasions he even saved a
certain number of Maquisards, described as terrorists, from the
Gestapo. But to put it briefly and perhaps too simply, he believed,
like Laval, for whom he had no liking, that Germany would win
the war. Michel, perhaps with Claude, was by far the most intelligent of us. He was certainly, like Brasillach, of whom I've already
spoken and with whom he had nothing in common, the most mistaken of us. Without modesty I can say that the least intelligent of
us was certainly Philippe. But some obscure instinct, an impulse of
nationalism, a vague sense of tradition, and above all his irrational
conversion to de Gaulle saved him from disaster. All the exceptional
qualities of Michel Desbois led him irrevocably to catastrophe. I
remember his astonishment when he realized that the conflict between Hitler and Stalin was not enough to draw Philippe and me
onto the side of the Germans. "I can understand Claude," he said.
"I can easily see that the Russian-German war would serve rather
to confirm him in his mad beliefs. But you! You!" Ideas are often
in a very unstable equilibrium with one another, and may be transformed in a moment. It is not so much ideas as circumstances and
temperaments—which are at the same time more superficial and
more profound—which decide the fate of men. The fate of Michel
was sealed. He was to pursue it through collaboration, blind fidelity
to the directives of the marshal, and perhaps—perhaps—to a share
of responsibility, not, as has often wrongly been maintained, in the
handing over of communists to the occupying authorities, but in
representations to those authorities in favor of some suspect or
hostage, representations which automatically diverted German repression toward others—i.e., usually toward communists.

You can easily imagine Claude's reactions to Michel's attitude.
And here comes a surprising episode in the family chronicle. It
concerns Claude, Anne-Marie, and Michel Desbois. During the war
Anne-Marie had emerged from the adolescence she had been lingering in even at the time of her forest rides with Robert V. or with
Major von Wittgenstein. Wearing her woolen-soled shoes, often on
a bicycle, with an imitation-leather handbag slung over her shoulder, she had fulfilled her promise: she had forgotten Robert V. and

become a girl of dazzling beauty—in fact, a young woman. My grandfather never suspected it, but I am afraid Anne-Marie had lovers. If the war, at the time I'm speaking of, hadn't filled the whole of the landscape, I would have devoted a few pages to this unheard-of event in the family history. In our family, girls did not have lovers. Women did, perhaps. But girls, no. It is not difficult to imagine civilizations in which women are faithful and girls free. But with us it was rather the opposite: young girls who were single were not free, and young women who were married were free. It was often just to become free that girls got married, even. And did wives, in our family, take advantage of their liberty? I must admit I don't really know. I've already mentioned that my great-grand-mother was said to have bestowed her favors on the duc d'Aumale. Perhaps other wives in the family kicked over the traces, but we didn't know about it. If they deceived their husbands, it was in the deepest secrecy. But there was no secrecy for girls: they were virgins up to the altar and their wedding night. And if there was no altar and no husband and no wedding night, well, they remained virgins up to old age and death. But were things different in the past? In the seventeenth or eighteenth century, for example, were manners freer for the girls in our family? There again I don't know. But I'd swear by my right arm that since the Revolution and the Resto-ration our girls did not have lovers. They read with amazement and enthusiasm the fantastic novels in which women like Mathilde de la Mole or Charlotte de Jussat (do you even know who she is?) awaited their lovers. They themselves could not await any lovers because they hadn't any. But Anne-Marie had. She hadn't met them at dances, horse shows, or country weekends. She had met them during air-raid alerts and meetings where they listened to the radio from London. Anne-Marie's rendezvous were underground in ev-ery sense of the word—political and emotional. Uncle Paul had spent his youth reading the novels of Octave Feuillet. Anne-Marie now threw herself into those of Roger Vailland. She made love in maids' rooms with boys whose names she did not even know and who had won her over, under false identities, by means of staff maps and uncertain quotations from Clausewitz and Hegel. Can you see how the whole climate of an age slowly changed? First of all, externally, there was the evidence of the Germans in our streets and in the main courtyard at Plessis-lez-Vaudreuil. Deeper down, there was the torrent of hopes and hatreds, beliefs and ideas, which gradually made their way through the country market places and the cafés in the big towns, through events, newspapers, rumors. And deeper still, in people's secret hearts, the sensibility of an age and its inner metaphysics were gradually being overthrown without any sign of these subterranean revolutions being apparent, until suddenly, to everyone's amazement, they emerged into the light of day in the shape of manners and morals completely revolutionized.

Anne-Marie, like Claude, had thrown herself into the struggle against the Germans. But of course she still continued to see Michel Desbois. Michel, who was now quite an important person in the new regime, was well protected, and Claude had the idea of seizing Michel with the help of Anne-Marie and her lover of the moment. Readers who are interested in these obscure aspects of the history of the Resistance and the fight against Vichy will easily find specialized books on the subject, or memoirs with details which I hesitate to dwell on and which do not, I think, belong in the pages of this chronicle. Suffice it to say that the operation did not succeed. It was a mixture of farce, practical joke between cousins, punitive expedition, and detective story. It also had a tinge of Labiche and a touch of thriller. A few months later Claude and Anne-Marie and another lover who had succeeded the first (no, actually it wasn't really the first) laughed at their abortive kidnap plot and used the experience they derived from it to help them organize a much more decisive and successful attempt: a little while before the Liberation they all took part in the execution of Philippe Henriot, whose dreadful eloquence had caused such ravages on Radio Paris.

Perhaps it would have been better if Claude and Anne-Marie's attempt against Michel Desbois had succeeded. At least it would have stopped him from making mistake after mistake throughout the spring of 1944. At the end of 1942 and even more at the beginning of 1943, after American power began to move into action, after the Allied landing in North Africa, the victorious resistance of the Russians at Stalingrad, and Montgomery's successes in Cyrenaica and Tripolitania, Michel Desbois realized that the man in London had been right despite the evidence against him, and that something astounding was happening: the most formidable military instrument of all time was going to lose the war. He suddenly saw things clearly. But already it was too late.

For a few weeks, or perhaps only days, Michel thought he might be able to link his fate to that of Pucheu, who was just going over to North Africa. But the execution of Pucheu threw him back into his old paths. He knew now, however, that they led nowhere. Worse, they led to catastrophe. Because he would not, or could not, go back on all he'd said, all he'd done, all he'd been, Michel deliberately reinforced the disastrous image of himself which he'd presented to his enemies. He began to receive insulting and threatening letters, even little coffins sent through the post. He didn't want to seem afraid. Despite Anne's objurgations, he bound himself closer and closer to the Germans, though he knew they were lost. He made one statement after another—desperate, crazy professions of faith. But despite his errors and faults, Michel Desbois was a decent man. I know the expression "decent" has long had a pejorative meaning. Yet the word applied to him in every sense. He had become a member of the upper middle class, attached to a certain order, blinded by anti-bolshevism, and now he plunged deliberately into all the dying agonies of collaboration. I repeat, he didn't hand over either Jews, communists, or members of the Resistance to the Germans. But it's true that he did encourage young men to work for the marshal and in the legion of volunteers fighting with the Germans on the eastern front. He had believed in Hitler's victory, though all Hitler's principles were alien to him, and he had thought that France's interest lay in ranging itself—"honestly," as he said, or even "honorably"—on the side of the victors. It wouldn't have been impossible for him in 1943, or perhaps in 1944, or after the Pucheu affair, to go over to those who now quite clearly were going to win. But, apart from his own interests, something inside him prevented him from changing sides. It was not so much fidelity to his own beliefs, for these beliefs were intellectual rather than emotional, and nothing changes more rapidly than intellect and ideas—much more rapidly, anyway, than the movements of the heart. No. His real motive was a need to punish himself for his own blindness, by following his shattered system through to the bitter end. How could he bear to witness the punishment of those whom he had led astray, those whom he had guided toward shame and death, death in shame? He could still get out of it—but only by abandoning those who had obeyed him, those who had trusted him and followed him. Everything in him revolted at the mere idea. My sister had lost no time in choosing the side opposite Michel's. Week by week, almost day by day, I watched the tragedy of their relationship, and the moment when Michel realized my sister's ideas were winning out over his own. Nothing else she could have done would have so encouraged him—in the name of what honor he had left—to persist in his madness. I think I have already mentioned the trust and tenderness that existed between Michel and Anne. It was when Marshal Pétain and Pierre Laval were triumphant that Anne grew a little away from Michel. But as soon as the side he had committed himself to was lost forever, she became close to him again and encouraged him to support ideas which she herself had never shared, and which he now, but too late, knew to be useless. Claude had no pity for Michel. "You have to pay for what you do," he said. He would dig me in the ribs and laugh at my timidity. He would stop laughing to ask me, with mock gravity, if I really had gone over to the side of treason. No, I didn't say Michel was right and Claude wrong. But I was filled with compassion at the sight of this useless courage, all this intelligence spoiled, expended on nothing.

What followed ... Some of you will still remember it, I imagine. Michel's trial was briskly dispatched. Michel and Anne, at the Liberation, had succeeded in reaching Switzerland, then Spain. But after a few weeks they could bear it no longer and returned of their own accord to France. Michel was arrested immediately. But I managed to persuade Claude not to testify against my sister's husband. For my grandfather, for Pierre, and for me, only just back from Poland and Germany, but for Anne above all, the sight of

Michel standing between his guards, hooted at by the crowd, appearing before the High Court of Justice presided over by the huge Mongibeaux, with his fur collar and his pointed white beard, was frightful torture. It all took place in a light at once tragic and unreal.

I thought of Plessis-lez-Vaudreuil, of our forbidden games in the attics filled with huge dust-covered trunks, the first lesson given by Monsieur Jean-Christophe Comte, and how Michel had looked, his head thrown back in surprise and concentration, as he listened passionately to words the meaning of which we did not yet understand because we were still too young: "Memory, memory, what do you want of me? Autumn ..."

Suddenly Michel caught sight of me among the hostile faces of the public, behind the policemen and the lawyers. He threw me a smile, a sort of grimace. And for me those lines by Verlaine—I could still hear Jean-Christophe quoting them in his warm voice, with its southwestern accent, rugged and full of light—at last took on all their heart-rending meaning.

Fortunately Monsieur Desbois, Michel's father, had died during the war, only a few weeks after my mother, who for the previous two or three years had been brought to the brink of madness by her almost atheistic mysticism. So he wasn't there to hear a bearded character with a Roman nose and spectacles, muffled up to the ears in his ermine cape with the red cravat of a commander of the Legion of Honor, calling for his son's death. The attorney-general, Mornet, proclaimed that Michel Desbois had behaved badly during the war and worked with the enemies of France. Michel's two defending lawyers did what they could. The prosecution's evidence rested on several statements, a few letters to Germans, and above all two or three recordings. These recordings made the court ring with Michel's voice—clear, terribly clear, and rather weary, as if worn out. I saw the two defense lawyers exchange a silent look. When the recordings were over, there was a long silence. Michel's trial was over. The attorney-general had only to draw the obvious conclusions from what all of us had heard. I have a confused memory of two or three incidents, the lawyers' closing speeches, a few shouts, the jury's withdrawal and their return. I can still see Michel, his lawyers, his warders, the attorney-general, the judge, and a collapsing Anne: Michel was sentenced to death.

What a strange thing a family is! The one who now emerges from the darkness in which we have left him is the eldest of the cousins, Pierre. You will remember his connections with the world of politics, from which he had been removed by his marriage to Ursula. But he kept a certain nostalgia for that world, the feeling of a career nipped in the bud and a life left suspended. After Ursula's death Pierre showed no sign of following in the adventurous footsteps of Philippe and Claude. Many of those who met him, dressed in a severe and already rather old-fashioned style, never in a hurry, looking like some connoisseur or distinguished idler, in the streets of Vichy or Lyons, and later in a Paris which some somber miracle had freed of all traffic, took him for one of the aristocrats who had been swept away in the debacle, a member of the upper middle classes overtaken by events, rejected by history, and abandoned on the banks of time like monuments to a fabulous and now reviled era. And perhaps he did partly correspond to this rather superficial description, which gradually superseded the memory of Ursula's husband and Mirette's lover. But at the same time, quite calmly and quietly, outwardly all indifference, Pierre had returned, in a certain form of resistance to the invader, to the political activity and interest in public affairs which he had once sacrificed to his vanished love for Ursula. For almost two years, without ever abandoning a way of life that was perhaps rather ruffled, though never really upset despite the very serious risks it entailed, he helped in the creation of the underground press, in particular an influential paper called *Défense de la France.* Claude was arrested by the Germans in 1943 and escaped eight months later. I was deported in January 1944, and Jean-Christophe died in my arms at Auschwitz in April. Philippe landed in Italy at the end of 1943, under General Juin. And Pierre went through the troubles airily and elegantly, never bothered by the authorities and perhaps never even suspected. At the Liberation, between the beginning of the free press and the advent of television, he was in the position of influence and power that belonged to anyone involved with the five or six major newspapers which formed the basis of the famous Fourth Estate, perhaps a more decisive one than the other three.

I don't suppose you find it very easy to imagine Pierre fighting on the barricades in the boulevard Saint-Michel or outside the Prefecture. Neither do I. But he did something else, if not something better. After his escape from Germany, Claude was one of the leaders of the Resistance in Paris, acted as a link between the police and his communist friends, and played an important role throughout the summer of 1944, before joining the Alsace-Lorraine Brigade under the orders of Colonel Berger, better known as André Malraux. Philippe, at the request of General Leclerc (he too was a relative of ours, like Admiral de Laborde, like quite a few collaborators and like quite a few members of the Resistance), was among the first to come from Normandy and enter Paris by the pont de Sèvres, or the porte d'Italie, I can't remember which, on a tank covered with flowers, acclaimed by the crowd and kissed by all the girls. Pierre, between games of bridge at an elegant club where Gaullism did not, to put it mildly, enjoy the odor of sanctity, went on writing regularly for the newspaper, contributing fiery articles under names like Villeneuve and Saint-Paulin. And he strolled nonchalantly through Paris, never more beautiful than in those scorching days of the summer of 1944.

I was not with Claude in his secret hideouts, his suburban houses crammed with explosives and machine guns, or his middle-class apartments in which he shot down with his own hand at least two or three of his comrades convicted of treason. I was not with Philippe and his triumphant tanks when, after four years, they kept the promises de Gaulle had made on the radio from London. Nor, unfortunately, was I with my cousin Pierre. But he has told me so often about the Liberation of Paris that I sometimes almost think I was actually there. In the streets of the capital, still covered with the vaguely Gothic notices of the army of occupation, Pierre had seen the fever of upheaval gradually mounting. Scarcely two or three months had swept by since the last visit of Marshal Pétain, who had come to Paris for the funeral of Philippe Henriot, executed

by a commando group which included, as you will remember, my
cousin Claude and Anne-Marie. The old warrior had once more
attracted enormous and enthusiastic crowds. Opinion polls did not
exist then, but if they had, the people—despite a growing sympathy
for de Gaulle and the Resistance—would probably still have given
an overwhelming majority to Pétain. But now the west wind had
succeeded the east and changed all that, driving away, with the hum
of countless engines and the scent of liberty, the last whiffs of
collaboration. Cobblestones were torn up, tricolor flags appeared at
the windows, processions of young men went singing through the
city. One fine, very hot August day—he thought, laughing, that the
world needed to be on fire for him to stay in Paris in August—
Pierre, coming from the rue de Varenne, was crossing the place de
la Concorde (on foot, of course) on his way to his club. The club
remained open that summer because practically nobody had gone
away. For by that astonishing intermingling of elements which is
always so badly conveyed by textbooks and learned studies, ordinary life went on with only imperceptible changes through the
tumult of history, just as it had gone on, I imagine, through other
changes, in 1793 or 1830, 1848 or 1871. Just as he had crossed the
bridge and was entering the square, Pierre noticed a car driving
rather fast two or three times around it. There was a man on the
running board—in those days some cars still had running boards—
waving his arms, as if asking the passersby to stand aside. To his
amazement, Pierre recognized Claude. Before he had time to wonder what his brother was doing there, leaping about on that car
whizzing around the Obelisk, the first shots rang out: it was the
attack by the police in the French Admiralty building. In a few
seconds panic had broken out. People were running in all directions,
as in the pictures which used to fascinate us in Jean-Christophe's
time, pictures of the Nevsky Prospect during the Russian Revolution. Pierre found himself in the Tuileries Gardens. There was a
chatter of machine guns and the sound of one or two German tanks
starting up. Pierre, helpless, hesitated a moment: he was due that
evening at an important meeting of the chiefs of the underground
press. The Germans had closed the gates leading into and out of the

Tuileries. He hurried toward the river, on the other side of the park. But there too the S.S. were already taking up their positions. A lieutenant came up to him and asked for his papers.

"They're forged, aren't they?" said the lieutenant. He was tall and fair, very good-looking and rather attractive, and he spoke in a jesting though rather cynical tone.

Of course the papers were forged. Despite his appearance of complete detachment, Pierre led two or three secret lives, each kept strictly separate from the others. To go to his club, he was carrying the forged documents that would probably be necessary in the course of the evening. But the lieutenant looked at them, shrugged his shoulders, and gave them back. Pierre, to thank him and to show his appreciation as discreetly as possible, muttered a fragment from Goethe:

> *"Unsterbliche heben verlorene Kinder*
> *Mit feurigen Armen zum Himmel empor ... "*

"You speak German?" said the lieutenant.

"I used to," said Pierre. "And perhaps one day I will again."

As he went over the Solferino Bridge, Pierre almost tripped over a couple of corpses lying there spreadeagled across the road. The bridge has been demolished now: and thus pass away cities, customs, whole ages. I remember a time when elderly people who had once known the Palace of Saint-Cloud, or dined at the Maison Dorée from which Odette wrote to Swann, seemed to me to have come from another world. Pierre thought to himself that his own life might have ended there, one hot summer day toward the middle of the century, just outside the Tuileries Gardens. What a pity that would have been! He still had things to do. That evening he took part in one of the meetings which decided the fate of the press after the war. Among those present were Georges Bidault, with his metallic voice and obscure utterances; Alexandre Parodi; Pierre Lazareff, in his suspenders, his glasses pushed up on his forehead, intelligence personified; Pierre Brisson, with his green pencil in his hand; Robert Salmon; Albert Camus; Hubert Beuve-Méry; and sev-

eral others whose names he hardly knew but which would soon be
on everybody's lips. *France-Soir*, the new *Figaro, Le Monde*, which
replaced *Le Temps, Libération, Combat*, and *Le Parisien libéré* were
all in the process of being born. By an amusing reversal, Pierre was
involved in a new distribution of wealth, a devolution of at least the
intellectual means of production, almost a revolution—his enemies
would call it theft. After many meanderings—through the Dreyfus
affair and the duchesse d'Uzès; through our rejection of the modern
world and our reconciliation with it through the Remy-Michaults;
through the Masurian Lakes which had given us Ursula; through
the vice-consul in Hamburg who had lent us Mirette; through the
abstract painters and Negro musicians of the rue de Varenne;
through Wall Street and the Spanish Civil War; through the crisis
of 1929 and the Communist Party; through the lessons of Monsieur
Comte; through the sailor from Skyros and the whore from Capri
—after all these, Pierre, Claude, and Philippe brought the family at
last to the shores of today.

Pierre threw all the power and influence he had acquired into the
balance for Michel Desbois. Once the High Court had sentenced
him to death there was only one resource left: General de Gaulle.
In the following hours and days, Pierre moved heaven and earth. He
telephoned or sent telegrams to André Malraux, General Leclerc,
General Juin, Georges Bidault—everyone who was important in
the current constellations. He was told he ought to apply to General
de Gaulle, try to move him through those about him, ask to see him.
Pierre wasn't quite sure how to go about it. He decided on the
simple approach. He got in touch with Claude and Philippe and
arranged for them to come and see him. He managed to persuade
them, easily in the case of Philippe, with a certain amount of difficulty in the case of Claude. Then he applied through four or five
intermediaries, and asked General de Gaulle if he would consent to
receive this family delegation. I myself got back from Germany just
before the trial, in a rather lamentable state, after a period in a
hospital in Nuremberg; I'll spare you the details.

"Perfect!" Pierre said to me. "A nationalist soldier, a communist
member of the Resistance, and a journalist who's a politician. A

battered-looking deportee in striped pajamas was just what we needed. And he's the brother-in-law into the bargain . . . Well"—to me—"here you are. Off we go, then."

One Thursday afternoon at six o'clock, all four of us were ushered in to see General de Gaulle. In those days his offices were still in the rue Saint-Dominique. We went in through a door that was almost directly opposite a shop run by the Samson sisters, where Aunt Gabrielle often used to take prints and engravings to be framed. Philippe, in a uniform of the utmost correctness, looked very handsome. Claude was in one of those strange get-ups exhibiting the mingled influences of the Resistance and the army. Pierre and I were in civilian dress. We were greeted by a member of the cabinet who, in the course of a brilliant career, was twenty years later to succeed Chateaubriand as French ambassador to the Holy See. I think his name was Brouillet. After a few moments he took us to the general's office. On the way we passed a young man of about thirty or thirty-five.

"Excuse me for a moment," said our guide. "I want to have a word with Monsieur Pompidou."

It was to the sound of that name that de Gaulle's door opened to us. The general shook our hands.

"Remind me where we met before," he said to Philippe and Claude.

"In Algiers," said Philippe.

"In London," said Claude. "In July 1940."

The general raised his hands. The gesture might have meant either that he remembered or that he did not, either that all those things were ancient history or that those were the days. He was silent for a while. We didn't want to break the silence. Although the setting could not have been more simple, there was a whiff of greatness in the air—a sort of natural majesty which owed nothing to "production." Of course it had something to do with the knowledge that the man sitting there in front of us, in a double-breasted lounge suit, embodied power. But above all was the indefinable but very strong feeling that after so many vicissitudes and successfully surmounted trials, he was indistinguishable from the history which he had foreseen and dominated more than any other man of our time.

The silence continued.

"Well?" said the general.

Pierre launched out and in a few minutes explained most of what you have already learned in the preceding pages: our childhood at Plessis-lez-Vaudreuil, the part played by Monsieur Desbois, our lessons with Jean-Christophe, and the fact that Michel Desbois was like a brother to us.

"So," interrupted the general, flicking through a thin file of papers. "A typical story of the days of oil lamps and sailing ships. But I believe your friend is a traitor, isn't he?"

I took my courage in both hands.

"He made a mistake, sir. In good faith. He didn't understand what was happening. Like Pétain, he believed that it was in everyone's interest to come to terms with the Germans. But I assure you he neither respected nor liked them."

"The Germans were the enemy. I call that treason."

To my great relief I heard Claude intervene. I had been afraid he might not speak.

"He never handed anyone over to the Germans, sir. And he saved some members of the Resistance from them."

"Not very skillfully, if I'm to believe what I'm told. And perhaps with something that was worse than clumsiness. People say now that Vichy hadn't many trumps up its sleeve. Do you think that de Gaulle had many, when he was on his own in London, both in the worst years and in the best? There was you," he said, looking at Claude as if the two of them had been the sole bastions of Free France. "But there were very few others. It is in dealings with those who claim to be friends that one needs to be most careful, most intransigent. If, in order to save members of the Resistance on his own side, Monsieur Desbois couldn't find any better method than sending to their death communists who, in their own way, were also resisting, do you think he really served France? If one absolutely has to choose victims and heroes, it's better to choose oneself. There's always time later to try to win other people over. In politics, as in other matters, there's only one position from which to judge men and events—the clearest, and the highest. I'm afraid your friend did not keep to such a position."

As far as I can remember, that's more or less what passed between us and General de Gaulle. Philippe added that if Michel didn't die he might still perform great services for France. The general asked, with somewhat bitter irony, if it was altogether impossible that some photograph might be produced showing Michel in German uniform, or that some proof might be adduced showing he had links with the Gestapo. Excluding error or accident, all four of us vouched for Michel Desbois' real feelings. Claude was a Companion of the Liberation. Philippe's services, first in Italy, then in France, had won him the Croix de Guerre with several bars, and made him an officer in the Legion of Honor. The general stood up and added a few last words, very polite and more relaxed. He told us he would settle the Desbois affair, one way or the other, with Michel's lawyers. And he shook hands with us. A few days later we learned that Michel's sentence had been commuted. In 1949 the case was reviewed in the light of new facts and services to the Resistance. Michel was sentenced to ten years in jail. In 1952 he was set free. In 1953 he went to America with my sister Anne. He was greeted there with warmth, and was able to begin again a life which had been interrupted by history.

We went on with our own lives in Plessis-lez-Vaudreuil. We had found the old house ravaged by war, by the passage of rival armies, and by the explosion of two or three bombs which had very nearly destroyed the whole place. Everything was changed, the intangible atmosphere even more than the actual setting. My grandfather had remained loyal to Pétain to the end. I admit that it might be regarded as inconsistency on his part, but for months I watched him passionately following the progress of the Allies, while at the same time lamenting the fate of the marshal. In 1943, and still more at the beginning of 1944, commando groups of the Resistance installed themselves, under Claude's orders, in the forests around the house. On the other hand, in Plessis-lez-Vaudreuil, Roussette, and Villeneuve, at the head of a group of local worthies, veterans of the

First World War, nuns, shopkeepers, and peasants, my grandfather clung desperately to the now shaky myth of Pétain. But during the eight months that Claude was in prison in Germany, my grandfather saw to it that the Maquis received necessary supplies, including, two or three times, arms. At the Liberation, there was a move to denounce my grandfather's attitude and his loyalty to Pétain. Claude and Pierre put an end to that in just a few days—the family genius still survived. But not everyone got around that difficult corner so smoothly: news reached us from the Haute-Vienne and the Lot of cousins and friends who paid dearly, sometimes with their lives, for the vagueness of their opinions during the occupation. Even among ourselves, consequences were not slow to follow. My grandfather and Claude had got on quite well together during the dark years. But they came close to rupture at the moment of victory.

My grandfather quite accepted the idea of seeing the victors dispose of the vanquished. Hadn't we ourselves, for centuries, massacred those we'd conquered and been massacred by those who'd conquered us? No, what angered, indeed infuriated, him was the victors' claim to be dispensing universal justice. In this attitude he dimly perceived reflections of Rousseau or of some extreme left-wing Hegel. So he looked everywhere for weapons with which to defend his own cause. He had no difficulty in finding them. Hiroshima and Katyn were exactly what he required: these contributions to victory did not seem to him sufficient justification for the claim to be imposing a moral order. In his view, the atomic bomb and the whole bolshevik heritage up to Stalin and Vyshinsky discredited the claim to international jurisdiction. If anyone mentioned Coventry, he replied with Dresden and Hamburg. The idea of having supporters of Hitler judged by supporters of Stalin struck him as farcical, and to Claude's indignation he didn't scruple to say so, amid all the acclamations of victory and the restoration of freedom. For Claude, there could be no comparison between fascism and Stalinism. Fascism was an attempt to dominate the world through force, not based on any principle. Communism was based on the idea of justice, though that justice might sometimes take strange forms. On one side was absolute evil. On the other, a terror which never quite effaced the image, distantly perceived through torture, show trials, and the realism of the Russo-German Pact, of the future happiness of humanity.

The trials in Paris and Nuremberg caused serious conflicts in the family. I don't know whether I've made it sufficiently clear to those who did not actually experience those intoxicating days of resurrection, with all their nuances and subtleties, that there was no question of my grandfather's defending Goebbels or Himmler, the methods of the Gestapo, or the concentration camps. Two of his grandsons had been deported. All of them fought against the Germans. Jacques had been killed in 1940. No one in the family could forgive Ravensbrück, Oradour, or the Warsaw Ghetto. But what astonished my grandfather was the clandestine rebirth, within that very democratic and republican ideology which had so violently condemned it, of the notion of collective responsibility. At the risk of tarnishing my grandfather's memory in many people's eyes, I must state clearly, in order to show the real sentiments of a traditionalist and of course reactionary old man at the intersection of two worlds, that he did not hold the German people, nor even the German army as a whole, responsible for the crimes which had been committed in their name by many of their members. He considered that leaving part of Germany to the mercy of communist tyranny was to fly in the face of human rights, and to repeat the madnesses and mistakes once attributed to Hitler.

My grandfather is dead now, and he didn't mince his words. I can say without modesty that my cousins and I had, each in his own way, made our little contribution to the common cause of national liberation. I see no reason why I should not now say quite openly what my grandfather thought. He thought that concentration camps, the torture of prisoners, the persecution of the Jews (who were not his friends), and the massacre of communists (who were his enemies) were abominations and crimes and should be prosecuted as such. But he also thought that the Resistance, to which his grandsons and great-grandsons had belonged, was made up of *francs-tireurs,* irregular soldiers, and that the laws of war, which he respected, gave the army of occupation the right to fight against them and to shoot them—to shoot them, but not, of course, to torture them. That was the nub of the matter. He thought that if the Germans had won and set up some nightmare Nuremberg of their own, they wouldn't have had much difficulty in showing that the atomic bomb and Stalin's repression were crimes against humanity. He was beginning to think—perhaps only because history was getting too much for him—that justice is not only thwarted when it is weak, but usually ceases to be just when it is strong. Like the Greek tragedians and Simone Weil, whom he had never even heard of, he saw justice as a fugitive from the camp of the victor. Such a modification of Pascal, who thought justice and force should be brought together, drove this elderly Christian, on the brink of death, into a kind of cynicism and skepticism.

I can still hear my grandfather, a few years, months, and weeks before his end, fulminating away like a prophet of woe. He said the whole moral system set up by the victors was a fowl that was bound to come home to roost. He repeated to all and sundry that the triumphant bomb would soon become the cross mankind had to bear, their terror. He said all that was needed was opportunity, and this might not be slow in coming, to make the victors in their turn perceive all the virtues that resided in torture and concentration camps. That it wouldn't be surprising to see communists and Jews pass from the role of victims to that of torturers—some of them had already done so—and adopt, with the approval of their own people, the method of burning villages and shooting hostages. According to him, all these horrors were born out of a kind of irresistible contagion of evil. Also, and above all, out of a more and more inextricable confusion between justice and force. "We are not only entering into an age of violence disavowed by everyone and practiced by all," he would say. "We also remain more than ever in an age of hypocrisy. After communism, Hitlerism and the struggle against Hitlerism, after the atomic bomb, Yalta and the dividing up of the world, there will be no crime which will not give itself out as justice—human justice, of course, which has replaced the justice of God. The Inquisition, so often denounced in the past, will in its

new forms have a great future. But for causes which will produce
fewer saints, less beauty, less greatness, and less hope." One of the
minor results of the crisis that the world had just gone through was
that my grandfather, a man of tradition and faith, began, like so
many others, not to believe in anything much any more. Too many
principles, too much of all that was sacred, too many of the fortresses of honor and respect, had been undermined. And even those
familiar things which still managed to remain upright could be seen
collapsing on all sides.

What I loved Claude for, on the other hand, was his enthusiasm,
his new-minted faith, the confidence he had in the future, perhaps
a confidence inherited from the lessons of Monsieur Comte. In 1944
and 1945 he firmly believed that man would improve. At a time
when my grandfather was seized with skepticism, Claude took over
from him, but instead of looking backward he looked forward: he
believed in a new press, in public virtue, in a socialist humanism, in
a science linked to morals, in progress, and in all the futures promised by technology and full of beauty. I think I have already,
somewhat boldly, mentioned the paradoxical element of Marxism
in my grandfather. Like the Marxists, my grandfather believed for
a long time in history, reality, and force. At least as long as we
ourselves were strong, he didn't bother about abstract justice, which
he could only conceive of as something existing within a given
order, a given system, a hierarchy slowly brought to maturity
through custom and time. But because he was a Christian he tem-
pered force with pity. But Claude, who was a communist, or had
been, and who had been a Christian, rejected force and refused
charity—justice was what he wanted. A universal and absolute
justice incumbent on all. And my grandfather did not believe in this
justice.

These new dissensions within the family were perfectly embodied in the great trials of the Liberation, the trial of Michel, of course,
but also those of Pétain and Laval and the trials at Nuremberg. My
grandfather was for shooting without trial, because they had been
conquered, a certain number of guilty officials and obvious criminals. And he was for freeing all the rest—the army chiefs, the

theorists, the journalists, Maurras, Brasillach, and, of course, the marshal.

If you include the interruption of his days in the wilderness, de Gaulle's rule over French history extends through some thirty years: from June 18, 1940, to the end of the 1960s. After the military glory he won in the First World War, Pétain's rule was shorter: from June 17, 1940, to the Liberation. But in the case of both men, their mystical presence in people's minds lasted much longer than the years during which they were actually present, in power or even in the world itself. Fifty years after their deaths, the names of de Gaulle and Pétain will probably no longer have any influence on the course of events, but they will go on awakening passions in the hearts of the men who followed, admired, loved, and above all sometimes hated them. My grandfather was shattered by Pétain's trial, and his being sentenced to death for treason. The family was probably more concerned and divided by Pétain than by even the Dreyfus affair. The positions were reversed: the democratic and progressive Left had gone over from the defense to the prosecution, and my grandfather had ceased to be attorney-general and had become the defense counsel. I don't propose to say anything here about the guilt or innocence of the accused. I repeat, contemporary history interests me here only insofar as it concerns my family. So I do not make any judgments: I don't feel capable of doing so, nor do I want to. I merely relate what we used to talk about between ourselves, when we met in Paris or at Plessis-lez-Vaudreuil. From Dreyfus and Hitler on the one hand to religion and sex on the other, there was no family problem we spent more time discussing than the fate of the marshal. Fifteen years, twenty years, twenty-five years later, in the absence—alas!—of my grandfather, we were to be concerned once more about the fate of the general. And we, the survivors, were to be as shattered by the French people's condemnation of the general—perhaps even more shattered—than my grandfather had been by the High Court's condemnation of the marshal. Our family probably had need of legends and myths. In the case of Pétain, the myth of the humiliated father, of greatness in misfortune, of abnegation. In the case of de

Gaulle, the legend was more real—the legend of victorious solitude, of ordeals surmounted, of glory submerged and then recovered, and of a genius for history. Everyone has need of myth. Everyone has need of legend. Lenin, Stalin, Trotsky, Hitler, Mussolini, Salazar, Franco, Roosevelt, Churchill, Tito, Nasser, Khaddafy, Perón, above all Mao Tse-tung, Pétain, and de Gaulle: the twentieth century, the century of progress, science, and rationalism, will, more than any other century, have been a century of myths and legends.

As I reread, now, these few pages on my family during the troubles, I feel a doubt. Might not an unprepared reader see my grandfather as a pale form of collaborator? I should feel very guilty if I permitted the least ambiguity on the subject. My grandfather felt for Pétain a mixture of loyalty, respect, and immense pity. He had more esteem for him than for Attorney-General Mornet, or for Maurice Thorez, who returned victorious, or for Stalin and Vyshinsky, who caused a new moral order to prevail over Europe in place of that of Hitler. Perhaps my grandfather was wrong. I can't say. If you want to know, I myself was closer to Claude's ideas at that time than to those of my grandfather. But my grandfather was attached to Pétain. Only at the same time, in the same breath and with the same heart, like the Parisians themselves when they acclaimed the marshal, he was on the side of the Allies against Hitler and his followers. And I hope you don't imagine that Bir Hakim and Strasbourg, Leclerc and Koenig, were matters of indifference to the old soldier *honoris causa* (he had never borne arms) that my grandfather was still. He respected Rommel. He respected Montgomery even more. He hated and despised such men as Goebbels and Himmler. And, more than anyone, he admired Churchill, his fierce humor, his courage, his obstinacy. There was nothing surprising in this: Winston Churchill was almost one of the Marlboroughs, who were so dear to us. Try to disentangle all that if you can. History is not so simple.

On the day of the Liberation procession, my grandfather, aged about ninety, was installed at the Rond-Point of the Champs-Elysées, on one of the balconies in the Figaro building. Pierre had gotten the seat for him, and from it he could see his grandson

Philippe going by in a tank, and his grandson Claude going by at the head of his partisans. Two of his great-grandsons who had been in the Maquis were among the young men coming from the direction of the Étoile. General de Gaulle walked at the head of the immense flood coming down the avenue which other processions, a quarter of a century later, were to go up in the other direction, as if the political career of the greatest of all Frenchmen, returned at last from exile, existed between two crowds dominated by his name, just as his fate was played out between two appeals: the inspired message of June 18, 1940, and the brief declaration of April 28, 1969—"I cease to exercise my functions as president of the Republic. This decision takes effect today at noon." On that day of Liberation General de Gaulle was greater than the others who marched with him. There was his appearance on the balcony of the Hôtel de Ville; the *Te Deum* in Notre Dame, with bullets whistling down the nave; his opposition to the Allies who wanted to abandon Strasbourg; his implacable determination to unify the country under the legitimate authority he derived neither from heredity, nor from God, nor from some uncertain suffrage, but from history subjected and a nation fascinated; finally there were the people of Paris, all of them behind him between the Étoile and the place de la Concorde. After four years of struggle, courage, and passion, the legend was being installed. Behind Leclerc's soldiers came firemen, postmen, railwaymen, nurses, men with armbands waving banners, gas and electric men, and street sweepers who had been in the Resistance. As the old man was leaving the balcony and thanking Pierre Brisson for having him, Pierre asked him his opinion of what he had just seen. "Not bad," said my grandfather, who could still make out dimly in the distance some marshals of France riding on horseback under the Arc de Triomphe. "Not bad. A bit untidy."

2

The Evening Breeze

MARIANNE WAS BACK AGAIN. HER IMAGE drove out the Frankish battleax, and resumed its place on the ever-lighter coins—so light one no longer even bothered to slip them to the choirboys on Sunday at mass in the old church at Plessis-lez-Vaudreuil. Under the direction of Monsieur Coudé de Foresto and others, we used up the last of the meat and bread coupons which for hundreds of weeks had played an unprecedented role in our daily lives. As you may imagine, the black market was unknown to us. Shoes reappeared, together with leather, wool, bicycle tires, and gasoline. Turnips and Jerusalem artichokes returned to the void from which they had emerged for four interminable years. Those were the last days of the Citroën *deux-chevaux.* Just a little more time and Brigitte Bardot would enter our lives. It would be the era of St. Tropez, the portable transistor radio and television. New names appeared on radio and in the papers, and children, as usual, but rather more than usual, were growing into men.

My grandfather was getting old. Two or three times already—it was as if he'd waited for France's troubles to be over before he began to weaken—we had had false alarms. First his lungs, then his kidneys, underwent seizures. But each time he had recovered. In the restored Republic, as if it had never ceased to be dear to us, in

new-won freedom, as if we had always revered it, we had celebrated
his ninetieth birthday, all together—at Plessis-lez-Vaudreuil, of
course. He was still strong and almost cheerful, despite the melancholy arising from his great age and his opinions about life. Uncle
Paul was no longer there, nor my mother, nor Jacques, nor Ursula,
nor Monsieur Desbois the elder, nor Monsieur Comte, nor old Jules,
who in the days of Jules his father and Jules his grandfather had
been young Jules. Nor Michel Desbois, in prison at Fresnes, and
then at Clairvaux. But Pierre and Philippe and Claude and I were
there, and so was Aunt Gabrielle, an old lady with white hair, and
my sister Anne, and yet another Jules, heir of the marvelous old
days. There were also young men and women who I must admit
were beginning to astound us: these were my cousins' children,
whom we had some difficulty in recognizing in their new roles.
They were all between about sixteen and twenty-five: Jean-Claude
and Anne-Marie, Pierre and Ursula's children; and Bernard and
Véronique, Jacques and Hélène's children. Jean-Claude, the eldest,
had followed Claude into the Resistance; Véronique was getting
ready to sit for her baccalaureate; and Bernard, who had just passed
his baccalaureate, spent eight months doing liaison work with
groups of the French Forces of the Interior. Only Hélène's youngest son, Hubert, with his fifteen years and his round cheeks, could
still pass for a child. We were fond of him because he was the
youngest, the gentlest, and the most cheerful. And there was a new
face, too, which I haven't yet had time to mention. This was a
Jewish girl, a communist studying psychoanalysis, quite pretty and
with very red hair. Her name was Nathalie. She was Claude's wife
—or perhaps, as people used to say then, his "girl"—a locution
which was outrageously modern at the time but is now already
old-fashioned. And, by one of those paradoxes which make life so
charming, my grandfather and she got on marvelously together.

It was plain that everything was changing, everything was going
on changing. "The way we're going to have to live is going to be
very different from what we've been used to," Pierre and Aunt
Gabrielle would say. The cost of living kept on rising and the value
of money kept on falling. Where was it all going to end? Immedi-

ately after the war and the victory, say between 1946 and 1952, before the new problems which were to arise for us out of the collapse of the empire (the colonial empire, remember?) and out of the shadow cast by the absent general, what stands out for me about the middle of the century, as it had already at the beginning of the thirties, is, I regret to have to tell you, money. Money problems. Neither Jacques' wife nor, as you may imagine, Claude's had brought much into the family treasury. The Wittgensteins were completely ruined and practically poor, their immense estates fallen into the hands of the communists and their factories destroyed. And Pierre and his children hadn't many resources left. Later, and quite quickly, in less than ten or twelve years, the Wittgensteins, allied to the Krupps, would regain their former power. But under a new system which was very foreign to us. As for me, I was good for nothing except ... but I believe I have promised not to talk about myself. There was only one person in the family able to earn a bit of money. Try to guess who. You never will. It was Anne-Marie.

I must admit, but I assure you without any shame, that we had had long family discussions, usually amid laughter, about the last resource of ancient ruined houses, the *ultima ratio regum,* which was certainly not anything to do with guns: a marriage of convenience (which according to our theories would have changed immediately into a marriage of love) with the heiress, if possible the sole heiress, to a fortune in wool or oil or steel. For Jean-Claude and Anne-Marie, and even for Véronique, who was only seventeen or eighteen, we had found candidates who wouldn't have done our affairs any harm and would have helped to put some butter on our parsnips and some new tiles on our dilapidated roof. But unfortunately this device, which had been successful for so many centuries, no longer worked very well. What a pity! Jean-Claude split his sides laughing, Véronique gave a faint smile, looking frankly shocked, and Anne-Marie spent all her time in a series of improbable love affairs which had nothing to do with matrimony. Even my grandfather no longer really believed in this traditional system, in which, on every side and as far back as everyone could remember, he had

been brought up. Aunt Gabrielle was the only one who was surprised that things had drifted so far from the rules which she had
once known and against which she had, as a matter of fact, spent
a good deal of her life cheerfully struggling. But the do-gooder of
Plessis-lez-Vaudreuil had finally won out over her former avatar of
the rue de Varenne and its forgotten audacities. Forgotten? Forgotten by us, perhaps. And perhaps even by her. But the painters she
had helped were now shown in museums, the poets were represented in school textbooks, and the work of her composer friends
now began to be played in almost classical concerts, of which the
proceeds went to charity or religious institutions. She had become
a terribly correct little old lady, with hair that was quite white and
a black silk ribbon around her neck, and the young people would
laugh when some elegant or cultivated old gentleman told them that
this dowager had once, in her own way, been a revolutionary. And
yet her name was beginning to appear in memoirs, in art dealers'
catalogues, and in histories of music or the cinema. At the very
moment when she retired forever into the bosom of the family and
of the strictest tradition, we discovered with some shame that she
alone of all who bore our name was going to leave behind her a
slender wake of talent, perhaps even a shade of genius, and to enter
through a charming and audacious little door into the corridors of
history.

Ah! Youth, youth. Nobody thought any more about Aunt Gabrielle unless, by a marvelous paradox, it was the lovers of old things
and the archivists of the past. It was Anne-Marie's name which now
began to shine. Modestly. It was to be read in small letters in *France-
Soir* and *Combat* and on the posters in the Champs-Elysées. It sailed
on the still-uncertain waters of the collective memory. Young fanat-
ics already repeated it. As you will already have guessed, Anne-
Marie, irresistibly, in accordance with one of the clichés of the
period, had gone into the cinema.

The beginnings of this career were looked at askance not only by
her great-grandfather, but also by her grandmother and her father,
who both, in their own way, had braved public opinion. It began
almost by chance, with vague propositions following a brief appear-

ance in a documentary on horse shows. Then came tiny parts in films directed by Jacques Becker and Marcel Carné, and a role scarcely more important in a film by René Clair. And then suddenly interminable telegrams began to arrive at Plessis-lez-Vaudreuil from Italy and America, with propositions that might almost be described as flattering. Rossellini had noticed her one evening at the Florence or at Jimmy's. The family at once played the Pauline trick on her: she was forced to change her name and adopt, for the screen, the instantly famous pseudonym which I will not reveal, out of posthumous obedience to the wishes of my grandfather and Aunt Gabrielle, though I imagine many of you have already guessed it. For ten or twelve years, right up to the beginning of the New Wave, her notoriety, celebrity, and finally her fame increased. And today people who have never even heard of our name know the five flamboyant syllables of Anne-Marie's pseudonym, scorned by the family or what was left of it, though with a tinge of satisfied vanity and secret pride.

Like Claude before the war, though for different reasons, Anne-Marie drifted away from us. We no longer saw her much. With her impresario and her directors, her hairdresser and her manicurist, and soon with her legend, she went from grand hotel to grand hotel in an aura of luxury and rather terrifying frivolity sometimes almost bordering on scandal, preceded and followed by public discussion and the devotion of young men. Amazingly, Anne-Marie's beauty, perhaps her talent and her ambition, quite a new thing for us, had succeeded in unleashing on our ancient family a great wind of youth which at once frightened and enchanted us. Did she ever dream still of her rides with Robert V. in the forest at Plessis-lez-Vaudreuil, or of the silent shadow of Major von Wittgenstein, dead at Stalingrad, of the young Marxists of the nights in Paris, or of the tall curly-haired Maquisard at La Flèche? I don't know. Sometimes she would talk to me about these already faded images, but rather in answer to my own curiosity and thirst for a vanished world than out of any need of her own to remember. Too many men had passed too swiftly through her life, a life ravaged by her own beauty and success, by applause and sheaves of flowers in dressing rooms. She

had become one of those goddesses of our modern world, so far
from all we used to be, so opposite to our faith and our old ideas
about greatness and decency. She drove men mad, but they no
longer really mattered to her. Her real lovers were anonymous
crowds, a somewhat bitter glory, and money.

But one summer evening Anne-Marie came back to Plessis-lez-
Vaudreuil. She was not yet at the height of her fame. She had come
from America. She had crossed the Atlantic because Hubert was ill.
His illness had begun quite lightheartedly, with an attack of appendicitis. It wasn't anything much. We took him to Le Mans and he
had an operation. It was almost a little celebration of affection amid
the torpor of the summer holidays; we just paid slightly less attention to the Tour de France, which had started up again, and in
which Bartali and Robic had begun to triumph. And we would sit
laughing around Hubert's bed. Naturally Aunt Gabrielle, who took
her role as grandmother very seriously, was somewhat upset. But
we knew enough not to be too frightened by the outmoded specter
of appendicitis. We kept saying that nowadays appendicitis was less
serious than a wisdom tooth, and Aunt Gabrielle calmed down.

Two or three days went by after Hubert got back from Le Mans.
Then, going into his room one morning, I was struck by how pale
he looked. He'd spent a restless night, he had a severe pain in his
stomach, and his temperature had gone up. What a nuisance! There
was talk of adhesions, of postoperative pain, of scars not closing
properly, and we even went so far as to wonder if the operation had
been a success, though this did not mean anything much. Aunt
Gabrielle was alarmed again. The doctor in Roussette was sent for
urgently. He was a distant successor of old Dr. Sauvagein, and had
had to attend two accouchements and one case of chickenpox that
same day. His sight wasn't very good. He thought it would pass off.
Hubert was a bit better. Already he had less pain. But that evening
he started to vomit.

He didn't have a good night. He was shivering, and it seemed to
me that his features were growing more and more drawn. The
doctor came again and said something which frightened us all: he
talked of obstruction of the bowels. That evening we called in a

professor from Rennes, an old friend of my grandfather's, and a doctor from Angers whom our neighbors in the country had spoken well of. They came the next day. Hubert had grown worse. He was suffering from shivering fits, nausea, severe abdominal pain, and fever, and his pulse was rapid and weak. And he showed a lassitude, almost prostration, which pain alone could interrupt. The two specialists met in the drawing room. It all looked rather like a play in which everyone was playing a part—theirs was polite knowledge; ours, discreet uneasiness; and that of Hubert, up in his room with its phonograph records and photographs of actresses, a very correct kind of suffering. We were much reassured by the presence of the two doctors. With their preoccupied and self-important air, they would sort everything out. They washed their hands and then went up to see Hubert, separately at first and then together; then they came down again and consulted with each other in a corner of the billiard room. They rejoined us, murmuring phrases which we couldn't understand and of which we could remember only terrifying scraps: peritonitis ... septicemia ... penicillin ... God! Perhaps they would have to operate again. God! Right away? Well ... no, not at once. They must wait a little, they would have to see. The pundits hesitated. There was an infection, and the first thing to do was to fight that. The boy was very weak. An immediate operation was too risky. There were other words in the air, but we did not utter them, as if silence might still ward off the evil and keep pain away from the body of our little one. Come from we knew not where, from the distant reaches of the family of which we were so proud, or perhaps just by chance, tuberculosis and cancer lurked about us in the suddenly hostile corridors of Plessis-lez-Vaudreuil.

It was a bolt from the blue. Hubert! Have I told you about him? He was a wonderful little boy, with very round cheeks and a rather startled look. He was almost grown up, but because he was suffering we suddenly saw him again as he used to be—as a helpless child. Did children still die? Could they still, in our day, after so much progress, fall ill and die? Come, come! But all the same I went to the post office. I telephoned Claude, who was in Paris: he said he would come right away. I sent a telegram to Anne-Marie, who was in Los Angeles. I said: HUBERT ILL. COME IF YOU CAN. QUICKLY. LOVE. And I signed it: UNCLE JEAN. She was there by the following day. Hubert was very ill.

I don't know whether, in your own family or in one near you, you've ever seen a child dying. I hope not. The death of someone we love is always sad. But it is the way of the world, and we all know it's a cruel world. But the death of a child is unjust: it is horror carried to absurdity. It is against order, monstrous, revolting, impossible. God has no right to change his own laws and make the youngest die before the eyes of the oldest.

It was as if Hubert, to show for the last time that he belonged to us, had waited to die until all his family were gathered about him. We stood around his bed and pretended to smile. He was trembling violently and no longer even complaining: fever, pain, and nausea were now so strong that he had entered that merciful state in which suffering and anguish are stifled and grow dim. Hubert gazed at us mildly, with a sort of silent yet puzzled trust. We saw a reproach in his look. Why were we letting him suffer? Why were we letting him go? No, I don't think it was really a reproach he was trying to convey. It was worse than reproach: it was resignation. He was no longer putting up a fight. He had suffered too much. He wanted it all to end, he wanted to be allowed to go. But perhaps at the same time he still dimly hoped we would hold him back? From time to time he thought it might be possible to stay and yet not suffer any more. Then he would smile. To tell us that he trusted us, and to reassure us. But then the pain would come back, the torture, the great waves of suffering. And then he would shut his eyes.

Now and then he would ask something in a faint, heartrending little voice: whether his cousin Anne-Marie, whom he admired very much, was there, or if his temperature had gone down. We answered quietly, and as calmly as possible. We wore broad smiles. Hélène went out of the bedroom to weep in silence in Claude's or my arms. Two or three times I had to struggle to hold back my tears. I could see my grandfather's lips tremble as he looked at the child. He leaned on us: the child's suffering had made him suddenly grow old. Meals were dreary affairs, and the evenings were spent in waiting. My grandfather kept saying he hadn't deserved, at the age of over ninety and after a life which had not been dishonorable, to see his son die, and the son of his son, and the son of his grandson. Even his name, he said, using an astonishing phrase which at any other time would have made us laugh, no longer gave him any pleasure. What could we say in reply? At night, before taking turns going to bed and pretending to sleep, we all prayed together. I saw Claude and Nathalie kneel down with us and pray for the child to a cruel and silent God in whom they did not believe.

At last, one morning, after two or three days, Hubert felt a little better. We breathed again. We managed to eat something, and to sleep for an hour or two. We were going to save him. How? We did not know. But we were going to save him. Already he was better. We'd just gotten worked up over nothing again. What an ordeal! But now everything seemed trivial and easy. There was only one thing in the world that mattered, and that was the life of a child. We telephoned to Le Mans, to Angers, and to Rennes. Yes, yes, the news was better. The doctor would come back the following day. There was talk of an operation if the patient's general state would permit: a laparotomy. The young dean and the doctor from Roussette came to lunch. We were just having coffee when Hélène rushed in and said in a hollow voice that the boy was not doing well. We rushed up the stairs, our minds blank, our hearts heavy, our heads reverberating with the words: "He's not doing well!" We stopped to get our breath back before going into the bedroom, as casually as possible. But one glance was enough: Hubert was dying. His face was covered with sweat, his cheeks had disappeared, all that could be seen was his nose, which was now like that of my grandfather. We were all in the room. I don't know how the news had got around so fast. Old Estelle was standing by the door with young Jules beside her. We joined the doctor and the priest around the bed. The doctor was no longer of any use. He stood a little to one side, yielding his place to the dean. The dean took the child's hands and asked him: "Can you hear me, Hubert? Can you hear me?"—bending over him until he almost touched him. Hubert opened his eyes. Yes, he could hear him. Then the dean began to recite, with us, the prayer for the dying.

The murmur filled the room and died away. The dean stepped aside. Hélène and my grandfather together approached the bed where the youngest of our name had almost finished suffering. They both knelt down and each took one of the dying boy's hands. We were all weeping, but without making any sound. Looking back, it seems to me we waited an eternity for death to come. We wanted him to die now, and for this agony to be over. He died almost in silence. I realized that he was dead when I saw my grandfather bow his head to kiss his hand.

We still had some happy times at Plessis-lez-Vaudreuil after that, but never the same as before. Many of our family, men and women, had died in the old house. But the death of the youngest among us was like an augury, like a knell for all the family. We buried him in the graveyard at Roussette, after a mass in the chapel where we had married Anne and Michel. Michel Desbois was a traitor, and in prison, and Hubert was dead. Something had changed in the family and in the house, not only for Hélène, of course, but also for Anne, for my grandfather, for all of us. We found it hard to laugh or feel happy. After so many centuries, so many ordeals survived, so much sorrow and so much joy, Plessis-lez-Vaudreuil was drifting away.

What a paradox! Plessis-lez-Vaudreuil had never been nearer, more comfortable, more agreeable. Do you remember those long journeys at the beginning of the century when we came to settle for six months in what seemed some distant province? Before the Second World War, we already used to come for just a few days, for shorter and shorter vacations, not only for Easter and Christmas, but also for Whitsunday or All Saints'. And now we came for the weekend or even just for Sunday, in our Citroëns or our Peugeots. We brought friends for lunch or dinner. They spent a few hours there and then went away again. We were within easy reach of Paris. It was no longer a chateau, it was a weekend house, a very comfortable country place, or, to use the hated phrases of building societies and tax declarations, a second home. There were now four bathrooms, running water almost everywhere, and oil central heating which had cost a fortune. "Modern!" my grandfather would say, with a grimace of disgust. But the tiles on the roof were in a bad way. And the woodwork was crumbling. Monsieur Tissier, the tiler, and Monsieur Naud, the carpenter, had warned us: if we wanted to avoid imminent disaster we must undertake urgent repairs. God! Was it true? Yes, it was true. We looked at the walls: they were crumbling. We looked at the turrets, which were supposed to derive their amazing shapes from Burgundy, or Bavaria, or Byzantium, or Persia: they swayed in the wind. The great rains of autumn, the storms we used to love so much, had become our enemies. We suddenly discovered that our stonework and woodwork, like our ideas, were falling into ruin. Age and the past, which we had revered, were betraying us.

We had to find means of repairing our beams, our gutters, our tiles, our ceilings, means to keep up our oak trees. We discovered with horror that we had scarcely any means left, though we had ceilings, tiles, gutters, and beams enough and to spare. And oak trees too, thank God. As a matter of fact, we used to sell them. We would gather around my grandfather in the evening and open the big ledgers in which our trees were recorded. We would count up all the different kinds. The oldest were the finest. It was one way of living in the past still. We felt at home in the plans that Monsieur Desbois had drawn up. Since Jacques' death, it had fallen to me to look after the forest. I didn't do it as well as Monsieur Desbois had. The forms, the taxes, the rules, the classifications became more onerous every day: how we used to hate those questionnaires we couldn't make head or tail of! The modern world appeared to us in the form of a forest of papers more numerous than our ancient oaks, a jungle of calculations and administration. We had fewer and fewer staff to reap the meadows and look after the roads, more and more expenses and less and less income. Every detail gave our grandfather an opportunity to conjure up times gone by—the duchesse d'Uzès in at the death by the pool of the Quatre-Vents; some ridiculous scene with the V.s at the crossroads of the Arbres-Verts (ever since Robert's death we refer to them as the "poor V.s"); some conversation with Jules in 1880 or perhaps 1881. Beneath the felled

oaks, beyond the scarcity of money, there arose a colorful world,
a lively world: whole packs of hounds fighting over a stag, or what
was left of it; horsewomen pursued by wild passions; pink coats full
of insolence, jauntiness, and strength; faithful servants who had
their own place in the system and touched my grandfather's hand
as they raised their caps. All that was dead.

We sold trees, whole forests. The oak trees tumbled into the abyss
and were not enough. My grandfather used to go and see them one
last time, before the ax and the sawmill. He would stand in front
of them and gaze. The woodcutters would wait. At last he would
go away again without a word, slightly stooped, his hands behind
his back. Then the woodcutters would spit into their hands and say:
"Here goes!"

Nor was there good news from Paris. Our property in the boulevard Haussmann no longer brought in very much. My grandfather
was astonished: what was happening? For a hundred and fifty years
we had lived off our trees and our houses in Paris. What was going
on, then, in this amazing world? We would launch into expositions
of social theory and economics which it would have been simpler
to sum up in a few words: the world was changing.

Because we weren't very intelligent, we made one monumental
error after another. We missed old Desbois. And we missed Michel
even more. We were losing a lot of money. And there was a cruel
rumor, which finally came to our ears, that we had made even worse
mistakes, and that if we'd been quicker, better managers, less backward, we could have saved Hubert. Thirty years ago, of course, he
would have died. But in our day and age he could have lived, he
ought to have lived. We had acted, of course, as people would have
acted thirty years ago, and he was dead. The modern world overwhelmed us with its increased possibilities and its great hopes. We
felt we were no longer up to it, that it was beyond us, that we were
no longer capable of mastering this speed, these complications. We
had had too much misfortune. And suddenly everything was giving
way. What was the use? So we started to sell. It was the simplest
thing to do. Houses, pictures, a field marshal's baton set with precious stones, trees and more trees, always trees. How horrible! With

a mixture of irony, sadness, and bitter satisfaction at having understood before everyone else, Claude murmured: "It's all over."

We scarcely bothered any more about memories, the spreading of the faith, the testament of St. Louis. We were preoccupied with frozen rents, farms which didn't bring in anything any more, fluctuating rates of exchange, crumbling stones and splitting tiles. Of course, we knew we were still high up among the small number of privileged in this world. But the system in which we had lived was collapsing. We didn't complain: in spite of everything, thank God, we still knew how to behave, and we could still see clearly enough to recognize that in a way we had brought it all on ourselves. We were our own victims, or perhaps rather the victims of a past in which even the most liberated among us were still held prisoner. How hard it is to change one's past, one's social class, one's economic and intellectual constellation! Thanks to the Remy-Michaults we had managed to work, to make money, to adapt ourselves to the modern world, as individuals. But for the family as a whole, that myth embodied in the stones of Plessis-lez-Vaudreuil, it was difficult, almost impossible, to adapt to the new structures—not only to their demands but, also by an astonishing paradox, to their advantages and pleasures. I think Claude and Pierre, and perhaps I too, understood quite well what was happening. But there was nothing much we could do about it. We accepted, we even went so far as to approve of what was crushing us. But my grandfather did not approve of it. He was too old to approve. But he accepted too. We all accepted. What else could we do but accept history? A history that was insidious, rather low, rather vile. We had prepared ourselves for heroic deaths, for the cross and the scaffold, for confessions of faith. But we had few arms against devaluation, the rise in the cost of living, economic and social changes; against justice and the future and intelligence; against all the shifting sands in which our house was sinking, under the triumphant eye of Karl Marx, Lord Keynes, Dr. Freud, Einstein, and Picasso (how right we had been to mistrust genius!).

Socialism. We sold. Psychoanalysis. We sold. Abstract art. We sold. Phenomenology and existentialism. We sold. Fortunes made out of oil and real estate. We sold, we sold. What had we to do with this age which was overwhelming us on every side? That Marxism and revolution should be banes to us—fair enough. But the very order of money and the bourgeoisie was alien to us. The future rejected us—very well. But for years and years a past had been building up which we could no longer recognize. We were betrayed on all sides, by the socialist future and the bourgeois past. We sold. But we couldn't leap over the centuries and go back to take our stand on Henri IV and Sully and St. Louis and Suger, on the thousands of émigrés, on Thomism, on the Counter Reformation and feudalism. Were there no more crusades? We sold. We knew very well that economic and social history was our Nessus' shirt. We no longer even thought that God and his truth and his justice were on our side. And, more than by ruin and helplessness, it was by this abandonment, this departure of God that we were overwhelmed.

One fine day, quite soon, we found ourselves shut up in Plessis-lez-Vaudreuil as on an island. The boulevard Haussmann, the farms in the Haute-Sarthe, and most of the forest had been sold off. Only the house and the oldest of the trees remained. When we turned and contemplated this shipwreck, its suddenness terrified us. Time, on which we had based everything, had reversed itself in a flash, and everything was overthrown. We were still sitting all together— those of us who were left—around the stone table. The lime trees were still there, slightly fewer, slightly thinner; death had struck among them, too. We talked as we used to, of the government, the neighbors, the mass on Sunday, and how the children were getting on at school. But there was something indefinable which was not as it had been before. It was not just that there was no longer any snow in winter or sun in summer; it was that the past and the future were both collapsing around us, and we seemed to be under a stay of execution.

It had all happened very fast, I thought. And then I remembered that twenty or thirty years before, and forty years before, and fifty years before, we were already saying the same things. And now, because we were getting old, we had the feeling that the end of the

world was near. But Jean-Claude and Anne-Marie and Véronique
and Bernard looked at us and laughed. We too had laughed as we
listened to Uncle Joseph and Uncle Charles and Great-Uncle Anatole. I shrugged my shoulders. The fact was that everything was
just continuing, the enormous mass of interests, feelings, passions
and memories, hopes and fears, wisdom and folly which made up
our world. The world went on. But differently. And there was,
after all, something that was nearing its end: Plessis-lez-Vaudreuil.

Sometimes, in the evening, before dinner, I would stand at my
window and look out at the old trees, the lake in the distance, the
limes, the stone table, all that peaceful and familiar landscape which
had stretched out in front of us for century upon century. It was
the time of day when a great silence fell and the birds were still. You
could see them flying past soundlessly, high in a sky from which the
clouds were disappearing. We were linked to, bound up with, those
gentle outlines, those rather faded colors, that incomparable perfume which I could smell from where I stood. I closed my eyes.
Neither Pierre nor Claude nor I myself was, like my grandfather,
rooted exclusively in this land which had produced us. Only Philippe, perhaps ... But we all felt at home here, and we were all
attached to it by the heavy yet beloved chains of tradition and
memory. Those trees, that little hill, that sky over there, so ordinary
yet so irreplaceable, was us. The stone table was us. The lime trees
were us. And were we going to have to leave all that, so near to us,
flesh of our flesh, our dead, our vanquished hopes? Yes, we had
really had it. Everything was changing, I knew that very well. A
great quiet murmur rose up toward me. Beyond the lake and the
forest were millions of men with their problems and interests which
had no longer anything to do with ours, and which for so long we
had ignored. Enduring their own misery and unhappiness, which
we did not share. This wise and untouched nature, this silent beauty
so harmonious and so well-groomed, was a marvelous privilege
which we alone enjoyed. And on the trees, the sky, the surface of
the lake, and above the stone table a single word was written, four
simple but sinister letters: over, over. We lingered on for another
two years, just as Hubert had lingered on for six days. We tried to

cling on. It was a slow torture, punctuated by taxes and frenzied calculations. We became miserly, gloomy, strange. Millions of francs went down the drain in the form of social charges which we never stopped worrying about—in gardeners' wages, in repairing the woodwork in the chapel, in mending the tiles on the roof. The difference between income and expenses only grew larger. Under the pretext of tradition, we no longer thought about anything but money. Now and again my grandfather would still make us laugh. Under the Second Empire and at the beginning of the Third Republic his father had employed three men just to look after the roof. He wondered if it wouldn't be cheaper to go back to the old system. We did our figures again, especially the subtractions. We needed about five million francs a year just to look after the roof. The trees in the forest, which had been cut down as severely as possible, brought in only four or five million. "Well," my grandfather would say, "we'll have to retrench." This was a phrase we now heard at least a couple of times a week. And he proposed we should survive with two men to look after the roof instead of three, and three gardeners instead of seven. If you have ever had occasion, going through the Haute-Sarthe, to stroll through what remains of the gardens at Plessis-lez-Vaudreuil, and of its famous kitchen garden and maze of yew trees where we ourselves never set foot, you won't have any difficulty in realizing that three gardeners were not a lot. But they were still too many. And there was something comic about a penury which still included two or three gardeners (we couldn't quite make up our minds), several housemaids (who by now were Spanish), a cook (who would soon be black), and Jules, unchangeable, still corresponding to our dreams, another phoenix arising from his ashes. We were still proud in our ruins. But we were already ruined in our pride. Claude was right: it was all over.

Beauty was expensive—we realized that. And I assure you, we also realized how easy it was to laugh at us, how ridiculous we were. Not with the ridiculous grandeur of the beginning of the century, but with the pitiable ridiculousness of those whom life had conquered. Perhaps I am not conveying this very clearly. We weren't dying of hunger. We still had cars, elegant clothes, expensive silk shirts made to measure, and luxurious habits. We still lived in a style which many people might envy. But now it was only out of inertia, weakness, inability to think of anything else. With a mixture of grandeur and hypocrisy, in a last spasm of self-righteousness, we ourselves were ready to say we did it out of duty. What can I say? The best way to put it is that our "structures" were collapsing.

I include, of course, our moral structures, the values, as people used to call them, according to which we had lived, blindly, for centuries. But people still manage to accommodate themselves to collapsing moral values. The most intelligent and magnanimous of us—you will realize that I am referring to Claude—had already changed. What were also breaking up now were our economic and social structures. And Claude himself, because despite himself, almost unconsciously, he had never ceased to be one of us, was also caught up in the catastrophe. He was caught up in it because he still loved Plessis-lez-Vaudreuil with every fiber of his being; because ideas are nothing in comparison with one's way of life, which is everything; and because memory suddenly awoke out of its ashes. I sometimes used to think that Claude suffered more than the rest of us. The contradictions which afflicted him were more cruel than those which afflicted us.

How we struggled! For tax reasons, Plessis-lez-Vaudreuil was made into a corporation in an attempt to anticipate difficulties still lurking in the future. My grandfather hated the very word and idea of a corporation, with its concomitant financial maneuvers and dividing-up of shares. But what else could we do? I've already had difficulty in talking about my grandfather and my father and Uncle Paul: I have had to simplify. But in addition to his brothers and sons, whom we've seen appearing and disappearing, my grandfather also had two married sisters and three daughters—my father's and Uncle Paul's three sisters—who did not live with us but who naturally had a right to a share in the inheritance. We still made only moderate use of birth control, and each of these daughters had had children. In Uncle Paul's generation, counting all the boys who fell in the war, there were seven children. In my generation, there were thirteen of us: Anne and me, my four cousins, and my three aunts' seven children. In the generation of Anne-Marie and my nephew, not counting the dead and those who did not marry, there promised to be a good twenty of them. To my grandfather's great satisfaction, Claude had just married Nathalie because they were expecting a child. That made one more. Twenty-one or twenty-two. And how were all these going to divide up Plessis-lez-Vaudreuil? One day when we were discussing the problem for the hundredth time, Bernard let fall a terrible witticism which went back a long way into the family subconscious. "It's a lucky thing Hubert died," he said. I can vouch for the fact that Bernard was fond of Hubert. But in his cynical modern way, which nevertheless had something of the reflexes of the past, he was expressing a profound truth. At last the family was coming up against the consequences of the Revolution and the abolition of the right of primogeniture. History always catches up with us in the end. We had always known that these two events—it was their avowed object, they did not hide it, and I don't even say that they were wrong—that these two historical events signified the end of our family as a social unit. We had held out a good long while. But now we were going to die.

I too still tried to live on a little while at Plessis-lez-Vaudreuil. I buried my head under my own words, as we used to bury our heads, ostrichlike, under the gravel on the paths. We came and went, we attended mass, we pretended to go on hunting and riding, we didn't want to know about the dangers which threatened us. But our hearts were no longer in it. There was something baleful in this long-drawn-out play-acting. Even the pheasants and the hares became scarce, as if they wanted to make an end of it. From time to time we could still get up a rather attenuated hunting scene outside the house. But it was only one more pretext for conjuring up memories—the fabulous hunting scenes of the beginning of the century, with their huge bags and the antiquated figures which were now disappearing into the darkness. No, hunting too was no longer what it used to be. The youngest of the family, Véronique and Bernard, only thought of getting away. Hubert had already gone. Bernard and Véronique wanted to leave us too. We used to hear them, on summer evenings, listening with a sort of envious passion to the syncopated echoes which their radios and record players brought them, of St. Tropez, of fashionable beaches, of all the places where other young people of their age were enjoying themselves. I still used to stroll quite often around the lake with my grandfather. He was over ninety now, but he still walked with a firm step. Our walk was exactly the same as in the days—Heavens! Was it so long ago?—when he used to question me about Claude's vocation, Uncle Paul's business affairs, the relations between Pierre and Ursula and the rumors they gave rise to, and Anne-Marie's studies. And now we said the same things about other people and over events. We were among the last people in the West to have spent our whole life in the same landscape, unchanged, untouched, with the same trees casting the same shadows on the same paths where we walked at the same hours. How could our ideas have failed to be equally rigid and immutable? Still nothing changed in the setting that surrounded us. A few trees had been felled, that was all. But people's minds changed, and their souls, and the speed at which time passed: every day it brought our downfall closer. My grandfather knew this. Sometimes he reproached himself for having lasted so long. And now he talked to me about the children, about those who after him, after me, were going to continue our name. He was worried about Anne-Marie. He was fond of the others, but he didn't understand them. "We are fighting," he would say to me, "for something they do not love." As always, the dead were our consolation. "Ah, Hubert! If only . . ." my grandfather would murmur. And it seemed as if Hubert, if he had lived, would have succeeded in saving everything, in marrying the Begum, repairing the house, replanting all the trees uprooted by age and the wind, checking all that rose as we descended—socialism, abstract art, the concrete music that my grandfather found so hideous, oil companies and real estate, the pornography which was already rearing a timid head through the holes of history—in short, in restoring to our name and to the house which embodied it all their vanished splendor. Ah, Hubert, Hubert . . . It was the story of Robert V. all over again, only more cruel. In his lifetime we had never surrounded him with such love and attention. But what could be more natural? We loved only eternity. And Hubert, in his turn, before his turn, had entered into eternity.

After Hubert, my grandfather would pass on to the death of Uncle Anatole, the death of Aunt Yvonne, the death of my great-grandmother, who fell off her horse at the crossroads of the Arbres-Verts, and the death of my great-grandmother's great-grandmother, who was guillotined. No doubt about it, we had spent most of our time dying. Everybody in the family had ended up by dying. But no one ever forgot. It was this prodigious, mystical collective memory which made up the name, the family, the house. And it was this chain, stretched out in defiance across our eternal enemy, time, that my grandfather did not want to see broken.

But it was breaking. For fifty or sixty years, occasionally through the agency of Albert Remy-Michault, offers to purchase Plessis-lez-Vaudreuil had not been lacking. One after the other, a Russian grand duke, Basil Zaharoff, the Duke of Westminster when he was thinking of marrying Mademoiselle Chanel, Charlie Chaplin, and a Greek shipping tycoon had offered us sums which, at least nominally, grew larger and larger with each offer. We had either not answered at all or replied, if not with insult, at least in extremely curt and imperious terms which must have seemed almost offensive to people who, after all, in their clumsy fashion (though one could scarcely maintain that the Duke of Westminster or Grand Duke Vladimir lacked *savoir-vivre*), were really paying us a compliment. "What about our name?" my grandfather would growl. "Perhaps they'd like to buy that at the same time?" Now the offer did not come from a grand duke or even a great actor or shipping magnate. It came from a big development company with American capital and barbarous initials, COPADIC or FORATRAC or something like that. You should have seen the rage and contempt with which my grandfather would utter the name. Ten or fifteen years later, the development company was to link up with such important concerns as the Société des Bains de Mer and the Club Méditerranée. The company wanted the house and all that was left of the land and the trees to set up a hotel in the country-club style, where guests could ride and play tennis and golf and bathe in a swimming pool

which some overelegant gentleman who came down in a white
Mercedes proposed to build beyond the stone table. We hurried my
grandfather back to his room lest he have apoplexy. Pierre, rather
pale, had long discussions with advisers and experts who changed
every week and represented various groups of subsidiaries and holding companies with impressive and interchangeable names, all mixed
up with one another so as to dazzle customers and confuse the tax
authorities. References to the leisure activities of the masses, to
highways and airports, fell from their lips like diamonds and pearls
from the lips of the princess in the fairy story. They made great
play with millions too, causing Pierre to look pensive and Véronique and Bernard to jump up and down with excitement. But no,
it was impossible. Already we were not alone when we took our
coffee around the stone table. We were surrounded by shades which
were no longer the ghosts of the dead members of the family rising
up from the past, but the ghosts of strangers rising up out of the
future. Even while the house still belonged to us, a whole anonymous crowd of golfers wearing caps and vulgar tennis players
jostled us shamelessly. We hesitated, hung back. The others sensed
it. The millions increased. This decided us, but of course in the
opposite direction from that which was expected. "People who
offer you a pound one day and two pounds the next because you
don't accept it!" said my grandfather furiously. "How can they
possibly be honest?" He stopped for a moment, pretending to think
it over, seeing frightful images in his mind's eye, like some topsy-
turvy temptation of St. Anthony: people in shorts or suspenders,
sunbathers, accordions . . . Then he burst out: "They'd be capable
of playing bowls outside the chapel, drinking frightful concoctions
imported from America." It was impossible. We said no. Much to
the stupefaction of the others, who had even offered to let us go on
living in the house for a while, to act as "hosts" and organize the
leisure activities.

Victory! We were staying on. There was a cloudburst, a section
of the forest caught fire: we lost another few hundred thousand
francs, perhaps a million. We raised a mortgage, we borrowed. We
knew very well now that catastrophe was inevitable. We could

almost calculate the date, which was not far off, when we would no longer be able to pay Jules, nor our taxes, nor the bills for the electricity and the telephone which my grandfather regretted having had installed so irresponsibly at the beginning of the century. Anne-Marie sent money she had earned from a film in which she appeared—though my grandfather didn't know it—in a bathing suit and a nightdress. Aunt Gabrielle and Pierre scraped up what they could from the remains of the Remy-Michault fortune, the vastness of which had disgusted my grandfather at the end of the Belle Epoque. But these were mere drops in the ocean that was carrying us away and the house with us. Philippe, who always got excited and liked to dramatize, came down to breakfast one morning—my grandfather fortunately still had his breakfast in his room, but the rest of us came down to the dining room because there were not enough servants for everybody to breakfast in his room—and threw a folded newspaper down on the table amid the bread and butter. The Sainte-Euverte family had dynamited their Henri IV chateau in Normandy, which was anyway rather ugly, having been somewhat over-restored around 1880 by an immensely rich grandmother, née Rufus Israël. "Good riddance!" said Pierre, without lifting his eyes from his cup. But Philippe was easily carried away, and the idea took root in his mind. He didn't dislike the idea of some final catastrophe, something which would be a protest against an age and a regime which the general himself had abandoned to its fate. General de Gaulle at Colombey, the Socialists in power, and Plessis-lez-Vaudreuil in flames: this was a conjunction of misfortunes which rather appealed to Philippe. Wasn't such a Twilight of the Gods on our own small scale better than creeping out on tiptoe, leaving the key under Jules' doormat for future owners who would certainly have striped shirts and modish ideas? Claude raised one eyebrow and shrugged: Philippe hadn't changed, that was certain.

Everybody's mood was affected by this mixture of uncertainty and anxiety. The Tour de France, the weather, the peas and the milk, the attitude of such keepers and gardeners as remained, the manners of the young, the ways of the family itself—in short, nothing was what it had been. The pears were not so good. My grandfather had always been a connoisseur of pears. From their appearance, their taste, almost—with his eyes shut—from their smell and touch he could tell the difference between a Conférence and a Louise-Bonne, a Doyenné de Comice and a Passe-Crassane, and distinguish a Duchesse d'Angoulême or a Comtesse de Paris from a Sucrée de Montlucon, a Bon Chrétien William from a Beurré Hardy. But they didn't seem to be worth anything any more. We were amazed. The pears had always been one of the prides of Plessis-lez-Vaudreuil. Pierre made inquiries. He discovered that the pears from the orchard were being sold in Angers or Le Mans by the gardeners, whom we no longer paid sufficient wages. And the pears which came to the table were from Paris. There comes a moment in scientific theories, art forms, governments, and families where everything which has hitherto functioned correctly and harmoniously begins to stutter and break down. People invent remedies, substitutes, theories of correction, modifications of every kind —sometimes with success. There are certain autumns in history which are the equivalent of its springs. And there are triumphant declines. Justinian, Belisarius, and Hegel each mark the end of something which had never been greater than when its evening was illuminated by their genius. Nevertheless the Roman Empire fell, and philosophy is dead. I suppose the idea of fate, which haunts men in a thousand different forms, derives from this strange coalition between the forces of destruction—from the impossibility of arresting what is hurrying to the brink of the abyss. You repair one hole, and it is replaced by ten others. You correct the tiller, and the storm grows fiercer. It is as if decrepitude, decadence, and downfall fed on, and were fascinated by, their own momentum. There is nothing to be done against erosion, there is nothing to be done against time. We had relied on time to build up our power: now it was turning against us and thrusting us back into the past which we had so much loved. Elsewhere it was building up new theories, dazzling visions, wonderful hopes. But we—we were breaking up, going to pieces. At God's pleasure. Never again would we know the delicious but lost flavor—delicious and lost, delicious because lost—of the pears of Plessis-lez-Vaudreuil.

Yes, we still had some good times at Plessis-lez-Vaudreuil. Véronique and Jean-Claude were both married on the same day in the
old chapel which you already know, full of memories and friends.
The hunting horns were there. They burst forth at the elevation of
the Host, and everyone was startled. A bright sun shone in the
courtyard and over the park. The children looked beautiful. But
they were no longer children. Through them, in them, I could see
other children: the children they had been, the children their parents had been. The children we had been. It wasn't only their games,
their expectations, their youth, their wonder, which were revived
and filled in spirit the crowded little church: it was ours. What love
of life! What gaiety! With all our faults, I think we had a genius
for celebration. Our dances, our hunting parties, our birthdays, the
feast days of our saints, our weddings, our funerals, even our tea
parties were incomparable. The conquering bourgeoisie had taken
them over from us, but it never succeeded in reproducing our
gaiety, which was shared by the firemen, the woodcutters, the
photographer, the teacher—all the people on our estates whom we
had loved and who had loved us. Do you remember Anne's wedding? Véronique's marriage to Charles-Louis, Jean-Claude's to Pascale, were as like it as peas in a pod. That was another form the
genius of our family took: we abolished time through repetition.

I can see it now, the courtyard at Plessis-lez-Vaudreuil, under its
summer sun, and the two couples drinking champagne with Jules
on one side and the dean on the other! Have a good look! I said to
myself. I looked because we already knew, all of us, that this vital
beauty was going to be snatched away from us. In the evening, after
supper, in the open air, under the lime trees around the stone table,
my grandfather, in an unheard-of fit of audacity, had made a
concession to modernity and secretly organized a surprise perfor-
mance of what he was the last person in France to refer to as the
cinematograph. Although he knew nothing about this modern art
form he had chosen with unerring accuracy, presumably because
of its title, a film that might have symbolized us: *Gone with the Wind.*
We were Southerners ravaged by disaster. Horses, carriages, black
servants, crinolines, happiness, and ruin danced around us. When

the last image flickered out over the ghosts of Melanie, Ashley, Rhett Butler, Scarlett O'Hara, and their vanished loves, all of us—the house, the lake, the stone table between the lime trees, our dreams, our follies, our illusions, and ourselves—we too were phantoms in a night that was ending. Already in the distance beyond the night we sensed a new day trying to dawn. Another day. Another dawn. Another time than ours.

By the next morning the children had gone, for two months—Jean-Claude with his young wife, Véronique with her husband. Anne-Marie flew off to Rome, New York, Hollywood, and Rio de Janeiro. Bernard hastened to Cannes—in fact to St. Tropez, but he said Cannes for my grandfather's sake. My grandfather had a soft spot for Lord Brougham. And we, the old people, were left alone. We suddenly felt a hundred years old. The double wedding, the sunshine in the courtyard, the mass in the chapel, the gaiety, the friendliness, the old carefree attitude, had only been another respite. *Gone with the Wind*—how apt! Our life was over. An evening breeze was carrying it away.

That was our last summer at Plessis-lez-Vaudreuil. Hubert had rendered us one last service by dying: he had given us an honorable excuse for leaving a house whose weight we now found crushing. Hélène could no longer bear Plessis-lez-Vaudreuil, where her son had died. She hardly ever went there any more. Aunt Gabrielle was ill and spent most of her time in Paris. How strange it was: my mother, Ursula, Aunt Gabrielle, Anne, Hélène, Anne-Marie, and Véronique had all been taken away by death, illness, fame, marriage, history, or grief, and the only woman left with my grandfather and his four grandsons was a young red-headed Jewess who admired two old men: my grandfather and Stalin. We led a very straitened life. We scarcely ventured as far, any more, as the stone table, the lime trees, the lake. We had our coffee on the steps of the drawing room, on the stones of the ancient drawbridge. It was as if we were just camping temporarily at Plessis-lez-Vaudreuil. We no longer even repaired the tiles or the beams. We were already drifting away in spirit from the house of our fathers. When we got an offer from a big textile firm in the north which wanted to use the house for children's holidays during the summer and for study groups and conferences for the rest of the year, we were no longer able to put up any resistance: our nerves and our strength were exhausted. Children's holiday camps had already been familiar before the war, but words like "symposium," "seminar," "executive conference," and "manpower retraining," which were already beginning timidly to make their way in the world, were even more certain to exasperate my grandfather. "Pap!" he would growl furiously, from old habit wielding his stick, which was provided with a minute hoe at the end, and gouging out a weed from the allée des Platanes or the allée du Roi. But, when all was said and done, technocrats were better than sharks. Professors of social science and economics were not my grandfather's dream, but they couldn't be worse than organizers of leisure activities. My grandfather, who had never known many people and now knew no one, asked Pierre, who was on familiar terms with everyone in Paris, to find out about the company in question and the people who ran it. Pierre came back with files full of figures, balance sheets, details about cash flow and investments. "That wasn't what I was asking you," said my grandfather. "What about religion and morality? I don't dare to think that there are still monarchists in big business. But are they Catholics?" Pierre pursed his lips. He knew the managing director was a womanizer and kept two mistresses, and that one of the vice-presidents, at least, was openly homosexual. But, like a coward, he said nothing: the morals of the directors would have sabotaged the whole deal. So he told our grandfather that on the whole it was a Catholic firm, which was true, and that the people who ran it were right-thinking—an expression I'd heard all my life but didn't think had survived the war. He added for good measure that the managing director—the one whom the vice squad had a file on and who had been prevented from standing for the senate because of a vexatious affair concerning the seduction of minors—was very right-minded. So I realized Pierre had decided to sell. The funny thing is that the firm really was one of the bastions of the Christian Democratic Party in the department du Nord, and twenty years later, with the advent of the bold younger generation, became a center of the wildest and most advanced Catholicism. It took an active part in the events of May 1968, and to the great scandal of employers in general supported some very outspoken publications. On two or three occasions it almost outdid the Communist Party by measures which were very close to power-sharing. By a rather pleasing twist of history it was at Plessis-lez-Vaudreuil that, over a period of ten or fifteen years, Jesuits, rebel intellectuals, and journalists belonging to the Catholic Left worked out between them some very untraditional doctrines which would have made my grandfather turn in his grave.

They—we called them "they" or "the buyers," not out of resentment or contempt but because my grandfather, who didn't know much about board meetings, had never been able to make out who really had the power to make decisions—offered us a sum very much less than the one suggested by the innkeepers who had wanted to turn the house into a country club. But they very cleverly undertook to manage the forest in accordance with our own plans and customs, said they would not touch the chapel, and promised to leave intact our fourteenth- and fifteenth-century tombs, the lime trees, and the stone table. For one night my grandfather hesitated. Then he accepted. It was a quick decision, taken with an ease which astonished all of us and perhaps astonished him too. There was a certain base and incongruous relief in such a rapid conclusion to a history which had lasted eight centuries. But we'd talked and discussed and suffered too much already. And we were going to suffer still.

Pierre, Philippe, Claude, Nathalie, and I were having breakfast when our grandfather appeared, already dressed and shaved. We stood up to say good morning to him. He hadn't slept very well. He still stood very straight, but with that tired, worn-out air which made us say every now and then: "Well, after all, he is ninety-two or ninety-three." He sat down with us. "I didn't have a very good night," he said. And then, immediately afterward, in a low and almost ashamed voice: "Well, I think we're going to have to sell." There was a long silence. But we couldn't let him take the most painful decision in the long career of the family upon himself alone. "I think so too," said Pierre. And Claude and I said the same. Phi-

lippe didn't say anything, but just threw out his arms in a gesture
of helplessness: I think he would have liked to die on the spot amid
his family, like the captain of a sinking ship, with his country's flag
flying from the mast, singing hymns. Despite the horror of the
moment, there was almost a kind of pleasure in the decision that had
at last been taken. The anguish of uncertainty gave way to the
urgency of all the arrangements that had to be made. Pierre had
already seized a pencil and paper and was noting down dates, people
who had to be consulted, details which had to be kept in mind.
Claude drew up a list—a very short one in the last fifteen years, and
shorter still in the last five—of the gamekeepers, gardeners, and
carters who had to be given compensation or gratuities according
to their length of service. To this list he added the old people, the
pensioners, the nuns at the old people's home, the five or six remaining gymnasts, whom he'd once described as fascists, and the Plessis-
lez-Vaudreuil Society, whose motto was the same as ours: "At
God's pleasure." We couldn't go away without attending to all
these. Our grandfather was sitting at the table, motionless, silent,
absorbed in some dream or in his memories. Suddenly he was overcome by a wave of emotion. Pierre was sitting on his right, Claude
on his left. He clutched the hand of each of them, and said in a low
voice: "Only one thing matters: the family. Stick together."

Getting ready to move did a great deal to occupy us. We stopped
thinking and suffering in order to throw away the broken vases we
found in the cupboards, and the odd volumes of *L'Illustration*
which had survived from the distant past. In them we found, between photographs of the Kronprinz of Germany and the Prince
of Wales, of the end of the Dreyfus affair and the beginnings of
flying, pictures of great-grandmothers in outrageous dresses which
made Véronique laugh. Pierre hauled me over the coals for reading
these treasures instead of just throwing them away. He wanted me
to help take down a portrait by Champaigne of some duke and peer,
or to sort out the innumerable packs of cards my grandfather used
to play patience with in the evening—he needed to be patient, for
three times out of four the game didn't work out. All the games had
different names: the Clock, Belle Noémi, the Naval Officers, the

Blonde and the Brunette, the Three Musketeers, Zigzag, the Court of Love, the Wedding Rings, Marie Antoinette, Obsession, Royal Wedding, Leapfrog. A year of our life, one whole year during which we didn't breathe and didn't dare talk to one another, passed away like that, ransacking our past. We divided up the clocks and the Louis Quatorze commodes, and we gave away the hunting horns, which no longer served any purpose. Hundreds of lives, generation after generation brought up to worship the past, had left behind them, like the moraines left by glaciers, traces of their passage through a world of marvels and sorrows which now consisted only of memories: we tried as hard as we could to efface them. We weren't merely sad; we were seized with a sort of shame. Did we have the right, for our own personal comfort and convenience, to consign to nothingness the past which God, the family, history— were they not all the same thing?—had spent so many centuries handing down to us? I suddenly felt close to Philippe and his despair. How many times did I hesitate, with an old photograph in my hand, or a faded garland of flowers from under a glass case! Then Pierre or Claude, who suffered just as much as I did but had more courage, would clasp me on the shoulder and say that my grandfather was waiting for me under the lime trees to go for a stroll around the lake, and they would take the useless but sacred object out of my hands and go and throw it for me into the wastebasket in the kitchen. We used to read lots of books in which brothers and cousins tore each other to pieces. But with us, perhaps in obedience to my grandfather's instructions, it was rather different: the world, time, and history had all turned on us to destroy us. But we—we loved one another.

Every so often, polite and learned gentlemen would arrive at Plessis-lez-Vaudreuil and go around the drawing rooms peering at the consoles, the demi-lune commodes, the Louis Quinze armchairs, the portraits of marshals decorated with the Order of the Holy Ghost or of cardinals clad in purple robes: these were the experts. Their looks and comments expressed a kind of admiration for the splendor of the place, and a shade of scorn for the mediocrity of the objects it contained. After two centuries of legacies and dividing up, there wasn't much of any value left in our ancient house: the commodes were fakes, and the cardinals copies. The originals were in London or New York, in villas in Cannes or Florida, in museums in Detroit or Chicago, perhaps in vaults in the Bahamas or Switzerland, or, at the best, hanging on cracked walls in some ruined cottage in the Vendée or Burgundy, carried there by the hazards of legacies and furniture allocated in lieu of money. My grandfather remembered that in the course of divisions which had taken place in previous generations, his grandfather, who had nine brothers and sisters, not to mention priests and nuns and two children who died in infancy, had handed over two Gainsboroughs to one dependent, three chairs by Jacob Riesener to another, and a set of Flemish tapestries to a third. Through the years, Plessis-lez-Vaudreuil had gotten poorer and poorer in order to survive. We had never actually sold anything during the whole of the nineteenth century and the beginning of the twentieth, but we had divided it all up. And now the pictures, vases, *objets d'art* and furniture were scattered all over the world. Nothing remained of the gold plate that had been a gift from Peter the Great, or of the thirty-six Gobelin tapestry chairs on which mythical heroes successfully confronted fabulous beasts. One had been discovered near Niort, another in the house of Uncle Adolphe's granddaughter, who lived at Mazamet, and three others at Ferrières, in the Rothschild chateau. The scales fell from our eyes: we had been living among shams. The exquisite taste which was connected with our name and which we had embodied with such pride had flaunted itself among fakes. The enormous red-tasseled pouffe with a palm tree on it, the big Spanish desk, the portrait of Louis XIV in armor and ribbons, in which we persisted in seeing the hand of Rigaud—all these amused our visitors rather than otherwise. We were advised to get rid of them as fast as we could at a local sale. With the pictures taken down from the walls there were dreadful patches left, some made pale by the absence of dust, some made dark by the absence of sun. We didn't know where to sit any more. Some straw-bottomed chairs and deal tables had been brought up from the kitchens. Sitting around in a void which every day became more oppressive, we were entering a universe alien to us. We had spent our lives among antique chairs and knickknacks, and now we looked like characters in some modern play with no décor.

We were learning what anguish was. Not merely misfortune and sorrow, which we had experienced like everyone else. But anguish, which was new to us. We used to wake up at night with a start, bathed in sweat, with an iron hand clutching our hearts. It was the modern world, playing cat-and-mouse with us. My grandfather did not wake up; he hadn't even been to sleep. We used to hear him walking, before dawn, along the corridors, amid muffled knocks and rustlings; groping in the dark, he would run his hand along the walls stripped of their engravings and their hunting trophies.

We knew that things, like men, could die. The chateau was dying before our eyes. We had killed it. History had killed it, and demography, and the rise of the working classes, and socialism, and economic development, and the end of privilege. But we had killed it too. We had done so because we didn't want to cling to its ruins and go down with it. The very time, as it went by, made us suffer. And yet perhaps we were never so great as in this misfortune. When I stood looking out of my bedroom window in the evening, hardly able to breathe for a suffering which never left us now, I could see, through the tears in my eyes, my grandfather sitting with Philippe and Claude at the stone table. Motionless. Silent. What were they thinking of, so different and yet so near to one another, united by something which reached down deeper into the earth and into men's hearts than passing vicissitudes and political opinions? There was my grandfather, still very upright, his hair very white, his chin resting on his stick, which he held with both hands. Philippe was still very good-looking, and tenser than ever from the inner struggles in which he was always defeated. Claude was consumed by a future that was turning against him, and more torn than any of us between a dual loyalty: to a future he did not wish to betray, and to a past he had neither the heart nor the right to renounce. They were silent. They looked neither at the lake, nor at the old trees whose every branch they knew, nor at the familiar sky, nor at the paths disappearing in the distance between the great oaks of the forest. They were looking into themselves. From time to time my grandfather would pass a hand over his eyes, Claude would light his pipe. They stood up. It would soon be time to go to bed in the empty house, to wake up next morning amid the trunks packed for a departure that was to be forever.

The local people came one after the other to pay visits of condolence which ended in tears. Even those who liked us least—the schoolmaster, the manager of the café, the spinster who ran the post office, the retired railway worker who was head of the communist cell and a friend of Claude's, with whom he had fought in the Maquis in the heroic days—even these said they would miss us. Together, in the kitchen, where there were two or three sticks of furniture left, or in the big drawing room, now stripped, we would have a glass of port or Pernod with them. Claude would shake hands with them, and my grandfather would embrace them.

One Sunday morning when the weather was still very fine, we attended our last mass in the village church. We still sat in the front row, on chairs upholstered in red and carved with names the youngest of us no longer even recognized—the names of great-grandparents, great-great-uncles and great-great-aunts. All the rest of the church had straw-bottomed chairs, the kind that Péguy loved. Each bore a little label with the name of the member of the congregation to whom it belonged: the right of property and the love of possessions struggled successfully, in the very bosom of the Church, against the Gospel's call to poverty and renunciation. Our scarlet and somewhat tattered chairs accentuated still further the metaphysical and religious hierarchy to which we had always been so attached: they were a patch of pride standing out amid the straw and wood polished by time. According to tradition, when the priest climbed up to the fine eighteenth-century pulpit almost in the middle of the church, on the right of the nave, we were supposed to turn our red chairs slantwise so as to have a better view of him. The altar was a long way from the congregation in a large choir surrounded by wooden stalls with carvings that were almost famous, and the officiating priest, naturally, still turned his back to the faithful. In church, at least, things hadn't changed very much since my grandfather's childhood. It was after our departure that the upheavals and the decisive changes were to occur: a portable altar at the entrance to the choir, the priest facing the congregation, all the prayers in French, the Host put into the hands of the communicants, the kiss of peace between neighbors sitting anywhere they liked. But at the end of our reign, only about twenty years ago, the church, like the chateau, was still one of the favorite refuges of that Sleeping Beauty who, despite technology, science, progress and revolution, was for us indistinguishable from history.

One Sunday recently I went back to hear mass at Plessis-lez-Vaudreuil. Time had gone by as on the face of a friend one hasn't seen for thirty years. There were no more red chairs. The priest, a young man, no longer went up into the pulpit, but spoke standing up, leaning carelessly against his makeshift altar. Syncopated rhythms had driven out Gregorian chant, and French nationalism had gotten the better of the mystery of Latin. But in the interest of truth I must admit that children no longer played marbles on the steps of the altar, and that the three old spinsters who took communion in our day had been transformed into two long lines in which young people and children predominated. "Yes, monsieur," said the young dean, whom I didn't know but whom the young women addressed familiarly, "they take communion. But they don't come to confession any more." What he said made me reflect about myself and about our past. How badly I have described it, that vanished past—I believe I have scarcely mentioned the enormous importance in our lives, especially in the lives of my grandmother and great-grandmother, of the pangs of confession, penance, repentance and abstinence which preceded communion, and the anguish caused if the slightest drop of mouthwash or rain crossed our lips after the last stroke of midnight.

That day we sat on our immemorial chairs. The whole church was looking at us. They all knew now that we were on the point of leaving, and many had come to see us for the last time. Instead of the congregation of twenty or thirty who came on ordinary Sundays, there were fifty or perhaps even sixty of us. It was clear that in the race for fame and popularity, Anne-Marie had beaten us by several lengths. "*Introibo ad altare Dei. Ad Deum qui laetificat juventutem meam* ..." At the very first words, which only ironically referred to youth and joy, we knew that the mass was going to be said for us, a funeral mass, and we were the dead. Our minds were blank, we stared in front of us, jaws clenched, on the brink of tears. We'd never cried so much. All that was needed was for our grandfather to meet some old farmer or gamekeeper, or to come across a letter yellow with age sent by some great-aunt at Claude's birth or Hubert's death, or to catch sight of the roofs of the house around a bend in a hedge-lined path, and the tears ran down his face. He was kneeling on his ebony and red-plush priedieu with his face in his hands. We surrounded him like a guard of honor and of sorrow, like a group of nurses ready to come forward in case of weakness or accident. But he didn't move. I thought it would be a good death for this old man of ninety-two or ninety-three to collapse quietly on the priedieu of his fathers in the heart of his church. But he wasn't dying. He was lost in thoughts which must have been dim and dreary. I wondered what he could be thinking about. I suppose he was seeing again in his mind's eye all the sorrow and all the happiness that had gone in procession through this church. The bereavements, the hopes, the family secrets, the unsatisfied passions, the triumphs and failures—right up to this final catastrophe, after which there would be nothing more. Everything took on a kind of sweetness amid the incense and memories: through the centuries, sorrows and even deaths had come to find peace here, had been absorbed, in memory, into the sacred alluvium of past and tradition. There was only one horror, only one unforgivable sin: and that was the torture we were now living through, of departure and desertion. We were breaking the thread, we were ending the past, in our secret magic we were indulging in the unpardonable act which reproduced in the negative, upside-down, mockingly, all that had been sacred in the divine decision to preserve and save. What we stood for was rupture and oblivion.

"*Credo in unum Deum, Patrem omnipotentem, factorem coeli et terrae, visibilium omnium et invisibilium.*" The service went mercilessly on and, like us, hastened toward its end. I remembered the interminable masses of childhood, in this same church at Plessis-lez-Vaudreuil or in the chapel. It used to seem to me then that time went on and on, and that it always had to be urged to give way to the future. Now I would have liked to let it linger a little, to see it slacken its pace at last; I would have liked this evening mass never to end. But it was ending. Already the dean was in the pulpit and we had turned our chairs to listen to him more comfortably. I noticed a slight spasm of pain pass over my grandfather's face. Everything he did for the last time, even the most insignificant gesture, was a source of pain. Tradition is not only memory; it is also habit and repetition, even routine. And that is why it is at the same time a strength and a weakness. Almost everything we did that terrible autumn day we were doing for the last time; all our gestures were simultaneously mere mannerisms and part of a fidelity stronger than death. When he twisted his red chair in the church at Plessis-lez-Vaudreuil, my grandfather knew that he was taking part for the last time in the slightly ludicrous little ballet, the unchanging rite, which brought smiles to the faces of the little girls from the village school, sitting in rows behind us. My grandfather was this red chair, just as he was his horse, his hunting horn, his tattered pack of cards, his old-fashioned suits. Because he was the past, he continually merged with things, with the gestures, the customs, and the thoughts which came from the past and conjured it up. As he turned for the last time toward the dean climbing up into the pulpit, my grandfather's distress was enriched by one more little detail of suffering.

"After having offered God our prayers for the living, we will pray also for the dead ..." After the sermon the dean's voice had risen to a high, unwavering, ritual note. But that day it was for us the voice was praying, not among the living, but already among the dead. "... Especially for the former deans of the parish, the former vicars, for its children fallen in battle, for all our dead, for the benefactors of our church ..." There was a long silence and all eyes turned toward us. My grandfather, his four grandsons, and, behind us, Nathalie, between Jean-Claude on one side and Véronique and Bernard on the other, had all stood up. "... In particular for Canon Mouchoux, Canon Potard, Dr. Sauvagein, for the following families

..." There followed the endless, tireless enumeration. Familiar
names which we knew by heart, and which had made us laugh so
often. "... Onésime Coquillerat, Ophélie Botté, Ernest Malatrat,
father and son, and the Thoumas-Lachassagne family who today
offer the consecrated bread ..." My grandfather stood motionless;
the whole church held its breath, awaiting the final, inevitable an-
nouncement. "... Above all, my brethren, we pray for those who
in a few days are going to leave us, and who will leave behind the
cherished memory of a faithful Christian family ..." My grandfather hadn't moved, but he no longer even tried to hide his tears.
They ran down his face and fell onto his old jacket.

   "*Vere dignum et justum est, aequum et salutare... Praeceptis salutari-
bus moniti... Domine, non sum dignus... Benedicat vos...*" The mass
was ending. All was just and equitable, and we had not lacked
admonitions from the Lord. One last time I tried to draw a breath
of that cool, that mustiness, that smell of incense. I tried for the last
time to decipher, inscribed beneath the statue of Joan of Arc, the
names of the fifty-seven children of the parish who had fallen in
battle, together with the list of the eight victims of the 1940–45 war
which had been added below, looking rather new and meager beside
the ranks of their predecessors. I tried for one last time to hear the
voices of Estelle and Madame Naud and Madame Tissier as they
sang the responses, far too high and accompanied by the harmonium and the twittering of the schoolchildren. I shut my eyes.
The responses spoke of acceptance, acquiescence. The whole
church was hymning that pleasure of God which was now tearing
us from the land where we were born, where we had lived, and
where—the first of our name—we were not to die. And we hymned
that acceptance too. But we were already swept up in the din of
chairs pushed back on the tiles, in the little whirlpool moving toward the door where, after the half-darkness of candles, hymns, and
incense, we were enveloped by the sun which had been awaiting us
under the porch.

   And then there was our last meal. There was practically nothing
left: no more china, no more knives and forks, no more glasses, no
more serving dishes. All that was left was the bell in the main

courtyard. At half-past twelve sharp it rang for the last time. Distraught but punctual, we had a snack lunch in the big dining room, off chipped plates and out of odd glasses. We were thirteen at table, but bad luck held few further terrors for us. There was my grandfather, his four grandsons, Aunt Gabrielle, who had aged thirty years and looked older than her father-in-law, Nathalie, Véronique and her husband, Bernard, the dean and the doctor, distant descendants of Canon Mouchoux and Dr. Sauvagein, and, on my grandfather's right, Jules, as much an embodiment of the tribe as we were, in his somewhat threadbare gamekeeper's livery. Jean-Claude and his wife were staying with Anne-Marie in America. Anne was busy with Michel. Hélène had left for Paris, where she was preparing for our withdrawal. We had drunk a drop of champagne, left over from previous parties. My grandfather was sitting in his traditional place, from which he had organized so many hunting parties, dances, and gymnastic parades. He was eating tuna fish and fruit, because that was the easiest. We no longer ate what was healthy or delicious. Overtaken at last by modernity, we were reduced to eating what was convenient. Oblivion works so fast that we already had some difficulty remembering with any exactness the engravings and paintings which had left square or round, oval or oblong traces behind them on the walls. "What used to be there?" asked Claude, pointing to an oblong patch between the two windows. And we couldn't remember whether it was a hunting scene or my grandmother's photograph. "Just you see," Bernard had whispered as we sat down at table. "It will be like Daudet's story about 'The Last Lesson.' " And although there was no blackboard on which to write "Long live the family!" nor any Prussian bugles to sound under our windows, the effect was the same: "It's all over . . . be off with you." During this last family meal in the big dining room at Plessis-lez-Vaudreuil all the shadows of the past bent over our shoulders with old Estelle as she served the dishes. She didn't serve them very well; she offered them from the right instead of the left because she was crying so much. So, in a sort of bitter and ridiculous communion, we all ate some of Estelle's tears mixed up with the salad. When, with the cheese, my grandfather offered wine to Jules with a hand

trembling with age and emotion, I thought that our last meal at
Plessis-lez-Vaudreuil was not only like Daudet's "Last Lesson."
There was another shadow around the table beside those of dukes
and peers and marshals astonished to see us going. A shade with
more pity for our pain than contempt for our cowardice. Our last
meal was a sort of profane replica of another farewell meal. We too
were about to leave the kingdoms of this world. But there was no
other Judas at our table than history, which, after so many kisses,
would never have done betraying us.

We did not speak. There was a tinkle of forks and glasses, though
we tried to stifle them. From time to time my grandfather looked
out of the windows at his trees, his lake, his stone table between the
limes, and raised both hands. Two or three times he tried to begin
a story: to tell us about a hunt, perhaps, or a visit by some farmers
or the duchesse d'Uzès, or to recall an occasion when the Wittgensteins were staying at Plessis-lez-Vaudreuil. But he couldn't finish.
So Pierre took over and chatted about anything that came into his
head, and then let silence fall again upon our grief and distraction.

We were not very hungry. And the little we did eat we had
difficulty in swallowing. Usually, history unfolds with an insidious
slowness in which causes and effects, beginnings and declines, are
inextricably intermingled. But there, that day, we were going
through an end that was bare and unadorned. The exploits of Eleazar fighting against the Saracens were ending in cottage cheese and
a few strawberries. The marshals, the ambassadors, the ministers of
Henri II, Louis XV, and Charles X, the archbishops and cardinals,
the cavalry charges, the looting, the balls, probably the cruelties, the
selfishness, the unawareness, all the upheavals of the most lofty and
the most charming kind of life, so many triumphs, so much courtesy, so much elegance and blindness, so much piety and pride, were
coming to an end at last with the end of the last meal. The dean
stood up to say grace.

We all stood up. For weeks and months we had been dreading the
moment when we should leave forever this indoor table, which
together with the stone outdoor table had been at the center of our
family life. How we'd laugh, sitting around that table! At Canon

Mouchoux, at the folly of the Wittgensteins, at Jean-Christophe Comte's ties, at the government, at the Remy-Michaults, at the V.s' snobbishness, at ourselves, and at this march of time which was now getting the better of us. We laughed. Despite our sternness, our severity, our memories, and our piety we were a surprisingly cheerful family. There had been nothing more full of life than the world which had been ours and which was now about to die. We all stood up. The mutterings of the dean did not really break the crushing silence which had fallen on the huge room. Estelle stood motionless behind Jules, twisting her apron the better to mop her eyes. Hubert's name could just be sensed on the dean's lips. My grandfather leaned with both hands on the huge oak table. Around this old table we had also known much bitterness and sorrow. The death of those we loved, the receding into the past of all that we admired, unsatisfactory elections, the coming of the enemy—in short, passing time and the change we hated so much had brought us much suffering. But now our suffering and gaiety, sorrow and laughter, were reconciled in memory, and grew so close as to merge together in the treasure which had been entrusted to us and of which perhaps we had been no more than unfaithful stewards: that treasure was the past. It took on a heart-rending sweetness in which good and evil both attained a kind of divine and adorable dignity just because they were gone. Even all our failures, even Hubert's death, even our decline and fall became dear to us and linked us to the vanished days in which bereavement and disappointment had not spared us. Subject as we were to God's pleasure, we made a choice in his eternity. We preferred what he had already created to what he was still going to create. My God, my God, why have you created a time which wipes out the past and lets it fade away in the forgetful memory of men? That was the real prayer which arose from our hearts as the dean was saying grace. Yet we should have realized—though for that we would have needed a lucidity we did not possess—that such a prayer was meaningless. For we loved the past just because it was the past. We loved Hubert's dying because it was our past. We loved our death throes because they were our past. We ought really to have thanked God for this passing time too, because

the past was born out of it and because, with our weakened vitality
and our inability to confront the world, it was the past that we
loved. And our tragedy was really only this: that having already
given up the future and the present, now, in departing from our
cradle and our refuge, we were giving up the past.

Because we were giving up the past, we were looking for the first
time toward the future. When the dean had finished mumbling
grace, my grandfather hesitated for a moment. We all thought he
was going to talk again about the pleasures and bereavements of
Plessis-lez-Vaudreuil. But he merely raised his glass of inferior
champagne—he had again succeeded in turning a day of sorrow
into a celebration—looked at Véronique, and said: "I drink to you,
my dear, because you are the youngest."

We left the table and went out of the dining room. My grandfather lingered behind a little, looking at the bare walls, the high
ceiling, the windows looking out on the trees. Véronique stayed
behind the rest of us and went over to him. As we passed into the
other room she leaned toward him and said something. They came
into the drawing room together, the old man leaning on the young
girl's arm. And to our profound astonishment in that time of sorrow, his face seemed to be lit up with peace, almost with happiness.
It was not until two or three weeks later that we discovered the
secret she had just told him, on the last day of Plessis-lez-Vaudreuil.
The sixth generation you've known of our family was taking advantage of our collapse to manifest itself. Véronique was expecting a
child.

Finally there was our last visit to the stone table and our last walk
around the lake. After the coffee, which was quite undrinkable but
was served in one of the blue Gien porcelain services with the
flower design which I can never see now without thinking at once
of Plessis-lez-Vaudreuil, my grandfather rested for three-quarters
of an hour. Then, while Pierre, Claude, and Philippe saw to the
preparations for departure, he asked me to go with him on a last
tour of inspection—a tour by a master in the process of becoming
a stranger. He took my arm and we walked away from the house.
We went under the lime trees, by the stone table. We looked at the

tree trunks where the children had always written their names, at
the branches, the leaves, the blades of grass. Everything was full of
memories, everything spoke of us. After our last meal together I
feared the worst, but this last stroll was as cheerful and animated
as the lunch had been silent. We were straining it a bit, no doubt.
But a little of our strength came back among the trees, under the
bright sun. My grandfather talked. He told me the story of his life.
I was amazed: it suddenly seemed to me I knew nothing about it.
Had I really had to wait for the moment when the guillotine was
about to fall on our necks to understand at last something about this
old man who, perhaps only because he had lived so long, had occupied so extraordinary a place in a dozen different lives? I suddenly
realized that he had seen, guessed, judged everything that we had
thought most intimate, most secret. Nothing had escaped him, from
Uncle Paul's marriage to Anne-Marie's escapades, the schemes of
the Remy-Michaults, Pierre's adventures and Claude's anguishings.
He had been not only the chief but also the center of the family,
and, like one of the old oak trees among which he had lived, he had
held out, blasted but indestructible, through storm and temptation
for nearly a hundred years.

We came to the end of the lake. As we walked around it the house
suddenly appeared to us through the approaching evening. It was
marvelously beautiful with its pink bricks and roof of black tiles.
The setting sun shone on it with a declining light, rich and heart-
rending. My grandfather had a sudden moment of weakness. The
sacrifice was too harsh. I felt him weighing slightly more heavily
on my arm. His life, all our lives, the lives of all our family through
past generations, was standing there before us. And we were going
to part from one another. Silence fell on us once more. We walked
along slowly, slowly. For we knew that when we got back to the
house it would only be to see it disappear forever before our eyes,
as in one of the fairy tales where mirages vanish as soon as they are
reached. The mirage was our past, our family, our name, the only
value still left standing, upon which the whole world rested that we
had respected and loved. During the twenty minutes it took us to
get back to the house, I came to know how time must disintegrate

for a condemned man as he walks toward the scaffold. Our scaffold
was our life, which was abandoning us, or which we were abandoning.

During the last few minutes of our walk, endless and yet too brief,
I was carrying rather than supporting my grandfather. It is well
known that emotion is the response of the individual to the circumstances of life when they become too difficult. And the body acts
as a regulating mechanism for emotions. It comes to their aid by
growing weak or fainting when they become too acute, as emotions
themselves come to the rescue of reason when it is overwhelmed.
My grandfather was so exhausted he no longer had time to suffer.
While we were still a long way away from them the benches around
the stone table had already, thank God, lost all emotional significance. They were only a haven of refuge and rest for an old man
at the end of his strength. My grandfather's body had taken pity on
him.

The list of our ordeals was not quite complete. We couldn't just
leave Plessis-lez-Vaudreuil as one leaves a hotel. There was still one
more station of the cross. We had to say goodbye to all those who
had lived through, with us, the end of our glory and our death
agony. As I was walking around the lake with my grandfather,
Pierre, Claude, and Philippe had gathered together in the big drawing room, now as empty as the dining room, all those who in some
way or other had been involved in our life. They included all that
remained of the gardeners and carters, the gamekeepers and road
menders who in the days of our splendor had made up our feudal
family's personal army. There was also the mayor and the dean, the
saddler and the painter, the nuns from the old people's home, the
socialist schoolteacher, the spinster who kept the post office, all
those—or their children—who had once been present at our weddings and other celebrations. Philippe and Claude had gone in the
car to collect those who lived farthest away—the farmers and keepers in the most distant parts of our far-flung forests. Most of them
had already come to see us separately, overcome with emotion,
when they had learned that we were going. Now they were all here
together, waiting for us.

When my grandfather and I entered the drawing room they were all standing around with glasses in their hands, talking very quietly, as though at a funeral. When my grandfather appeared there was first a stir, then a silence. He went forward slowly and sat in a chair that had survived the shipwreck. Véronique stood near him. My cousins and I chatted to our friends. We tried to talk about trees, harvests, hunting, everything that interested them and us. But everyone was thinking of only one thing, though neither they nor we knew how to express it. They just said: "Oh! Monsieur Pierre . . . Oh! Monsieur Claude . . ." And we shook one another by the hand. We were drinking champagne again, with those long crumbly biscuits dusted with sugar which I think are called boudoirs. I have disliked them ever since. Pierre talked at random about those who were going to come after us, singing their praises. But the farmers and the keepers shook their heads and wouldn't listen. The representative of the company that was to replace us had been to see one of them and talked to him. The experience had left him unimpressed: "He was trying to be charming but he was boring. Don't tell me, Monsieur Pierre! You'll never persuade me they're not just nobodies." With an inspired tact which came from the heart they spoke ill of the others, the newcomers, in order to please us. Claude talked about the war to his old comrades from the Maquis; it was torture to him to be forced into this feudal role. Véronique and Nathalie went around pouring drinks and offering cigarettes. It was getting late. The sun was low. Then my grandfather stood up and, in an inaudible voice, said a few words which I have completely forgotten or which I never really heard. Then he went over and spoke to each person separately, these men who had often hated him, who had fought against him because he was the incarnation of the chateau, of reaction, clericalism, and Vichy; because he was not really a republican and not much of a democrat. But now, I could see, they were dismayed to see him beaten at last. Talking to me about the scene afterward, Claude said, and perhaps he was right, that it was a marvelous example of paternalism. He said he could hardly believe it had happened scarcely twenty years ago. We obviously had a gift for these discrepancies in time, these living anachronisms. Do you remember the menus of the dinners Pierre and Ursula used to give in the late 1920s, which continued the 1900s and the Belle Epoque well on into the twentieth century? The scene that day was no less extraordinary. We might have enacted it in 1880, or 1820, or even 1785, if we had been ruined then by unsuccessful speculation. But it wasn't speculation which had ruined us now: it was nothing other than history and passing time, and this farewell picture owed its bizarreness to the fact that, fixed and immutable in the person of our grandfather, we had survived them beyond all hope and expectation.

He walked around, leaning on Pierre. The first in the row was an old gardener. My grandfather talked to him about a father and grandfather who had been gardeners like himself; about a little girl he had lost; and about how they both tried once to make a palm tree grow in Haute-Sarthe. After the first few words the old man, dressed in his Sunday best, burst into tears. My grandfather was weeping too. They fell into one another's arms and stayed like that for a few seconds. Thus, one after the other, my grandfather embraced all those who had come to tell us they didn't hate us, or didn't hate us any more, because misfortune had clothed us at last in a new dignity. He embraced the lady from the post office, the nuns, the chief of the fire brigade, the schoolteacher. It was an amazing sight. Everyone was weeping. My grandfather, exhausted, his eyes full of tears, distraught, no longer knew where he was. When he came across me, exchanging a few words with the secretary from the Town Hall, he didn't recognize me at first and asked me faintly if I'd been here long and if I'd known his father. I said I'd come there as a child, that I'd known almost everybody, and that I intended to write a memoir about the vanished past. Claude burst out laughing and there was something terrifying in his laughter. For a moment it was as if the shades of madness hovered over our collapse.

Through the windows, the sky was darkening. The last day at Plessis-lez-Vaudreuil was ending. Night was already about to fall. The keepers, the gardeners, all those who had been with us through the years and to whom we were linked by bonds which Marxism cannot entirely explain, our servants and our friends, one after the other, left us. There is a Haydn symphony in which, one after the other, the performers blow out the candle which lit up their score, and leave a lively and cheerful scene to sink gradually into solitude and silence. It was performed for the first time in 1772 for our cousins the Esterhazys. It is called the "Farewell" Symphony, and it was a symbol of our ancient chateau. We knew very well that the house would survive us, that it would go on after us, that the earth was not going to open up and swallow the stone table at the very instant of our departure. But without us the stones, the earth, and the trees could only live a life that was as dull and devoid of significance as our own life would be without our trees, without our earth, and without our stones. Systems collapsed because they were systems. But because they were systems, the elements of which they are composed remain for a long while unused after the wholes of which they were part have fallen. Without any meaning or any connection with anything else, they have great difficulty in reorganizing themselves. And in fact they manage to do so only by forming new systems just as inspired but just as unjust as those which went before—perhaps a little more inspired and a little less unjust? That is the question—but which, in any case, will in their turn be destroyed. That is what is called history, which, like the theories of physics which explain things now by waves and now by corpuscles, can be read equally well either as the different stages of consciousness on the way to its fulfilment, or as an indefinite succession of forms, evolutions, and cycles, a series that is more or less meaningless, in any case one which is richer in illusion than in progress.

We were just marking time now. The wheels had gone full circle. Bernard told how one of the carters was going around the countryside, around the restaurants and the cafés, making rude remarks about the recent charade at the chateau. Claude was inclined to be of his opinion. Whether he liked it or not he was one of our order, and, especially at a time when that order was in the process of collapsing, he made common cause with us. But when he looked at it from outside that rigmarole of attitudes and tears, the disguising of real situations, if not of real interests, under sentimental appearances, rather sickened him. He was less given to embracing people than my grandfather. He was less given to weeping in public. Perhaps this was because he was younger. Perhaps too it was because he thought that, after all, our going was sadder for us than for those who remained behind, the gardeners and the keepers, the spinster at the post office and the schoolteacher. Bernard's carter went around saying it was a funny idea to feel sorry for employers when at last their victories were replaced by defeat, and that he knew a whole lot of decent people who were more to be pitied than we were, and had been for a long time. In an attempt to soften my grandfather's grief Claude allowed that there was something in what the carter said; that we had always had luck on our side and that others were still imprisoned, much more than we were, in misfortune. My grandfather was silent for a moment, thinking perhaps of those who had never known anything but failure. "They don't want masters any more," he murmured. "Well, they'll have bosses." Claude threw up his arms in disagreement and helplessness. That evening he didn't feel like continuing an argument which was painful to him in every way and for many reasons, and which made him feel not only helpless but also bound hand and foot by feeling, reason, and history. Anyway, we were going.

The cars were waiting for us in the main courtyard, which had seen our coaches, our carriages, German tanks—so many different ways of going away and coming back. But this time we were going away without hope of return. And after so much effort and so many rearguard actions, we didn't know what to do with the little time that remained. Each of us filled the last moments of the disintegrating dream with a kind of mechanical activity which finally revealed, in its aimless panic, his secret preferences, his real attachments, what it was about the disaster that hurt him most. My grandfather went and sat by the stone table, all alone among his dead. Philippe went to the kennels and the stables, long abandoned by our dogs and horses. Avenger was dead too. Fortunately. Philippe wandered about amid memories which had vanished before we did. Pierre and Claude had taken one of the cars to drive around for a quarter of an hour among the lakes and the great oak trees of the forest, amid one last vision of bicycles, of bathing parties, machine guns, and youthful love affairs. Now they were all back again, silent at first, then giving orders for our departure. As for me, I went for the last time—how often we had used that phrase during those three or four months—through all the places where our life had been spent and which had become so familiar to us that we no longer even noticed them: the marble staircase, the billiard room, the dreary series of high-ceilinged drawing rooms, the two dining rooms, the libraries where I had passed so many hours and days, stretched out with a beating heart and all our treasures spread around me on the floor, the big room on the ground floor where we left our guns beneath the mounted antlers with their magic inscriptions:

> *Tonnay-Charente Hunt*
> *Started at La Paluche*
> *Taken at the Croix des Quatre-Chemins*
> *Laid on by La Verdure*
> *November 7, 1902*

or:

> *Pique-Avant*
> *Nivernais Meet*
> *Started at the Arbres-Verts*
> *Taken at the Grand-Bois Lake*
> *Laid on by La Rosée*
> *January 19, 1927*

I inhaled, as in the church, the incomparable aroma which had survived the scattered pictures and sold furniture—an aroma of the past, of wood, of mustiness and love which made my head spin. I was walking like an automaton amid forty years of memories and eight centuries of ghosts. These colors, these sounds, these windows open on the park, that faint sound in the distance, that fragile perfume—I mustn't end by forgetting them all. I tried to steep myself in them, tried to take in all that had been our life, so as not

to let it fall into the void and disappear altogether. I was laying in
stocks of memory. It was in thinking of the future that I found
myself again in the past.

Voices were calling me from the courtyard. I opened a window:
Pierre, Claude, Philippe, Nathalie, and Véronique were already
gathered around my grandfather and Aunt Gabrielle and were
beckoning me to come down. I looked around me. I saw the evenings of long ago, those I had not known but which the family had
spoken of just as they'd spoken of those I had known: Boris bursting
in among the violins and dancers of another age; my grandfather
playing patience; the visits of the dean and Monsieur Machavoine;
the coming of Jean-Christophe; the determination of Monsieur Desbois; weddings and dances, lunches, my grandfather's outbursts
against the government; waiting for news during the war; Colonel
von Witzleben coming into the drawing room; I could hear Hubert's laugh and Claude's silences, the rumbling of tanks, whispered
conversations about the follies of Pierre and Aunt Gabrielle or
Michel Desbois. Had not the fate of the world been enacted in these
huge rooms, under these vast ceilings? They had for me at least,
because I had lived there. I went back swiftly, in a maelstrom of
vanished events, through the funeral procession of deserted drawing rooms. I shut all the doors behind me. I went out. There, in their
mechanical incarnation, stood the instruments of God's pleasure:
one Renault and two Peugeots. The engines were already running.

There was a peal of laughter. It was Bernard. God, what had he
found to laugh at? I jumped in and sat beside my grandfather in the
leading Peugeot, which Philippe was driving. And now we were
moving off. None of us looked around. It was all over. A new life
was opening up before us, a life which was at last like everyone
else's.

A few hundred yards from the house the road rises a little. From
a bend in it, there is one of the prettiest views of Plessis-lez-Vaudreuil. As the Peugeot was taking this corner, my grandfather asked
Philippe to stop. Philippe glanced at me. Was there going to be
trouble now? My grandfather got out of the car and gazed for a few
moments not at what we used to see when we looked from the

house at the lime trees or the stone table, but at what strangers saw when they were coming to see us or going away. It wasn't yet night but with every minute darkness was gaining on the last gleams of day. The chateau was drawing farther away in time, in space, and also in the light which now lit it up but faintly. My grandfather looked. I didn't look at the house. I looked at my grandfather, saw how beaten he looked. The second Peugeot drove up with Claude at the wheel. He didn't get out. I could feel that he was tense, almost hostile. Hadn't this nonsense gone on long enough? He had suffered just as much as we had, but the expectation of a new world now beckoned him forward, to look toward the future without turning around at every step. And now the Renault appeared. It stopped. Pierre came over to my grandfather and stood for a few moments motionless beside him, watching the house disappear in the darkness. I stood a little way off. It struck me as an astonishing sight: the family contemplating itself, in its gravest crisis since its time began, through its chief, the stones of its name, and its past. The old man walked back toward us, and Pierre put an arm around him. "Come," said my grandfather, and he got back into the car.

We drove on. It was dark. I could no longer see my grandfather. I could guess his shattered expression through the darkness. I would have liked to be able to take him in my arms, tell him that we loved him, that nothing mattered in the world except the love that bound us together. I would have spoken to him about our name, too, about his past, about his honor. I didn't really know myself what the honor of our name meant now, but I did know that, for him, everything rested on that value and on that myth. But my throat was tense, and I couldn't get a word out. I simply took his hand and squeezed it. And I heard a sob burst from the lips which for months had not uttered one complaint: "Oh, my boy! If only you knew . . ."

There are many things I haven't known in the course of a life which you will do me the justice of admitting I have scarcely mentioned. Like Pierre, like Claude, like Philippe, I have made many mistakes, committed many faults and many follies. But in the silent darkness of the Peugeot carrying us toward Paris, lit up now and then by the flash of headlights or, as we went through a village, the

revolving rays of street lights, I said to myself that perhaps I might
redeem all the debts I had accumulated in my useless and undistinguished existence. The idea came to me of bringing to life again
what was dying. There weren't many of us left now who knew or
could guess what my grandfather was thinking, what he had
suffered, his pride, his crazy ideas, the picture he had of history and
of his own decline and fall. Sitting beside him in the car that was
carrying me through the night, taking me from a world that had
disappeared forever, I had the same feelings as I had had ten or
twelve years earlier, listening to Claude and Philippe sitting around
the stone table and telling about their Spanish Civil War and the
contrasting choices they had made. It had seemed to me then as if,
through the family, I was watching history in the making. And now
too, in this absurd apocalypse, the family expressed history still—
a different history from the history of battles and ideologies, a
history that was slower, more secret, more collective, perhaps less
sensational and probably more important, but in fact the same history under different appearances. For it was the insidious history of
economic fluctuation and social evolution that was driving us out
at last, after so many obstinate efforts and struggles, from Plessis-lez-
Vaudreuil. The Peugeot drove on through the night, toward the
northeast, toward Paris. My grandfather had fallen asleep. Or was
pretending to sleep in an attempt to suffer a little less. His head was
on my shoulder. I was still holding his hand. I put it gently to my
lips, as he had put Hubert's to his lips when he was dying. Nothing
could ever give back to us what had just faded away in the darkness
of the past. But out of filial piety toward my grandfather, toward
all the dead whom we had left around the stone table, toward God's
pleasure, to which we had always submitted, there was one thing
I could try to do: it was to help the others, those who would come
after us, to remember the buried world we were leaving behind us.
To preserve something still of its allure and its weaknesses, its grandeur, its absurdities, its follies, all the selfish and ingrown sternness
which brought about its destruction and death. Yes, perhaps I could
do that. And that—a sort of play upon words—would be my answer to my grandfather's sorrowful cry as he tore himself away

from Plessis-lez-Vaudreuil: "Oh, my boy! If only you knew ..."
Somewhere between Plessis-lez-Vaudreuil and Paris, between the
past and the future, between the imaginary world and the real
world, between memory and hope, I vowed to devote a part of my
wasted life to giving back to those I loved something of the inimitable flavor of their vanished dreams. I ask my grandfather's forgiveness for having let so many years go by after his death before raising
this wretched chateau of words in place of the chateau of glory and
stone he loved so much.

3

After the Deluge

FOR A LONG TIME I INTENDED TO FINISH these memories of the vanished past with the end of Plessis-lez-Vaudreuil. As the cars drove on through the night, a whole age of our collective life was finishing. The adventure begun by old Eleazar in the Holy Land was ending eight or nine hundred years later with the collapse of that part of our name which was embodied in stone and wood. It was plain to all of us that the family would not survive the upheaval which was uprooting us, depriving us at one stroke of our most important reason for living, and flinging us into a world from which we had done our utmost for so long to stand apart. We had known other misfortunes and run other risks. War, the Reformation, rebellions, the Revolution, the guillotine, and money had all, more than once, almost put an end to our solidarity and our pride. But this crisis, without any doubt, was the most terrible in our history. It deprived us of hope. When we climbed the scaffold and the erstwhile victims were changed into executioners, we knew, of course, that after all the violence perpetrated on our part with a greater or lesser degree of justice, we, who had once been so strong, had at last become the weak ones. But God, the king, and the Church had not disappeared. We expected them to return.

More: even if we'd known that neither God nor the king nor the Church would ever come back again, we wouldn't have stopped believing in them, nor above all would we have stopped believing in ourselves. But now Plessis-lez-Vaudreuil was lost forever. And there on the road to Paris, neither Pierre nor Claude nor Philippe nor I believed in ourselves any longer.

I won't go into detail about our settling in in Paris. There are already enough books which tell, with a greater or lesser degree of skill, about everyday experience: life in big cities, its anonymity, the awfulness of the shapeless crowd cut off from its origins, restless and indifferent. We were like peasants driven out of a countryside which was in the process of disappearing, lost in the city, tossed to and fro by events they did not understand. Pétain and de Gaulle had both gone: Pétain was in prison and de Gaulle in exile—after exile overseas, exile in the marches of the East. I rather envied Claude, who at least still had some belief in those incarnations of the sacred which we had so much difficulty in doing without: for him what was holy was the people. With General de Gaulle absent and the Communist Party still there, people took the place, for Claude, of the declining family.

We needed fathers, lands, leaders, things to support us and people in whom to believe. But we were losing everything at the same time: the chateau, the forest, the marshal, the general. And we were going to lose the empire, those orange and blue patches in Africa or Asia which used to give us so much pleasure: Pondicherry, Yanam, Karikal, Chandernagore, and Mahé—substitutes, in the context of a slightly larger community, for the Arbres-Verts and the stone table. And in the end we were going to lose the last treasure which remained to us—morals. Morals—an intangible reality which was no longer to be seen on maps, a kind of pure form which belonged to no one and yet belonged to everyone and was in everyone, something imperceptible and indistinguishable from the spirit of the age, something which had connections with order. The three centers of our racked existence became Colombey-les-Deux-Églises, Dien Bien Phu, and St. Tropez, the three centers of a new and usually painful sensibility. The army was breaking up. So were morals. The Church still held out. But that too would soon be put to the test. It was only a matter of time.

Pierre, Philippe, and Claude had gone to live in the avenue d'Eylau and the rue de Courty and the rue Bonaparte. The house in the rue de Varenne had long since been sold, and was now occupied by a government ministry which we looked on as rather like one of those coarse and tactless birds which install themselves in another bird's nest. I have already described how files and bureaucracy took the place of evening gowns and the aesthetic extravagances of the declining upper middle classes. My grandfather and I moved into a modest apartment in the rue de Courcelles, all that was left of our boulevard Haussmann property. There were only five rooms, and my grandfather could scarcely breathe in them, but he lived on for almost two more years. He was very weak when we got back to Paris, and although he needed open air and space he hardly ever went out. Paris frightened him, with its crowds and its traffic. Out of his natural habitat, he was like those postmen you hear of who die as soon as they retire. He died in our arms one winter morning without having suffered too much. He was ninety-five. The last day, when he was delirious, he asked if there was straw in the street. We didn't understand. But we soon remembered that, until the beginning of this century, when someone was dying, the servants used to spread straw on the street outside to deaden the sound of the wheels on the cobbles. So my grandfather died as he had lived, absorbed in memory and in the past. He left practically nothing: two suits which he wore alternately regardless of the weather or the temperature; a few hats; a fur-lined cloak; a dozen stiff, mostly wing, collars, and a few dozen pairs of gloves; some sumptuous silk shirts. He had been one of the last examples of this everyday mixture of simplicity and splendor. The money from the sale of Plessis-lez-Vaudreuil had already been divided up among the children and grandchildren, and so scattered, lost. He left his only treasure to me: a huge missal stuffed with pious pictures and mementoes of all our dead. The most recent photograph in it was of Aunt Gabrielle. She had died three months earlier, knocked down by a car on the esplanade des Invalides at the beginning of autumn. A police car just got her to Lariboisière Hospital in time for her to draw her last breath.

I sat down by the window in the tiny apartment. The uninterrupted murmur of cars in the street below floated up to me. I thought vaguely of Plessis-lez-Vaudreuil and my grandfather's long reign among his trees and memories. He had been the last of the dynasty, the one whom history overthrows and strikes down, the one who gathered the fruit of the efforts of all of our line throughout the ages, but who in the end had to pay for their crimes and their errors. History often sells things on credit. But someone has to pay in the end. And it was with my grandfather that all the debts of our history, which the Revolution hadn't been enough to cancel, had come home to roost. His father and grandfather had still lived in the reverberations of an older world. And those who came after him would soon get used to the troubles of the new one. But he had been torn between the past and the future. I thought, with some bitterness, that if we'd held on two more years, amid difficulties no doubt, and perhaps the beginnings of poverty, we could have let my grandfather die at Plessis-lez-Vaudreuil like all the rest of them. I was seized with regret, remorse, a certain amount of shame. Oh, I knew very well that compared with the life of a miner, a Polish Jew, a peasant in the Andes, or one of those still-mysterious Chinese who appear from time to time in history after a long eclipse, my grandfather's existence was some Western, aristocratic fairy story, miraculously preserved from fire and tempest. But we hadn't let him enjoy this privileged existence to its natural conclusion, as dictated by custom and tradition. Who can ever know what men suffer? I should hate to offend those who have experienced, either in the flesh or in their affections, more cruel ordeals, but perhaps my grandfather, in his own way, touched the depths of the pain and anguish which I read of on every page in that old, thick missal, worn with age and use, in the images of those who were no more, and whose heart-rending voices, coming from the Book of Ecclesiastes or the Wisdom of Solomon, implored us to remember. I flicked through them absent-mindedly, and the shades of those whom he had gone to join rose before me.

Those who knew and loved her
Remember in your prayers

CHARLOTTE MARIE EUGÉNIE, MARQUISE DE . . .
née WILLAMOWITZ-EHRENFELD
born Graz, April 7, 1862
called to God at Plessis-lez-Vaudreuil
August 2, 1918

Holy Virgin, have pity on those who love one another
and are separated (Abbé Perreyve)

or:

Remember in your prayers

CHARLES ANATOLE MARIE PIERRE
Colonel Comte de . . .
born Plessis-lez-Vaudreuil, December 18, 1869
died for his country, September 8, 1914

Sacred Heart of Jesus, my trust is in Thee!
(7 years ind.)
Our Lady of Lourdes, pray for us!
(300 days ind.)

Above the various texts were photographs of dreamy young girls
or spruce elderly men, usually in uniform. The back of a photograph would occasionally have extracts from letters written by the
deceased or his or her friends. For example, "She called up visions
of the Christian ladies of old for whom this world was no obstacle,
and who traveled through it with their eyes fixed on another life."
Sometimes there would be passages from sermons or diaries; sometimes lines from Racine or Péguy or even Victor Hugo, especially
in the case of young men who had been killed in the war. Nearly
always there were brief quotations from Lacordaire or the Pope:
"He preserved up to the end the heritage of his faith and the honor
of his fathers." Or "Weep not, I shall love you beyond life: love is
in the soul and love does not die." There were also military citations,

eulogies by bishops or generals, phrases from the dead person's will or last words. Very often there was a prayer to the Virgin: "Remember, O most merciful Virgin Mary, that there have never been any who have appealed for your holy protection, implored your assistance or asked for your help in vain . . ." or: "Holy Virgin, in the midst of your glory, forget not the sorrows of the world . . ." Or there would be a prayer especially apt for these cruel circumstances, and worth a plenary indulgence for the souls in Purgatory (provided there was also a prayer to the intention of the Supreme Pontiff). It began: "Behold me, good and gentle Jesus, prostrate before you. I pray and implore you with all my soul . . ." and ended with a somewhat audacious turn of speech, written above a picture of a crucifix: ". . . having before my eyes the words which the Prophet David put into your mouth, O gentle Jesus: 'They have pierced my hands and feet: they have told all my bones.' So be it."

I thought of my grandfather again. All of us—the lawyers, the businessmen, the buyers and sellers, history and the spirit of the age —all of us, more or less unwilling executioners, had pierced his hands and feet, had told all his bones. And we had thrown his poor body out of its garden. We took it back again, but it was too late, and life and soul were gone. One rainy morning we buried our grandfather in the family chapel in the cemetery at Roussette. That day I noticed again something I had already suspected: the youngest of us felt the same sorrow as we older ones did at being cut off from their origins, but in their case the feeling was mixed with a kind of relief. Of course, all of us felt sad; there is something melancholy about the end of any story. But whereas the end of Plessis-lez-Vaudreuil placed an unbearable weight on the memories of the old people, it took a corresponding weight off the hopes of the younger ones. The vanishing of the lime trees and the stone table, the dining room with all its rites, and so many centuries of custom, unchanging routine and immobility, allowed Jean-Claude, Bernard, and Véronique—not to mention Anne-Marie—to enter into the world of freedom. They had no more attachments. They could go where they wanted. They hesitated a little—but they liked that feeling of independence and uncertainty. Perhaps they didn't even find insecurity disagreeable. Hubert had been the last child to remain faithful forever to what was eternal in Plessis-lez-Vaudreuil—because he had died there. But the others were almost happy to be freed at once from the privileges and the burdens, the greatness and the servitude. They went away, often a long way away. Greece, Italy, and Spain were too near for them. They started to look toward the Sahara, the Amazon, Afghanistan, Nepal, Ceylon. A life of liberty which could be shared with everyone was more important to them than memories and constraints which could not be shared. Later on, the family would be replaced by more extended communities. But seven or eight years after the end of the war, at the beginning of the fifties, it was still the age of rediscovered pleasures and individual liberty.

The death of our grandfather had invested Pierre with new functions: he was now the head of the family. For many reasons, this was a dignity which had lost much of its glamour. His authority and prestige were much diminished by the mere fact that Plessis-lez-Vaudreuil itself no longer acted as a unique center and rallying point. Our grandfather had acted the part of patriarch with great solemnity right up to the end, but this was no longer possible. And yet, with age, Pierre had taken on an attitude which gradually relegated to an inaccessible past the previous stages of his life, although they did emerge from time to time. Who now remembered his dreams of happiness, his political ambitions, the scandal he had been mixed up in? When, ten years or so after our grandfather's death, the young ones saw him coming out of midday mass at Saint-Honoré-d'Eylau, or, on the Sundays when he went to lunch with his brother Philippe, at Sainte-Clotilde, little remained of the vanished splendor of the Masurian Lakes, or of the mixture of distress and pride which Ursula had stood for, or of the adventures of Mirette and the vice-consul in Hamburg, or of the rumors, muffled by time, of resistance to the Germans and activity with the underground press. All that was left was an elderly gentleman of sixty or so, antiquatedly elegant, with completely white hair, walking with the aid of a stick, and remarried to an American who was some vague cousin of the V.s'.

After his grandfather's death Philippe had gotten into the habit
of inviting his two brothers, his sister-in-law, and his cousin to come
and see him every second or third Sunday. The two brothers
brought their wives, Ethel and Nathalie. The sister-in-law was Hélène. She was a grandmother now. The cousin came alone—the
cousin was me. I suppose that I had gotten older, like the rest. But
I was the only one who didn't see it, who couldn't see it. Philippe
had always suffered on France's account. He had started to suffer
with Maurras and Léon Blum, with Bainville and Daudet, with
Mussolini, and with Franco and Hitler. He had suffered a great deal
with Pétain. And now he was suffering with de Gaulle. He had
clung to de Gaulle with the desperation of a drowning man. First
de Gaulle had saved him, then he had abandoned him to his fate.
And now Philippe, who had remained the youngest and handsomest
of us all, or rather the one least touched by age and its assaults, spent
his time lamenting the fate of France, which, in fidelity and despair,
he had put in the place of the family when that was torn apart.
Claude had replaced the family—scattered, threatened, almost destroyed—by the people. And Philippe had replaced it by his country. But the country did not seem to be getting on much better than
the family had: no sooner had victory come than everything was
in disarray. He found a sort of awful pleasure in this ordeal. After
having fought with the Free French he was infuriated and disgusted
by the excesses of the Liberation. He almost became that curious
phenomenon, a supporter of Vichy in retrospect. Many collaborators had belatedly discovered that they were really supporters of
the Resistance. Philippe's case was the opposite: he was a faithful
but disillusioned Gaullist, and he found it more and more difficult
to contemplate what was happening to Pétain and those who had
followed him through misfortune and resignation. The break between America and Russia, the Iron Curtain, the Cold War, the
horrors of Stalinism, and the rise of the Third World filled him with
horror and bitter amusement. In his worst rages, on evenings when
everything seemed unbearable, he would go so far as to think with
nostalgia of the German army, which he had helped to destroy.
When open war broke out in Indochina, Philippe could stand it no

longer. He got himself attached to General de Lattre de Tassigny as war correspondent for a big Paris newspaper, and spent all his time with the Legion or the parachutists in their red berets. Over fifty years old and in civilian dress, he was with General de Castries during the battle of Dien Bien Phu. He was taken prisoner by the Viet Cong. And by an irony of history, it was Mendès France, whom he hated, who got him released.

Politics, expelled from the citadel of Plessis-lez-Vaudreuil by the reactionary genius of my Grandfather, now seemed to have invaded our life. Politics was everywhere. Had it ever stopped being so? The revolutions of 1830 and 1848, the coup d'état in 1851 and the Commune in 1871, the Dreyfus affair, Vichy, the 1914 war, the Popular Front—it was impossible to deny that politics had always been the ruling factor. But it had been disguised—or we had disguised it. We had disguised it with pleasure, good breeding, religion, tradition. But with the triumph of democracy and the irresistible rise of socialism, with the Russians on the Danube and the Elbe, a few hours from the Rhine, with the atomic bomb, politics was more and more closely intermingled with our daily life. It was no longer possible to camouflage it with a mixture of solemnity and triviality. We depended upon it for our survival. And its pressure became more hostile every day. The growing permissiveness in morals—we often congratulated ourselves that our grandfather was no longer there to witness conquests and successes that would have scandalized him—led, paradoxically enough, to a lessening of the part played by love in our civilization. And the ground lost by love was occupied by politics.

Because, like art or philosophy, it was an agent of destruction, love had never been accorded a place of prime importance in our family. Yet the world around us was steeped in it. For centuries, love, the affections, and amorous conquest had played an essential role in literature, the theater, and people's everyday preoccupations. And as the obstacles put in its way by morals crumbled and yielded, so writers, poets, sociologists, and moralists all vied with one another to celebrate its triumph. But it was not long before the abolition of obstacles made the whole thing meaningless. No one has more need of resistance than Lovelace and Don Juan, or even Tristan and Romeo. The liberalization of morals did not enhance the role of love, which needs to be nurtured on misfortune, difficulty, and opposition. The tolerant society we were embarking upon was the emotional equivalent of a scorched-earth policy: there was nothing left to burn. And suddenly energy turned away from battles won in advance. Only novelists—and perhaps not the best of those—still insisted on inventing love stories which went around and around in circles and interested no one any more. The Cid, Adolphe, and Fabrice del Dongo still had some meaning. With Julien Sorel, love was overshadowed by the class struggle. Porto-Riche, Octave Feuillet, and Paul Bourget came on the scene much too late to occupy the place they hoped for in the history of love. Marx won out over Racine, and revolution over the analysis of feeling.

Claude was the first among us to understand this change. His life, instead of being traditional or emotional, was first and foremost political. And he inclined toward Karl Marx just as my father, once, to the scandal of the family, had inclined toward Romanticism. But during the war Claude had neglected Marx for de Gaulle. After de Gaulle retired for a decade or so, Claude returned to Karl Marx, and his hero was Stalin. I might almost say that in Stalin he found, if not a father figure, at least a grandfather figure. In recent years, either for the rest of the world or for us, Pétain, Churchill, de Gaulle, and of course my grandfather had represented Moses leading the Israelites. Now it was Stalin's turn. He appeared as a mixture of Charlemagne and the bogeyman, with the sinners on his left, where it was better not to be, and the righteous on his right, a position which was not much better. Never mind—Claude admired him and loved him. Never mind if there were rumors about the real relationship between Lenin and the future marshal, about the camps in Siberia, or about the brutality of Stalin's dictatorship: Claude waved aside these polemics as mere fascist propaganda. To doubt Stalin was to choose Hitler. Once de Gaulle went into the wilderness, Claude had no doubts. He went to Prague, Warsaw, Budapest, Moscow. He was what was called in those days a good fellow traveler. He wasn't a member of the party, but, as in the years before the war, he identified himself with it. So, for him, 1956 brought a series of events more tragic than the end of Plessis-lez-Vaudreuil was for the rest of us.

Before the winter was over he heard with horror Khrushchev's revelations to the twentieth congress of the Soviet Communist Party. In the autumn there was Budapest. Communism was destroying itself. None of these blows could have been struck from outside. It was as if the only way to act upon communism was by becoming part of it. No one would have dared to say about Stalin what his own people said about him. No one would have dared to send tanks into a communist country except another, and the most powerful, communist country. Philippe was triumphant. Claude, for the second time, saw his world collapse. The first world he had been born into, and he had left it because he thought it unjust. The second he had chosen. And it turned out to be worse than the first.

I saw a lot of Claude at that time. Again, he was very unhappy. Everywhere, toward the end of the fifties, it was as if hope had vanished like a mirage. In less than twenty years the world had gone from the depths of 1940 to the delirious hopes of 1944 and 1945, only to fall back again into the risk of war, the heaping up of ruins, disorder, skepticism. Neither evils nor their cure left one stone standing upon another. People began to whisper that Hitler might have lost the war, but he was going to win the peace. Not only the Russians and the Americans, but also the Jews and the communists, whom, for a time, Hitler had thrown into the same camp, began to hate and perhaps to destroy one another. Violence and terror revived everywhere under cover of the affectation of tolerance and the proclamation of the rights of man. Claude's disillusionment was worse than other people's because he had had more faith in human progress. Now even science abandoned him. Ten or fifteen years after the war, science began to be called in question, sometimes even accused. From beyond the grave, and of course in conditions very different from any he could have imagined, my grandfather was avenged on the modern world which he refused to accept and which he had denounced in advance.

In those days Claude would often say to me that he had wasted his life, that he had been wrong about everything, and that he could no longer believe in anything. After a thousand years of use, our past had collapsed, and his own future was collapsing before it ever began. As you may imagine, Philippe was delighted with this admission of defeat. But even he couldn't do much more than rejoice at other people's misfortune: his world too, our world, continued to be engulfed by the waves of history.

You may remember our somewhat uncertain relationship with the notion of country, empire, and national authority, embodied successively by Robespierre's Jacobins, a Corsican general, the son of a regicide belonging to a younger branch of the Orléans family still not to be trusted, and by the republicans of big business or the Popular Front. We were divided between tradition and purely political frontiers. Spain, Austria-Hungary, the Papal States, and all the Germanys were at least as close to us as the Marseilles of gangsters and socialists, as Lyons with its silk and its sausages, as Lille with its looms. As a matter of fact, we were Europeans born too soon. How hard we had tried to become republicans, patriots and Frenchmen at last! We had gotten ourselves killed on the battlefield, rallied to the "Marseillaise" and the tricolor, entered both democracy and business, averted our gaze with difficulty from the past and looked toward the future. And now the future—no doubt that was its fate, but we were so slow that it went faster than we did—was turning into the past. We were always a generation late, always one system or one revolution behind, which hastened to destroy that which we were just catching up with at the very moment we were resigning ourselves to it. We had just brought ourselves to give up Plessis-lez-Vaudreuil and to kill our grandfather so as to merge at last in the community and the Republic, one and indivisible. And the community was dissolving, the Republic disintegrating.

Stalin and Budapest tortured Claude. Indochina and Algeria crucified Philippe. God hadn't quite abandoned us: he distributed trials, suffering, and injustice very fairly between East and West, between tradition and socialism, between the past and the future. If, as Hegel put it, history is a judgment of God *(Weltgeschichte ist Weltgericht),*

the Almighty must have had difficulty in deciding between Philippe
and Claude. So he afflicted both of them. Claude was in much the
same despair as he'd been plunged into by the pact between Ribbentrop and Molotov. He tried to understand how *Das Kapital* had led
to the camps in Siberia, and the Communist Manifesto to the tanks
in Budapest. For Philippe it was simpler: he was dying.

He was dying. And for nothing. As you are beginning to realize,
we had often died in the course of the centuries. And not always
as victors. But at least our deaths, on the most wretched battlefields,
in the vilest prisons, even on the scaffold, had always remained with
us as an example of greatness to be cultivated by our children. We
always managed to salvage our deaths. They were never wasted.
But Philippe didn't really know why he had chosen to die. It was
in truth a kind of suicide through contrariness.

I suppose, in order to give a clear account of our adventures in
those days without structure but not without passion, I ought to
devote whole pages to political, intellectual, and ethical history.
Before, at the balls or dinner parties at Plessis-lez-Vaudreuil and in
the rue de Presbourg, psychology played an important part, because we lived in closed universes where the individual was supreme. From Racine to Benjamin Constant, Proust, Gide, and
Mauriac, the slow progress of sentiment in the souls of princesses,
adolescents, mature women, homosexuals, and citizens of Bordeaux
took up a great deal of space and a great deal of our time. But after
the undermining of the rue de Varenne itself, speed, the image,
television, a mixture of socialism and money, the heritage of Morand and Malraux, in short, the modern age, had abolished all that.
We have already seen how economic and social considerations gradually prevailed over emotional preoccupations. Now it must be
added that action, behavior, and politics prevailed over psychology.

Everything became fast, rough, often strong, sometimes rather
unfeeling—and everything was interconnected. Plessis-lez-Vaudreuil had been an island surrounded by time. Now that the island
was submerged and ruined, we entered into the modern world, into
its limitless prospects and dizzy whirlpools. No one any longer had
the time, the wish, or perhaps even the ability to understand his

neighbor or his enemy as we used to understand my grandfather or Aunt Gabrielle, Racine's Phèdre, the maternal feelings of Madame de Sévigné, and to imagine their tricks, their ambitions, their generosities, and their intentions. The universe had become a juxtaposition or an interpenetration of opaque mechanisms and actions which for the most part fought against one another and then sorted things out as best they could. They were born out of chance and necessity, education, social class, economic facts, heredity, and environment. Anything might happen, but in any case psychoanalysis and Marxism would always offer an interpretation. People had stopped understanding; instead they explained.

This was the time when Anne-Marie was transformed into a star and when her name began to shine from screens all over the world. Books came out full of photographs of her—often without very many clothes on. She lived a crazy sort of life, incomprehensible even to herself. She would pass from gaiety to dejection, high spirits to depression. She spent a lot of money, she wasn't very happy, she had everything, and she wept. When we saw her in Paris, or in Rome shooting a film, or when she had us invited to stay with friends of hers in Provence on some huge Greek yacht flying the Panamanian flag, we were astounded by the contrast between our memory of her riding a bicycle along the paths at Plessis-lez-Vaudreuil in her white pleated skirt, her long hair streaming down her back, and the picture of her now with her whisky, her tumultuous love affairs, her huge and fickle public, her jewels and paraphernalia, the Italian sailors she slept with, the American lovers she destroyed with drugs and humiliation. Sometimes, in the evening, after a violent scene and before going off to forget everything in the arms of an oil magnate or a racing driver—who made me think of a bullfighter and took me back thirty years to the memory of Ursula, my cousin and Anne-Marie's mother—she used to talk to me still about her childhood. And I would talk to her about mine. And because they both took place against the unchanged background of Plessis-lez-Vaudreuil, under the eyes of my grandfather, the two childhoods seemed to merge into one despite the twenty years or so which separated them. The sky above us now was almost the

same as the sky at Plessis-lez-Vaudreuil, with the same stars performing the same evolutions. How peaceful! How serene! With our
glasses in our hands and the murmur of music in the distance, we
tried in vain to read our fates in the stars. A sort of numbness crept
over us, tinged with sweetness and melancholy. It seemed as if
nothing mattered in this limitless universe, and as if minutes, months,
and years existed only to be swallowed up in nothingness. She was
drunk. So was I. We didn't speak. In this space, this time, we were
mere specks of dust whose happiness consisted only in confusion
and annihilation. How far away we were from the established grandeurs, the fixed rules, the immutable terrestrial and celestial order
whose decline we had witnessed! Anne-Marie, Pierre, and I, or
Anne-Marie, Nathalie, Claude, and I, would be drawn by a mystic
communion around the stone table. The table was still there somewhere in the distance, but all that had given it meaning had been
engulfed in the void. We no longer existed, and yet we were reliving
our youth. We went on drinking. I seemed to glimpse my grandfather and Aunt Gabrielle between some Italian starlet and a former
brothelkeeper who had married the owner of three of the biggest
newspapers in the United States. I burst out laughing. Anne-Marie
stared at me. She wasn't happy either. She threw herself into my
arms and wept. Three-quarters of an hour later, irresistible, pitiless,
she would cause a scandal in a fashionable nightclub.

It wouldn't be difficult to write a long book about Anne-Marie.
Quite apart from the essays and coffee-table books which quite
openly make her their subject, I know at least two or three novels
in which the fictional heroine is obviously based on her beauty and
her follies. When I think about her now I see a composite figure.
For that matter, whenever I try to summon up any member of my
family I am more interested—perhaps you've noticed?—in their
remembered image than in any particular detail or anecdote. But of
course I like these images to be as true, as exact, and as detailed as
possible. And however fixed they may be, like the image one has of
the elderly Hugo or Rimbaud as a young man, they do develop with
time. Anne-Marie was no longer the little girl having lunch with us
in the children's dining room at Plessis-lez-Vaudreuil, nor the young

woman in love with Robert V., nor the already widowed pseudo-fiancée haunted by Major von Wittgenstein, nor the mistress of the curly-haired lad fighting for the Liberation. She had become a star, the successor of Ava Gardner and Marilyn Monroe, the archetype, together with Brigitte Bardot and Jeanne Moreau, of the international film star. And we would see her standing beside Onassis, or the irresistible Kennedy, or Prince Orsini on the front page of *France-Dimanche* or the cover of *Paris-Match*. But within her life as a star there were stages. Throughout the fifties she continued to mount the invisible ladder of popularity and success. And then suddenly—because of a migraine, a change of hair style, an exhausting journey, or a meeting with a friend she hadn't seen for two or three years—she started to look old. At the beginning of the sixties she was still marvelous, adored and triumphant. But the decline had already set in. She still went on trying to drown her sorrows, but she could feel the old life she had pursued so passionately coming apart in her hands. Sometimes she would be seized with panic. Then she would behave worse than during the years of her rise to fame. Even her father could do practically nothing with her. Only Claude and I could calm her a little. When we weren't there, there were terrible scenes, with processions of lovers, furious and angry dreams we never suspected, and nightmares in which the high gilded ceilings of Plessis-lez-Vaudreuil and the lakes in the forest found a place.

All these different versions of Anne-Marie would crop up in society conversation, in actors' autobiographies, in novels by Norman Mailer or Truman Capote, or in the fireside gossip, in Scotland or in a drawing room in the avenue Montaigne, of some elderly uncle from the banks of the Rhine come to shoot grouse or Roman princess passing through Paris to buy new dresses. Anyone who had never known Anne-Marie and heard people talk about her like that might have wondered whether it could really all refer to the same person. Having refused, one after the other, the fates that were offered her, she ended by leading five or six different lives. Only last year I met two men quite advanced in years who must once have been quite good-looking, and who in their totally different ways had been important. Each of them had dreamed for several years of marrying Anne-Marie. How time flies! Anne-Marie would soon be forty. And, having refused and driven crazy so many men of charm and talent, she now did her best to get married to a fat, rich Lebanese in the oil business. It was the time of the Algerian troubles. The Lebanese not only possessed a fortune which caused all doors to be opened to him; he was also very intelligent. He realized, before most other people, the way things were going to turn out. And right in the middle of the Algerian War, over the head of the French government, he was negotiating with the big oil companies, with Enrico Mattei, the F.L.N., and the G.P.R.A., the Provisional Government of the Algerian Republic.

I remember one evening in Rome—so many years after those nights of our adolescence, when Claude and I, with Marina, used to stroll by the Tiber and the Colosseum—when Anne-Marie had invited us to one of the sumptuous palaces her lover used to rent. The company included Claude and Nathalie, Philippe, Pierre and Ethel, a few actors and actresses, a few fashionable princes and princesses, a few businessmen, and myself. It was a year or eighteen months after the triumph of *La Dolce Vita*. For a long time we had acted out our own *Leopard* at Plessis-lez-Vaudreuil. Now we were acting their *Dolce Vita* in rented palaces. We drank. Probably we all had something to forget. So we forgot it in drink, drugs, gambling, and with the boys or girls we happened to come across, and whom most of the group made use of irrespective of sex. But was this way of life so new, this fashion that was the child of the Roaring Twenties finding its second wind thirty-five or forty years later in London and St. Tropez, Rome and St. Moritz? Of course, it formed a startling contrast with the stern nineteenth century, the puritanism of Queen Victoria, and the severe habits of Plessis-lez-Vaudreuil. But perhaps it only linked up with more ancient traditions, with the frivolous shade of the Regency and the end of the eighteenth century, with the lusty appetite of the Renaissance, and with the pleasures of the declining Roman Empire. As well as those who are inclined, by faith or hope, to see history as indefinite progress mingled with certain irregularities, there are also those who see it

as a perpetual cycle returning to parallel situations indefinitely repeated. We were emerging from a long ordeal, many of our deepest
springs of action had been broken, the future was uncertain and our
values shaky: no doubt all this was enough to give us a thirst for
pleasure in which the moralizing historian would have no difficulty
in detecting all the seething monsters of anguish, inflation, the absence of the father, and abandonment. I think that, in our case, we
were very much influenced by the disappearance of Plessis-lez-
Vaudreuil: Claude, Philippe, Pierre, Anne-Marie, and I were all
linked to that nature and that art, that savagery and that refinement
in which our name was embodied—and we were linked too to their
sudden absence. It was hard for us to get over this rupture with our
past and with our habits. I suddenly realized how middle-class that
pastoral life of ours had been. We imagined we were still leading
the same lives as our ancestors. More probably we were just leading
the lives of the ruling classes at the end of the nineteenth century.
Can one escape from one's own time? One can be superior or inferior to it, one can struggle against it as we always had. But in the
end it always gets you and marks you with its imprint. I began to
understand the truth there was in Claude's opinions. Despite our
long hatred of money and big business, of Louis Philippe and of the
Republic, despite our hunting horns and our love of Saint-Simon,
we had become middle-class. Upper-middle-class, but middle-class.
And perhaps we were now more middle-class than ever in realizing
at last that we were so, and in rebelling against the discovery. While
we were still at Plessis-lez-Vaudreuil it would never have occurred
to us to see ourselves as bourgeois. But as soon as we realized that
we too had become members of that detested class we rebelled
against it with drugs and baccarat, with Arab revolutionaries and
Italian actresses. And nothing could have been more bourgeois than
all these reactions and our refusal to admit to our new condition.

That evening, in the Quirinal Palace or the Piazza Ognissanti
rented by Anne-Marie and her Lebanese lover, the company was
mostly of the Left. But I hadn't yet come to the end of my naïve
discoveries, and this atmosphere suddenly seemed to me quite different from Claude's rebellion and Claude's hopes. Seen from Plessis-

lez-Vaudreuil, the Left was one uniform nightmare, a monolithic
monster. But now it seemed full of nuances and divisions. Perhaps
the Right too, looked at from some socialist or communist observa-
tory, gave an impression of unity? Yet what was there in common
between fascism and us, between the Employers' Federation and us,
I was almost going to say between the comte de Paris and us? At
all events, I could see divisions forming within the Left which we
used to consign in its entirety to horror and reprobation. I looked
at Claude: he suddenly seemed the image of my grandfather. A
modern image, of course, transformed, turned inside out, upside
down, if you like. But the image of him, just the same—my grandfather brought back to life. I don't think he himself was unaware of
this reversal, this eternal return of things in our inexhaustible yet
limited universe. I had noted long before that, far removed as they
were from one another, so contrasted, such fierce enemies, Stalin
and my grandfather belonged to the same world of archetypes and
eternal ideas—the world of the father and the model. Claude had
cut himself off—as he thought forever—from our system of tradition and decadence; he had gone over to the side of the most
unconditional enemies of our hated past. But now, before my very
eyes, I could see things, events, and men arranged in a very different
fashion. Now it was Claude who embodied the morality of my
grandfather, with his love of order and equity, of history and its
principles. It was simply that time, with its procession of novelties
and transformations, had passed above everything, throwing a veil
of obscurity over what was really self-evident.

Or perhaps I was dreaming. The future would tell. In any case,
Philippe didn't see things the way I did. In his view, it was all mere
abomination, content to disguise itself with the most diverse of
masks. Claude, the Lebanese, the businessmen of the Left, the lesbian
princesses, all were just the multiple faces of what we had always
hated. He couldn't help retaining a paradoxical affection for Claude,
yet at the same time he detested him. He was overflowing with
indignation the whole evening, which was only a slightly more
emphatic repetition of many similar experiences. If I were writing
a novel and had the skill, no doubt I could describe those hours in

the vivid style of a Styron, a Malcolm Lowry, or a Norman Mailer. What shall I say? At Plessis-lez-Vaudreuil we were close to the life we led. That evening in Rome we were surrounded by gulfs; every word opened precipices at our feet. We were all unhappy, guilty, haunted. Every sentence we uttered was eaten away from below, and referred to fantasies, tragedies, secrets, vanished dreams. Incest, madness, and crime were among us. Everything was false, doubly or triply false. Everything was full of sin or stifled remorse, and death was everywhere. Without drink and gambling, drugs and eroticism, most of those present wouldn't have been able to go on living. Our least words were tinged with bitterness and each of us, often unwittingly, was pursuing someone else's death or his own. Amid so many ruins we were amazed still to be standing, and we weren't too sure we were pleased about it. It wasn't only the world that was on the brink of the abyss; it was ourselves. Everything was toppling, and so were we. We were the tightrope walkers of modern times, the mountebanks of a twilight trying in vain to be a dawn.

Philippe dimly perceived the destruction that lay behind all our attitudes. And he hated them. He had already had a violent argument with the Lebanese about abstract painting and modern art. He hadn't said anything very intelligent, and the Lebanese had outmaneuvered him, almost made him look ridiculous. I can still see them, in the huge, sparsely furnished room with cushions on the floor and a vague murmur of music coming from somewhere, glasses of whiskey in their hands and fury in their hearts. They didn't know each other, but they hated each other already. There was no reason why they should: they didn't love the same woman, they didn't owe each other money, their countries weren't at war, they weren't interfering with each other in business or ambition. And yet everything set them against one another. But I could vaguely guess what irritated Philippe about this marvelously cultivated Arab who spoke French better than we did and was so much at home in this new world which he amused himself by dominating. He was Anne-Marie's lover. We were beginning to get used to Anne-Marie's lovers. It was understood that she trailed all hearts behind her because she was beautiful, and because she naturally shared in the celebrated family charm. It was also understood that she really cared only about us, and that all the rest, the cinema, her love affairs, her world triumphs, were just an unimportant game. She looked down on it and laughed at it, and we, the younger ones —younger, I mean, than our grandfather, to whom it would never have occurred to laugh at such adventures—we smiled at it indulgently. But that evening it was the Lebanese who was smiling. He knew—we all knew—that in the struggle for recognition which may be one of the forms of love, it was he who was winning. How many young men had I seen dragged along in Anne-Marie's wake, enchanted by her legend and terrified at the idea of losing her and never seeing her again! But time had had its effect on bodies and hearts as well as on ideas and morals. I looked at Anne-Marie. Yes, she too, whom we had thought to be unchangeable, she too had grown older. How sad! There were two lines by her mouth, her skin was less smooth than it had been, her eyes were slightly puffy. Of course, she was still beautiful. But she was afraid. Afraid of passing time, of failure, of no longer being attractive. She was afraid of losing this lover who was not so good-looking as many others had been, though they had been scorned, dismissed, forgotten long ago. Perhaps she loved him less than she had loved those others, too, but he had one enormous advantage: he had come on the scene at what was for him the most propitious moment—the moment of anxiety, of the decline after the triumph. Did Philippe realize all this? I don't know. But he sensed it, I am sure. A kind of jealousy, not amorous but social, a group or clan jealousy, seized him at the idea that the niece he was so proud of and who belonged to us was about to forget the family for an Arab, a businessman, an obvious product of the new world Philippe hated so much. The other man, of course, was already relishing his somewhat dubious success. And he was forcing Philippe right up against the wall. Pierre had already left. Claude said nothing. Like my grandfather in the old days, he didn't agree with anyone. His world and his hopes were already elsewhere: they too were being swallowed up by the past.

Philippe couldn't transfer the battle to sentimental grounds. He struggled on the battlefield of ideas, morals, aesthetics, politics—

perhaps, in fact, that was the real battleground. I would have been hard put to it to say whether the hostility involved was political and social or emotional and to a certain extent erotic. Each grew out of and strengthened the other. The argument became more and more heated. The two principals were now a spectacle for all the others, and could no longer moderate their positions. Philippe had never been good at arguments. He soon lost his temper, and for us who loved him it was almost unbearable to see him falling into his adversary's traps. The Lebanese mocked him, forced him to contradict himself, drove him into blind alleys which made the onlookers snigger. Philippe was gradually losing ground, and rushed headlong into platitudes of ethics and tradition which the others anticipated and gloated over. Words like "honor" and "patriotism" were drowned in laughter. Someone called him a fascist, and I saw him hesitate and begin to panic: was he, who had fought against the Germans ("And you, what did you do during the war?"—and everyone started laughing again), was he going to react to the insult or accept it as a challenge, since after all he had been a fascist for ten years out of scorn and hatred for just this kind of people? But already the argument, with its rapid associations of words and ideas, its sudden shifts and subtle nuances, had passed to another subject —Algeria—which didn't improve matters.

I knew, from the very beginning of these reminiscences, that our slightest words and deeds were linked to a whole world of customs and events. No sigh is ever breathed on earth which doesn't call in question the order of the heavens. Everything is interconnected. There is no love which is independent of politics or art; no human or social relations, however insignificant, which do not reflect the state of morals, the evolution of religion, everything that contributes to the spirit of an age and the atmosphere of an era. And what was happening in France in 1960? The Algerian War, the tragedy that was to deal the last and most terrible blow to Philippe's hopes, and transform them into illusions. I might have written a book about Anne-Marie and her wild life. I might also have written one about Philippe's role in what happened in Algeria. And, in their opposite ways, those books would in a sense have been the same, for

Anne-Marie and Philippe, in their very different ways, both represented the same era and a comparable constellation.

Philippe had thrown himself body and soul into the cause of Algeria's remaining French. You have already seen how he was not sufficiently wary of history and its reversals. Of course he was one of those who had helped to bring General de Gaulle back to power. After that, and a brief period of exaltation, his life became just one long ordeal. Every Frenchman has rubbed shoulders with supporters of French Algeria and supporters of de Gaulle. Most Frenchmen have seen people change sides and either abandon de Gaulle after having acclaimed him on May 13, or, conversely, follow him in his policy of independence where once they suspected him of being a fascist or called for his return so that he might keep Algeria French. Philippe's tragedy, which led to his death, was that he remained, or tried to remain, to the end, a fanatical supporter both of French Algeria and of the general. Philippe was perhaps the simplest of us all: a nationalist, a patriot, a conservative, he had none of those complications and refinements which he hated in the modern world. And yet, three times, history managed to drive him into paradoxes from which he could not escape. An admirer of nationalism, he had admired the nationalism of others which had been turned against us, and for a couple of years, until salvation was brought by de Gaulle, he had been in the extraordinary situation of a nationalist looking on with uncertainty and horror as a foreign nationalism triumphed over our own democracy. De Gaulle and de Gaulle alone had enabled him to get out of the impasse, and Philippe could never forget it. But at the Liberation—and this was like the second test in a Breton or Arabian fairy story—the Gaullist in him was opposed to the purging and persecution of the Pétainists. He found himself on the side of those he had fought against and whose errors and illusions he understood because he had once shared them. And now, for the third time, he felt trapped by history.

Philippe, like the rest of us, was no longer a young man. He was well over fifty. He would soon be sixty, like Pierre. But because he had never married, and because he still had almost as many women trailing behind him as Anne-Marie had men, he still retained something of his adolescence, a freshness, a capacity for enthusiasm, an almost childlike naïveté. His love of women was very strict. He was as severe as my grandfather had been against homosexuals, against eroticism, against any form of scandal, against modern music and painting (he was apt to see these as a form of pederasty), against anything he did not understand, and with age he tended to conform to a somewhat old-fashioned type of antiquated gallantry. He looked to his country's past for remedies for its present decadence, which he was always castigating with a surliness that made the young people laugh. To a certain extent he shared popular taste: he liked military music, he liked the Fourteenth of July celebrations, and unlike our grandfather would never have missed them on any account; he sympathized with the war veteran's mentality, and adopted it in place of the fascism of his youth, perhaps in order to exorcise it. The events leading up to May 13, 1958, had plunged him once more into the atmosphere he loved best: the atmosphere of military plots and national conspiracies. For two or three weeks he was involved in the process begun by de Gaulle. Once again he took part in a kind of patriotic and clandestine activity, behaving like the hero of a cloak-and-dagger novel or of one of those slightly satirical films alternating between sentiment and violence. Once the general was back in power, he had the feeling that he had contributed to the resurrection of France.

Perhaps, for reasons I have often suggested, there are already too many deliberately historical and social references in these reminiscences. I have no intention of following in the footsteps of all the colonels and diplomats and journalists who have traced the development of General de Gaulle's Algerian policy. First of all, I don't know much about it, and moreover my intention is not to retell the history of recent years but simply to show how it, just as much as and perhaps more than emotional experiences or the famous years of infancy, entered into and modified the behavior of individuals. Did General de Gaulle change his mind about Algeria between 1958 and 1960, or, for anyone who could understand, were all the future developments already there in embryo in the speeches which aroused such enthusiasm in the Forum or in the rue d'Isly? Frankly,

I don't know. What I do know is that Philippe—perhaps because he wasn't very intelligent—was absolutely convinced that with the general as president it was certain that Algeria would remain French. He could see there might be another policy. But he could not see that such a policy could be followed by de Gaulle. De Gaulle's strength and genius was in the fact that many, both among those who supported integration and among those who supported independence, made the same mistake as Philippe. The general moved to and fro among them all with incomparable skill, relying sometimes on one side and sometimes on the other, sometimes simultaneously on both, and maneuvering all at the same time. Many of those who backed the myth of de Gaulle did not approve of his policy, and most of those who did approve of his policy didn't want to see it applied by him, whom they hated. These uncertainties and reversals gave rise to strange episodes which were far beyond Philippe's ability to imagine or adapt to: he had neither the virtues nor the vices necessary to dominate his age.

What he did have was sincerity—an old-fashioned sincerity which looked toward the past. It wasn't enough. Sincerity has never been enough to win the place in history that is accorded to guile, ambition, the ability to foresee the future, intelligence, and genius. Philippe flung himself into all the illusions of fraternity between the French and the Moslems. He had fought in Italy and Germany with Algerian units whose respect he had won and among whom he had made many friends. I can't believe he was ever mixed up in murder or torture. He just tried, as he put it, to bring men of goodwill together and galvanize their energies. He had no official position, but he was one of those always to be found hanging around the bars of the Aletti and the St. George Hotel in Algiers, hatching plots and political coups in a strange and oft-described atmosphere of clandestine adventure and patriotic responsibility. But as the days and weeks and months went by, Philippe was forced to realize that the general's intentions were not, or were no longer, what he had persisted in attributing to him. The end of Plessis-lez-Vaudreuil had been a terrible blow to Philippe. Perhaps the revelation of the general's Algerian policy was an even worse one. The world around him did nothing but die, and history did nothing but betray.

It was in these circumstances that I met Philippe again in Rome, at Anne-Marie's. His nerves were raw. Everything hurt him. Anne-Marie along with everything else. She was amused by Uncle Philippe's adventures and pretended to put them on a par with her own sentimental escapades. This comparison exasperated Philippe. When it came to the Lebanese, it was unbearable. The Lebanese, Anne-Marie's way of life and reputation, the absence of Plessis-lez-Vaudreuil though it was always present in the background, the dissolution of the family, and finally the incomprehensible attitude of General de Gaulle over the death throes of French Algeria, everything combined to demonstrate that the world Philippe had loved was receding every day further into the past. Anne-Marie's lover was not slow to understand the situation, and pressed his advantage. He attacked all Philippe's sensitive spots, he made him contradict himself and the general. It was a dreadful spectacle. The argument became a single combat that was tragically unequal. Philippe, covered with sweat, drawn, his hands trembling, downed every drink as it was handed to him. I tried two or three times to intervene, to calm him down and make him leave. But he couldn't leave. He was fascinated by what he hated—by subtlety, irony, the rejection of the past, ideas which looked to the future, Anne-Marie's hostile attitude. Surrounded by his Danish starlets and his Roman princes, the Lebanese looked on smiling at the collapse of his enemy. He went so far as to express admiration for de Gaulle, and said he saw him as the instrument of the march of history. The disoriented Gaullist was caught off balance. The Lebanese completed his work with small, subtle touches, such as putting his arm around Anne-Marie's neck, completing the abasement of the uncle in the affection he showed to the niece, laughing aloud as he wrung the life out of Philippe. Dawn was breaking over Rome when Philippe and I stood once more in the square where, so many years earlier, Claude and I had looked on at the birth of fascism. My cousin was tottering with drunkenness, fatigue, humiliation, and despair. He babbled

with impotent fury. He wept. I held him up. He reproached me for
not having helped him against the coalition of starlets, degenerate
aristocracy, and revolutionary capitalism. I tried to console him
briefly, pretending to laugh. But he had been mortally wounded. He
kept saying: "And de Gaulle! De Gaulle!" I realized that the name,
to which for so long he had attached all his disappointed hopes, now
stood for an immense weariness, for all the bitterness of a future
which he was no longer able to keep up with. There was nothing
more for him to do. He was too old: it was not a question of years,
but of history. We staggered along, with me holding him up, stopping every so often for an attack of weakness to pass, or for him
to weep, once or twice for him to vomit. It was a comic scene. But
it didn't make me laugh. That night in Rome, Philippe was already
dead. Poisoned by words. Strangled by ideas which he could no
longer understand. Executed by history.

I wasn't very surprised, five or six months later, to hear about the
deaths of Philippe and Anne-Marie, only a few weeks apart. My
cousin had been found in a blind alley in Algiers with a bullet in
his head and a revolver beside him. I was sure of only one thing:
he had wanted to die. As for the rest ... There were different
theories. There was talk of suicide; of an execution by the F.L.N.;
of a settling of accounts by the O.A.S., because of Philippe's contacts with the Gaullists; of a liquidation by the Gaullist secret
service because he was too involved with the O.A.S. Everyone had
some reason to wish him dead—and he as much as, or more than,
any of them. All sorts of elaborate stories were told. Two young
Italians came to see me in Paris—friends of Giorgio Almirante, and
mixed up to some extent in neo-fascist activities. By an irony of
history they had been sent to me by a politician of the extreme
Right who was the son of somebody you've most likely forgotten:
the socialist schoolmaster at Plessis-lez-Vaudreuil, whose hand my
grandfather went and shook just before war broke out. The Italians
told me that my niece's Lebanese lover had close connections with
the leaders of the F.L.N., and that he had told them my cousin was
extremely hostile to Algerian independence. They offered, for a
considerable sum of money, to give me photocopies of irrefutable

evidence. But almost at that very moment the family lawyer sent me a recent letter which Philippe had written him. The letter spoke very violently against certain of our compatriots, and did not accord with the revelations of my two Italians. The evidence of various friends and relations seemed to point to a serious nervous breakdown. Pierre and I set out for Algiers. We stayed there a week or so, but didn't find out anything definite. In the plane, on the way back, Pierre said that the saddest thing about it was that Philippe had always dreamed of dying for France. It was a strange idea, perhaps, and one without much meaning any more. He was dead. But for what? Did we have the right to put on his grave the old-fashioned words which still were to be seen on the graves of his brother, of my father, of so many uncles and great-uncles, and which he would have been so pleased with: "Killed in action" or "He died for France"? But could such words still be used in the age of Dien Bien Phu, of the battle of Algiers and the O.A.S., an age that would soon be that of the Vietnam War, an age in which young men lay down on railway lines to stop military equipment from reaching the army? We were all living in the past. Philippe had taken from it what had irremediably aged in our modern world of machines: the military spirit, chivalry, the myths of medieval heroism, love of discipline and authority—everything which nowadays was not only forgotten but also scorned and hated. "You know," said Pierre, "it might be better to think he really wanted to die with Plessis-lez-Vaudreuil." Yes, it was better. And it was probably true. But then, in a world which was collapsing, it was hardly worth bothering about details.

It wasn't long before the Lebanese abandoned Anne-Marie. I scarcely knew him, and can't even remember his name exactly, but he played a certain part in the history of the family. Philippe was dead. Anne-Marie was taking drugs. She had been admitted as an emergency case into a hospital in New York. Do you remember the dazzling young actress who came across the Atlantic to see her cousin die? I've often told you how strong our family feeling was. I flew in the opposite direction to see my niece die. After all, all those who had the good fortune to know her had at some time or

another been in love with her—her uncles like everyone else. She
wasn't dying. Not yet. But when I went into that room in one of
the most expensive clinics in New York, my heart stood still: it was
an old woman lying there in the bed. Nowadays, if you told young
people she was once beautiful, more than beautiful—enchanting—
and that she won the hearts of all our cousins in the country, officers
in the Wehrmacht and the Luftwaffe, members of the Resistance
and show-jumpers, Italian actors and Greek oil magnates, they
would only laugh. Fools—you don't know what I have learned at
the cost of my life, that there is only one force in the world and it
is called time. The blows I have seen it strike around me!—old men
and children, stones, ideas, morals, memories, and the gods. It wasn't
enough to say that time ruled the world. The world was time. It was
the time of pleasure and the time of pain, the time of youth which
doesn't worry about time and imagines it isn't passing, the time of
rain and sun, of storms, of the clear air around the isles of Greece,
the time of disasters and the time of love, the time of memory and
the time of oblivion. Everything which unfolded before the eyes of
generation after generation was nothing but time. It was embodied
in museums, churches, cemeteries, houses which first were built and
then began to crumble, in journeys, in money which first circulated,
then accumulated, then circulated again, then melted away and
vanished. It was embodied in failing health, in gathering or dispers-
ing clouds, in the earth and the trees, in feelings, in ambition, in
works of art and in war, in passion and in history. It was embodied
in Plessis-lez-Vaudreuil and in each one of us. And my grandfather
was dead, and my father was dead, and so was Uncle Paul, and Aunt
Gabrielle was dead, and Jacques and Hubert and Philippe were
dead. And Anne-Marie was no longer beautiful.

Sitting beside Anne-Marie's bed in the New York clinic, I understood what had been so fundamental in my now disintegrating
family: it had struggled against death, it had struggled against time,
seeking in history and in a memory transmitted from generation to
generation and mortal to mortal something stronger and more dura-
ble than the individual who perished. The age we were now entering upon was the triumph of the individual. That was a great and

good thing. Liberty, happiness, all the pleasures of this world had been too little known to us. But now many people would know them. I didn't disagree with those who were glad of this and who mocked and hated us. I myself might not have loved the family if I hadn't been born into it. But I was born into it, and I did not repudiate it. And I admired its efforts to survive. Once again, by Anne-Marie's bed, I experienced the heart-rending realization that there was one world which was falling to pieces and another which was being born. Anne-Marie, like Claude, though in a different way, was the link between the two worlds. More than anyone else, she had enjoyed the delights of the new world. And now she was also learning that those delights must be paid for. Despite her triumphs and her glory, she was the first of our name to be afraid of dying alone.

Neither Anne-Marie nor I had any children. Nor had Philippe. And Hubert had died long before he was old enough to have any. There were more and more dead branches on the family tree. That wasn't the most serious thing. There had always been branches which did not continue, and Pierre, Claude, and Jacques had sons and daughters. No, what was serious was that even with these sons and daughters, the family was doomed. And not only our family. All the others, all the families, the family as such, the form and idea of the family. And—was it cause or effect?—with the family, history, the past, memory, tradition, a love of what is unchangeable, an impulse towards eternity, had all received their death blow.

There hadn't been very many of us at Plessis-lez-Vaudreuil, apart from Jules and my grandfather. Despite the lake and the forest, the stage was a small one and the audience few. But there were people present at our birth and there were people present at our death. The king died only once—in 1793. For centuries and centuries, up to the blow struck by Sanson and the roll of drums on January 21, the king had never been dead. And we did not die either. We fell asleep in the bosom of the family and of the Roman, Apostolic, and Catholic Church, and in the peace of the Lord. And the genius of the family, without which we were nothing, enabled us still to survive, through name and memory, in succeeding generations.

But Anne-Marie was not falling asleep in the peace of the Lord. And the family were not there. She was too far away and they had too much to do. She seemed to suffer a great deal. She had left the dusty little old theater of Plessis-lez-Vaudreuil, she had been applauded by millions of hands, millions of hearts had beaten for her, and now she was all alone in this New York clinic. The most expensive clinic, perhaps. But all alone. She was glad to see me. She held out her famous arms which in just a few months had become very thin, and she murmured that she wanted to die in San Francisco—she said "Frisco," as people do in cheap novels—or in Los Angeles or Santa Barbara, where Michel and Anne had a house. And she too wept. She still wanted sunshine, champagne, noise, applause. I think she had loved the life which had given her everything. It wasn't negligible. But she found it hard to leave it. As I emerged from her room, I encountered a doctor and two nurses. They were great admirers of Anne-Marie. They were very sad to see her in her present state. I asked if she would get over it. They were afraid not. And they didn't seem very sure that it was to be wished for. I told them she wanted to go to California and they thought it was a good idea. I found myself out in the street again. It was pouring rain. And I didn't feel very cheerful.

Anne-Marie lingered on for quite a while. She managed to leave the clinic. She was even offered a part in a second-rate film. But it was the part of a crazy old woman. She was still hesitating whether to accept it when all her problems were solved at once. She died of heart failure one evening in Hollywood, at a party held at Frank Sinatra's villa. As they didn't know what to do with the body in the middle of the champagne and caviar, they took it to her room at the Beverly Hills Hotel. Five or six people, including Michel and Anne, came to pay their respects. She was buried in California under her dazzling pseudonym, and our name does not appear on her grave.

That year, on All Saints' Day, a few survivors gathered in the cemetery at Roussette, where my grandfather and Philippe were buried. Mass had been said for the repose of the souls of the family dead, in particular, to use the dean's expression, for the intention of my grandfather, Aunt Gabrielle, Hubert, Philippe, and Anne-Marie. There were beginning to be a lot of dead people among those we had known. Uncle Paul, Ursula, and cousin Jacques had already entered into a sort of prehistory. Véronique had had the child whose advent she announced to her great-grandfather the day we left Plessis-lez-Vaudreuil. She had called him Paul, in memory of Jacques' father. On this early November day, still marvelously mild, he was ten or perhaps eleven years old, and the crisis of 1929, the bold doings in the rue de Varenne, and even the death of Jacques, his grandfather, meant very little to him. How long ago it all seems! Even Claude and Nathalie's son, who was three years older, had difficulty sorting out all those names of people whose faces he had never seen. My grandfather often used to recite to us the names of his two grandmothers, his four great-grandmothers, his eight great-great-grandmothers and so on back to the seventh or eighth generation. Between games of patience and the visits of Monsieur Machavoine and Dean Mouchoux, that was one of the treats, one of the favorite distractions in those glorious and dreary days at Plessis-lez-Vaudreuil. Young Paul, and even Alain, Claude's son—between the two boys, who were almost contemporaries, there was the genealogical refinement my grandfather liked to describe as a generation gap—already found it hard to remember the name of Ursula von Wittgenstein zu Wittgenstein, their aunt and great-aunt respectively, or that of their grandmother or great-grandmother, Gabrielle Remy-Michault. In their defense it must be admitted that the ins and outs grew more and more difficult every day. It was no longer only the dead that the family lost en route. There wasn't much left of the last double wedding at Plessis-lez-Vaudreuil. Jean-Claude was divorced, and Véronique was about to be. I got the impression they were both going to marry again quite quickly. Divorce has become one of the elements of social life, just as hunting and visits from country cousins used to be. The family tree was going to become endlessly complicated with some branches disappearing and others being grafted on. As we came out of the church I was astounded when Claude leaned toward me and said this sort of thing would never have happened in our grandfather's time, the days of Plessis-lez-Vaudreuil. I looked at him. The revolutionary and communist sympathizer had, in his turn, changed gradually into a conservative old gentleman. Time, which touches everything, overthrows even upheaval, destroys even destruction. Everything changes, even change. That is why, in the long run, in this agitated yet immobile universe, everything is always being transformed and nothing ever changes.

Everything passes, everything dies. Death is the only thing which escapes time and never dies. Hence, I suppose, the connection between death and eternity. At the beginning of July 1963, Jean-Claude and Bernard decided to go sailing together, from St. Tropez to Sardinia, perhaps as far as Sicily. The two first cousins had always remained quite close, perhaps out of a vestigial sense of family tradition. But God's pleasure decided otherwise: they were both killed in a car crash on a dangerous stretch of the road between Montargis and Nevers, where there had already been a dozen or so accidents. The highway there had not yet been built. There was a young woman with them who was expecting a child. She was Jean-Claude's new fiancée. She died after three days in the hospital at Briare. Pierre died of rampant cancer a year later. His only son was dead. And so were Jacques' sons. Philippe never had any children. So Claude, the last of the brothers of the elder branch, the last descendant of the Remy-Michault clan, became, in his turn, the head of the family. The king is dead, long live the king. But though all these things were sad for the individuals, it no longer had much importance in relation to the fate of the family. For some while already there had no longer been any king, there had no longer been any head of the family, there had no longer been any family.

I saw that family, my family which I loved, disintegrate and vanish. God's pleasure, which it had taken as its own, had turned against it and dealt it a mortal blow. Each time another crushingly commonplace tragedy struck it, I was filled with the same desire that I'd felt two or three times in recent years: not to tell the family's history, nor to descend to anecdotes, nor to rise to morality, metaphysics, or politics, but just to fix forever, in images which would never change again, events and people that become more distant and elusive every day and that nobody, soon, will be able to remember. Manners, mannerisms, ideas, beliefs, ways of being. Cars and clocks. Ceremonies and clothes. Virtues and vices. On different levels of economic and social organization, I think any other group would have followed a pattern comparable to that followed by my own family. But perhaps because of its cohesiveness and its primitive and old-fashioned structure, my family presented me with a convenient and special example. Like the donor or artist in an old painting, hidden away among the faithful at the foot of the saint's bed or behind the executioner, I would re-create scenes in which I myself had somehow taken part, a silent witness standing motionless in a corner, absent yet always present.

I had felt this irresistible need to ensure the survival of something of our inconsistencies and our vanished hopes when Philippe and Claude were reunited at the end of the Spanish Civil War. I had felt it again, more strongly, the day when my grandfather looked for the last time at Plessis-lez-Vaudreuil. I felt it again in Rome in the Piazza Venezia with Philippe, in the New York clinic with Anne-Marie, in the cemetery at Roussette with Claude, on that All Saints' Day when he seemed to me to have taken up what remained of the more than half extinguished torch fallen from my grandfather's hand. For a long while the family name, embodied in the stones of Plessis-lez-Vaudreuil, had outlived its members. But now, with every passing day, the house and the family became more and more the prey of God and his pitiless pleasure. All I wanted to do was revive their image and preserve—not, alas, as in the past, for centuries, but merely for a few years of these troubled times—something of their memory as it vanished into the darkness.

The Exile

AT THE END OF AUTUMN 1969, THE WORLD was fairly quiet. For the last ten or fifteen years the specter of another world war had gradually been receding. Men were setting off to land on the moon. Vietnam was still in flames, but the Czechoslovakia affair was slowly falling into oblivion. At the beginning and end of every weekend, on Friday and Sunday evenings, there were long lines of cars on all the roads in and out of Paris. Buses with platforms were only a memory, and Monsieur Georges Pompidou had been president of the Republic for a few months. The Communist Party was still the vanguard of revolution, but it revealed at the same time an almost middle-class aspect which reassured some and exasperated others. Young people everywhere, perhaps weary of more than twenty years of almost universal peace, were restless. Just before Christmas the papers and the radio reported a series of incidents which might have been isolated episodes or might have been politically motivated. Banks, boutiques, and private houses were attacked one after the other with an accuracy and imagination which seemed to denote a worthy successor to Arsène Lupin. The remarkable thing was that the carefully chosen victims rarely met with any sympathy. On several occasions the action of these lawless elements, to whom at least a section of public opinion was far from hostile, only preceded, or perhaps caused, the intervention of the forces of law and order, who often discovered that the victims themselves were guilty. But the most astonishing thing was that the mysterious organization involved gave away all its loot to the underprivileged. This second phase of their operations was often more risky than the first, because, by its nature, it had to be done openly. Five or six days after an attack on some dubious building society, or some art dealer who took advantage of a gullible public with a unique collection of statues and masks he had picked up cheap in an African republic, everyone would hear that a kind of fair was to be held somewhere, and food and money were going to be given away. The problem was to guess where. The police discreetly took up positions outside the hospitals of Lariboisière and La Pitié, and at Aubervilliers, around what remained of the shantytowns where the Algerians, Portuguese, and Senegalese who had managed to survive the crossing of the Pyrenees huddled together. But it wasn't very hard for the successors of Mandrin and St. Francis of Assisi to find some poor people who were not being watched. In any case, these benefactors with hand grenades and machine guns seemed indifferent about who was to benefit from their largesse: the important thing was carrying out, even on a modest scale, a redistribution of wealth which combined all the attractions of justice and adventure, and might later spread and take on unpredictable proportions.

What struck me about all this, and reflected in a commonplace enough way a whole new intellectual orientation, were the leaflets the organizers of these festivities left behind them at the scenes of their exploits. They were written with a great deal of energy and skill, and some of them were entitled "At the People's Pleasure." As you may imagine, I pondered that a good deal, and also the idea of history being subject to the people after having been so long subject only to God.

I admit I didn't see right away the more direct links between this minor aspect of contemporary history and Plessis-lez-Vaudreuil. Claude and I were now approaching the age at which you met our grandfather between the war of 1914 and the war of 1940: it was only scientific and medical progress that kept us from being quite

old men. We had foolishly chosen to grow old at the very moment
when the world suddenly remembered, and grew younger than
ever, how old Alexander and Mozart were, Masaccio and Giorg-
ione, the Grand Condé when he won the battle of Rocroi, and the
generals of the Revolution. For a long time we had been prevented
by history from understanding the modern world, and now age was
added to history. Our only connection with the events which were
as much beyond us as big business had been beyond our great-
grandfather, or the Spanish Civil War beyond our grandfather,
were through Alain, Claude and Nathalie's son. Of all that large
family, he and his little brother, who was five or six years old, were
the only survivors of their generation to bear our name. War, drugs,
chance, cars, guns, cancer, and, of course, time, had done their work.

There are many *longueurs* in these reminiscences, many clum-
sinesses and imperfections. But there are no descriptions: "The
house was a tall stone building covered with slates, flanked by two
enormous towers and with a multitude of little turrets; it turned
rose-colored beneath the setting sun . . ." Or: "Pierre was the only
one of us with a round face, and almost blue eyes which he inherited
from his mother . . ." No. I haven't described either Claude or Aunt
Gabrielle, nor even my grandfather, who was far from inconspicu-
ous. You probably know that my grandfather was rather tall, that
Aunt Gabrielle had been very beautiful, and that there was something wrong with Claude's left arm. But that's all. Instead of describ-
ing my characters, I would have been quite content to give the sort
of stage directions you used to find in certain plays: one person
moves off opposite prompter, and another enters, prompt side. Our
"prompts" were of course economic and social on the one hand and
on the other had to do with belief. I wouldn't have minded giving
the reader a kind of do-it-yourself kit, with rows of squares for
heredity and environment and customs, and almost abstract shapes
to put in them which would only have taken on weight and color
through the situations they were placed in. Not the ideas—the
situations. I think this would have been a kind of true realism, for,
after all, everyone knows now that, what with change and necessity,
we are practically nothing but the product of the circumstances in

the midst of which we struggle and which make us what we are. And, to crown all, there might almost have been something modern in an evocation of the past which was subject to these laws.

So, if you don't mind, let's try not to describe Alain. As you may imagine, he had long hair and a beard and wore a sheepskin jacket in winter and a windbreaker in summer, and, by way of a challenge to centuries of convention, he never wore a tie. He was tall and slightly shortsighted, he stooped a little but was quite good-looking. We criticized him for being dirty and unkempt, for being, to use a favorite expression of ours, less *soigné* or well-groomed than we used to be. The chief thing was that everything we did or said or thought, everything we had done or said or thought—and God knows we had never thought anything but trivialities—seemed to him monstrous. I think that, after all the trouble it had gone to, he hated the family.

In a certain sense he wasn't disloyal to the heredity he loathed and which weighed so heavily on him. Claude, his father, had once denounced and renounced the family. But the revolt of the son projected the father into the past. Claude had become the family, bequeathing to his son the task of challenging it. Not long before, I had been pondering the fate of Anne-Marie. And now I sometimes thought about the future of my first cousin once removed. And of course I thought that he too eventually, like one of those struggling swimmers who have to be knocked on the head in order to be saved, would be destroyed by time and then restored by it. For the moment, at any rate, he had ventured a long way from our shores. Every belief rejects time, the erosion past and to come, experience, the lessons of history. Alain believed. In what? Simply in the rejection of the past which we had so loved; of experience; of history. He had no positive beliefs, only negative ones. He rejected, denied, demolished. As for constructing, we would see later. I have to admit his strongest belief was that we had always been fools and perhaps rogues. This was a bit of an exaggeration. But I could see what he meant.

By a paradox which wasn't too difficult to explain, I perhaps better than Claude could understand his point of view. Naturally there were many things which the father and son had in common. But there were also many points of opposition. In the two previous generations, after a long period of immobility, the present had attempted to take the place of the past and had then, in its turn, become ancient history. First my father, then Claude had represented the successive stages of these adaptations, which Alain saw merely as conscious or unconscious camouflage, perhaps more to be condemned than the very systems they attempted to hide. Claude had made superhuman efforts, despite and in the face of the family, to try to stand at the spearhead of democracy and the Republic: but Alain scorned both the Republic and democracy. He despised them as my grandfather and my great-grandfather had once despised them: like them, but differently. Marx and Freud had had their effect.

Father and son had endless discussions about Marx and Freud. Some Sundays I looked on, as an outsider. I didn't know anything at all about *Das Kapital* or the unconscious, but I often found myself closer to Claude or even to Alain than they were to each other. Though they both believed in them, Marxism and psychoanalysis were beginning to separate them from each other as sharply as the idea of monarchy had once separated the Legitimists and the Orleanists. As far as I could understand his somewhat obscure ideas, Alain accused Claude of lyricism and moralism, and there was in fact some truth in his view of my cousin's universe. Claude, on the other hand, accused his son of worshipping two or three new and, to Claude, strange, gods: language, sex, and an attitude toward the use of violence which he, Claude, perhaps because of his age and the passage of time, could not approve of.

I expect you have forgotten the way we used to venerate the language of Racine and Chateaubriand at Plessis-lez-Vaudreuil. Even English, which the V. family, for example, used frequently, could not affect our admiration for French. A snobbish love of things English and American, and certain mannerisms in French, seemed to us mere affectations of the upper middle classes. We at Plessis-lez-Vaudreuil spoke with the words and the accent of Bossuet and Saint-Simon, of our carters and of Jules—who, in his turn, spoke exactly like us, with the same forthrightness and the same elegance. Like religion, like the forest, like the family name, like Plessis-lez-Vaudreuil in its entirety, language played a magical part in our dignity and in our happiness. But these were not at all the sort of concerns which motivated Alain. For him, language, though he was quite a serious student of linguistics, was not intended to narrate or even to convince. His charm did not consist in being amusing, like my father, nor in being, like my grandfather, rather stiff. There was never anything either funny or polished about Alain. To us at least he seemed both very relaxed and serious to the point of downright lugubriousness. He was usually rather difficult to understand, too, because he by no means used the same words as the factory workers with whom he claimed solidarity. At the same time he hated puns, irony, and lightness, and the taste which we had always had for form, clarity, and rigor. For him language, like everything else, was first and foremost an element of revolution— not at all because of its lucidity, but because of the internal capacity for destruction linked to its obscurity and to the analysis of its structures. The role played by sex in Alain's scheme of things also very much astonished Claude, who had retained much of our traditional family puritanism, and perhaps even carried it somewhat further. Alain's attitude seemed to him the opposite of what for Claude himself had been the keystone and meaning of the socialist revolution—the dignity of man. When Alain saw his father riding the broken-down hack of humanism and the dignity of man, he looked at him pityingly. Then Claude would call his son a fascist. All we needed was Philippe.

A year or eighteen months earlier, in two of the most memory-laden cities of old Europe, there had been, separated by a few weeks, two series of incidents which seemed important to us then, and which may perhaps remain important in the eyes of history. In a way they were contrasted; in another way, they may have belonged to the same spiritual movement, though lent different colors by the prism of circumstance and ideology. These two sets of events were those of May in Paris, and the crushing of the springtime in Prague. Again, I don't propose to give a history lecture, or even to indulge in retracing events which everyone remembers. I shall simply continue the story of what happened in our family, or what remained of it, in what my grandfather had for fifty years been calling "these troubled times." In February or March 1968 I had lunch at Claude and Nathalie's, together with Véronique and her second husband. Alain had brought three friends I didn't know: a rather distinguished-looking youth, another who was a bit fat and puffy, and, in particular, an amazing redhead who seemed much more gay and amusing than most of the youngsters of his generation. I'd almost forgotten them when I saw them two or three months later on television: they were Sauvageot, Geismar, and Cohn-Bendit. I only mention them here because their faces, like those of Dreyfus and Hitler, though in a more modest way, were among those specially involved in the family chronicle I am trying to tell. Despite their insignificance, and because of their three-week celebrity in the midst of firecrackers and overturned cars and whiffs of sulfur from a revolution that was neither political nor social nor economic, but strictly speaking moral in the sense that it had to do with *mores*, these young men took their place in our photograph album beside my grandmother in her little veil, Pierre in his boater, Pétain at Vichy with two little girls in Alsatian costume presenting him with flowers, and General de Gaulle, arms uplifted, standing on some balcony, delivering in his inimitable accent a few words of English, German, Spanish, or Russian, in honor of the French.

The events of May, as they were called, and the Russian tanks in Prague, whose very existence the leaders of the Communist Party denied, had, both for Alain and for Claude, relegated Soviet communism to a place among the forces of oppression. But my cousin and his son drew very different conclusions from this. Claude admitted to me that once again, this time forever, after the mock trials in Moscow, after the Russo-German Pact, after the disintegration of Stalin's image, after Budapest and the camps in Siberia, his illusions had collapsed. Stalin was no longer there, and Prague had been invaded. He gave up the Revolution. He went back gradually, if not to the ideas of my grandfather, at least to the liberalism of my father, who, after opposing the fanaticism of his own day, had in his turn embodied the modern form of old-fashioned conservatism denounced by Alain. But according to Alain, far from looking backward, one ought to throw oneself forward. Toward what? Toward a liberating minority working for the masses, toward a counterviolence which at last unmasked the hidden violence of the classes of oppression and secret domination. Claude saw the Russian tanks in Prague as being on the same side as the extreme Leftist groups in Paris, since both tanks and Leftists claimed Marxism as their authority. Alain saw them as on the side of repression and the C.R.S., or riot police—which with charming naïveté he compared to the S.S.—since both tanks and C.R.S. were employed against the people, as personified by its young men and its students. Both Claude and Alain condemned Prague. One emerged from all this as an anti-Marxist, the other as an ultra-Marxist. People's minds were confused. We even had a fiercely reactionary old great-great-aunt somewhere in the Vendée or near Niort who, perhaps inheriting the obsessions of Philippe, had hailed the Soviet army as the one surviving remnant of the military spirit and the forces of law and order. And of course nothing could shake the opinions of the considerable masses of people who persisted in seeing Moscow as the hope of the Revolution. All that was really clear was that everyone made haste to call everybody a fascist who didn't think as he did.

Alain's emotional life was a mystery to us. Sometimes it seemed he had none at all. Even in our straitlaced family most of us, in obedience to a convention which now seemed to belong to past civilizations, were very fond of women. Alain, who was always talking about sex, didn't really like women. His mother, who pretended to be very avant-garde in matters of education, couldn't help asking me if I suspected Alain of being a homosexual. But no, Alain, who possessed nothing of the seductive charm once exercised by the famous uncle in Argentina or by my cousin Philippe, or even by Uncle Paul in the distant days when Aunt Gabrielle fell into his arms, had none of the classic homosexual characteristics which were depicted, to our horror, in the books of Proust and Gide, and of which we found traces in various distant members of our inexhaustible family. On the contrary, it was as if, in Alain, everything,

including love and desire, was theoretical. Strangely enough, despite his beard and his long hair, which were probably some kind
of compensation, the idea of nature, in him as in many lads of his
age, had weakened at the same time as the idea of culture. Was this
the influence of machines and technical progress? I don't know. But
we, who'd spent our lives amid convention and artifice, were certainly, in many ways, closer to nature than he was. Nothing struck
him as self-evident and irrefutable. Everything was subject to experiment and discussion; if everything wasn't uncertain—for he was
somewhat categorical, often even peremptory, in his assertions—
then at least it was unpredictable. For a long time, on the other hand,
our ideas and reactions had been almost disgustingly predictable.
Everything had always been foreseeable for us in the closed universe in which we lived, surrounded by barriers and parapets. For
him nothing was impossible or forbidden or sacred.

Perhaps, above all, it was this idea of the sacred which separated
us from Alain. We had been steeped in it as in some permanent holy
oil, as if in the only kind of air that was breathable. Everything
might partake of the sacred, from mealtimes and New Year greetings and aunts we had never heard of, to respect for the dead and
the mystery of the Immaculate Conception. It wasn't altogether
impossible to see the idea of the sacred slowly evolving. By almost
imperceptible transitions it came to apply not only to loyalty to the
king but also to the blue line of the Vosges and to the tricolor flag.
But in one form or another, from the unchanging Holy Father to
ever-changing fashion, the presence of the sacred had dominated
our whole life. Bread was sacred. And then, a little later, so were
ideas and books. The poor were sacred, probably in a dual sense:
they were always with us, and we had to love them. And perhaps
they had to be always with us for us to be able to love them. Just
strain your memory again, will you? Do you remember the idea—
God! how long ago it was!—of things being what they are? But
things were no longer what they were. They were undermined
from within, they were divided against themselves, they had broken
the moorings which tied them to law and order, and were about to
float away on the high seas, tossed by the waves of doubt and

contestation, eaten away by a salt that corroded the sacred. There was another phrase which we used to repeat from our tenderest infancy and which was a faithful reflection of our submission to what was sacred: "There are certain things which are done." Our life had been full of things which were done. To die for one's faith or one's country was a thing that was done. So was to kiss ladies' hands, and the rings of bishops. Acting with courage, elegance, integrity, a certain blindness, perhaps hypocrisy, were things that were done. But for Alain, things were no longer done. One changed them.

You have been good enough to follow me as far as the dawn of the future which the songs used to promise us. You know already that we were narrow-minded, stupid, buried in the past as in some protective slime, and that we hated change. Alain lived only to see life change. To see men, history, the music of things, the spirit of the age, all change. For him, the future would never again be what it was, what it had always been. It was no longer a continuation and projection of the past, something forever compromised, forever mortgaged. It was something radically new.

It was absolutely amazing to see change burst in upon stability like this, to see a family which had always obstinately looked toward the past suddenly fling itself into the future in the incarnation of the last of its members to bear its name. This new tendency of time to give the future and revolution preference over the past was a thing we felt all the more strongly because my grandfather had still been alive when Alain was born. In a few years we had passed from the court of Louis XVI or Charles X to the permissive society and the expectation of a world without classes, without army or police, without Church and without state.

When I talked to Alain—I was very fond of him, and I think he quite liked me, in spite of my liberal-reactionary temperament—and when I remembered our grandfather, I was struck by the symmetry between the old man and his great-grandson. They made such a perfect contrast that they came to resemble each other. They had the same intransigence, the same certainty that they were right, the same faith (whether believing or unbelieving), the same scorn for skeptics, liberals, and agnostics. My grandfather derived from Bossuet; Alain, from Hegel. There were subtle differences, of course, but neither of them had anything in common with Montaigne, Voltaire, Renan, Anatole France, or André Gide. If anyone incautiously referred to the typically French divergence between the schools of the intellect and those of liberty, they would both shrug their shoulders or start to laugh. Many of my grandfather's characteristics quite appealed to Alain. He laughed when I told him the famous sally: "Tolerance—I suppose they mean licensed brothels." Of course, Alain didn't agree with it. Not because it was contemptuous of tolerance, but because it was contemptuous of women. What did either Alain or my grandfather need with liberty of thought or tolerance? Both of them possessed the truth. One of them had God and the king, the other had Marx and Engels, and there was no place in either of their systems for the criminals and fools who persisted in defending error, heresy, schism, or the joys of living.

They didn't like the present very much. They rejected it. They were like those statues of Janus in which the god is divided and turns his back to himself, one head looking toward the past, the other toward the future. They were both opposed to continuity and the flow of time. My grandfather consigned the present to the past, and denied the future. Alain projected the present into the future, and wiped out the past. The future according to my first cousin once removed was as immobile as the past according to my grandfather. Both of them, rigid, happy, safe from change and tempest, immune from crime and injustice, shone forth in a sky that was out of time.

I used to tell Alain that we had died of blindness. But mightn't he be heading, along a different path, for a similar fate? I sometimes used to think that between the past and the future there had been a brief moment when time had once more begun to function according to its own laws, a time when the future was safe and when hope could still be born. It was what I used to call my father's moment. Alain hesitated to say anything disagreeable about my father. But he had his own opinions. Bourgeois liberalism, for him, was nothing but an unstable and impermanent instrument of destruction in which bad conscience disguised itself as tolerance, cynicism or lyricism, elegant morals or depravity, jesting and pleasure. My grandfather used to say exactly the same thing. Probably out of family partiality, and through the prism of memory and increasing age, I saw the age of my father, with his painters and writers, his musicians and scientists, as a culminating point in a civilization of pleasure, comparable perhaps to the Renaissance or the eighteenth century. But my grandfather and Alain saw it merely as a passing stage, decadent according to one, revolutionary according to the other. Full of weakness and hypocrisy and signifying either the downfall or the advent of the Kingdom, the end or the beginning of the Golden Age.

"And what about the proletariat?" Alain would say to me. Children of eight pushing carts in Welsh coal mines weighed very heavily on the consciences of people like Alain. What could I say? That I approved of slavery, exploitation, of some people enjoying leisure and prosperity at the expense of the misery of others? Frequently, when I was talking to my young relative, and I talked to him quite often, he made me feel—and it was a success for him and a failure for me—that talking was useless. We each followed our own paths, merely passing and greeting each other on the way. He would say that the past was unjust, and I would say that Stalin was as unjust as anybody. He would say that Stalin was only a human being, and that the world yet to be built would be juster and more beautiful. I would say that it was a funny idea, building a just and beautiful world with drugs and hostages, violence and bombs. He would say that the violence we were always talking about was only counterviolence, and that real violence was our arbitrary law, repression disguised as justice and order, our infamous prisons, barracks, factories, schools, police stations, and law courts. I said his future was only a dream, and even the thought of it a bit sour. He answered that my path had unfortunately been no dream at all, and that the future hadn't yet begun.

He would talk about factory life in Zola's time, about the life of peasants depicted by Le Nain or during the Thirty Years War, about Aristotle's slaves. I would cough and hide behind my age and

talk about Mozart and the Acropolis. Bad luck! Apparently all this
was just the reverse side of exploitation. Alain hated Greece. And
he hated reason and culture as much as he hated humanism. This
contempt was, for me, both the reflection and the opposite of my
grandfather. Alain used to talk about us. So did I. I told him about
some of the absurd and typical incidents described in these reminiscences. To him they seemed ridiculous, often repugnant. I told him
I was thinking about writing this book. He didn't see the point, and
pulled it to pieces before it was even written. That shook me
slightly. I tried to defend myself. The past had made us, we were
its children, we ought to know it even if only to change it . . . But
Alain rejected it with stupefying violence. Had Claude, nearly half
a century before, been so rough? Things, events, men had been very
different then. Claude had had a sort of hatred. But in Alain it was
more a kind of implacable gentleness. He waved bombs around, but
never stopped talking about love. He lit furnaces, and would see
only their light.

He didn't mean to refuse us as individuals—my grandfather, all
those you have seen moving in procession through these pages—he
didn't mean to refuse us the virtues of courage, goodness, and even
intelligence, which I knew, better than anyone, to be limited. But
he dismissed them all as masked violence, hypocrisy, criminal frivolity, scorn for humanity. "Puppets," he would say, "who unfortunately at the same time were policemen." I couldn't really see my
grandfather as either a policeman or a puppet. "My poor Alain," I
said to him, "are you quite sure you yourself won't look like a
puppet to those who come after you? Are you quite sure that, in
relation to those who don't think as you do, you're not even more
of a policeman than your great-grandfather, your grandfather, or
even your Uncle Philippe? I'm afraid those whose myths are still
floating about in the future are in the long run much less tolerant
than those whose myths are already safely in the past." He looked
at me—I think he thought I was an imbecile. I didn't argue the
point. I was quite prepared to agree.

It occurred to me that, prisoner as I was of my ghosts, my
obsessions, my memories, I might really be too buried in the past

about which I have talked to you at such length to be able to understand what was still being born. Can anyone ever understand what they themselves are not? Like my grandfather, Alain didn't bother too much about trying to step outside his own system. My weakness and my strength consisted in trying to enter it.

Well, one autumn evening a few years ago in my apartment in the rue de Courcelles, in the heart of one of the most middle-class districts in Paris, I was reading, with a mixture of somewhat forced sympathy and an effort to overcome my own amazed incomprehension, the leaflets which had come into my possession entitled "At the People's Pleasure." The title had given me food for thought. But it wasn't until I'd read them right through that the light dawned. "Law and order, morality, justice, necessity, the force of circumstance, the dignity of labor, good sense, honor, and God's will have never been anything but the will of the feudal authorities, big business, the heads of the Church, the army, and the police. We will replace it with the will of the people. God's pleasure is dead. Long live the pleasure of the people!" There was only one person in the world who could have written that. Alain.

It *was* him, of course. It was only out of modesty that he wrote anonymously. With admirable simplicity, he insisted on the communal nature of his appeal and his plans. But that didn't stop him from talking to me about them with the greatest enthusiasm. He even suggested I should help him. It was a strange idea—I hadn't any of his own gifts for organization. So he just made me promise to keep his secret for at least three years. That was four or five years ago. Listening to him, I spent the most amazing night of my life. My head went round. I had to make an effort to convince myself that the young man sitting there in front of me was really the grandson and great-grandson of so many men of order and tradition. Sometimes he seemed to me to be a monster, sometimes a saint, a fool, a cynic, an agitator like the heroes he so profoundly despised. He spoke with a chilly enthusiasm which terrified me. This youth of twenty spoke of heads of state as if they were his equals, and felt about them very much as my grandfather had felt, though with more reserve and courtesy, beneath the towers of Plessis-lez-Vaudreuil. The redistribution of money, food, and other goods in which he had been involved for the past few weeks was merely a preface to an infinitely more ambitious plan which was made, very intelligently, to depend on the exploitation of the new virtues born out of liberalism and democracy: solidarity, the horror of violence and cruelty, mass sentimentality infinitely multiplied by developed means of communication. The idea—it was really inspired—was that after two thousand years of humanism and Buddhism and Christianity, after a century of socialist ideals, the bonds between men were now so close that it was no longer necessary to strike at those on whom one wished to act: it was enough merely to attack the first comer. In the past, knights had endeavored to capture the king, Richard the Lionhearted or John the Good. Later, thugs with a petty-bourgeois mentality kidnapped Lindbergh's child or that of some big industrialist, or the wife of a millionaire. But now that family and country were being replaced by a much wider community, these primitive efforts had become old-fashioned. You could do things on a bigger scale. In this famous world that was both unified and shrunken, you could get anything by threatening anybody. The press, radio, and television, immune from all governmental pressure at least in the West, fell over themselves to take the place—and with advantage—of the absurd blackmailing letters which used to appear in novels written in letters cut out of a newspaper. Of course, there was no longer any question of anyone limiting his ambitions to ransom in money. It was possible to obtain anything, in any field, by threatening with death or torture a handful of poor orphans snatched up without too much difficulty outside their school, or some popular singer whisked off from in front of ten million fans. The important thing was that everything should be made public. And, of course, everything would be made public.

You can imagine the horror with which I listened to these ravings. I said to myself, yes, no doubt about it, my nephew was crazy. I looked at him. He smiled. But he spoke so deliberately, so calmly and forcefully, that I hesitated to take a stand. He might have been delivering a lecture on economics or contemporary sociology. He paced back and forth, talking all the time. The surrealists, he said, shouted the odds clamoring for a revolution they never made and proclaiming, though without taking any risks, that the purest surrealist act consisted of going down into the street and firing into the crowd. Everybody thought that was marvelous. But there was nothing simpler than putting these two propositions together and at last making the transition from the words which dishonored literature to execution. All you needed to do to get government to comply with what you wanted was to kill a dozen or perhaps a hundred people, a thousand or two at the most. And wasn't this a mere drop in the ocean compared with the countless victims of capitalism and reaction? It was much less than one year's useless slaughter on middle-class highways. And anyway, you couldn't make omelettes without breaking eggs, or revolutions wearing kid gloves.

You could just take people at random, or you could have fun picking out distinguished people. There was nothing against choosing the victims from among one's class enemies. It was very easy to find people who were famous enough to stir up public opinion, and yet who were unprotected—a cardinal, for example, or a little-known writer (the French adore writers), a successful actress, or a reactionary journalist.

"And how about the Pope?" said Alain. "Eh? Kidnapping the Pope would be something, wouldn't it? You could get anything you liked—the abolition of military service, everybody let out of prison . . ."

"But my poor Alain," I murmured (I couldn't think of anything else to call him), "my poor Alain—what about the police and the army and public opinion . . . ?"

"You must be joking," answered Alain. "Public opinion in France will never again be unanimous about this sort of thing. Either the government will give way, and we will have won, or it won't give way, and when someone strolling through the forest of Fontainebleau (it can be very deserted, you know, during the week) comes across the bodies of eight little schoolgirls selected at random from smart Sixteenth Arrondissement schools, raped and drugged to death, or the crucified corpse of the speaker of the National Assembly, it'll cause a commotion, believe me, and it won't do the system any good. I wouldn't like to be in the shoes of the minister of the interior or the prefect of police. And have you thought about fires? And blowing up dams? And derailing trains? And making planes crash? I only mention bombs for the record; they're rather out of date, rather folksy, don't you think?" He laughed.

"When there's a forest fire—of course it won't always be us who did it—or when a school or a hospital or a department store is burned to ashes, people will come to see everything as our doing. We won't even need to put our threats into effect. We shall just say: 'Watch out!' and wag our little finger. And all this rotting filth will disintegrate on its own. We can't lose, whatever happens! Suppose the impossible occurs and there's a terrific offensive against us— police everywhere, permanent alert, a cop behind every tree, out- side every school, at every counter in every airport, all over every forest, the army on a war alert and trucks full of troops in all the towns . . . You can imagine the atmosphere, the rage of the people, the sarcasm of the newspapers . . . But the marvelous thing is that in our struggle against the vileness of liberal democracy, we win not only when the enemy weakens but also when he tries to be tough. We want to make them unmask their violence. And how? With violence. Nothing is more contagious than violence. It spreads like typhus and is only strengthened by meeting obstacles. We shall be both force and counterforce, we shall be strengthened by whatever opposes us. We shall loot banks, blow up theaters, give our lives in exchange for luxury hotels and smart residential areas, we shall create a reign of terror. Then, when the state collapses or there's a military dictatorship, life will become impossible. And that's exactly what we want. We don't want money, or reforms, or a new set of puppets. We want to bring to birth that which exists. There's no point in getting worked up over all that nonsense about values, or about sham idealism. For the moment, destruction is the thing. It's not very difficult."

"But, Alain," I stammered. "People will hate you, drive you out . . ."

"Don't you believe it!" said Alain. "You'll see, the victims themselves and their parents and friends will end up understanding us,
perhaps helping us. I don't say we ourselves mightn't get a bit
damaged in the process. So what? We're prepared for it. And anyway, if they arrest three or four of us, we shall just kidnap a dozen
kids at random in the smartest part of Paris. I can just see *Figaro*,
Le Monde, and *France-Soir* with their headlines and their polished,
ponderous, cowardly lead articles, their liberal indignation, their
impotent humanism. Perhaps there'll be a call to arms, a call to
national resistance? A dozen schoolgirls in exchange for three members of 'At the People's Pleasure'! Is it a deal?"

We'd already had some madness in the family. One of my grandfather's sisters had died in a rather special nursing home on the
outskirts of Paris. She had had visions and received messages from
the Virgin Mary for Monsieur Fallières and Monsieur Loubet. And
one way or another we were all a bit strange, eccentric, what my
grandfather used to call "funny customers." Well, the last of our
name was certainly a funny customer. I went on with the hand-to-
hand struggle.

"And what's it all for?" I asked. "Why all that bloodshed, all that
pain, all that suffering of the innocent?"

He looked at me pityingly. Was it still possible to distinguish
between guilty and innocent? Everyone was guilty, everyone was
innocent. The guilty were innocent and the innocent were guilty.
Hadn't we, at Plessis-lez-Vaudreuil, been guilty? What about Captain Dreyfus, and the children of coal miners, and the millions of
lives sacrificed throughout history for the benefit of our family and
people like the Remy-Michaults? What we had to do was add
Nietzsche and Marx and Freud all together, take advantage of the
immunity of violence after Hitler and Stalin, and, under the appearance of violence, bring about the triumph at last of justice and truth.

"And what do your friends think about all this?" I asked.

"What friends?" he said.

"I don't know ... Geismar ... Cohn-Bendit ..."

"Pooh!" he answered. "Petty-bourgeois reactionaries!"

For more than fifty years I had heard people predicting the end of a pleasant way of life and of civilization. And in the hundred or hundred and fifty years before I was born, the same cry had gone up amid the ruins of privilege and tradition. We had heard the cry, because it was we who had uttered it. But throughout the ages, others had always wept over the ruins of their houses, their temples, their morals, and the end of their world. Everything had always been collapsing—in Babylon, Jerusalem, Rome when the Barbarians came at the beginning of the fifth century, Samarkand, Constantinople in 1453, among the Aztecs and the Incas, at St. Petersburg and in Vienna. I didn't see the end of the world in Alain's ravings. The annals of history had contained much worse: epidemics of madness and collective suicide, massacres of whole nations, terrifying kinds of religion, bloodthirsty monsters ruling whole countries. But the distinguishing thing about Alain, so obvious that it hurt me, was that he demonstrated the end of something which was still very dear to me despite its errors and absurdities: the end of the family. We had spent a good deal of time compensating for one another, balancing things out. Perhaps our family feeling resided precisely in these reversals and recantations. We had included Catholics and Protestants, generals of the emperor and émigrés and even friends of Lafayette, many anti-Dreyfusites and a few who had supported the captain (mostly, I must admit, in retrospect), supporters of Franco and Spanish republicans, admirers of Marshal Pétain and Gaullist members of the Resistance, puritans and roisterers, believers and skeptics. But after every squall we closed our ranks; we helped one another even if we were enemies; we respected one another even if we fought; we were converted before we died; and the unity of the family was always preserved. But I didn't see how Alain could ever take his place again in the bosom of our holy family.

There had been misfortunes greater than this end of an era. There had been catastrophes. There had been the bomb. I couldn't even convince myself that this mixture of Ravachol, Lenin, Jarry, and Uncle Donatien which Alain was getting so worked up about would ever really come to anything, would ever really be changed into actual events. There was something absurd mingled with the horror. But, horror or absurdity, the family would not survive it. The past, which had lasted so long, had been interrupted. The future was starting again from scratch. It was quite possible that the fate of the future was, in the first instance, to change. Perhaps the paradox really lay in the family, all whose efforts had been bent toward subjecting the future to the domination of the past and toward making the future and the past, through the elimination of time, as indistinguishable from each other as twins. Anyhow, the madness of one member of the family was putting an end to its paradox. Was this really progress? The world was prevailing over the clan. And the fluctuations of time, its seductions and dreams, its unlimited treasures but also its terrors were prevailing over the rigid splendor of immobility.

As you know, nothing ever came of Alain's imaginings and his unprogrammed revolution, or almost nothing. A few Palestinians belonging to the Black September organization, some Japanese belonging to the so-called Red Army, and a few outlaws who wanted to join their wives or be received in audience by the Pope did hijack a few planes. The Baader-Meinhof gang did slightly better in Germany. I've sometimes wondered if there wasn't some connection between the Baader gang, the Japanese Red Army which crucified its traitors, and Alain's visions. But these others were not concerned with the feast of the future and bloodshed which my nephew had foretold. Every time I heard about some hostage being taken or some school set on fire I used to look for traces of Alain; but I always looked in vain. He had disappeared. I hadn't forgotten him. I hadn't forgotten our amazing conversation that evening. And yet sometimes I came to wonder if I hadn't dreamed it. And other times I asked myself whether what he said that night was really so much worse than the great slaughters of history celebrated in legend, in books, in institutions, in memory, by our enemies and by ourselves. The Holy Inquisition, the extermination of Protestants and Jews, the September Massacres and the Commune, centuries of torture and crime, and the wars toward which we had always been so indulgent—wasn't all that both more real and more terrible than

Alain's fabrications? The slaughter of the innocents was certainly
nothing new. There was nothing at all really new about Alain's
plans. Happiness, peace, and justice were very fragile. My grandfather had often said so. But that was no reason for being so afraid
of undermining the existing order that you never dared to touch it.
On the contrary. The ground seemed to tremble beneath me. The
words "equity" and "truth" came to be empty of meaning, leaving
the way clear for every kind of inversion and atrocity. But the cult
of the family was still so strong in me that I missed my nephew. I
should have liked to be able to go on talking to him about the
murder of hostages, the burning down of forests and schools, and
the very familiar theme of the awfulness of governments. But he
wasn't there any more.

By a common enough paradox, Alain, whose whole efforts consisted in freeing himself from our idea of the sacred, had ended by
creating a new one of his own. Together with a group of other boys
and girls, most of them extremely young, he organized secret ceremonies, part training camp and part black mass, which showed
traces of the teaching of Gurdjieff and Georges Bataille, of some
sort of Indian esotericism and of the wildest kind of National Socialism, the whole thing, naturally, under the combined aegis of Lenin,
Nietzsche, and Uncle Donatien. This was what he called the plant-
ing of spiritual bombs. As the result of certain incidents which I
shall refer to briefly in due course, the police and the newspapers
interested themselves in these somewhat obscure affairs. But secrecy, fear, and confusion have always made it impossible to see
them quite clearly. The meetings were sometimes held in a barn or
a cave, but usually in the open air, in a clearing where a bat or an
owl had been crucified. Those present flagellated one another a
little, made love, and, for practice in street fighting, fired real bullets
at desperadoes in American army jackets. Alain would read aloud
from de Sade or some Zen apologist, or sometimes it would be a
speech by Trotsky or Goebbels, or a page from the New Testament, Lautréamont, or Jarry. Then they would all take a meal
together called the Supper or the Symposium, consisting chiefly in
an exchange of drugs, from hashish, which made them laugh, to

heroin and LSD. I still don't quite know what part Alain played in all this: some regarded him as their leader, others as a dreamer they made fun of. The link between this group and the "People's Pleasure" organization wasn't very clear either: sometimes they seemed to merge and sometimes they seemed quite different. Sometimes they even vanished, and reporters and other inquirers would write them off as the result of invention or mass hallucination. But there were some tangible traces left, such as crucified owls, incurable drug addicts who called for Alain in their delirium, the leaflets which had so impressed me, the tragedy which I shall tell you about, and my nephew's disappearance.

The newspapers of the day—it was 1970—devoted a lot of space to the story of a girl of scarcely sixteen who according to the law had to remain anonymous. She was Gisèle D., and she too was to play a strange and sinister role in the history of the family. After the astonishing night I had spent with Alain, I pondered for a long time about what I ought to do. As a reactionary on the side of repression, and in order to avert tragedy, I thought I ought to warn the police. But I had promised secrecy. And then, Alain was my cousin's son, and I had transferred to him a good deal of the affection and even of the admiration I'd always felt for his father. Anyway, what could I have said to the police officer? That a young relative of mine had said ... that he read subversive literature ... that he had strange ideas and disturbing plans? He would have laughed in my face. So I kept quiet. And in the months that followed I didn't see much of Alain and his tall, rather nearsighted figure, like some luxury tramp. But I was uneasy and preoccupied, in something of the same state of mind as Inspector Ganimard waiting for some new exploit by Arsène Lupin, or Dr. Watson waiting for news of Sherlock Holmes who had somehow got confused with Professor Moriarty. When I got a telephone call one morning from a police inspector asking to see me "on a matter concerning your family," I felt a mixture of anxiety and almost relief. It had happened, Alain had been caught and they knew something about him. But no, they didn't know much. A few minutes later, Claude rang up. Alain's name had been mentioned among many others, and as they hadn't been able to get hold of him they wanted, just on the off chance, to determine if his family knew anything. His father had been sent for, and Claude summoned me to the rescue.

It was a ghastly story. Gisèle D. was found lying on a stretch of moorland near the River Sarthe—about forty kilometers from Plessis-lez-Vaudreuil. Her eyes had been gouged out. But she was still alive. They were able to question her. She maintained that she had put out her own eyes with a red-hot stake. Why? To punish herself. To punish herself for what? The explanations became confused. There was mention of drugs, incest, a kind of mystic exaltation, penance for some terrible sin. The investigators were rather skeptical. They didn't believe a girl of sixteen could have blinded herself like that. They did believe it was some sort of punishment, but it was not clear who had inflicted it. The girl, gradually emerging from a kind of coma, mentioned her brother, whose mistress she apparently was; Alain, with whom she was perhaps in love; and five or six other boys and girls. On this lonely moor, only a little way away from the most French of landscapes, a landscape whose serenity and grace has been celebrated by so many poets, this group had enacted scenes of horror which terrified even the police, used to more traditional tales of respectable blackmail or three straightforward bullets in the stomach.

Two young children had disappeared in the district. Their bodies had not been found, but the gang was suspected of having kidnapped them and made use of them for some mysterious practices. The girl either would not or could not say anything about it. She shrieked and threw herself about in fits which a few centuries earlier would have been taken as proof of possession. The doctors put an end to the interrogation. So the investigators' reconstruction of the affair was incomplete. The charges which hung over Alain were serious, but vague—some business of corruption of minors, incest, kidnapping, perhaps murder, and causing grievous bodily harm. Above all there was the extraordinarily murky atmosphere arising out of the domination of minds and bodies, inverted mysticism, black magic mixed up with drugs and machine guns, and, lastly, possession. The devil was lurking there somewhere. In contemporary dress, with a very up-to-date vocabulary. He was hiding practices dating from the Dark Ages beneath the appearance of a modern young man.

Of course the police searched the house where Gisèle D. and her parents lived. It was an extremely comfortable, almost luxurious apartment near the rue de la Pompe, between the rue de La Tour and the rue Desbordes-Valmore. The family's secrets were dragged through all the newspapers. The husband had mistresses, the wife had women friends. One of these friends had also slept with the father and made some approaches to the daughter. It was all terribly commonplace and I don't suppose you expect me to repeat the half-veiled details purveyed by the press. Eric, Gisèle's brother, was a rather strange character. He claimed to be Alain's best friend, though he didn't share his views, and I myself had met him two or three times. But, for my part, I'd have sworn they hated one another. Eric collected Wehrmacht helmets and S.S. belts, and went about in long, improbably colored capes. He cultivated an overbearing manner, a taste for money and enjoyment, and a liking for a very *recherché* kind of poetry, esoteric and rather lofty. Under an affectation of virility he was fighting an obvious tendency toward homosexuality.

Gisèle kept a diary. The police found it. It was a big notebook with an imitation-leather cover in which she had been recording, for three or four years, everything that was important to her. Overnight, this schoolgirl's diary, which had no literary merit and wouldn't have been accepted by any publisher, became worth astronomical sums. Newspaper editors and publishers, crooks on the make, fought one another for it. The black book, to give it the name by which it was known in the papers, was in theory under seal. But as a result of sordid scheming—Eric had made a photocopy of it—and in contempt of the law, flouted yet again, a well-known magazine printed long extracts from it. The magazine paid enormous sums for the scoop and gave it great publicity; it was a huge success. It was a heart-rending mixture of schoolgirl meditations and very naïve demonology. The girl mentioned her brother, of course, her

parents, her friends, and Alain. No surnames appeared in the published version, but all the Christian names were there. I had no
difficulty in recognizing them. And to my amazement, in what must
have been obscure to the majority of readers I found traces of the
family, traces I never expected to see in a sensational weekly over
the signature of a total stranger who was a victim in a news item
and perhaps implicated in ritual crime. "Alain." "At God's pleasure." (This phrase, according to the magazine, was underlined in
red ink.) "God's pleasure. I don't believe in God any more, but I still
get a kick out of the idea of his pleasure. Alain talks to me about
the people. I prefer God, our God, the absence of God." Then there
were entries about the Beatles and the Black Panthers.

Once again my family seemed to me to have reached the end of
its career: it had gone through a complete revolution, in the astronomical rather than the political sense. Its shadow had been
visible, surrounded by all the pomp of the Church and of tradition,
in the chronicles of Joinville and de Villehardouin, in Bossuet's
Oraisons Funèbres, in the memoirs of Saint-Simon and Chateaubriand and in the letters of Marcel Proust. And now it haunted the
pages of a sensational magazine, among the news items, or, more
accurately, scandals. But was it still the family? It was its negative
—inverted, different, the shadow of itself, unrecognizable and yet
identical. It was (as with God) its own absence, its own negation.
Two or three weeks later, Gisèle D. groped her way to the window
and threw herself out. She didn't escape her destiny a second time.
She wasn't killed outright, but died four days later, after more
suffering. I haven't known many men or women to whom fate has
been more cruel.

Eric and Alain were ordered to appear as witnesses. They had
crossed the frontier on the very first day. They were reported as
having been seen—but was it really them?—in Macedonia, Iraq, and
Afghanistan. A film director claimed to have met them in Nepal.
To me, nothing seemed more likely. Six months or so ago, a young
man died of typhus in a hospital in Nouméa, the capital of New
Caledonia. He had given a false name and his identity papers had

been clumsily altered. It didn't take long to establish his real identity: he was Eric. This news, which would have caused a sensation two or three years before, just made a two-line item in the local paper. The Paris press, the weeklies which had fought over photographs of Gisèle and her brother, and the magazine which had published the extracts from the black book didn't even mention it. There were elections on at the time, I think, or some new scandal which drove out the old ones, or perhaps the automobile show, or one of those Tours de France which used to fascinate my grandfather in the days when our decline was still splendid. I believe it was Merck who won that year, or perhaps Ocaña. But now that Aunt Gabrielle and my grandfather are dead, there are none of us left— I am the only survivor—to take an interest in the Tour de France. I sometimes wonder whether, after so many years of triumph and glory, the Tour de France, like the family, hasn't, in the end, grown old.

I still get a postcard from Alain from time to time. He isn't dead. He doesn't say very much. He never signs the cards. But I recognize his writing and I know they are from him. They come, sometimes several of them together, from all over the world, from Manaus and Kigali, Scutari and Kobe, New Orleans and the deserts of the Yemen. I suspect my nephew of playing with me and trying to establish a legend that he is ubiquitous. He is posing as an evil genius. Whenever there is some disaster—an opera house burned down, a train derailed, a massacre in California, or a big plane crash—I get a cryptic message from him. It's as if his work of destruction is being carried out all over the world. It's probably just chance, or perhaps, at a pinch, an accidental convergence of separate unrelated crimes, of which, in his madness and against all probability, he pretends to be the center and the master. Believing—and I'm not sure that he was wrong—that our family and its peers had for centuries stood for oppression, he eventually came to identify himself not only with the fate of a world in revolt against law and order, but also with everything which wears away under the hand of man and everything which disintegrates in nature. I can easily imagine him as some Vidocq of contestation, an ultramodern Robin Hood, a nightmare Arkadin or Vautrin, the head of some imaginary revolutionary Mafia on a worldwide scale, a Che Guevara of the People's Pleasure, seen in his stormy, fiery delirium as indistinguishable from the sinister pleasure of a god of vengeance and crazy justice.

So this is what we have come to, twenty years after the end of Plessis-lez-Vaudreuil. In my seventy years I have seen everything die around me, everything change, everything be reborn differently, and, if the young people will forgive me, I don't understand much about this world I am about to leave. Of the large family I have tried to show you, without either vaunting it to the skies or crushing it with contempt, there only remains, in my generation, one sister whom history has made an American and your humble servant who is writing these reminiscences. All the rest, up to us, have ended up returning in peace to the Lord. Claude died of grief a little over a year ago. To employ the expression used on our tombs, he had come back to the faith of his ancestors. I can bear witness to the fact that he came back to it with ardor, but with a kind of heart-rending lassitude. When he said to me, "There is nothing but Christ," it seemed to me it was no longer a youthful cry of triumph and enthusiasm, but rather an admission of the futility of men's dreams of happiness.

Claude had been very much struck by something that had happened quite recently. We had relatives in Bohemia who by a strange coincidence had followed a path very similar to ours. It was a family in the ultraconservative tradition but, as a result of the resistance against Hitler, two of its younger members had evolved toward the Left, even the extreme Left. The events in Prague and Budapest shook them, but did not make them deviate. They became passionate participants in the springtime of their own country and helped to draw up the famous Declaration of Two Thousand Words. The younger of the two, Jan, was condemned to death in 1969. The other, Pavel, was arrested a year or two later. Claude and I knew him very well. He professed to be an out-and-out atheist, with a kind of aversion to the Church and its rites, and for us, even for Claude, his intransigence was an inexhaustible theme for jesting.

After he was arrested we sometimes managed to get information about what had happened to him. To our amazement, the reports all said that he was now a militant Christian.

Six or seven months before Claude's death, we got some more details through Czechs who had been let out of prison and had managed to leave Czechoslovakia. Pavel's conversion was not a miracle. It was rather—how shall I put it?—an arbitrary but at the same time almost inevitable choice of the only opposition doctrine which was not compromised. He could no longer call himself a communist, or a monarchist, or a capitalist, or even a socialist or a liberal. So he called himself a Christian. He had become that surprising phenomenon, a Christian atheist or perhaps even a sort of Catholic who was not merely nonpracticing but in fact scarcely even a believer. One of his friends, almost as amazed as we were, said he had only one hope left now—to die for a faith which he might not share, but which at least he could still respect, admire, and love. History had already shown victims of the Inquisition, or of the mock trials in Moscow, blessing as they died those who had sent them to their death. And now, in the midst of our intellectual confusion and the famous crisis of values, of surrogate protest and of substitute belief, here was a faith that was embraced with the sole idea of finding at last, even equivocally, something to die for. Lord! What sort of an age were we living in, when the first thing people did was choose their enemies and when many, to justify their death, died in borrowed or merely improvised beliefs! But anyway, for dying, and for showing the meaning one attached to life, which perhaps had no meaning, there was still no substitute for the lessons of the Beatitudes.

I have considerable qualms about discussing the end of Claude's life. How can I be sure that I really understood it? And in any case it belongs only to him. But I think that after so many tragedies and disappointments and after the follies of his son, which shortened his life, the example of our cousins in Bohemia had given him much material for meditation. In the end, Claude, like all of us, remained closest to Christianity. Can one ever quite do away with the crushing weight of the past, its good side and its bad, its living aspect and its dead? And, though he looked in some very unlikely places, had Claude ever sought anything but the spirit of the Gospel? And now those words of Christ which he had once renounced reappeared, but in a rather surprising new light, as the faith of those who had exhausted all the illusions of this world and perhaps of the other, as the hope of those who had no more hope. It was as if the spirit of the family had succeeded, by the most roundabout means, in bringing Claude back to the tradition of his fathers. Faithful to our customs, I was at his deathbed. I don't think he believed in anything much any more. But like my father, and my grandfather, and my great-grandfather, he professed, at the very end, an obstinate and perhaps desperate faith in something supreme—in this world or another? How do I know? Did he know himself?—something which Christ had spoken to him about and which was indistinguishable from love. I asked him if he still remembered that stormy night when we had left Rome and when he placed his hope in men and God. He answered me with a murmur in which I alone could divine a smile: "If I were the Pope . . ." But although I bent over him, I could hear no more. He was dying, rejoining in memory all those of our name from whom, well before his son, he had parted.

I should have liked to write and tell Alain that his father was dead. But I didn't know where to reach him. From time to time I would still get cards from him, sent from all over the place, rejoicing in disasters that had actually happened or looking forward anxiously to hoped-for cataclysms. But I had no way, I still have no way, of answering him and telling him about his father. Perhaps it's because I can't talk about Claude to his son that I talk about him to you. What else can I do to keep the family from disappearing into the void? There are days when I think that God's pleasure isn't the most cheerful thing in the world.

Easter Sunday

God gave hope a brother: his name is memory.
—Michelangelo

❖ NIGHT IS FALLING, BUT IT IS SPRING.
Everything around me is full of life, joy, and hope. The world is new. For so many young men and women, it is spring. As we are quite long-lived in our family, perhaps I shall see another five or six springs, perhaps even ten, before I go and join the other members of the family outside time, which destroys everything. So let me look back once more on the vanished things which I have tried to bring to life again as far as I am able. I don't matter—what matter are the shadows of my family which I have tried to revive in my memory and in your minds. So I hope due allowance will be made for any lack of skill on the part of the author. The past I have been talking about deserved not more respect and love than I could give it, but more talent and strength.

We weren't saints. We weren't geniuses. I am not even sure, though we had almost everything, that we lived as well as we might have, as well as we ought to have. We might have been freer, more amusing, happier. We should have had more generosity, more heart and intelligence, more imagination, more talent. But, as I hope I have shown, we were the prisoners of too many ghosts. Others, in this century and the last, pointed toward the future. We pointed only

toward the past. Others shone for the world at large. We shone only
for ourselves, for our cousins in Germany and Bohemia, for the
people in Villeneuve and Roussette who were our friends, for a few
snobs whom we looked down on, and for Jules, whom we loved.
Of course, it is quite possible to be very hard on us—as hard, for
example, as Alain was, although he was one of us, or even Claude
before him. I myself wasn't always very indulgent. Jean-Christophe
Comte, Marina, the sailor from Skyros—many of those who crossed
my path, even the humblest of them, were much better than we
were. And there were, among us and in us, many different tendencies and contrasting temperaments, and a multitude of different data
and choices. And yet, up to quite recent years, there was a family
spirit which restored unity to this diversity. It is this family spirit
that I wanted to keep alive through changes of minds and manners,
through time. Everything, everywhere and always, is time and
nothing but time. But probably in no other age did passing time
prevail so fast and so strikingly over time which endures. Our whole
history can be summarized in a few words: we were born in a
certain place—Plessis-lez-Vaudreuil, with its perfume of eternity.
But at a certain date the history of the twentieth century suddenly
fell upon us. What I have tried to do is quite simple: I have tried
to describe the struggle to preserve an essential stability in the face
of fashion, progress, and time, and the triumph of time over our
eternity.

It would never occur to me to complain of our defeat. There is
no denying that, in a sense, we embodied death—our avowed goal
was to arrest time. But movement and life always prevail in the end
over immobility. So movement has prevailed. And life. What could
we do, even with the support of Bossuet and Saint-Simon, Chateaubriand and Barrès, Barbey d'Aurevilly and Maurras, against
Voltaire and Rousseau, Hugo and Rimbaud, Breton and Gide? Our
death was inscribed in our life, we lived only to die. But we were
not low, or cowardly, or even completely blind. Perhaps we shall
seem less at fault, less ridiculous, in the eyes of more distant history
than we appear in the eyes of immediate history. We simply came
at the end of a long cycle. We belonged to a doomed race, pitiable,

yet sublime; the race of fallen masters who see their age coming to an end. Now it is the time of slaves—our slaves? Now it is the time of victims—our victims? It is the time of their revolt and their triumph, and these are very fine things too—but honor also to those who went before! We were not innocent. Who is? But we were no more guilty in our day than many of our critics today who, unlike us, are always talking about justice and equality, but who are very far from living as they think. We did live as we thought, and we thought as we lived, a century or two behind the times.

Many people nowadays, perhaps almost everyone, wants to begin something, to invent something new, to open up fresh, perhaps unheard-of paths. My ambition is more modest: it is to finish, to close. I don't wish to be the one who showed the way. Loyal to my family and their blindness, I merely sprinkle tears and a handful of earth, like a mute offering, on their forgotten graves. I am quite incapable of being the first of a line. So let me at all events be the last. For many long years we were the last. And I shall be the last too. The last! No one, after me, will be able to talk about the life they never knew. They might invent it. They might reconstruct it from letters and books, from the monuments of history. But they won't be able to remember it any more. But I did remember Claude, Philippe, Michel Desbois, my father, Aunt Gabrielle and Uncle Paul, the Wittgenstein zu Wittgensteins and the Remy-Michaults, Mirette, the sister of the vice-consul in Hamburg, Jules and my grandfather. And I tried to bring them to life again. I wanted to make a book that would take the place of the memory of the family, in the process of disappearing into the void. If I have succeeded, justly and accurately, in contributing something however little toward the analysis of a system which has created, in daily life as well as in literature and art, so many masterpieces of elegance and strength, as well as so many errors and offenses against intellect and taste, I shall have fulfilled my purpose. It is impossible not to see that we are at the end, not of the world, but of the age to which I belong, and am glad to belong. In a little while, all that is of that age will be more foreign to us than the manners of the remotest inhabitants of New Guinea or untamed Amazonia, crossed by highways, carved up by bulldozers, penetrated by the West. It will be stranger than the stones on the moon. And perhaps I shall have saved something—an attitude, a few words, a gamekeeper, a clockmaker—from a submerged kingdom.

But I don't imagine that my family alone embodied the history of the world, or that it symbolizes the past. Perhaps that's what the family itself thought. But it didn't deserve such honor—nor such dishonor. It played a sufficiently vigorous part in the past in which it shut itself up to have remained, in my eyes, almost indistinguishable from it. But of course I cannot bear witness to all the inexhaustible riches of days gone by. I have been able to conjure up only a small number of shapes and particular situations. My older readers will each have his or her own treasures, treasures which for them too merge with the days of their childhood: the garden of an old house in some little provincial town; a father or grandfather going to or coming back from the war; silent evenings containing nothing but happiness in Brittany or Auvergne; or echoes from a distant and amazing world—Nungesser and Coli crossing the Atlantic, Carpentier's matches, the king of Yugoslavia being murdered in Marseilles, Stavisky committing suicide in a chalet in the mountains ... If I have recounted these memories about my own family, it was in the first instance in order to go on speaking about them, and so that they wouldn't die entirely. But it was also to talk to you about yourselves and so that you should remember, in your turn, yourselves and your own families.

Am I, by any chance, ignorant of the fact that I lived in a privileged world, and that the universe I have summoned up was in the sun and not in the shade? Am I ignorant of the fact that many others have fled from the past as from some hateful nightmare? May God's pleasure be to end nightmares and make the sun shine! I can never say often enough that I don't see the past as a model for the future. It was because she looked back that Lot's wife was changed into a pillar of salt. But neither do I see the past as an abomination of abominations that has to be thrown down and forgotten in order to build cities of happiness in its place. We have known worse, since, than Sodom and Gomorrah. I expect many will also try, though in vain, to escape from the future. And, when the future has in its turn become the past, we shall see if it looks any better than our own vanished days.

Is there anything more absurd than reproaching Aristotle for having had slaves, and my grandfather for having lived as he lived? And could there be anything more repugnant than wanting to restore slavery in our own days, or more foolish than trying to live now as my grandfather once lived? Every age has to live according to its own techniques and its own morals. Could even the wisest of the Greeks, who had no machines, have imagined the abolition of slavery? If we are talking only about force, let the weaker brethren yield: I can say that quite simply because all that our past life stood for has long gone over, bag and baggage, to the side of the weaker brethren. But if we want to talk about morals, what is more obviously necessary than putting situations and people back into their historical context? In his own time, for his own time, my grandfather was just. He was one of the just men, one of the respectable people, who were meat and drink to the right-thinking novels and to the conformists of those days, and who, in the opposite sense, are still meat and drink to the conformists of today. It takes a kind of genius to see tomorrow's morality arising slowly out of the manners of today and the hopes for the future. It is plain we did not possess that genius. And so, at the end of our history, we shall leave behind only the faint trace which I have tried to describe. I am quite prepared for us to be criticized, my grandfather and my father and Plessis-lez-Vaudreuil and all of us, for being out of step with the modern world, or, if you insist, for stupidity. But I won't agree to our being accused of injustice. What about Dreyfus, someone will say, that thorn in our flesh? What shall I say? Well, at least, in that past we are speaking about, a Dreyfus affair did occur. How many Dreyfuses have there been since who haven't even had that much fuss made about them?

Tomorrow is another day. It will have its own joys. Yesterday had its joys too. Tomorrow will have its honor, yesterday had its honor too. Do we nowadays still have that blind faith in the future which wise men had at the end of the last century? Are we still quite sure of our triumphant mornings and futures full of promise? But it is no cheap skepticism which teaches us about the flux of time and its continuity. Tomorrow has to emerge from yesterday and relegate yesterday to the past. What would God's pleasure be if it were not for time, which we hated for so long? I ask my grandfather's forgiveness, for he did not love it, but it is with the triumph of time that this history of the past ends. What could be more natural? There is only one way to escape time, and that is to choose to die. And that is what we did.

I wonder if Alain himself didn't share, in his own paradoxical fashion, in this desire to disappear from a world which was continuing. He too wanted an end to time and history. He wanted an imaginary kingdom, a Utopia, like my grandfather. But whereas my grandfather saw them before the Revolution, Alain saw them after. I am closer to my father, who placed his hopes in change, assisted by memory. Like him I am divided between those two opposite worlds, both full of strength and delights: the world of change and the world of memory. I decline to choose between them.

And I am like my grandfather who, when he had to leave it, turned to look back at the house of his fathers. I too have difficulty in tearing myself away from its shades. And when I cast a last look at the stone table under the limes at Plessis-lez-Vaudreuil, and on the ghosts of my family fixed forever in the immobility of death, how can I not see, with wonder and terror, all that has changed in this world? For the worse, of course—in my grandfather's time there were forests, the villages were prettier and the towns more habitable, there weren't so many cars, and there was no bomb. But also for the better. I am still, with all my heart and soul, a disciple of Jean-Christophe. I believe—it's as good a belief as any other and, because happiness and unhappiness are never comparable, I don't need to justify it—that good is the ally of time, and that gradually, imperceptibly, irregularly perhaps, with sudden slowings-down and temporary reversals, good triumphs over evil. Neither my grandfather nor Alain was fond of that rather ludicrous myth called

progress: my grandfather would have none of it, and Alain didn't
believe in it. They were both attracted, rather, by the idea of catastrophe, wished for by one and dreaded by the other. Progress and
the science from which it is inseparable are not very popular nowadays. Once everybody swore by them, but now they are decried.
Nothing changes so fast as intellectual fashion. I am careful not to
take sides in the quarrels of our philosophers. I simply desire, like
my father, that nothing should ever be lost, and I look on this
entertaining world with curiosity and sympathy.

On the world of yesterday, the world of today, and also the
world of tomorrow. At the end of the last century, when it grew
dark, the liveried servants—can you see them?—used to go through
the rooms and anterooms, the billiard room, the dining rooms, the
drawing rooms, the boudoirs, and light, one after the other, as in
some fairy play, the oil lamps which shone on my father's childhood. Then the darkness was filled with a shadow show which you
and I have never seen. An old man was there, but it wasn't my
grandfather; it was his father. My grandfather was still a young
man, between thirty and forty. He kissed his mother's hand. There
were uncles, great-uncles, great-aunts, and aunts. The bishop might
be there, the priest, some general like a character out of Prévert, a
couple of colonels, unknown visitors who had been staying for five
or six months, cousins from Brittany or Provence. There was no
prefect, and there were no bankers. And all this charming vanished
group, escorted by footmen in blue eighteenth-century livery, carrying torches, would pass in procession into the dining room. I can't
even remember what time it was: a quarter past seven, perhaps? Or
half past seven. Or perhaps seven o'clock. I don't know. My only
excuse is my absence: I hadn't yet entered, half an hour before the
grown-ups, surrounded by English nannies and nursemaids in caps,
into the children's dining room. We won't try to imagine the conversation at my great-grandmother's table. I don't suppose it was
very witty or intelligent. But its tone is inimitable. History has
secrets which books and the cinema can scarcely restore to us.
There are things more completely lost than the name of the Man
in the Iron Mask, or the mystery of the Temple: the words of my

grandfather, the attitude of my grandmother, the atmosphere of the time, the spirit of the age, all the commonplace, incomparable aspects of everyday life. We are familiar with the clothes, the setting, and often the words. But we do not know the tune. We shall never know how Malibran sang, how Pavlova danced, or how Berma acted. It was to remind myself as vividly as possible of my grandfather's intonations, his incomparable scent, his imperceptible gestures, his charm, that I have written these reminiscences. But, perhaps imprudently, I expect as much delight, different but as much, from the world into which we are now entering, a world my grandfather would, I am sure, have viewed with horror.

Instead of just thinking about my grandfather or great-grandfather, I sometimes put myself in their place, and wonder what would have surprised them most about the pleasures and troubles of our own day. I don't think they would have been the least bit fascinated by all the scientific progress. They might well have been delighted to take a Boeing 727 to throw themselves at the feet of the Pope, or be operated on for prostate by the most modern methods. Why not? And I don't say that the conquest of the moon wouldn't have impressed them. Even if the parallel with the discovery of America had made them uneasy—was the five-hundred-year-old precedent such a fortunate one?—the parallel with the Crusades would not have displeased them. But I doubt if they would have found any charm in city traffic or color television. You know what they thought about science, technology, and progress. It's not to their credit, but curiosity about the future was unfortunately not their strong point. I can just see the expression on their faces when confronted with speed, advertising, new discoveries, love of sensation, all our retrograde progress. They would simply have been bored and indifferent. But our morals and our ideas would certainly have shocked them. I have already talked about sex and language in connection with the relations between Claude and Alain. One could go on for hours about the respective ideas of my great-grandfather and his great-great-grandson about love and language. But perish the thought. And one could also go through each of the minute and countless details which cause the present and the future, every day, to relegate the past to the fabled distance. I am not fit for such an enormous task. But there is one institution which has changed a great deal, and about which I ought to say a word, for, as my grandfather revered the Church, so he would have been aghast at what has become of it.

Since everything was changing, why shouldn't the Church change too? But it didn't begin to change until after my grandfather's death. I thank the Lord and his priests for this respite. The Church of his childhood, the Church of time immemorial, was the last bastion on which his universe rested. It held out a long time—longer than all the rest. Whatever my own opinions may be—and I am still careful not to pass judgment—I am grateful to fate for not having let my grandfather see that image of tradition and eternity grow uncertain or collapse.

My grandfather realized that storms and whirlpools were building up in that direction. But he mistook the nature of the danger. He imagined that the Church, the last bulwark of the past, would be swept away in the tempest. He hoped, of course, for its final victory, which in his view would be the victory of order and good. But he thought that in the meanwhile it might know collapse and disaster, its bishops might be martyred, its temples profaned. I suppose he could see himself walking up to the scaffold or the stake together with the dean, exchanging a few words with him about the glory of the elect and the immortality of the soul. What he couldn't imagine was a Church which would turn away from the past and from tradition, and which, instead of being destroyed by revolution, would become, to a certain extent and in some of its aspects, not only its accomplice but also one of its auxiliaries, like the historical or dialectical materialism which, here and there, it would ultimately come to take over from, no longer in the name of science but in the name of justice.

If one wanted to be pedantic, it wouldn't be impossible to trace the frontiers which separated the succeeding generations of my family on two or three of the questions we have discussed. Claude, who was attracted by communism and had fought in Spain on the side of the republicans, remained very close to my grandfather as far as language and morals were concerned. There, it was between Alain and Claude that the barrier lay. On the other hand, on the subject of the Church, because my cousin was of the Left, it was between Claude and his grandfather that the division existed. In this field as in the others, Alain was of course beyond any kind of evolution. For him, who totally rejected everything we had loved, liberalization was never anything but a camouflage of the past and an aggravation of oppression. For Claude, what had changed in the Church toward the very end of his life corresponded quite closely to what had changed in him. I can imagine the astonishing conversations between grandfather and grandson I could have described to you if the change in the Church had come about twenty years earlier. But we had to wait a little for the holy alliance between the Church and the past to be broken. And it was perhaps because the Church, at the time of his death, was no longer the Church of his grandfather, that Claude in his turn, despite and yet because of what he thought, had gone to rest, like all his family, beneath a cross which had been the cross of slaves before becoming the cross of a god, and which perhaps was only going back to its origins in humility and upheaval. We mustn't expect too much of the ghost of my grandfather. The slaves' revolt had little to do with his picture (probably distorted by the magnificences of history and of Rome) of the peace of the Lord and the throne of St. Peter.

The world changed a good deal in my grandfather's lifetime, between the First World War and the fall of Berlin in 1945. Perhaps it has changed even more during the twenty or twenty-five years since his death. Not only God and art and love, but also education, politics, business, war, the Champs-Elysées and the Côte d'Azur all present completely new faces which he would not recognize. Even revolution and the future have been changed. It is better that he isn't there to get angry and to grieve. His shade—it is in the order of things—has joined the shades of all our family around the stone table. But the movement of things goes on even beyond the grave. What has changed most is that we are no longer there to go on worshipping our ancestors under the limes at Plessis-lez-Vaudreuil. Before, there was continuity within this continuity, to withstand death and the series of generations. But Alain will not remember us. Even in the void and beyond, change has prevailed over permanence, and the family has ceased to be that image of eternity which it tried to represent, despite everything, through so many centuries.

I am incorrigible, and now and then I still find reasons to see hope shining dimly in the future. I have said several times that after the deaths of Hubert, Jean-Claude, Bernard, Pierre, Philippe, and Claude, and not counting the girls who no longer bear our name, Alain and I—the one absent and the other an old man—were the last of our old tribe. For this I must apologize to a little boy who is just ten years old, my nephew and my godson, almost my son, whose name is François-Marie-Sosthène. Sosthène, like his great-grandfather. But we call him François, because no one's called Sosthène now. He is the son Claude and Nathalie had sixteen years after Alain. He's a very hard worker. He's first in his class in what still remains of French and History, and in the New Math which has replaced our Arithmetic. He will carry on the line. But he's still too small to talk to about Plessis-lez-Vaudreuil and our family portraits.

He will carry on the line . . . Does this soothing phrase still mean anything? We shall probably love one another as people in families do, perhaps very warmly, and then he will go out alone into a new world. At God's pleasure, if you like—it's like saying "at random." Plessis-lez-Vaudreuil has vanished. The honor of our name no longer exists. Does family mean anything any more now than birth and friendship, a last resort in case of emergency? I don't know. François is very strong. I am rather afraid, I must admit, that for this last of the Mohicans there's nothing to wish for but good health, money, perhaps a little happiness—at the best, success. In the days of our splendor we hoped for a little more than that.

There is no longer any torch to hand on with one's last breath. No more estate, no more line. There is some beauty and grandeur in this new situation. But it's up to the individual to make his own fate and his own life. Each of us is alone in the world. Each of us will choose, according to the people he happens to come across, his

friends and his tribe. People talk a great deal nowadays, using a lot
of long words, about man's solitude. I think it comes from the
destruction of the family.

I don't deny any of the virtues of the systems yet to come. The
individual will be freer and the group will be larger. One way or
the other—I can hear myself speaking like my grandfather, and in
his disillusioned tones—we are moving toward socialism. I don't say
socialism isn't the fairest system. If it keeps its promises and over-
comes its obstacles, if anything of socialist dreams survives in socialist society, it may be at once a liberalization and a collectivization.
And I am far from claiming that the family was never on the side
of oppression and hypocrisy. A whole enormous sector of twentieth-century literature, probably the best of it, from Martin du
Gard to Gide, Mauriac and beyond, is an accusation against the
family. My own family had its limits, it had many faults, including
its blindness, its group egoism, a mass of absurdities. But I maintain
that it also had its greatness, its honor, many virtues which are
denied it and which people laugh at but which they will never
replace. It is dead. Let's not talk about it any more. On the scales
of a future which is now the only thing that counts, my family will
not weigh very heavily. But it was mine. I will not disavow it. And
as far as I can, by telling what it was like, I will perpetuate and
celebrate it.

Since Anne-Marie is dead, since, barring some miracle, Alain is
lost forever, I sometimes dream of François' future. Because he is
one of us, he still sets out in life with more advantages and privileges
than many. Perhaps, in this new world which I can no longer even
imagine, he will do the great things which for so many centuries we
have ceased to do? For although we lived in legends, we didn't make
them much any more; even in the bosom of the family, they tended
to turn against us. My role is to remember. His will be to invent.
And—I say it with affection both for him and for us—let him not
walk in our footsteps! Let him go elsewhere. Farther. Let him live
and think without the family. And, in a way, against it. Let him
forget us—and yet, let him try sometimes, with amused indulgence,
to remember the past.

Our foolishness long consisted in not seeing that the past had no meaning except insofar as it served the future. Alain's foolishness consisted in imagining that the future could deny the past. Children, of course, are the death of their parents. But they are their descendants too. They kill them, but they continue them. I wish many things for my youngest relative, but perhaps first and foremost that he should know how to reconcile within himself the past and the future. They have never been so hostile to each other as they are today. I have conjured up a past which every day grows fainter. The future has no need of me. It will come into being without me, aided by many others. But because there is such a thing as history, tomorrow is linked to yesterday. May past and future not ignore one another. May they remember that the future, in its turn, will one day be the past. May they not allow time to destroy eternity.

When I try to pay my family the respects of the past, I am also, by accepting time, trying to salvage my part of eternity. In this world where everything changes and fades away, I clutch at my dead, I clutch at François like a man swept away by the raging torrent of days, months, seasons, years, which add up so soon into centuries. I am drowning in that torrent because I am going to die. But let our name, my name, not quite perish! I know how reactionary and backward this desire for eternity is, and that many see salvation in the abandoning of one's name and of the selfish dream of a collective personality. But I cannot change entirely, either. I cannot strip away completely the old man who is a member of the family. I have had to struggle to reject the temptation of hoping to see Alain's name shining through his bloodthirsty follies, with a red-and-black brilliance of which we might still be a little proud, as of some Gilles de Rais or Uncle Donatien. And now I transfer to the ten-year-old François those long-lived hopes which cannot manage to die. I have no idea what he will do. If he remembers anything, let it perhaps be Aunt Gabrielle and her dazzling talents. Let him tear himself away from the past in order to remain more faithful to it. Let him make his fortune if he can, and if he really must. Let him be alone and strong amid the nameless crowd. Let him mark his time with his name so as to give the past all the colors of the future, let him go to the moon, to try at last to be at the beginning of things instead of at the end. Let him paint the sort of pictures which made my grandfather laugh, let him build the sort of houses where Jules would never have wanted to live. Let him compose music with the trumpeting of elephants and the clashing of ashcans. Let him write the sort of books about which Claude used to say that nothing ever happened in them. Perhaps the best would be for him to get to the head of some political party—a moderate party, a party of the Right, of course—the Socialist Party, for example. Or else, let him simply win the Tour de France.

It remains only for me to crave the indulgence of those who have been kind enough to take an interest in these graves and in this past. But I don't blush for this past full of marvels and delirium—it is my past and I accept it. And I am as proud of it as any Jewish merchant or Arab peasant or Red Guard is proud, and justly proud, of what his forefathers and he did in the past, the subject of their talk in the evening in their houses or tents, and which is called tradition. But my past is past, more past perhaps than the other pasts, and it is disappearing into the darkness. I turn to it as our cousins in Bohemia turned, when they were dying, to a faith in which they no longer believed. I no longer believe in many of the things my grandfather believed in: the return of the king, the nature of things, the immobility of time. But I salute and I admire what he believed and what he was, in this age when everyone else laughs at them.

I also salute my father, whom I scarcely knew. I can see him still, and hear him reciting old Hugo to me and laughing at the world, in which, gay and charming and oblivious of fashionable anguish and the contradictions of history, he was so marvelously at ease. The future did not frighten him because in him curiosity and tolerance were joined to loyalty. I should like to possess, as he did, a loyalty always on the watch for the future, and an amused tolerance.

I salute my mother, who loved sorrow, and Jules, and Jean-Christophe, and Monsieur Machavoine, who wound our clocks, and Dean Mouchoux, who crunched up candles and whole nuts—all of them, and Aunt Gabrielle, who had too much talent for us, and the beautiful Ursula, and Hubert, who died when he was fifteen, perhaps partly through our fault, and Claude and Pierre and Jacques and Philippe, and Anne-Marie, who was so attractive to men, and Monsieur Desbois and Michel and Anne, and the sailor from Skyros and the whore from Capri, and Pauline, the bareback circus rider, who loved her name, and the lost little sister of the vice-consul in Hamburg, and all the members of my family whom I loved because all of them, including Alain, were irresistible and unforgettable women or men of faith and fervor for whom, even when they made use of it with splendor and indifference, money did not matter, men who knew what they wanted and who, one way or another, often mistakenly, but always elegantly or with conviction, fought against the world; people whom one does well to remember. Far from the stone table, I remember.

I salute François because he is our future. It was raining hard the other day when I drove him out in the Peugeot to Plessis-lez-Vaudreuil. It was Easter Sunday. We wandered around the house, which he had never seen. I knew the caretaker. And you know him too. Guess who he was. He was the son of Jacqueline, made pregnant by a scoundrel just before Munich, in the time of Ciano and Goebbels, Litvinov and Daladier, the days when Anne-Marie galloped Avenger through the forest trails. He was the grandson of Marthe, cook at the chateau in vanished ages, and of Monsieur Machavoine. He kindly let us go as far as the main lobby, where the walls, now empty, had once been covered with guns and stags' antlers. For a brief moment after the door was opened, all the aroma of the past swept over me. And I closed my eyes to breathe it in more deeply, and to see again within myself all that had vanished. But the boy was bored. When we came out, I bought him an air gun and a Coca-Cola from a stall in the marketplace, decorated with already tattered posters of Marilyn Monroe and Johnny Halliday and Che Guevara. In one corner there was a slightly smaller poster with a picture of—do you remember?—the daughter of Ursula's bullfighter.

I am of little importance in this history of the world and of my family. Curious about the future, loyal to the past, I remain a witness, a kind of lookout watching to see what happens. Often the show gives little cause for laughter. But it amuses me and I like it. Among things and men, with affection and irony, I am, I try to be, amid the squalls of the wind of history, the watchman of God's pleasure.

Plessis-lez-Vaudreuil—Rome—New York—Paris
1938–1974

A Note About the Author

Jean d'Ormesson—youngest member of the Académie Française; chairman of the board of the newspaper *Figaro;* deputy secretary general of the International Council of Philosophy for UNESCO's Humanities Division; director of the philosophical-historical journal *Diogenes*—is the author of two nonfiction books and five novels. His last novel, *The Glory of the Empire,* won the Grand Prize for fiction from the Académie Française.

A Note on the Type

The text of this book was set, via computer-driven cathode ray tube, in Janson. This face is a facsimile reproduction of type cast from matrices long thought to have been made by the Dutchman Anton Janson, who was a practicing type founder in Leipzig during the years 1668–87. However, it has been conclusively demonstrated that these types are actually the work of Nicholas Kis (1650–1702), a Hungarian, who most probably learned his trade from the master Dutch type founder Dirk Voskens. The type is an excellent example of the influential and sturdy Dutch types that prevailed in England up to the time William Caslon developed his own incomparable designs from them.

Composed by Datagraphics, Inc., Phoenix, Arizona. Printed and bound by The Haddon Craftsmen, Inc., Scranton, Pennsylvania

Typography and binding design by Karolina Harris